Bleeding Through

Bleeding Through

A Rachel Goddard Mystery

Sandra Parshall

Poisoned Pen Press

Copyright © 2012 by Sandra Parshall

First Edition 2012

10 9 8 7 6 5 4 3 2 1

Library of Congress Catalog Card Number: 2012936476

ISBN: 9781464200274   Hardcover
       9781464200281   Trade Paperback

Poisoned Pen Press
6962 E. First Ave., Ste. 103
Scottsdale, AZ 85251
www.poisonedpenpress.com
info@poisonedpenpress.com

Printed in the United States of America

…when the wind begins to roar
It's like a lion at your door
And when the door begins to crack
It's like a stick across your back
And when your back begins to smart
It's like a penknife in your heart
And when your heart begins to bleed
Then you are dead, and dead indeed.

—*Old nursery rhyme*

For the Essential Four:
Carol Baier, Cathrine Dubie, Jerry Parshall
and Emma

Acknowledgements

My thanks, as always, to my indefatigable critique partners, Carol Baier and Cat Dubie, for their honesty, insights, and encouragement.

My husband, Jerry Parshall, serves as a first reader and editor, but he is also an essential part of the planning and plotting process with every book. Sometimes I think his mind is even more twisted than my own. He also restores my confidence when I reach that inevitable point where I'm convinced the whole thing is hopeless and deserves a swift burial in an unmarked grave.

My editor, Barbara Peters, is quite simply brilliant. Thank you, Barbara, for pushing me to make every book the best it can be. I'm also grateful to the wonderful staff at Poisoned Pen Press for making publishing feel like a family project.

Dr. D.P. (Doug) Lyle, as always, has been a great source of information on any crime-related topic. I recommend his Writer's Forensic Blog to anyone who aspires to write mysteries.

Thanks to the readers who let me use their pets in this book: Carolyn J. Rose (Max), Brenda Williamson (Lucky), and Mimi Stevens (Loki). I hope you'll enjoy your little ones' cameo roles.

I am grateful every day for my friends in Sisters in Crime, especially the Guppies and the Chessie Chapter. I love you all, and appreciate every pat on the back and every word of encouragement.

Hearing from readers and meeting them in person is always a pleasure, and often a rotten day is salvaged by a nice e-mail from a stranger who has just finished one of my books and wants to tell me she or he enjoyed it. Thank you for reading this book, and please let me know if you like it.

Chapter One

Two dozen teenagers tumbled out of the school bus and charged after Tom Bridger along the shoulder of the road, brandishing their litter spikes like warriors' spears.

Rachel Goddard parked her Range Rover behind the bus and walked up to wait for the last student to emerge. A blast of chilly wind whipped her auburn hair across her eyes and prompted her to zip her fleece jacket and tug the collar around her neck. They'd started three hours ago with a perfect April morning, but now clouds towered overhead, dragging their dark shadows across the mountain that rose on one side of the road.

The silver-haired bus driver gestured to hurry his tardy passenger. After a moment, seventeen-year-old Megan Beecher emerged from the bus. Clutching a plastic trash bag in one hand, she dangled her litter spike from the other so that it banged against the steps as she descended. While the other kids disturbed the peace with a chorus of some abominable rap song, Megan's pale face remained expressionless, her blue eyes blank.

"Are you okay?" Rachel laid a hand on her shoulder. Megan was a slight girl, several inches shorter than Rachel, and she'd lost so much weight in the last month that Rachel could feel her bones through her sweater. "I'll drive you home right now if you're ready to quit."

Megan shook her head without meeting Rachel's gaze. A long blond strand had worked loose from her hair band and fallen forward over one eye, but she seemed not to notice. Rachel almost raised a hand to tuck it back into place but caught herself in time to suppress the urge.

Why had she pushed the girl to join the litter cleanup? Megan, who planned to become a veterinarian, wanted to go to her Saturday morning job at Rachel's animal hospital as usual, but Rachel had insisted that she get outdoors and take part in the annual civics project with other Mason County High School students. She'd seemed okay when they started, but she'd been fading all morning. Now, at their third stop, she had retreated so far into herself that she barely seemed aware of her surroundings.

As Rachel and Megan caught up, Tom halted and faced the group. Even when he was out of his deputy sheriff's uniform and dressed in old jeans and a worn denim jacket, he looked like a cop, confident and authoritative. The boys treated him with respect. The girls, though…Rachel hadn't missed the way they ran their eyes over Tom's six-feet-plus of lean muscle, his strong features and olive skin, his thick black hair. He was trying so damned hard to ignore their flirtatious looks and smiles that Rachel didn't know whether to laugh or feel sorry for him. If he had the vanity to match his looks, she thought, he would be impossible to live with.

Tom waved a hand at the trash-strewn ravine that dropped down from the road. "Let's see who can fill up a bag first before the rain starts. The winner gets a free burger for lunch."

"What, no fries?" a gangly, freckle-faced boy asked. He flapped his trash bag until it caught the breeze and inflated like a balloon. "And how about something to drink?"

Tom laughed. "Negotiated like the son of a lawyer, Ansel. Okay, a free burger with fries and the drink of your choice."

All the kids except Megan swarmed down the slope, whooping and yelling as they slid and stumbled, alternately using their poles for balance and for spearing trash they spotted on the way.

"Don't they ever get tired?" Rachel said to Tom. She'd begun to think longingly of lunch and a place to sit down while she ate. "I hope all this exercise counteracts the cholesterol overload they're headed for at lunchtime."

"What, you don't think they'd be eating junk without my encouragement?" They both watched Megan begin a slow descent, placing her feet with care and using her spike to steady herself. "Poor kid," Tom said. "I thought this outing might do her some good."

"I should have left her alone and let her go to work today. At least she enjoys that." Rachel shook her head. "I can't even imagine what it's like for that family. Not knowing must be torture."

"It's been a month. They know." Tom patted her back as if she were the one who needed consoling. "But without any proof, it's hard to move on."

The Beechers needed a body to bury, Rachel thought. They needed certainty, and a way to say goodbye to Megan's older sister. A beautiful young woman, her adult life just beginning. Vanished.

A single raindrop landed on Rachel's forehead and ran down her nose. Swiping it away, she said, "We'd better get busy."

She and Tom pulled disposable gloves from their jacket pockets and tugged them on as they set off down the slope.

Rachel joined Megan and deposited the trash she picked up in Megan's bag. The girl kept her distance from the other kids, who spread out under the darkening sky to harvest the bonanza of litter, racing each other to stab debris on the ground and tug plastic shopping bags from among the fresh new leaves on tree branches. They stomped on beer and soft drink cans and bottles to flatten them before tossing them into bags. Birds in the surrounding trees, silenced by the students' noisy arrival, soon accepted their presence and resumed a spring chorus of chirps and whistles. A pair of large pileated woodpeckers swooped past the group at eye level, startling the teenagers into a very uncool fit of giggles. All except Megan, who didn't bother to look up to see what caused the reaction.

A tall, skinny boy named Jarrett stood a few yards from Megan and Rachel, poking an old mattress with his spike. "Hey,

Dr. Goddard," he said with a grin, "want to help me wrestle this into my bag?"

Rachel shook her head in disgust. "Why on earth would anybody throw a mattress off the side of the road?"

"So they don't have to pay at the landfill," Jarrett said, as if pointing out what should be obvious. He frowned when something caught his attention. He leaned down for a closer look.

"Leave it alone," Rachel told him. "It's filthy. The guys on the county truck can pick it up when they come to collect our trash bags."

Thunder rumbled in the distance and a few drops of rain struck her hair and shoulders. They would have to wrap it up soon. For now, she went back to work, plucking trash out of the leaf litter and tangled vines on the floor of the ravine.

"Oh, Captain Bridger," one of the girls called out.

Her teasing tone made Rachel look around. A pretty girl with curly brown hair held up a campaign sign that read *Tom Bridger for Sheriff.* She smiled at Tom, twenty feet away. "Is this trash too?"

The kids nearby laughed.

"I guess my competition's been down this road," Tom said. "Now I know where all my signs are disappearing to."

"Why don't you take it home with you," a smirking boy said to the girl, "and hang it on the wall next to your bed?"

"Well, I just might do that."

The boys snickered. Rachel saw Tom roll his eyes in exasperation before he bent to pick up a couple of beer bottles.

Suppressing a smile, Rachel told the girl, "I'm sure we can give you a new one that hasn't been lying out—"

"Dr. Goddard?" Jarrett called, his voice rising to an urgent pitch. "Captain?"

Rachel and Tom spun around. Using his litter pole, Jarrett had levered one edge of the mattress several inches off the ground. "There's something real weird under there."

Rachel and Tom exchanged a glance. Teenagers and drama. "What?" Rachel said. "Another dead possum?" The last one they'd stumbled across had set the girls to shrieking as if they'd come face to face with E.T. You'd think these kids, growing up in a rural mountain community, would be used to seeing the rotting carcasses of wild animals.

"I don't think so." Jarrett pushed the mattress up a couple more inches. "Oh, man. What is that? It's too big to be an animal. And it's got plastic around it."

That brought the other boys running. Most of the girls followed, converging around the mattress.

Rachel edged through the clump of kids, expecting to find a dead pet or farm animal somebody had dumped out here. She crouched to examine the partially exposed object.

For a moment her mind went blank, refusing to register what lay before her. Then with a shock she realized what she was seeing. Her throat tightened with nausea and she felt the blood drain from her head. She wobbled and had to brace herself with a hand flat on the ground. Unable to look away, she called out, "Tom? Where are you?"

"I'm right here." He'd moved close enough to startle her.

Rachel rose and stumbled back as Tom peered under the mattress. Jarrett still held it up, but his pole trembled in his hands.

"Jesus Christ." Tom caught the side of the mattress and shoved it off to reveal a body wrapped in plastic sheeting.

Gasps and strangled cries escaped from the gathered teenagers. Fat raindrops splattered the plastic.

Oh my god, no, Rachel thought. She couldn't let Megan see this. She jerked her head around, searching for the girl.

"Okay, you're done here," Tom told the teenagers. "Get back up to the road."

Nobody moved. Riveted by the scene in front of them, the kids didn't seem to hear a word he said.

"Go," Tom said. *"Now."* He stepped forward, gesturing, forcing them to shuffle away.

When Megan Beecher slipped past the retreating students, Rachel grabbed her. "No, Megan, don't. Stay back."

Megan strained against Rachel's grip, her eyes pinned on the thing lying at their feet. Her hands curled into fists. Her cry began as a low moan, torn from deep inside her, and it rose and swelled into a wail that echoed through the ravine. The other teens froze, their faces contorted by fear and horror at what they were witnessing.

Megan sagged into Rachel's arms, gulped and burst into sobs. "Shelley," she gasped. "It's Shelley. It's my sister."

Chapter Two

When they heard Shelley's name, the students crowded around again, mouths agape. Suddenly half a dozen were holding cell phones aloft as they jostled each other to get the best angles for pictures of the body in its plastic cocoon.

Tom swore under his breath. "Get back up to the road and on your bus," he ordered. "I need this area cleared. No pictures, for god's sake."

Megan sobbed in Rachel's arms. Some of the other girls began crying, their litter spikes abandoned on the ground.

"It's really her, isn't it?" Jarrett stared, pale-faced, at what he'd uncovered. "She must have been murdered, right?"

"What's she doing here?" the freckle-faced son of a lawyer asked. "I mean, she disappeared in Fairfax County, didn't she? Do you think—"

"What I think is that you need to show a little consideration for Megan," Tom said.

The boy glanced at Megan and ducked his head. "Sorry," he mumbled.

"Now go on," Tom said. "All of you."

They moved off reluctantly, glancing back over their shoulders as they climbed the slope. When thunder cracked directly overhead and the sparse raindrops turned to a steady drizzle, they picked up speed and scrambled for the shelter of the bus.

"I need to go up to the road to call in," Tom told Rachel. "I can't get a cell signal down here. I'll have to wait for backup before I can take Megan home and talk to her parents. Why don't the two of you get out of the rain?" All he needed was a storm, washing away trace evidence, reducing the crime scene to a muddy mess.

"Come on," Rachel said to Megan. "Let's go wait for Tom in my car." Rachel looked shaken, but she kept her voice steady and Tom knew he could count on her to stay calm for the girl's sake.

"No!" Megan tried to squirm free. "I can't leave Shelley down here all by herself."

Rachel held on, both arms around Megan. "We have to let the police do their job. And we have to take you home to your mom and dad. You need to be with them now."

Tom helped Rachel get the girl up the slope. One on each side, they kept her on her feet when she stumbled over rocks and roots and tugged her forward when she tried to turn back to her sister.

The students had boarded the bus, but half of them clustered on the side overlooking the ravine, some sticking their cell phones through open windows to snap more pictures. The driver stood in the doorway, looking confused. "What am I supposed to do?" he asked when he spotted Tom.

"Get them out of here." Tom was sure they were spreading news of the discovery by text and e-mail, and he was afraid Shelley's parents would find out through gossip before he was able to talk to them face to face.

"Settle down, you guys!" the driver yelled at the students. He slammed the door shut, slid behind the wheel and revved the engine.

While Rachel guided Megan into the back seat of her Range Rover, Tom dug his cell phone out of his shirt pocket. He ordered dispatch to call in all off-duty deputies. He made a second call to Sergeant Dennis Murray, asking him to pick up Daniel Beecher from his job at the McKendrick horse farm and drive him home. Next Tom phoned Dr. Gretchen Lauter, the county's medical examiner, and finally the State Police, to request a crime scene investigator.

With the necessary calls made, the school bus gone, and Megan slumped against Rachel's shoulder in the Range Rover, Tom had time to take a deep breath and think about what was happening. He stood at the top of the ravine, letting the drizzle soak his hair, staring down at the old mattress and the body it had concealed. He'd recognized Shelley Beecher instantly, even though slight bloating distorted the oval shape of her face. Long blond hair draped her shoulders, and the outfit on the body matched the description of what she was wearing when last seen: short blue jacket over a pink sweater, jeans, athletic shoes.

Tom had believed Shelley was dead since the day she disappeared in Northern Virginia, where she was a first year law student. So did the Fairfax County detective on the case. But she didn't look as if she'd been dead a month. Bloating and decomposition were noticeable but not advanced. The plastic was still clean. If she wasn't killed immediately after her abduction, where had she been for the last month? And, as one of the boys had asked, why did her body turn up here in her home county in the mountains of southwestern Virginia, hours away from the place where she went missing?

The sound of approaching vehicles broke into his thoughts. More deputies had arrived to secure the scene. Now Tom had to take Megan home to her parents and tell them their older daughter was lying dead in a ravine.

◇◇◇

The Beechers' two-story white house seemed eerily quiet and lonely when Tom turned Rachel's Range Rover into the driveway. After weeks of friends and neighbors streaming in to comfort Dan and Sarah, people had run out of things to say and turned back to their own everyday lives.

The house sat on a quarter-acre lot carved out of a patch of pine woods. In the flower beds along the front of the house, dozens of gold and white daffodils bobbed in the light rain. A broad yellow ribbon circled a maple tree, its bow drenched and drooping. Only Sarah's mini-van sat in the driveway. Dennis Murray hadn't arrived with Dan yet.

The last thing Tom wanted to do was give Sarah the news without her husband by her side, but he had no choice.

The second Tom braked, Megan burst from the back seat and sprinted for the house. The family's yellow Lab, Scout, rose from the porch, his tail wagging.

"Megan, wait!" Rachel pleaded, scrambling after her.

Climbing out of the vehicle, Tom called, "Megan, let me tell your mother—"

But she was already up the steps, wrenching the door open, screaming, "Mom! Mom, it's Shelley!"

Tom and Rachel hurried after her. When they stepped into the living room, Sarah was coming down the stairs. She halted, her gaze falling first on Megan's anguished face, then shifting to Tom and Rachel. A hollow-eyed waif, thin arms hanging at her sides, Sarah looked twenty years older than she had a month ago. Messy blond hair hung around her face. A stain that looked like egg yolk streaked her white t-shirt and the waistband of her jeans.

"I need to talk to you, Sarah," Tom said. "Let's sit down."

Megan bolted up the stairs and almost knocked Sarah over when she threw herself into her mother's arms.

Over Megan's head, Sarah's eyes met Tom's. "She's dead." A flat statement.

"I'm afraid so. I'm sorry, Sarah." He had nothing to say that would soften the blow. Every word he spoke would feel like a knife in her heart.

Sarah sank onto a step, pulling Megan down with her.

Beside Tom, Rachel turned away from the sight of the mother and daughter, a hand over her mouth.

Sarah's eyes blazed when she fixed them on Tom again. "Why in god's name did you tell Meggie first? What's wrong with you?"

"I saw her," Megan whimpered.

"What? What are you talking about? How did you—"

"We found Shelley while the kids were out on their field trip," Tom said.

Sarah expelled a breath as if he'd punched her in the stomach. "You found her here? But how is that—They said it happened in Fairfax County."

"We have a lot of unanswered questions. If I could have spared Megan—I'm sorry, but she was there at the time." Tom knew Megan would tell her parents every detail of what she'd seen, how her sister's body looked, how they'd discovered it under a filthy mattress. He felt helpless, knowing Megan would be haunted by the memory, that she would make her parents' pain a million times worse by planting those images in their minds.

Hearing a vehicle pull up out front, Tom looked to the open doorway. Daniel Beecher exploded from a Sheriff's Department cruiser and ran for the house. When he hit the porch the dog barked once and fell in behind him. Tom and Rachel stepped out of his way as Dan barreled through the door with Scout on his heels. Tom waved at the cruiser, letting Dennis know he could leave.

"You're sure it's her?" Dan's stocky body quivered with tension. Tears ran unchecked down his face and soaked his short blond beard. In his face Tom saw Dan hadn't given up hope, he wanted to hear that Tom still had doubts.

Tom laid a hand on Dan's shoulder. "Yes, I'm sure. I'm sorry."

At Dan's side, Scout barked again, begging for his master's attention. Rachel dropped to her knees and distracted the dog by scratching his head and soothing him with murmured words.

Dan twisted away from Tom and mounted the stairs. Pulling Sarah to her feet, he enclosed her in a tight embrace. Megan wrapped her arms around both her parents and sobbed against her mother's shoulder.

While the Beechers poured out their grief, Rachel slipped a hand into Tom's. Everywhere Tom looked in the living room he saw reminders that Dan and Sarah's lives centered on their daughters. Photos of Shelley and Megan, as alike as twins except for the five-year age difference, lined the blue walls and decorated the tabletops. Over the fireplace mantel hung a big picture of

Shelley in her university graduation gown, flanked by her smiling sister and parents.

Forcing himself to disconnect from the scene emotionally, Tom focused on all the things he must do in the next few hours. He had to get back to the scene, but first he would drop Rachel off at home and collect his cruiser. He—

"I'm going out there," Dan said, his arms still around his wife and daughter.

"I'm going too," Sarah said. "She needs her family with her."

Aw, god, Tom thought. "I know how you feel, but—"

"You don't have any idea how we feel," Dan said.

"I meant that I understand why you want to be there. But I have to ask you to stay away and let us do our work. You can see her later today, I promise." One or both would have to formally identify their daughter's body before it went to Roanoke for autopsy, but this wasn't the time to tell them that.

"I'm going," Dan said. "Sarah, Meg, you both stay here."

"I'm her mother, Dan," Sarah protested.

He kissed her forehead. "Honey, please just stay here with Meggie. Let me do this by myself. I'll be back soon."

No amount of gentle argument would deter him. Dan rode with Tom and Rachel a few miles down the road to Tom's farm, where the two men switched to the cruiser. Not wanting to set off another outburst, Tom held back the questions that crowded his mind. Dan remained stone-faced and silent until they reached the place where Shelley's body lay.

Chapter Three

Rachel sat on the screened porch, absently stroking her black and white cat Frank as he purred on her lap, while Cicero, her African gray parrot, squawked at a bluejay that taunted him from a nearby shrub. She wished she could erase the image of Shelley's lifeless body from her mind. She wished she could go back and do something to keep Megan from seeing her sister that way. The sight would haunt Megan forever.

The sound of an approaching vehicle made her glance toward the driveway. "Oh, no," she groaned. Ben Hern's black Jaguar pulled in behind her Range Rover. He unfolded his tall, muscular body from the low-slung car and headed for the front door. Ben was a close friend, but Rachel dreaded facing him now. She hoped someone had already told him about the discovery of Shelley's body, so she wouldn't have to break it to him. Nudging Frank off her lap, she rose and went to meet Ben.

As soon as she opened the front door, she realized that he knew. The effort of holding back tears twisted his handsome face into a mask of grief. Raking his thick black hair off his forehead, Ben choked out, "Is it true? She was wrapped in plastic and stuck under a dirty mattress?"

"Come in." Rachel pushed open the screen door.

Ben stooped in the hallway to pet Frank, but his stunned expression didn't change. He had the kind of Latin lover looks— his real name was Benicio Hernandez—that reduced a lot of women to simpering idiots, but an easily wounded heart beat behind that deceptive facade. He'd been a mentor of sorts to Shelley, and he was fond of the whole Beecher family.

"How did you hear about it?" Rachel asked.

"I was out at the horse farm when Dennis Murray came to get Dan." Ben stood, jammed his fists into his jeans pockets, hunched his shoulders. "It was a nightmare. Dan didn't want to believe it. He was yelling at Murray, saying it had to be a mistake, Shelley couldn't be dead. Joanna was crying. I've never seen her cry before."

Rachel felt a pang of pity for her friend Joanna McKendrick, who was Shelley's godmother. Rachel had met the Beecher sisters when she was living in a cottage on Joanna's horse farm, where Dan Beecher worked as a trainer. "I'll stop by and see Joanna later. She's probably gone over to the Beechers' house by now."

Ben wandered into the living room, his movements jerky with tension. Rachel followed, with Frank padding alongside her. "After Dan and Murray left, somebody called Joanna and told her all the details. Even offered to e-mail her some pictures of Shelley one of the kids took."

"Oh, god." It shouldn't matter. Shelley was dead, and what the killer had done to her body after taking her life couldn't hurt her anymore. Yet it deepened the wound immeasurably for those left behind.

"God damn it!" Ben's words burst out of him in a shout. The startled cat shot from the room and ran down the hall. "Who would do something like that? She was a good girl, she really cared about helping other people."

"I know. She had a good heart." *Shelley's never met a stranger,* Dan used to say, with obvious pride in his ebullient, friendly older daughter. Rachel wondered how he felt now about his daughter's open, trusting nature. Taking Ben's arm, she steered him toward the couch. "Come on, sit down."

He dropped onto the couch beside Rachel. "That's probably what got her killed, you know. She let a stranger get too close, she didn't see danger coming. Girls like Shelley are natural targets for perverts."

Rachel had no trouble imagining endless variations on Shelley's abduction and murder. "If I ever have a daughter, I'll make damned sure she looks at everybody with a healthy amount of suspicion. You don't have to be cynical to be careful."

"At least the waiting's over for Shelley's family. They know what happened to her." Ben's voice choked up again. "They can say goodbye now. Never knowing would have been a hell of a lot worse."

Rachel didn't answer. Ben had no idea how close to the bone his words cut. Although he'd been a friend since childhood, he didn't know the truth about her life, the secret she lived with. Every day for the past month, with all of Mason County obsessed with Shelley's fate, pictures of her smiling face posted everywhere, Rachel had been forced to think about the special brand of torment that followed a child's disappearance. For some parents, answers never came. Parents like Rachel's own.

Don't, she told herself, blocking the memories before they fully formed, silencing the question—*Have I done the right thing?*—before it took hold in her mind like some old song that repeated endlessly and wouldn't go away. Rachel had made the decision several years ago to leave things as they were. She couldn't erase the past. She believed she had good reasons not to try.

Ben looked at Rachel, his eyes widening as if a horrifying thought had occurred to him. "Oh god. Am I partly to blame for this?"

"What? How could you be to blame?"

Leaning forward with his elbows on his knees, he clenched and unclenched his hands. "I was the one who encouraged her to volunteer with the innocence project. She might never have gotten involved if I hadn't suggested it. And the project director might have turned her down if I hadn't been pushy about it. I mean, when your project's main source of money asks for something, you don't say no."

Ben was a serious artist, but he made his living—an extraordinarily lucrative living—by drawing a comic strip called *Furballs*, using his own cat and dog as inspiration. He gave away a lot of his money, and the Virginia Innocence Project was one beneficiary of his generosity.

"What does her work with the innocence project have to do with her death?" Rachel asked.

"She was making people mad by trying to get Vance Lankford out of prison. This whole county believes he's guilty, he killed that guy. I tried to talk her out of taking on a local case involving people she knew, because I figured she'd get a lot of blowback. There were other cases she could've taken on. I should have made her listen to me."

"Oh, Ben." Rachel sighed and rubbed his back. "Don't look for ways to make yourself feel bad. If somebody died of food poisoning at that soup kitchen you support, would you feel responsible? No, don't answer that. Of course you would."

"So would you. We're just alike that way, and you know it."

Rachel's cell phone chirped in her shirt pocket. "I'm sorry. I'll get rid of whoever it is." She frowned when she saw the name on the screen: *Michelle Goddard.* Her sister almost never called her—Rachel was the one who worked at keeping their relationship alive. A call from Michelle might mean bad news. "It's Michelle," she told Ben. "I have to take this. Don't leave. I'll keep it short."

Ben leaned back on the couch, blew out a sigh and nodded. "Tell her I said hello."

Rachel tried not to sound alarmed when she answered. "Hi, Mish, what's up?"

"It's me, Rachel." A man's voice. Kevin, Michelle's husband.

"Oh. Hi." Now she was really worried. If calls from Michelle were unusual, calls from Michelle's husband were, or had been until now, nonexistent. Suddenly Rachel couldn't sit still. She stood and began pacing the living room. "What's wrong?"

"Nothing, nothing." Kevin paused. "Well, actually—"

"Has something happened to Michelle?"

Ben sat up straight on the sofa, alert and concerned.

"No, no," Kevin said. "She's right here."

"Oh, good." Rachel sagged with relief, and she shook her head to answer the question on Ben's face. "You scared me for a minute."

"I'm sorry. I didn't mean to." Kevin's strained voice, with its edge of anxiety, ruined his attempt to reassure Rachel. "I—We, that is—"

He broke off, and Rachel heard a fumbling noise from the other end. Then her sister's voice. "Rachel, I need to see you. You're the only person I can talk to."

Another spurt of alarm. "Talk to me about what?"

In the background, Rachel heard Kevin protest, "You know you can tell me anything. I'm trying to understand, I just don't—"

"That's right, you don't understand."

"Michelle!" Rachel said. "You're freaking me out here."

"I don't want to get into it on the phone. I want to tell you everything in person."

Rachel hesitated. Michelle and Kevin lived in Bethesda, Maryland, outside Washington, D.C., hours away. Rachel had visited occasionally, but to drive all that distance just to talk? What could be that urgent? That bad? "I'll have to make arrangements to be away from work."

"Could I come out there instead?"

For a second Rachel didn't know what to say. Michelle had never been to Mason County, never shown any interest in visiting in the two years Rachel had lived there. Her sister had never met Tom, although Rachel had moved in with him months ago.

"I know I'm imposing on you," Michelle said into the silence, "but I'm desperate to get away for a while. If I could come and stay with you a few days—" Her voice broke and fell to a whisper. "I'm frightened, Rachel."

"Are you going to tell me what's going on or do you want to leave it up to my imagination? Which is running wild right now, by the way."

The response came from Kevin, who took the phone. "She says strange things are happening. She thinks somebody's getting into her office at night, moving things around, and she says she's getting anonymous phone calls. She believes somebody is stalking her."

"My god," Rachel exclaimed. "Have you called the police?"

Kevin sighed. "Yes, and they said they can't do anything because there's no proof. They pretty much said that unless somebody attacks her, she's on her own."

Rachel was silent a moment, registering the way Kevin had delivered the story: *she says, she thinks, she believes. There's no proof.* "Answer me honestly. Just say yes or no—do you believe those things are happening?"

Kevin took his time, and when he finally replied he sounded reluctant to speak the words. "I'm…I'm not sure. I'm just not sure."

◇◇◇

Tom had never seen a grown man cry the way Daniel Beecher did, unashamed among other men, making no effort to keep up a stoic front. In the month since Shelley disappeared, he'd been the strong one in the family, going to work every day, refusing to give in to despair. Now, with Shelley lying dead in the ravine below him, sobs convulsed his body, and he leaned a hand against a tree trunk as if he needed the support to keep from collapsing.

The rain clouds had drifted off, and Tom and Dan stood in a splash of pale sunlight at the top of the slope. Below them, Dr. Gretchen Lauter looked on as two young men lifted Shelley's body onto a stretcher and secured it with straps for the climb to the road and the waiting mortuary van. Several men wearing the brown uniforms of the Mason County Sheriff's Department formed a motionless line along the road. Waiting for orders, struck dumb by the naked grief of the victim's father. Some of them watched Dan with fear in their eyes, and Tom knew they were thinking of their own kids, imagining themselves in Dan's shoes. Tom felt an answering wrench in his own gut, and for once he was glad he didn't have children to worry about. To lose.

In Dan's eyes Tom saw a boiling stew of rage, barely controlled, and the force of it made him wonder if he'd be able to keep the grieving father at a distance from the investigation. He pulled a clean handkerchief from the back pocket of his jeans and pressed it into Dan's hand.

Swiping the handkerchief across his mouth and nose, Dan drew a deep breath and made an effort to calm himself. "I keep thinking we should have taught her to be more careful, not to be so friendly to everybody. She thought bad things only happened to other people, not to her."

"You can't raise kids to be afraid of the whole world," Tom said. "You cripple them if you do."

"And look what happens if you don't." Dan's face contorted and fresh tears filled his eyes. "Can't you get that plastic off of her?"

"It'll be removed in the hospital mortuary so Dr. Lauter can take a look at her before she goes to the medical examiner in Roanoke."

"Do they have to do an autopsy? Does she have to be cut up?"

"We can't investigate Shelley's death without an autopsy."

To Tom's relief, Dan accepted that. He pulled in a shuddering breath and said, "I want to see her before they take her off to Roanoke."

"We'll go to the hospital. I need you to give me a formal identification. Do you want to pick up Sarah so she can be with you?"

Dan shook his head. "She's not in any shape to go through that. I'll do it."

"She'll want to see her daughter."

"No. Not like this."

Tom doubted Dan was doing his wife a kindness by keeping her away, denying her the finality of seeing Shelley's body, but he wouldn't argue the point. Families had to live with the emotional fallout of mistakes they made at times like this. Tom had learned to recognize situations where his interference would only add to the turmoil.

The two mortuary attendants started up the slope, carrying Shelley's body on the stretcher between them.

"I want to ride with her," Dan choked out. "I don't want her to be alone."

"We'll be following right behind all the way." Tom laid a hand on Dan's shoulder. "We're going to need your help to find out who did this. I'll want to talk to you and Sarah both, probably more than once."

"You gonna ask us a lot of stupid questions about her boyfriend and her teachers? Like that detective from Fairfax County did when she went missing?"

"They're reasonable questions, Dan."

"It's a goddamn waste of time. I can tell you exactly who killed my daughter."

Chapter Four

Rachel paused in the hallway outside the bedroom, her hand on the doorknob, transfixed by the images that rose up in her mind. Her blond, blue-eyed sister Michelle. The blond, blue-eyed Shelley Beecher. So much alike. For one awful second she envisioned her sister staring through a plastic shroud with lifeless eyes.

"Oh my god," she gasped, bile rising in her throat. She swallowed. Why had her mind made that crazy connection? She shook her head, banished the terrible sight, and pushed open the door to the bedroom that had belonged to Tom's parents.

The cat and bulldog scooted past her, grabbing the chance to explore a space usually off-limits to them. Rachel had no choice but to put Michelle in here, since she and Tom occupied the only other bedroom. Their recent paper-stripping and painting binge hadn't extended this far, and they'd had no reason to change the room's contents either. Wallpaper splashed with red and yellow flowers. Braided rug. Early American furniture. Michelle would be appalled.

Well, that's just too bad, Rachel thought. *Welcome to my world, baby sister.*

The attempt to buoy her spirits lasted a split-second before she leaned against the door frame, overcome again by the anxiety the phone call had stirred up. Michelle had sounded desperate. Terrified. She was convinced someone was stalking her, breaking into her office. Yet the police refused to help, and her own husband seemed to doubt any of it was real.

Could it be possible Michelle had imagined the stalker? She'd always been emotionally fragile. She had never squarely faced the truth about their identity, about Judith Goddard, the woman who had raised them and pretended to be their mother. Rachel was also living a lie, but at least she had confronted the reality behind the facade of their privileged childhood. For a long time she had feared the past would catch up with her sister someday and crack the pretty glass bubble she lived in. Was it happening now? Was the stalker imaginary, representing the truth Michelle wanted to deny, destroying her equilibrium?

Rachel shook her head in disgust. *Psychobabble.* Michelle had her flaws, but she wasn't suffering from psychotic hallucinations. Rachel had to take her sister's account seriously. Some nut case was tormenting Michelle, and god only knew what he might do to her if he wasn't stopped.

Frank, the cat, leapt to the top of a small bookcase and watched the brown and white bulldog, Billy Bob, snuffle his way around the bedroom, probably taking in the lingering scents of Tom's parents. Billy Bob had been little more than a puppy when John and Ann Bridger died in an auto accident, but Rachel doubted the dog had forgotten his former owners.

Leaving the animals to their explorations, she walked down the hall to fetch clean sheets from the linen closet.

Tom had no idea yet that Michelle was coming. Rachel hated springing it on him at the worst possible time, at the start of a time-consuming, energy-draining murder investigation, but what else could she do in the face of her sister's distress?

Back in the bedroom, she dropped the linens onto a chair and pushed up a window to let in a fresh, cool breeze. The room hadn't been opened in so long the air smelled stale, and dust covered every flat surface. After she made the bed, she'd have to clean. She shook out a sheet over the mattress at the same time Frank jumped onto the bed. When the sheet descended on him, he wiggled around underneath, inviting Rachel to play. She tickled the cat through the cloth, her mind still on her sister.

She wouldn't bet on Michelle and Tom getting along. And Michelle did not enjoy the countryside. What if she suddenly decided after a day or two that she couldn't stand it here and wanted to go home? Kevin was driving her out, but if he couldn't come to retrieve her during the work week, Rachel would have to juggle her own schedule so she could take Michelle back to Bethesda.

Maybe I'll drop her off at the Trailways station. Rachel had to laugh at the idea of her fussy sister riding back to Maryland on a bus. Then she sank onto the unmade bed and caught her head in her hands. Frank popped out from under the sheet and butted her elbow. "She's not even here yet," Rachel told the cat, "and already I'm getting snarky."

Frank replied with one of his rusty-hinge meows.

After all this time, nothing had changed in the prickly relationship between Rachel and her sister. They still circled the ghost who stood between them, unable to lay Judith Goddard to rest, unable even now to talk about what she had done to them. Rachel could see the sad irony in a clinical psychologist's refusal to face childhood trauma, but she had suffered enough emotional pain herself to know she had no right to force it on Michelle. She wasn't willing to let her sister drop out of her life, so she'd accepted Michelle's rules, maintaining occasional, undemanding contact, skating on the surface while all the important things remained unsaid.

Now Michelle needed her again. She'd turned to Rachel the way she had when they were children and nightmares drove her from her bed and across the hall to seek safety and comfort with her big sister. How could Rachel say no? She was grateful that, unlike Megan Beecher, she still had her sister. She would do whatever she could to help. But she felt a deep apprehension and resistance building inside her as the weight of Michelle's problems settled on her, and she took it as a warning that they couldn't easily slip back into their childhood roles.

◇◇◇

Tom dropped a file folder on the conference room table and flipped it open. Inside lay three sheets of paper and a photo of

Shelley Beecher, twenty-two years old, first year law student at George Mason University in Fairfax, Virginia.

"The Fairfax County police have all the records on suspects and interviews, and they've never shared any of it with us," he told Dr. Gretchen Lauter and the two deputies seated at the table. "I asked a few people here some questions when she disappeared, but I didn't have any reason to think somebody in Mason County was responsible."

"Until now." Sergeant Dennis Murray, a lean deputy with close-cut dark hair and wire-rimmed glasses, sat directly across from Tom.

"It doesn't make sense," Brandon Connolly said, "that somebody would snatch her in Fairfax County and bring her body down here. What could be behind that?" The young sandy-haired deputy often acted as Tom's partner in investigations and Tom wanted him in the loop from the start.

"Damned if I know," Tom said. "Whether the killer lives in Mason County or not, he—or she—was taking a chance on getting caught by bringing her body all the way from Northern Virginia. It would make more sense if she was brought here alive and killed here. But that would have been a risk too, at a time when everybody was looking for her and her picture was posted everywhere."

"There has to be a reason the body was dumped here," Dennis said. "I can't even guess what it might be, though."

"Gretchen?" Tom said. "What do you think about cause of death?" After Dan Beecher's anguished identification of his daughter's body, Tom had hustled him out of the hospital morgue and driven him home rather than staying to learn what Dr. Lauter's preliminary examination revealed.

The medical examiner, a woman in her late fifties whose short curls were more gray than black these days, looked up from the batch of photos she'd been studying. "The autopsy may prove me wrong, but I'd say she died of strangulation with a leather belt or something similar, an inch or so wide with hard edges. Something that held its shape when it was pulled tight."

She handed Tom a close-up photo she'd taken of Shelley's neck. With her hair pulled out of the way, the ligature bruise was unmistakable.

"Did she have any other injuries? A head wound?" Tom couldn't help hoping Shelley had been knocked out before she was strangled. "Could you tell whether she was sexually assaulted?"

"I didn't undress her. I didn't want to disturb the body any more than I had to before it went to Roanoke, but I can say that her clothing was intact, nothing was torn. She had no head injury, and there's no blood on the body that I could see. She did have obvious injuries to her hands, though." She offered Tom a close-up photo of Shelley's hands, laid on her chest.

Tom slid the first photo across the table to Dennis and Brandon and took the second.

"Some of her fingernails were ragged, as if they were torn off while she was scratching something or somebody," Dr. Lauter said, "The bones in two fingers on her right hand were broken. Snapped, as if—I shouldn't be speculating, but what came to mind was somebody bending the fingers back until they broke. I'm inclined to think she put up a good fight. Unfortunately, the nails are so clean that I doubt the crime lab will find any tissue from the killer under them."

Tom stared at the mottled blue-green of Shelley's skin, the two fingers on the right hand that were twisted together like a pretzel. He could imagine the pretty young woman he'd known fighting, kicking, clawing while the belt tightened around her neck and stopped her scream, stopped her breath. Stopped her life.

Tom pulled himself back to the moment and slid the photo across the table to Dennis and Brandon. "What about time of death? She doesn't look as if she's been dead long."

Dr. Lauter hesitated before answering. "I'm not going to make any assumptions about when she died. She could have been killed in the last few days, but it's also possible she's been dead longer than it might appear at first glance."

"The body's in good condition," Tom said. "To keep it that way any length of time—"

"If she was killed soon after she was abducted, and stored somewhere cold," Dr. Lauter said, "decomp and the other processes would have been slowed down considerably but not stopped."

"Stored?" Brandon said, frowning at the photos.

"It's just a hypothesis. I mentioned it because she doesn't appear to have lost any weight, and if she'd been kept prisoner for a month—" Dr. Lauter shook her head. "Let's wait and see what the autopsy shows."

"All right," Tom said. "We don't know exactly when she was killed. But let's think about the way she died. Strangulation takes strength and time. The killer had to hold onto a healthy, athletic young woman for several minutes, while she was struggling."

"Probably a man," Dennis said. "Boyfriend? Stalker? Didn't the Fairfax cops check out those angles?"

"I'm sure they did," Tom said. "Her father thinks there's another possibility. I don't know how seriously to take it, but Dan thinks her murder's connected to her work with the Virginia Innocence Project in Fairfax County. I'm not sure whether she was doing it for course credit or just for the experience, but she wanted to prove Vance Lankford is innocent."

"Yeah, I know," Dennis said, his tone sour. He handed the two pictures back to Dr. Lauter. "The guy beat Brian Hadley to a pulp with a tire iron. Why anybody would think he's innocent is a mystery to me, and I don't know what an amateur could turn up six years later that would clear him."

"I don't either," Tom said. "My dad worked that case. The evidence was solid. But the Virginia Innocence Project's been able to get new trials for a few state prisoners, and they've found evidence to clear two people. The lawyer who runs it called me when she decided to let Shelley look into Lankford's case, and she sounds pretty sharp. I never expected it to amount to anything, but I doubt she would have gotten the innocence project involved if she didn't see some merit in it."

"Do you think one of the Hadleys could have been involved in Shelley's murder?" Brandon asked. "They haven't been too happy about her stirring things up, asking questions. To their minds, she was trying to set Brian's killer free."

"Dan told me Skeet Hadley's been harassing the whole Beecher family," Tom said. "For months, ever since he found out what Shelley was doing."

"That sounds like Skeet," Brandon said. "I went to school with him, K through twelve. He's got the worst temper of anybody I know, and he never lets go of a grudge."

"So maybe he went to talk to Shelley and ended up killing her in a rage?" Dennis asked.

"After driving for hours to get to Northern Virginia, probably stewing about it the whole time?" Dr. Lauter put in. "That's not spur of the moment rage. That's premeditation."

Tom closed the useless file. It would fatten up soon enough. "It's just one possibility we have to look at."

"So we start by talking to Skeet?" Brandon asked.

"After I see Shelley's folks again. I didn't get a lot of details from Dan earlier because there was so much going on." As he stood, Tom glanced at his watch. Almost time for dinner. He wanted to eat it with Rachel and take a break from bad news. "By the way, the Fairfax County detective who's been working Shelley's disappearance is on his way down."

Dennis grimaced and said something Tom didn't catch.

"He'll stop in Roanoke to see the body before he comes here. She could have been killed in his jurisdiction. Until we pin down the location of the murder, this is a joint investigation. Accommodate him as best you can—but don't share anything with him without my go-ahead."

Dennis grumbled, "Like we need some outside cop getting underfoot, telling us what to do."

Which was more or less the same thing Tom was thinking.

◇◇◇

Tom parked the cruiser on the side of the road a hundred feet from the Beechers' driveway, and he and Brandon walked to the house past cars and trucks lining both sides of the pavement. Vehicles filled the driveway bumper to bumper. In the front yard, half a dozen preschool boys played a clumsy, noisy game of kick-the-ball on grass still wet from the earlier rain, seemingly unaware of the turmoil and heartache gripping the family that lived here.

"My mom's here," Brandon said, gesturing at one of the cars they passed on the driveway. "The Beechers and my folks are good friends."

"Yeah, I guess you knew Shelley pretty well, didn't you?"

Brandon didn't answer, and after a few steps Tom realized the younger deputy wasn't keeping pace. He turned. Brandon stood on the driveway with his head bowed, thumbs hooked over his gun belt.

"You okay with going in there?" Tom asked.

Brandon drew a deep breath, squared his shoulders, and jutted his chin. "Yeah, I'm okay. Let's go."

Although Tom's family wasn't close to the Beechers, he'd known them as long as he could remember, and he wasn't any more eager than Brandon to wade into the sorrow this house contained. Teary-eyed women, men who didn't know quite what to say or do, Dan and Sarah and Megan in more pain than any kind words or gestures could alleviate. Every one of their friends and neighbors, faced with the loss the Beechers had suffered, would be thinking even as they offered sympathy: *Thank god it isn't us.*

Climbing the front steps, Tom admitted to himself that he would feel the same way if he and Rachel had children. He didn't want to imagine how he'd react if anything happened to his little nephew Simon, and at times like this, he wasn't sure he wanted any kids of his own to worry about. One more way to get your heart broken in a merciless world.

Aw, hell, who was he trying to fool? He'd marry Rachel today if she would say yes, and he would welcome and love as many kids as she wanted to have.

The living room was so crammed with women that Tom and Brandon had to shoulder their way in, trying to be polite about it. The combined odors of hairspray and perfume hung in the air. The two of them worked their way over to the couch where Sarah slumped, vacant-eyed, with Brandon's mother on one side and Joanna McKendrick on the other. Marie Connolly had apparently come straight from the bakery she and her husband owned, and she still wore her customary black slacks and pink shirt, with the logo *Connolly's Country-Fresh Baked Goods* stitched above her heart. She had an arm around Sarah's shoulders.

Joanna, a middle-aged blond woman dressed in the jeans and boots she wore around her horse farm, looked up at Tom with sad, weary eyes and shook her head as if she had no words for what she felt. She pressed a clean tissue into Sarah's hand and lifted the hand to catch a trickle of mucus before it ran down over her lips.

Tom realized all the women had fallen silent, waiting to hear what he would say to Sarah. "I don't have any news," he said. "I won't bother you with questions now, but I'd like to talk to Dan."

Sarah stared into space, giving no sign that she'd heard Tom. Joanna said, "He's on the porch."

With Brandon trailing him, Tom continued through the house. In the kitchen, platters and serving dishes covered with aluminum foil crowded the breakfast table and counters—hastily assembled condolence gifts from people who had little else to offer except their words and their presence. The aromas of beef, chicken, and freshly baked bread came as a relief to Tom after the chemical haze in the living room, but he wondered how long it would be before the Beechers felt like eating again.

They found Dan, and a dozen other men, on the big screened porch at the rear of the house. Dan stood at the screen, staring mutely into the backyard and the woods beyond. The family's yellow Labrador, Scout, sat at his side, leaning into his leg as if propping him up. The other men stood back, giving Dan space.

Tom touched Dan's arm, startling him into awareness. "Can we talk for a couple of minutes? I have to ask you some questions."

"What good are your questions now?" Dan's voice came out hoarse, his words a little slurred, making Tom wonder if he'd taken a drink to dull his pain. "She's gone. We've lost our daughter."

"I need you to focus right now on helping us find out who did this. That's the best thing you can do for your family. Can we talk somewhere in private?" Megan, Tom realized, had probably retreated upstairs, and he didn't want to go up there with Dan and disturb her. "Why don't we go out in the yard?"

Dan heaved a sigh and nodded. Tom pushed open the door to the yard and let Scout run out first.

On the small flagstone-paved area that served as a patio, several folded plastic chairs lay in a stack and a grill on wheels stood under a protective black cover. Dan followed his dog onto the lawn.

Falling in next to Dan, with Brandon on the other side, Tom said, "You told me earlier that you think Skeet Hadley had something to do with Shelley's death. I wanted to ask you—"

"He had everything to do with it." Dan swung around to glare at Tom. "I should've stopped him before it went this far. I'll never forgive myself for not—" He choked up and couldn't go on.

"Exactly what has Skeet done to make you think he would hurt Shelley?"

Swiping a hand across his face, Dan blinked back tears. "He's been over here I don't know how many times, telling me I had to put a stop to it, make Shelley back off. But damn it, she wasn't doing anything to the Hadleys. It didn't involve them."

"Did he ever harass Shelley directly?" Brandon asked.

"Oh yeah. He kept calling her, telling her what she was doing was wrong, she was just causing the family a lot of grief on top of what they already suffered. She bought a new cell phone with a new number just to keep him from getting to her. And I had to throw him out of the house every single time Shelley came home. He just wouldn't leave her alone about it."

"Today is the first time I've heard about this, Dan." Tom didn't try to hide his exasperation.

"Why didn't you report it?" Brandon asked.

Dan threw up his hands. "I wish to god I had. I wish we'd taken out some kind of order to keep him away from her. Away from us. But Shelley said she understood, and she didn't want to hurt the Hadleys by getting Skeet in trouble with the law. God, why did I listen to her? Why didn't I do something to protect my daughter?"

"Don't blame yourself," Tom said, although he knew he'd feel the same way in Dan's situation. "Aside from Skeet, can you think of anybody who would've wanted to hurt her?"

"I told you it's a waste of time to—"

"I know, I know. Just bear with me here. Was she having problems with her boyfriend?"

Dan pulled in a breath, let it out, as if forcing himself to be patient. "There's a boy she hung around with, but I don't know how serious they were about each other. We never met him. His name's Justin something. He's a photographer. Didn't sound to me like he amounted to much, but she liked him. I never got the feeling he was giving her any trouble."

Tom wrote down the first name. He'd have to find out more from the Fairfax detective.

"Skeet's the one you ought to be looking at," Dan said.

"I intend to. Meanwhile, I want you to stay away from him. Stay away from all the Hadleys."

Dan's jaw clenched.

"Think about Sarah and Megan. You don't want to do anything to make this harder for them."

Dan held Tom's gaze for a long moment, then shook his head. "I'm not making any promises I can't keep."

Chapter Five

Rachel pushed rice around on her plate with a fork as she tried to come up with words to tell Tom about Michelle's impromptu visit without making it sound as if a ton of trouble was about to crash down on them.

Since they'd sat down to dinner at the kitchen table he'd barely spoken, and he ate mechanically with a distant expression on his face. Rachel knew he was totally absorbed by the Shelley Beecher case. He'd changed into his brown uniform and planned to get back to work after eating. She might not talk to him again until morning, and she couldn't wait that long to tell him Michelle would be there in a few hours.

The mantel clock in the living room began chiming seven, as if nudging her to get it over with before she ran out of time. On the kitchen wall next to their table the bird in the old cuckoo clock popped out and added its raspy chorus.

Rachel waited until the clocks fell silent. "I'm sorry I can't give you more notice than this, but my sister's coming to stay for a few days." Her voice sounded like a shout in the quiet kitchen. "She'll be here tomorrow."

For a moment Tom seemed to have trouble focusing on what she'd said. He blinked. "Your sister?"

"Yes." Avoiding Tom's direct gaze, Rachel grabbed her glass and swallowed a gulp of water. "Michelle's having…a problem, a fairly serious one, and she needs to get away for a few days. She wants to talk to me about it."

Tom folded his napkin and tucked it under the edge of his plate. Rachel could tell he was trying not to show a reaction, but she caught the sudden wariness in his eyes.

"A marriage problem?" he asked. "Is she leaving her husband?"

"No, it's nothing like that. In fact, Kevin's driving her out here, but he has to go back on Monday because of work."

Frowning, Tom said, "She has a serious problem and her husband's going to drop her off and leave her?"

"Yeah, that surprised me too," Rachel admitted. "He's always so protective toward her. But he has something major scheduled at work, a negotiation of a settlement in a big lawsuit, and he's in charge for his firm. He can't be replaced." She paused. "You'll like him. He's a great guy. And I really am sorry to surprise you like this, especially now. Do you mind?"

"Of course not. She's your family. It's about time I met her. And her husband." Tom's words rang hollow, without the warmth of enthusiasm, and his smile looked forced.

Rachel's answering smile felt no more genuine on her face. *Just look at us. Just listen to us. You'd think we barely knew each other.* "Thanks. I know you're busy—"

"Yeah, and I will be for a while. I'll do my best to spend some time at home, but I can't promise anything."

"Don't worry about it." Rachel wanted Tom and her sister to spend as little time together as possible. Michelle could be charming when she made the effort, but she could also try the patience of a saint, and Tom was nowhere near sainthood. "It's just as well that we'll have some time alone together. I think she needs emotional support more than anything."

Tom gave Rachel a long, assessing look, the kind of scrutiny that told her he was picking up on every tremor of anxiety. He knew her relationship with Michelle was shaky at best, and he had to realize that only something extraordinary would bring Michelle all the way to Mason County to seek comfort from Rachel.

"You haven't told me exactly what kind of problem she's having," he said. "The longer you stall about telling me, the more I worry. Out with it. What's going on with your sister?"

Rachel pulled in a deep breath, released it. "Some guy is stalking her."

"What? Does she know who it is?"

"No, she doesn't, and she hasn't been assaulted or anything like that. But she feels threatened."

"Has she reported it to her local police?"

"Yes," Rachel said, "but they told her they couldn't do anything unless she's attacked or she can prove who's harassing her. She's scared, she feels defenseless, and I don't blame her."

"What did she tell you? What's happening?"

Rachel repeated what little she knew. "I know it might not sound like much to the police, but this kind of thing can be terrifying for a woman, even if the nut case never comes near her." She paused. "And I know from my own experience that sometimes guys like that don't stop with threatening phone calls."

"Right. To be on the safe side, you have to assume they're going to escalate." Tom frowned and raked his fingers through his hair. "Rachel, has it occurred you that this stalker might follow Michelle? If he's really obsessed with her, he could show up at our door."

Good god, Tom was right. Why hadn't the possibility even entered her mind until now? Rachel wavered. Her first instinct was to argue for the right to shelter her sister, but at the same time some part of her was reaching for an out, hoping Tom would provide it. "Does that mean you don't want her to come? You don't think it's safe?"

"Just hold on now." Tom raised both hands. "I didn't say that. She's welcome, her and her husband both. But I want to get more details from her. Unless there's some hard evidence, stalking isn't easy to prove in a legal sense, and the police can't do much about it."

"I'm not trying to hand this over to you to fix," Rachel protested. "You have enough to do without taking on Michelle's problems."

"Yeah, right, your sister's being stalked and you want me to forget I'm a cop and ignore it." Tom grinned, and the chill in the air between them gave way to a familiar warmth.

Rachel smiled. "Okay, I thought you might be able to do something, or give her some advice that would help. And if you can, I'm sure she'll appreciate it. But mostly I think she's just looking for a few days off the guy's radar." She scooped up a forkful of rice and went back to eating, hoping to signal her own confidence that it would all work out for the best. A confidence she didn't feel.

"Well, I have one more place to go before I can call it a day." As Tom rose to leave, he added, "I think you ought to know that Detective Fagan's on his way here. He's been working Shelley's disappearance."

Rachel's fork slipped from her fingers and fell onto her plate with a *clink*. "Have you been talking to him about the Beecher case for the last month? Why didn't you tell me?"

Tom gripped the back of his chair and sighed. "I've only talked to him two or three times about Shelley, and I didn't see any point in mentioning it. It didn't have anything to do with you."

She crumpled her napkin and threw it onto the table. "It's a good thing you're working the case now. I wouldn't trust Fagan to get anybody convicted for Shelley's murder. Considering his record."

Tom pushed his chair back under the table. "I'm not trying to defend him, but you know, it's not always the fault of the police when a jury acquits a guilty person and sends him to a mental hospital instead of jail."

That sounded like a defense to Rachel, and it stung. Had he been humoring her all along, secretly dismissing her anger at Detective Fagan as unjustified while letting her believe he agreed? She pressed her fingers to her side, where she felt the raised edge of a scar through the fabric of her shirt. The memory seldom invaded her conscious thoughts anymore, but now and then it still ambushed her at night, the whole terrifying experience playing out in her dreams, until the burning pain of the bullet slicing into her body jolted her awake. "Just keep him away from me while he's here," she said.

"There's no reason you have to cross paths."

Rachel rose, grabbed their plates and carried them to the sink. She took out her anger and disappointment on the dishes, scraping leftovers into the sink, jamming them into the garbage disposal. Tom hovered beside her as if uncertain what to do or say. "Go," she said. "You have work to do."

He laid a hand on her shoulder. Rachel froze.

"I don't want to leave with you mad at me."

Rachel closed her eyes, exhaled, forced her body to relax. She wasn't being fair to Tom. Whether he was right or wrong, whether he did it smoothly or clumsily, his first impulse would always be to protect her, and that was all he was trying to do now. "Michelle, Fagan," she said. "It's just a lot at once."

"I know." Tom leaned to kiss her on the cheek. "We'll have to make some time to talk. I'll try not to be too late."

Rachel turned to kiss him on the lips, reining in the urge to throw her arms around him and hold on. Then he was gone.

◇◇◇

Driving away from the farm, Tom tried to put Rachel out of his mind for now. He couldn't shake the feeling, though, that he'd let her down. He wished he'd told her earlier about Fagan working the missing person case so she wouldn't have been blindsided by the news that the detective was about to show up in Mason County.

As if hitting her with that wasn't enough, he'd come off sounding negative about her sister. Rachel had surprised him with the news that Michelle would arrive in less than twenty-four hours, and he knew he hadn't done a good job of hiding his feelings. Rachel loved her sister, but nothing she'd told Tom made him want to have Michelle as a guest in their house. She was dumping a huge emotional burden on Rachel, with her story about being stalked. Tom wasn't sure he believed any of it. Anonymous calls? Could be kids playing pranks. Things moved around in her office? The cleaning staff could be responsible. But if she really was being stalked, they had to worry about the guy following her to Mason County.

He drove a few miles down the road to the Hadley property. Blake and Maureen lived with their younger son Skeet and Blake's mother in a big white farmhouse that had been in the family for generations. The farm around it had gradually diminished in size as family members went into other types of work and sold off parcels. Brian, the older of Blake and Maureen's two sons, hadn't done any farming, but he'd built a small house of his own on the land when he married. His widow, Grace, still lived there with their two kids, a boy who probably couldn't remember his father and a girl born shortly after Brian's murder.

Tom parked in the gravel driveway and mounted the steps to the wide, covered porch. He rapped the brass door knocker, in the shape of a banjo, hard enough to be heard at the back of the house, in case the family was still at the dinner table.

Blake, the tall, broad-shouldered head of the family, swung open the door. When he saw Tom, he crumpled his paper napkin in one hand, raising ropey muscles along his forearm. Before Tom could speak, Blake said, "Soon as I heard about the Beecher girl, I knew you'd be coming around. We're finishing up supper. Might as well get the interrogation over with, I guess."

"I didn't come to interrogate you." Tom opened the screen door and stepped into a hallway that stretched the length of the house. Photos of several generations of Hadleys, all of them with musical instruments, lined the walls. "I just need to ask you a few questions."

"Well, you'll have to excuse me if I don't see the difference."

Blake led the way past the unused dining room to the kitchen, where the family sat at a big round table. Maureen, as rangy as her husband, sat next to Blake's frail mother, who had been in a wheelchair since suffering a stroke. Brian's widow, Grace, a pale-skinned young woman with brown hair and eyes, sat between her children. Crowded together in the middle of the table were several nearly empty vegetable serving dishes and a platter holding the remains of a chicken.

Skeet, the person Tom most wanted to talk to, wasn't there.

"Evening," Tom said to the women. "I'm sorry to interrupt your dinner. Is Skeet around?"

"Out with some friends," Blake said. He stood behind his wife with his arms folded across his chest.

Tom gave up any hope he'd had of going home to Rachel after he finished here. He wanted to talk to Skeet tonight, and he'd probably have to spend some time tracking him down. "I'd like to speak to the two of you," he told Blake and Maureen, "and you, Grace. One at a time."

"Oh no, you don't." Blake glared at Tom as if expecting a fight. "You're not going to separate us and try to get us to contradict each other. You'll talk to all of us together or you won't talk to any of us."

"Fine, if that's the way you want it," Tom kept his tone amiable. "I don't think the kids should be present, though. And I won't bother Mrs. Hadley." He nodded toward Blake's mother, who looked around in confusion, her paralyzed right arm pressed to her waist.

Grace said, "I'm staying here with Grandma and the kids. Lucy and Mark need to finish their dinner." She placed a hand on each child's head. Mark, a seven-year-old who had Grace's pale skin and dark hair, squirmed away as if embarrassed by his mother's protective gesture.

Tom wouldn't press Grace to talk to him now. As Brian's widow, she might seem to have the strongest motive for stopping Shelley's effort to free his killer, but she was the least likely of this bunch to abduct a girl, strangle her, wrap her in plastic, and dump her in a ravine. Unless, of course, she had help.

Blake and Maureen brushed past Tom and led the way up the hall to the living room. The two of them sat together on the couch, presenting a tense united front. Nudging a toy fire engine out of the way with the toe of his boot, Tom sat in an armchair across the coffee table from them. In no hurry to get started, he glanced around the blandly pleasant room, done in beige and several tones of green, distinguished only by the upright piano in one corner and the family pictures lining the mantel and covering every wall and tabletop. The Hadleys, like the Beechers, cared about family above all else.

Tom figured the silence would get to one of them, and less than a minute passed before Blake blurted, "The Beecher girl's death hasn't got anything to do with us."

"I hope it doesn't."

Blake jumped to his feet, fists clenched at his sides. "Whatever you came here to say, spit it out."

Tom remained seated, looking up at Blake. "When somebody is murdered, the first thing the police have to do is find out whether the victim's had any disagreements with anybody, whether somebody has a grievance against them. You understand that, don't you?"

"Sit down." Maureen grabbed her husband's wrist. "Let's answer his questions and be done with it. Then he can get on with finding out who really killed the girl."

Blake took his place on the couch, but he hunched forward, hands gripping his knees, poised to jump up again at any second.

"Thank you, Mrs. Hadley," Tom said. "I know you've all been unhappy about Shelley's investigation into Brian's murder."

"Investigation!" Blake scoffed. "She's just a kid. Was. What did she know about investigating crimes? Your own father found enough evidence to get Vance Lankford convicted and locked up for killing our son. Don't tell me you think your dad got the wrong man."

"I'm not investigating Brian's death. As far as I'm concerned, that's been settled by a judge and jury and his killer is in state prison. My job is to find out—"

The front door slammed. Skeet Hadley charged into the living room, his face red with fury. "What the hell are you doing here?"

Rising from his chair, Tom said, "I'm investigating Shelley Beecher's murder."

"And you came straight over here to accuse us." Skeet jerked off his black leather jacket and flung it on the chair next to Tom. A younger version of his father, Skeet had the same rugged good looks but was a little taller and more muscular, his curly brown hair long enough to hang over his forehead and brush his shirt collar in back. "Well, if you don't have the evidence to arrest one of us, you can leave right now. You're not welcome here."

The sour odor of beer wafted out on Skeet's breath. Not drunk, but almost there. "What makes you so sure that I suspect one of you of murder?"

Blake opened his mouth to answer, but Skeet cut him off. "Watch what you say, Dad. He's trying to trick you. Trying to make you incriminate yourself."

Skeet, Tom thought wearily, watched too many crime shows on TV. "I'd like to rule out all of you as fast as I can. Help me do that, okay?"

"You ought to be talking to her boyfriend," Skeet said.

"Or boyfriends," Maureen put in. "She probably had plenty of them, the way she flirted with everything in pants."

"When was the last time any of you saw Shelley or talked to her?"

For a moment none of them answered, then Maureen said, "We all went to see her when she was home for Christmas. We thought if we sat down with her, we could talk some sense into her. But she wouldn't listen."

"She blew us off." Skeet paced to the fireplace and back as he spoke. "She acted like she felt sorry for us because we couldn't see the truth."

Blake snorted. "She said if we cared about Brian, we'd want his *real* killer caught and punished. Well, my son's real killer is sitting in prison right now, and he's gonna stay there if I have anything to say about it."

"All that girl wanted," Skeet said, "was to make some kind of name for herself. It was just so damned obvious. She had this idea she was gonna be in the news for freeing an innocent man."

"I wouldn't be surprised," Maureen said, "if she already had her outfit picked out for going on the Today Show."

"Look at this." Skeet spun around, strode to the mantel and grabbed a couple of framed photos. He walked back and thrust them in Tom's face. "This was my brother. This is who Vance Lankford beat to death."

"Did you know he was about to sign on with a record company in Nashville?" Blake asked. "The rest of us, we always picked and sang at the festivals and the fair, but we were just amateurs, having fun. Brian was different. He had the talent to make it. He was gonna be a star. But now—" He broke off, shaking his head.

Tom looked at the photos Skeet held out. One showed a fresh-faced, grinning Brian Hadley with his guitar slung over his shoulder, his white cowboy hat cocked at an angle. In the other Brian stood at the center of his bandmates, including Skeet, who'd been a teenager then. Something was wrong with that picture, but Skeet pulled both photos away before Tom could figure out what it was.

"Do you have any idea how it made us feel," Maureen pleaded, "knowing somebody was trying to get Vance Lankford out of jail? Brian was murdered. His little children are growing up without their father. And here was this girl planning to make herself a celebrity by getting his killer out of jail."

Although Tom thought Shelley's belief in Lankford's innocence was misguided and her efforts to free him were a waste of time, he didn't let that skew his memory of her. The girl the Hadleys were ranting about didn't sound like the one he'd known. He could mention that her death wouldn't put an end to the innocence project's investigation, but he didn't want to deal with another outburst.

"Right now," he said, "the Beechers are going through the same thing you've been through. Their child has been murdered. My job is to find out who did it."

None of them answered. Maureen rubbed her hands along her forearms as if feeling a sudden chill. Blake stared at the floor. Skeet replaced the photos on the mantel and stood with his hands fisted at his sides, scowling at Tom.

"Was Christmas the last time any of you saw Shelley?" Tom asked. "That was more than three months ago."

"Well…" Maureen glanced at her husband beside her, then over at Skeet by the fireplace. "That was the last time all of us together saw her."

"But you've seen her since then separately?"

"I haven't," Blake said. "I've talked to Dan and Sarah, though. Tried to make them shake some sense into their daughter."

"Mrs. Hadley?" Tom prompted. "What about you?"

Another round of exchanged glances. The two men's stubborn expressions gave up nothing, but Maureen wavered and finally said, "I ran into her at the drugstore a couple of times. I tried to talk to her and she wouldn't listen."

"Skeet? I hear you've been to the Beecher house a few times by yourself."

Skeet kept his head down and suddenly appeared absorbed in the condition of his rough fingertips, rubbing them together, studying them. He was a guitar player like his older brother. Callused fingers came with the instrument.

Tom let the silence draw out. At last Maureen said, "Tell him, for heaven's sake. He knows already."

"All right, all right." Skeet swiped his curly hair off his forehead, then stuffed his hands into his jeans pockets. "I went to see her when she came home."

"Did you ever go up to see her at college?" Tom asked.

"No," Skeet said. Too quickly.

"I'll find out if you did, so you might as well tell me."

"I told you no, Sherlock." Sulky. Stubborn. Skeet acted like a kid ten years younger, stuck in a rebellious phase.

"You're sure about that?" Tom asked.

"Our son's not a liar," Blake said. "You got your answer."

An answer, anyway. But not the truth. Tom would bet on that.

"Listen to me," Maureen said, leaning forward, hands clasped in her lap. "The last thing in the world we'd want is for the wrong person to be punished for Brian's murder. We want his killer punished. And he *is* being punished. He deserved the death penalty, but at least he'll never get out on parole. I never believed Shelley was going to find anything that would clear a guilty man. How could she? We just wanted her to stop stirring up all those bad memories. We wanted to be left in peace."

"You can't seriously believe one of us would kill her over it," Blake said.

Tom could believe almost anybody was capable of almost any act, and these people had more motive than many killers did. He wouldn't get anything else out of them while they were together. "Well, thank you for talking to me. I hope you'll be patient and answer my questions if I need to come back to see you again." Blake gave a grunt of exasperation, but Tom went on without acknowledging the reaction. "I'll get this over with as soon as humanly possible."

Driving away from the house, Tom thought about the naiveté of earnest young people who got hold of a lofty notion and didn't think twice about bashing everybody over the head with it. It might not have anything to do with Shelley's murder, but he wanted to know what made her so sure Vance Lankford was innocent. Whatever she'd been up to, she should have been more discreet about it. The victim's relatives, still trying to accept their loss, had obviously felt she was taunting them with the idea that Lankford might go free. They were angry and hurting, and Tom wouldn't be surprised to learn that one of them had lashed out at her in an unguarded moment.

Chapter Six

Rachel's drinking glass slipped from her fingers, bounced off the edge of the bathroom sink and shattered on the floor. Water and glass shards sprayed the tile and her athletic shoes. Sighing, she leaned against the sink. Third time this morning she'd dropped something. Second time she'd broken something. She still had a few drops of milk on her shoes from the cereal bowl incident in the kitchen earlier.

Tom appeared in the bathroom doorway, buttoning his brown uniform shirt. "You're a nervous wreck. You're really worried about your sister, aren't you?"

"Yes, I am." *In more ways than you can imagine.* Rachel turned away, hiding her face from his scrutiny, and yanked a hand towel from the rack. She knelt to clean the floor.

Tom stooped at the same moment, and they bumped heads. "Sorry," he said. "You okay?"

Rachel nodded, fighting the urge to throw herself into his arms and pour out her anxiety. She wanted their normal Sunday morning routine, the leisurely breakfast, the shared run over the hills and through the meadows on the farm. But Tom had a murder to investigate and she had Michelle to deal with. *Get a grip, for god's sake.*

Silently Tom collected the pieces of broken glass and dropped them into the wastebasket while Rachel mopped water off the floor and her shoes with the towel. She dug a bit of soggy bran flake, a remnant of the kitchen accident, out from under a shoe lace.

After tossing the last sliver of glass into the trash, Tom rose. "I doubt I'll be able to do much, but at least I can give her some advice on how to deal with it."

If she'll listen to you. If she'll even want your advice. "Thanks," Rachel said. She stood at the sink and wrung the water out of the towel.

He kissed her. "I'll be home for dinner, I promise."

"Tom, wait." Rachel shook the water off her hands, then wrapped her arms around him, burying her face in his shoulder. She forced herself to voice a little of what she felt. "I'm so afraid the two of you will hate each other."

Tom laughed and hugged her. "Is that what's bothering you? I'll be on my best behavior, I promise."

"I know." Rachel kissed him and let him go. *It's not your behavior I'm worried about,* she thought as he walked off down the hallway.

How could she explain her conflicted feelings about Michelle, the longing mixed with apprehension, the tenderness that too often gave way to anger? Tom realized that Rachel wanted, needed, to help Michelle, but would he understand if she told him she was afraid to have her sister in their home? Not only because Michelle was bringing trouble with her, but because her presence would dredge up memories Rachel didn't want to face.

She had told Tom the bare facts about what had happened to her and Michelle as children. He knew about the kidnapping, about Rachel's privileged but loveless childhood as Judith Goddard's daughter, her search for her real parents, but for the most part she still kept the door into the past closed to him. Some things, including Judith's death and Rachel's role in it, remained impossible to talk about. Impossible to think about without bringing on a flood of anguish that threatened to destroy her.

Michelle was her only link to the past. If Michelle didn't exist, Rachel might be able to leave it behind and never look back. But then, if Michelle didn't exist, none of it would have happened in the first place.

◇◇◇

Detective Nate Fagan prowled the perimeter of Tom's office, examining the framed photos while Tom sat at his desk wondering how long the Fairfax County cop, who'd just arrived, would be underfoot. A tall, sharp-nosed man in his forties, Fagan had only a hint of bristly dark hair on his shaved scalp. His black suit, draping a bony frame, made him look like an undertaker.

Fagan paused before a picture of Tom's father and older brother Chris in Mason County Sheriff's Department uniforms. "Family? You all look alike. They still on the job?"

"No," Tom said. He added with some reluctance, "They both died in an accident a while back."

Fagan swung around. "Hey, that's rough. Car accident?"

Tom nodded. Fagan looked expectant, as if waiting for details, but Tom wasn't going to revisit the night that changed his life just to satisfy the man's curiosity. Leaning back in his chair, he broke eye contact and swiveled toward the window into the parking lot. A TV van from Roanoke sat out there, and a young female reporter with shoulder-length brown hair stood next to it, talking to a man with a video camera.

"What did you tell them?" Tom asked. "I noticed you talking to them on the way in."

Fagan followed Tom's gaze. "The vultures? I said we didn't have any information for them yet, but they'll be the very first to know when we do."

Tom gave a short laugh. Pretty much the same thing he'd told the reporter when she waylaid him. More journalists would be here soon. Dennis Murray had the patience to deal with them, and Tom planned to let the sergeant deliver short updates at broadly spaced intervals.

"The less they know, the better. Until we need them." Fagan moved on to a photo of Tom in his Richmond PD uniform, standing between his father and brother. Jingling keys in his pants pocket, the detective asked, "Richmond, huh? Why'd you leave?"

"Long story." One Tom had no intention of telling a stranger. "Can I get some coffee brought in for you?"

"Naw, I'm about maxed out on caffeine for one morning." Fagan settled in a chair in front of the desk, slumping and crossing an ankle over a knee. "So, is the sheriff coming in today?"

"No," Tom said. "He's on sick leave. I'm in charge."

"And running for the office, huh? I nearly plowed into one of your campaign signs when I took a curve too fast. When's the election?"

"In the fall. I'll worry about it when the time comes. Right now all I'm thinking about is this case."

Fagan scratched a spot on his chin. "By the way, where's the closest motel? I didn't notice anything driving in."

"I wouldn't recommend the fleabag motels around here," Tom said. "I know a couple of people who might rent you a room. I'll have somebody call around and find a place for you to stay."

Fagan shook his head, a bemused half-smile on his face. Tom could almost hear the man thinking: *I've really landed in the middle of nowhere.*

Enough chitchat. "You saw Shelley Beecher's body in Roanoke?" Tom asked. "What do you think about the condition of it?"

"I'm not sure what to think." Frowning, Fagan brushed a hand over his stubbly hair. "It's hard to believe she was alive most of the time she's been missing. I thought from the start we were looking for a body."

Tom fingered the one-page report on his desk, faxed from the medical examiner late the day before. "The M.E. won't even take a guess at time of death. Says he saw contradictory indications on his preliminary exam of the body."

Fagan nodded. "If she was killed earlier, not long after she was snatched, then the body had to have been hidden someplace cool and dry to be in the shape it's in."

"The M.E.'s definite about one thing, though. This wasn't a sexual assault. I guess a stranger could get off on choking her to death, but I'm more inclined to think the motive was personal and she was killed by somebody she knew."

"I couldn't find anybody she was on the outs with," Fagan said. "Other students, professors, friends—everybody seemed to love the girl. Did somebody here have a problem with her?"

Tom nodded. He told Fagan about the Hadley family's quarrel with Shelley over her work on Vance Lankford's behalf.

"That's a possibility," Fagan conceded. "But if she was abducted and murdered in Fairfax County, her killer's most likely walking around there right now, not down here."

"I want to hear what you've got on her boyfriend, teachers, school friends."

"Yeah, I'll fill you in." Fagan gazed absently into space as he tapped an index finger on the wooden arm of his chair. "Why bring her body out here? That's what puzzles me."

"I don't know, but it makes me think the killer's familiar with this area. Either came from Mason County or still lives here. But why would he go out of his way to bring his crime so close to home? Why not leave her where she died, or dump her somewhere far away, so he couldn't be connected to it?"

"People who do this kind of thing, they don't think rationally," Fagan said. "Their behavior's got its own logic."

"I realize that." Tom stifled his irritation at the other man's instructive tone. "But he had the presence of mind to either kill her and hide her body for a month or keep her captive for all that time. I think we're dealing with somebody who's organized and gives some thought to what he's doing."

"Maybe he got rid of her just because he needed room in his fridge for his next victim."

"Are you're suggesting this is a serial killer?" Tom asked. "What do you base that on?"

Fagan waved a hand as if trying to erase what he'd said. "Joke, joke."

Not a funny one, Tom thought, if you happened to have known the girl when she was alive and well. "There must be a reason why her body was brought here."

"You think the killer's sending us a message?" Fagan delivered the question with a heavy dose of condescension. "You know how rare that kind of thing is?"

Tom kept his own voice level and neutral. "It wouldn't have to be a message to the police. All I know is that she was brought back to her home county, and she wasn't buried. Whoever put her there knew she'd be found. We can't even be sure she was abducted and killed in Fairfax County. She could've gone somewhere with the killer voluntarily, if it was somebody she knew and wasn't afraid of. After she left the meeting with the innocence project team that night, she never got back in her car, did she?"

"No," Fagan said. "It was still parked in the lot, about a hundred feet from the door of the building. She probably never made it back to her car, but we didn't find any signs of a struggle."

"No witnesses?"

"No. The office is in a strip mall with small shops and a café. There were a few people around at the time, but we couldn't turn up a single witness who remembered seeing the girl. Whatever happened, it was outside the range of the security camera over the door, and it went down quietly." Fagan paused. "I believe she was murdered in Fairfax County, but I'll stick around here for a while and talk to people who knew her, see if I can pick up any useful information."

"Sure," Tom said. "You'll get more cooperation if you go with me, not alone."

Fagan didn't respond to that. "I want to take a look at where you found her. What kind of physical evidence did you pick up at the site?"

"Just a lot of trash, and I doubt any of it relates to the crime, but the state lab's going over all of it. Everything the crime scene guy found and everything the kids collected. The lab's got the mattress too."

"Well," Fagan said, rising. "Take me out there, will you?"

Tom was tempted to say he had more pressing things to do and send Fagan out with another deputy, but he thought better of it. He'd reached a conclusion that he hadn't shared with anybody else yet, and he wanted to see if Fagan, after viewing the body dump site, would come up with the same idea. He stood. "Let's go."

Chapter Seven

Rachel paused while dusting the coffee table for the second time. Was that a car pulling into the driveway? A jolt of anxiety set her heart racing, but she told herself it wasn't Michelle and Kevin, they couldn't be here already unless they'd left home well before dawn.

But when she hurried to the window to look, there they were, getting out of Kevin's silver Mercedes. For a second the whole scene felt like such a surreal blending of Rachel's two lives that she could only stand and stare.

While Kevin popped the trunk lid and walked around to the rear of the car, Michelle started along the front walk to the porch. Rachel stashed the dust cloth in a table drawer and ran to open the door.

As Michelle mounted the steps, Rachel barely caught herself before she blurted out her shock at her sister's appearance. The usual rosy blush of Michelle's cheeks had faded, and recent weight loss emphasized her high cheekbones. Dark circles under her eyes spoke of sleepless nights. Her blond hair, pushed back over her ears, looked as if she hadn't thoroughly combed it that morning.

Rachel stepped onto the porch and Michelle rushed forward and caught her in a tight embrace. Michelle's hair smelled faintly of apples, the perfume of the shampoo she'd used for years. She had always been slender, but now she felt alarmingly gaunt in Rachel's embrace, her ribs palpable through her blouse and sweater. She clung fiercely, until Rachel pulled away.

Sniffling, Michelle blinked back tears.

"Hey," Rachel said, then stopped because she didn't know what she could say that would make the situation easier. *Don't cry? Everything's okay?* If that were true, no power could have dragged Michelle out here to the mountains, the country, where she might actually encounter a wild animal or a bug. Rachel looked past Michelle to Kevin, a big, handsome guy who would have fit anybody's description of all-American. His face locked into a frown, his eyes haunted by worry, he climbed the steps with Michelle's blue suitcase and a black overnight bag.

"Thank you for letting me come," Michelle said. Her gaze darted around as if checking to see whether anybody lurked nearby.

Has it occurred to you that this stalker might follow Michelle? Tom's conjecture popped into Rachel's mind. But how likely was it that anybody would trail Michelle all the way out here? She was far away from the source of her problem, and she was safe. Rachel couldn't help Michelle if she gave in to paranoia too.

"Come in, come in." Rachel ushered the two of them through the doorway.

From the long center hallway, Michelle glanced right into the living room, left into the dining room. "What a homey little place."

A homey little place? Had she imagined the critical undertone to the comment? "I love it. It's comfortable, and I like having so much outdoor space."

"Well, you always were a nature girl," Michelle said.

Kevin stood inside the door, still holding the luggage. Billy Bob bypassed Michelle and headed straight for Kevin, who set down the bags and stooped to scratch the bulldog's head.

"Meet Billy Bob," Rachel said.

"What a great dog." Kevin laughed as Billy Bob angled his head to take full advantage of the scratching. "I've always wanted a bulldog."

"Oh, you have not." Michelle's indulgent little smile broke through her gloom. "You just want a dog, period."

She sounded, Rachel thought, like a mother who had long ago established that her child was not going to get a dog, however much he begged. "I'll show you your room," Rachel said. "Then we can relax and talk."

She forced herself to take the stairs at a normal speed instead of sprinting up two at a time. A mixture of excitement and apprehension kept her pulse pounding in her ears. When she reached the second floor landing she wiped her damp palms on the legs of her jeans.

The door to Tom's parents' bedroom stood open. Frank lay curled on the bed, fast asleep, his back against one of the pillows.

Kevin laughed. "This little guy hasn't changed much since the last time we saw him. Still enjoying a life of ease."

That coaxed another small smile from Michelle. Relieved by the break in tension, Rachel laughed and said, "I'll dislodge him."

As she started for the bed, Frank raised his head and blinked at them.

"No, it's all right," Michelle said. "Let him stay." With her arms folded tightly across her midriff, she surveyed the room as if she had her own doubts about staying.

"This room belonged to Tom's father and mother," Rachel said. "We've been doing some redecorating, but we haven't gotten around to changing anything in here yet. We don't normally use it, so…"

"It looks very comfortable," Michelle said. "You don't have to apologize."

Rachel almost said she wasn't apologizing, but she pulled herself up short. *Oh, yes, you were. And you will not do it again.* She drew a breath and let it out before she spoke. "You have your own bathroom here. Come downstairs when you've settled in. I'll make some tea, unless you'd rather have coffee. If you're hungry—"

"Tea's fine," Kevin said, giving Rachel a knowing, sympathetic little smile. "Don't go to a lot of trouble. We had breakfast so early that we stopped for an early lunch on the road. We'll be fine until dinner."

In the kitchen, Rachel put a kettle of water on the range, grabbed cups from a cabinet and placed them on a tray. She popped open the plastic container where she kept tea bags and surveyed the selection. What would Michelle like? Tom didn't drink hot tea, so all Rachel had were several of her own preferences. Michelle used to prefer Darjeeling, but did she still drink it?

Oh, for god's sake, don't worry about every little thing. Rachel gripped the edge of the counter with both hands. Tom was right. She was a nervous wreck. They still had to get through the evening. Would Tom and Michelle liked each other, or at least be able to accept each other? Any tension that developed between them would make it harder for Rachel to give her sister the emotional support she needed.

"Rachel?"

Kevin's voice made her spin around. He stood in the kitchen doorway, brow furrowed, hands jammed into his pants pockets.

"Could you go up and talk to her now?" he asked. "She says she just got one of those phone calls, and she's pretty upset. I'll get out of the way. Can I take a look around the farm, maybe take Billy Bob with me?"

"Sure, of course." Rachel brushed past Kevin and ran upstairs to her sister.

Chapter Eight

Tom handled the steep incline easily in his boots with ridged soles, but Fagan's dress shoes sent him sliding into the ravine like a skier making his first wobbly run down a slope. Every time Fagan collided with a rock, root, or scrawny bush, Tom grabbed him to keep him from tumbling head over heels the rest of the way.

"You okay?" Tom asked when they both made it to the narrow strip of flat land at the bottom.

Fagan leaned over, hands on his knees, trying to catch his breath. "Man," he gasped, "you must be part mountain goat."

Tom grinned. "Among other things."

Straightening, Fagan wiped beads of sweat off his upper lip and surveyed both sharply angled walls of the ravine. The one they'd just descended was a challenge but not impossible. The other side would require rock climbing skills. Fagan scanned the narrow area at the bottom, then looked up again. Tom guessed what he was thinking but didn't press him. Somewhere nearby a pileated woodpecker pair exchanged *cluk cluk* calls.

"Any other way to get in and out of here?" Fagan asked.

"No. If there was, we'd call it a hollow. Over here's where we found the body. Watch your step in all these vines." Tom walked over to a rectangular spot free of vegetation. "The mattress was laying here long enough to smother the vines and weeds under it. But I believe the body was brought here in the last few days."

Joining Tom, Fagan studied the space. "The plastic she was wrapped in was clean?"

"Spotless," Tom said.

Fagan looked upward again. "If the body was rolled or dragged—"

"The plastic would have been dirty, probably torn too."

Fagan was silent a moment, frowning. "If she was wrapped in a blanket, a sheet, something that protected the plastic—"

"It would have snagged in a dozen different places." Tom waved a hand at the wild rhododendrons and other stunted shrubs that clung to the slope like barnacles on a ship's hull. "There would have been plenty of fibers left behind, especially if a blanket was used."

"And the crime scene tech didn't find any fibers?"

"He picked up a few, but they probably came off the kids' clothes yesterday." Tom paused, then added, "You couldn't roll a body straight down, with all the vegetation in the way. Dragging it, yeah, that's possible—if the body was wrapped twice, then dragged carefully, weaving around a lot to stay clear of the brush, then the outer wrapping was removed and carried away."

Fagan stuck his right hand in his pant pocket and jingled his keys. "Lot of trouble to go to, out in the open where you don't know when somebody might drive by."

Tom hoped that thing with the keys didn't turn out to be a constant habit. He could get tired of it fast.

"How'd somebody get a mattress down here?" Fagan asked.

"Two guys standing at the top could throw a mattress, and it could make it all the way to the bottom before it hit. Two guys with enough muscle. The body wasn't tossed, though. It was carried." Tom cleared his throat and asked Fagan, "Are you thinking what I'm thinking?"

Fagan's eyebrows went up. "And what are you thinking, Captain?"

"That one person might have managed it with a lot of time and effort. But it makes more sense to think two people carried Shelley Beecher's body down here."

◇◇◇

Michelle sat on the edge of the bed, a hand pressed to her forehead. Frank, sitting up on the bed and tensed to bolt, watched her with wide eyes. When Rachel walked in, the cat leapt off the bed and trotted out.

Dropping her hand, Michelle watched Frank retreat. Emotion brought some of the color back to her cheeks, and tears rose to her eyes. "Even the cat doesn't want to be around me." She followed the words with a choked laugh.

Rachel sat next to her sister. "Kevin said you got a call that upset you."

"He didn't believe me." Michelle plucked a tissue from the box on the bedside table and dabbed her eyes with it. "He doesn't believe any of it."

"He knows you got a call," Rachel pointed out. "He was right here with you."

"No, he was in the bathroom, with the water running. And my phone log says the caller's number is blocked. I told him the caller spoke and used my name, but still—" Michelle blotted her eyes again with angry jabs. "I'm getting tired of my own husband looking at me like I've lost my mind."

"Mish—" Rachel searched for the right words. She didn't think Michelle would invent such things, but she hoped her sister wasn't in real danger. The harassment could be a prank, a nasty one that had gone on too long and had to be stopped. "Maybe Kevin just doesn't know how to handle it."

"Well, neither do I. Who is this person? Why is he doing this to me?"

"Are you positive it's a man?"

Michelle nodded. "When I first started getting calls, I couldn't tell. For a while he didn't say anything, he just...*breathed*, then hung up. When he started speaking, I knew it was a man. He whispers, a soft, creepy whisper, but I'm sure it's a man."

"What did he say on the phone just now?"

"He said, *Are you enjoying your little vacation, Michelle?* He knows where I am." A tremor ran through Michelle's body.

"That's what he wants you to believe. Maybe he's just angry that you're not at home and he can't find you." But what if he guessed where Michelle had gone and came after her? To reassure herself as much as Michelle, Rachel placed an arm around her sister's shoulders, the way she had so many times when they were girls, and automatically spoke the old, familiar words of comfort. "There's nothing to be afraid of. You're safe now."

Michelle jerked away from her and jumped up, an angry flush coloring her face. "Don't treat me like a child! You're just *indulging* me. I thought you'd understand after what you went through with Perry Nelson."

"The two situations aren't exactly the same," Rachel said, "but believe me, I do know how scared you must be." Nelson had been a charming, blandly handsome young client who brought his dog to Rachel for treatment and grabbed an opportunity to steal her prescription pad. When a pharmacist alerted her that Nelson had presented orders for narcotics in amounts not normally prescribed for dogs, Rachel had pressed charges against him. Nelson retaliated with a campaign of harassment and, ultimately, by shooting her. "I still dream about it sometimes. So please don't think I don't understand."

Michelle wrapped her arms around her waist and stood rigid as a statue. Her face displayed every emotion she was sorting through, as if searching for one that suited her. Stubborn anger gave way to grudging acceptance of Rachel's apology, only to be displaced by a fresh wave of anxiety. "I knew it was bad for you, but I had to experience it myself to really understand."

"I was lucky in a way," Rachel said, "because I knew Perry Nelson, I understood why he wanted to hurt me."

"The police knew who he was too, and they knew what he was doing, but they didn't do anything to keep him from hurting you," Michelle said, her voice rising. "He almost killed you, while the police stood by and let it happen. I can't even identify the person who's harassing me, so what hope do I have of getting any protection?"

Oh, god, Rachel thought, weary with tension. She felt helpless. Was there any right way to deal with this? Rubbing the knotted muscles at the back of her neck, she said, "Maybe Tom can help somehow. I promise he'll take you seriously. Come sit down, please. If you need to talk, I'm here to listen."

Michelle returned to sit on the bed beside Rachel, but kept her arms clamped around her waist. She rocked slightly, back and forth.

Everything in Rachel urged her to embrace Michelle, beg her to stop torturing herself, but she stayed silent while her sister groped for words.

When Michelle spoke again, her voice came out a whisper. "I've been thinking about Mother a lot since all this started. I still miss her so much."

Rachel's desire to comfort her sister vanished. "Well, I'm sure she'd be a big help if she were here. Maybe she could hypnotize you and make it all go away."

Rachel instantly regretted the words. She had to look away from Michelle's wounded expression.

"How could you say something so cruel to me?" Michelle's voice quavered. "So much for sisterly understanding."

"I'm sorry." This time Rachel meant it. She was fumbling for something more to say when footsteps sounded on the stairs. Michelle yanked a handful of tissues from the box on the bedside table and dabbed and wiped her face. Seconds later Kevin appeared in the doorway.

Chapter Nine

Detective Fagan frowned as Tom pulled onto the shoulder of the road in front of the Lankford house. "Are we going to have a pack of pit bulls jumping us when we get out of the car?"

Two PRIVATE PROPERTY—NO TRESPASSING signs hung on the five-foot high chain link fence and a third on the gate. A padlock secured the gate on the inside.

"You wouldn't put out the welcome mat either," Tom said, "if you'd been through what these people have. It's incredible, the crap they get thrown at them. Literally, sometimes." He plucked his cell phone from his shirt pocket. "Having a convicted murderer in the family doesn't make life easy."

Tom punched in the couple's home phone number and drummed his fingers on the armrest while he waited for an answer. Vance Lankford's parents lived in a residential area on the outskirts of Mountainview, where the lots were smaller and the houses closer together than anywhere else in the mostly rural county. Tom could remember when robust azaleas had lined the front of the white siding-covered house and the flower beds had overflowed with spring bulbs and colorful summer annuals. Now the azaleas looked sickly, with sparse foliage and only a few pink flowers dotting the branches. Several clumps of gold and white daffodils bloomed beside the front steps—you couldn't kill a daffodil if you beat it with a shovel, Tom's mother used to say—but the tulip leaves struggling up through the weedy beds looked like weak afterthoughts of bulbs long since spent.

Although the Lankfords' cars both sat in the driveway, the curtains on all the windows remained tightly drawn in midday. After the phone rang for the sixth time, Tom tapped his horn. One downstairs curtain flicked back a couple of inches, then fell closed again. A moment later, Jesse Lankford answered the phone inside the house. "What is it? What do you want?"

"I just came by to see if everything's okay here. Can I come in? I won't bother you for long."

Jesse sighed. "I'll be out in a minute." He hung up.

"He's coming to unlock the gate," Tom told Fagan. They both stepped out of the cruiser.

Slamming the passenger door, Fagan said over the car's roof, "These people are teachers? They teach in a public school when they have to live this way? You've gotta be kidding me."

"I don't know how they do it," Tom said, rounding the front of the cruiser. He lowered his voice when he saw Jesse Lankford emerge from the house. "Considering the shitty way teenagers behave sometimes."

Jesse, a tall, thin man whose stooped shoulders made him look shorter, hustled along the driveway with his head down as if he were running a gauntlet. Ten feet from the gate he glanced up and stopped in his tracks. His eyes, fixed on Fagan, widened behind his black-rimmed glasses. "Who are you?"

"This is Detective Fagan from the Fairfax County Police," Tom said. "Detective, this is Jesse Lankford."

Before Fagan could speak, Jesse demanded, "What do the Fairfax police want with us?"

Fagan stepped forward. "I've been investigating the Beecher girl's disappearance, and I'm down here looking into her death."

A blotchy flush traveled up Jesse's neck to his pallid cheeks. "We don't need to get dragged into that. It has nothing to do with us."

"We just want to talk to you," Tom said. "Can we come in for a minute?"

Jesse shot a look to his left. Tom followed his glance and saw the white-haired woman next door peering through a side window at them. Muttering something under his breath, Jesse yanked a key ring from his pants pocket and fumbled with the padlock inside the gate. He yanked it open, and without speaking again, wheeled around and hurried back up the driveway to the house.

Tom and Fagan made their way to the front door, sidestepping a mess of half-rotted fruits and vegetables strewn over the driveway, the front walk and the steps. Dents pockmarked the vinyl siding on the house, and the rocks responsible for the damage lay on the ground along the foundation. Sitting only thirty feet from the road and lacking a porch, the house made an inviting target. Even so, Tom figured you'd need a hell of a strong pitching arm to lob a heavy rock this distance.

A blood-colored stain and bits of red pulp splattered the glass in the storm door—an over-ripe tomato, probably thrown the night before, its acidic aroma still strong.

When they entered the living room, Jesse started to slide one of the three bolts into place on the door, then abruptly abandoned it. "Nobody's going to bother us with a police car parked outside."

Sonya Lankford stood by the fireplace, a big box of kitchen matches in one hand indicating they'd interrupted her as she was about to light the kindling and logs laid in the grate. With her free hand she tucked her shoulder-length gray hair behind her ears, tugged at the hem of her green cardigan sweater, smoothed the front of her brown skirt.

"Are you two all right?" Tom asked her. "Has anybody been bothering you?"

"What do you think?" Like her husband, Sonya wore glasses, and her thick lenses made her eyes look disproportionately small above her sharp cheekbones. "People were driving by half the night. Screaming and throwing things. Yelling that Shelley got what she deserved, and we'll get the same if we keep trying to get Vance out of prison."

"Why didn't you report it?"

"What good would that do?" Jesse said. "Are you going to park a deputy in front of our house all night, every night?"

"If it's necessary, yes." A rash promise, Tom knew, one he could keep only in the unlikely event that deputies volunteered their time.

Jesse snorted, dismissing the idea. "We don't know anything that'll help you with your investigation. Don't drag us into this. You'll just make matters worse."

"If you'll talk to us for a few minutes, we won't bother you again."

Jesse and Sonya locked eyes for a long moment, and Tom had the impression the two were debating without speaking a word. Then Jesse motioned the policemen toward the two easy chairs facing the sofa.

Tom and Fagan took the chairs and Jesse dropped onto the sofa. Sonya crouched by the fireplace and struck a match. For a second the sharp odor of sulfur stung Tom's nostrils. When she set the fatwood kindling ablaze, a strong but pleasant aroma of pine wafted through the room, carrying with it a jumble of half-formed memories and associations. Childhood. Holidays. Family. It was what Tom thought of as a happy smell, but he saw no happiness in the Lankford house.

With the drapes drawn, the two lamps burning on the end tables by the sofa cast more shadows than light. The room looked clean and neat, but Sonya roamed around, flicking her fingertips across tabletops, straightening a country print on a wall, tugging the curtains more tightly together. A photo of the Lankfords' only child, Vance, stood on the mantel. A high school picture, from the look of it, a reminder of better times. Tom wondered what the fresh-faced, smiling boy in the photo, ordinary but pleasant, looked like after a few years in state prison.

"I figured Shelley's body turning up yesterday might set things off again," Tom said. "I'm sorry about that. I don't know what gets into people."

"It's nothing new." Sonya paused by the sofa, her lips twisted in a sour imitation of a smile. "This has been our life since the day Vance was arrested."

"Nobody should have to get used to being harassed," Tom said. "I've told you before, get me some license plate numbers and I'll put a stop to it."

"We'd have to go outside to get the plate numbers," Jesse said. "We don't open our door at night."

"We know who's doing it, though," Sonya said. "Some of them are our own students. I see them smirking at me in class. I hear them whispering when my back's turned."

"Who are they?" Tom asked.

Jesse shook his head. "If we started accusing people, our lives wouldn't be worth living."

Are they worth living now? Underneath the pungent pine scent Tom detected layers of stale odors, as if the house had been shut up tight for years, the door never open long enough for fresh air to get in.

Fagan, who had been listening with a frown, now asked, "Why do you put up with it? Why do you stay here?"

Tom winced. The Lankfords focused twin glares on the detective.

"This is our home," Sonya said. "We were both born and raised in Mason County. We've got old people in our families that need us, our parents and aunts and uncles. We've been teaching here since we got out of college. We're not letting anybody run us out of our jobs and our home."

"But if your own students are harassing—"

"I taught Brian Hadley in my music class," Jesse broke in. "Coached him in the school band. Sonya had him for English. He was a good kid, and he had a lot of talent. We both encouraged him to go after what he wanted. Now everybody acts like we're to blame for him being dead."

"How closely were you working with Shelley on getting your son out of prison?" Tom asked.

"We weren't *working with* her," Sonya said.

"She talked to us a few times, that's all," Jesse said. "We couldn't tell her much. Hell, if we could prove our boy didn't kill Brian, we would've done it before he was convicted. Everybody thought we put Shelley up to what she was doing, but Vance was the one who got in touch with the innocence project and asked them to help him."

"Everybody hated us already because we wouldn't disown our son," Sonya said. "They thought we should be walking around in sackcloth and ashes, begging everybody to forgive us for raising a murderer. Then when Shelley started trying to get him out, that just made them madder."

A loud pop from the blazing wood in the fireplace made all of them jump. Jesse brushed past his wife, grabbed the poker, and stabbed the logs to settle them in the grate.

"Don't you believe your son is innocent?" Fagan asked.

Tom groaned inwardly. The detective was ripping into unhealed wounds.

"Yes, sir, we believe our son is innocent," Sonya snapped. She raked a hand through her hair on one side as if she wanted to tear it out by the roots. "We didn't raise a killer. And we didn't raise a fool. Any man would have to be a fool to murder somebody over that little slut."

Fagan looked at Tom, eyebrows raised inquiringly.

"I'll fill you in later." Before Fagan could say anything more, Tom asked the Lankfords, "Did Shelley ever tell you she had some information that might get Vance out of prison?"

"She believed he was innocent," Jesse said. He returned to the couch and tugged his wife's arm to make her sit beside him. "She said she was going to do everything she could to prove it. But she never gave us any details about what she was doing. We don't know if she really had anything or not."

"We didn't have any expectations." Sonya sat upright and stiff, her hands pressed together in her lap, palm to palm and fingers to fingers. "What could a first-year law student do that Vance's own attorney couldn't?"

Tom held a low opinion of the attorney who had represented Vance and suspected the defense could have been better. But he was also positive his own father's investigation had been thorough and the evidence had been corroborated. "The innocence project won't drop the case because of Shelley's death. If I can find out what she came up with, I'll let you know, and I'll make sure the prosecutor knows about it."

"Right." Jesse's face twisted in a sneer. "We'll pin our hopes on the prosecutor who sent Vance to prison and the son of the cop who arrested him."

Tom didn't bother to answer that. He didn't care what the Lankfords thought of him. He did care about their safety, though. "You've got all my phone numbers, don't you? Home, office, cell? I want you to call me when anybody comes around here harassing you. Day or night. Anytime. Call me."

They both looked dubious and didn't reply.

Tom rose and Fagan followed him to the door. Jesse trailed them outside.

After Tom and Fagan walked through the gate, Jesse said, "The Hadley boy's one of them. Brian's brother, Skeet."

"He comes by here at night?" This information didn't surprise Tom.

"Yeah. He was here last night, throwing rocks and yelling. Just so you know."

"You need to make a formal complaint."

"No. We'll wait it out. We've made it this far." Jesse slammed the gate and clicked the padlock shut. "Nobody's going to drive us out of our home. We're not leaving unless we go feet-first."

That, in a nutshell, was Tom's greatest fear for these two.

In the cruiser as they drove away, Tom's thoughts shifted to Rachel. He wished he could have stayed home today so he'd be with her when her sister and brother-in-law arrived. He didn't like the nervous, almost fearful vibes he'd been getting from her since she told him Michelle was coming. He didn't think her jitters had much to do with her sister's stalker story. Michelle herself was the source of Rachel's anxiety. When anybody needed Rachel, she was there heart and soul, but she wasn't approaching her sister's dilemma with her typical passionate abandon.

Fagan broke into his thoughts. "So what's the story? I'm starting to think the Beecher girl's murder might have something to do with the innocence project after all. Even the convicted man's parents didn't like her poking around."

"It's a small community," Tom said. "Things like that fester because everybody knows everybody else and they run into each other everywhere they go."

"So what happened? Who's the slut Mrs. Lankford mentioned?"

Tom slowed at an intersection, paying respect to the four-way sign without coming to a full stop when he saw no vehicles approaching in any direction. "Brian Hadley had a country music band, and Vance Lankford was in it. Played electric guitar, I think. He was a little older than Brian, and he was teaching biology at the middle school and playing in Brian's band in his spare time."

"And the girl?" Fagan prompted. "Who is she, and how did she figure in it?"

"Rita Jankowski. She was a singer." Tom drove into Mountainview, past a used car lot and an Exxon station. "She and Brian sang together. Brian was just twenty-one when he died, but he was already married, had one baby, another on the way. And he made the mistake of getting involved with Rita."

Now Tom realized what was wrong with the picture of Brian's band he'd seen at the Hadley house the night before. Somebody had cut Rita out of it. Not surprising. The family wouldn't want a reminder of her part in Brian's death.

"She was already paired off with Lankford?"

"She's never been the type to tie herself down to one man," Tom said, "but yeah, they'd been seeing each other, then she and Brian started up. Classic story."

Fagan was about to say something when the squawk of the dispatch radio cut him off. "Unit two?" the young woman's voice asked. "Are you on the road?"

"Unit two here," Tom answered, silently wondering, *What now?*

"We've had a call from Maureen Hadley about Dan Beecher causing a disturbance over there," the dispatcher said. "I sent Brandon Connolly out, but I figured you'd want to know too."

"I'm on my way." The fallout was starting already. Tom swung the cruiser around in a U-turn and sped south again.

When Tom slowed in front of the Hadley house, Blake Hadley and Dan Beecher stood three feet apart in the yard, screaming at each other while Maureen and Skeet watched from the porch. Brandon stood with the two men, gesturing and talking, but they didn't seem to notice he was there.

"Aw, crap." Tom braked hard enough to jolt Fagan forward against his seat belt. "Dan's gone completely off the rails."

He jumped out and jogged over to the men.

"I was afraid of this," he said when he reached Brandon. Dan and Blake went on yelling. "We'll have to babysit Dan when we should to be trying to solve his daughter's murder."

"Can we lock him up for disturbing the peace?" Brandon asked. "Keep him where he can't stir up trouble?"

"I'm tempted, but I don't have the heart to do that to Sarah and Megan." Hitching up his gun belt, Tom shoved his way between Dan and Blake. "All right, calm down and back off."

"How am I supposed to calm down when my daughter's dead?" Dan demanded. Pressing against Tom's shoulder, he pointed at Blake. "For months now the Hadleys have been saying somebody ought to make Shelley shut up. How do we know they didn't take it in their own hands and decide to shut her up themselves?"

"Dan, come on," Tom said. "You're not thinking straight."

"You calling me a murderer?" Blake shouted at Dan, close enough to Tom's ear to make him wince. "Go ahead and say it. You think I killed your girl?"

"I wouldn't put it past that boy of yours." Dan flung an arm toward Skeet on the porch. "The way he talked about her, like she was some kind of pest y'all wanted to get rid of."

"She was an ignorant little girl who didn't know what she was doing," Blake said. "Getting in over her head, acting like she knew better than the police and the courts."

"Yeah, and you hated her for it, didn't you?" Dan demanded. "Hated her enough to kill her over it."

"Stop it!" Tom shouted. "Both of you, shut up right now."

Blake sputtered, "I'm not going to let him get away with—"

"I said *shut up*. Now you listen to me." Tom planted one hand on each man's chest and shoved them a few inches farther apart. Tom noticed that Fagan had stayed with Tom's cruiser, well clear of the fray, and leaned against the car with his hands stuffed into his pants pockets. Probably jiggling his damned keys. Looking from Dan to Blake, Tom said, "Isn't this situation bad enough without the two of you going at each other? You've both lost children—"

"Yeah," Blake said, speaking to Dan. "Now maybe you know what we've been going through. How's it feel, huh?"

"You goddamn son of a—" Dan strained against Tom's hand, trying to get at Blake.

"Quiet!" Tom ordered. "Blake, can you keep your mouth shut long enough for me to get him out of here? Dan, come on, you're going back home where you belong."

He caught Dan's arm and pulled him toward the road. Tom didn't let go until they reached Dan's truck. "Are you all right to drive? You haven't been drinking, have you?"

Staring down at his feet, hands propped on his hips, Dan seemed to be struggling to pull himself together. "No, damn it, I haven't been drinking. God knows I could use a drink."

"What got into you, coming over here? What right did you have?"

Dan raised outraged eyes to Tom. "I told you what they've put us through. They didn't leave us alone till Shelley disappeared last month. Then all of a sudden we didn't hear a peep out of them. And you know why? Because they knew she was dead. They knew their little problem was done with. Skeet did it. I know he did. He killed my daughter." Dan yanked open the door of his truck. "Now you get him for it, you make him pay, or I'll do it myself."

Chapter Ten

Rachel kept an eye on the knife her sister wielded, afraid the blade might miss the mark any second and slice through one of Michelle's fingers instead of the ripe tomato on the chopping block. Although Michelle had changed into a fresh blouse and slacks, brushed out her hair, and applied pink lipstick, she was still distracted and tense. Letting her help with dinner preparation had been a mistake.

Frank had curled up on a kitchen chair. From the dining room Rachel heard the faint clinks of silverware as Kevin set the table. They all made a deceptively cozy scene, but the cat was the only one not being eaten alive by anxiety.

As usual after they said hurtful things to one another, Rachel and Michelle hadn't had a chance to clear the air. Hadn't made the effort, and probably wouldn't. After so many years, Rachel thought with grim amusement, it was amazing they could see each other through the smog of uncleared air between them. Hearing Michelle refer to Judith Goddard as Mother, hearing her say in that sorrowful voice that she still missed the woman, was almost more than Rachel could take. Yet she wasn't sure what she wanted Michelle to say instead. Rachel remembered a time before Judith. Michelle didn't. Despite seeing the proof of what Judith had done—the truth Rachel had shoved in her sister's face—Michelle had loved Judith as a mother and been loved in return. That was the only reality she wanted to acknowledge.

The knife slid into the tomato a hair's breadth from Michelle's fingertips. Rachel couldn't stand it anymore. "I think one's enough for the salad," she said. "Just add those slices to the bowl."

She turned away to spoon rice with raisins and almonds from a pot into a serving dish. Where was Tom? He'd promised to be home in time for dinner, promised to listen to Michelle's story and try to help. Rachel couldn't be angry if he got tied up with work, but—She noticed Michelle reaching for a second tomato, her movements mechanical, her eyes barely focused on the task. Rachel grabbed Michelle's wrist and took the knife from her. "One's enough. Why don't you help Kevin set the table?"

"For heaven's sake," Michelle said, pulling free from Rachel's grip. "That hurt."

Rachel sighed. *You're treating her like a child again. Stop it.* "I'm sorry. I was afraid you were going to cut yourself."

"I have used a knife before, you know." Michelle turned on the faucet to wash her hands. "And Kevin loves tomatoes. He always wants more."

Frank dropped to the floor and trotted from the room a second before Rachel heard the front door open and close. *Thank god, he's home.* She hurried out of the kitchen and up the hall.

Tom leaned down to pet Billy Bob and Frank, then greeted Rachel with a kiss.

"I'm so glad you're in time for dinner," she whispered.

A crease of concern appeared between his brows. "Are you okay?"

"Sure, I'm fine." But his expression told her that he sensed how frazzled she felt.

Kevin stepped into the hallway from the dining room, smiling and extending a hand. "Tom, hi," he said. "I'm Kevin Watters."

Returning the smile, Tom shook his hand. "Hey, Kevin, good to meet you."

"I'm sorry we descended on you like this, without much notice," Kevin said, "but I think some time with Rachel is exactly what Michelle needs right now."

Rachel noted with relief that Kevin made a favorable first impression on Tom. Sincere, obviously aware that their arrival could be seen as an imposition, but concerned about his wife. She cared much more about Tom's reaction to Kevin and Michelle than about their opinion of him. Even if they hated him, her feelings for Tom wouldn't change. But she was afraid he might see her relatives as additional unwelcome baggage in a relationship already shadowed by her past.

"Rachel's family is always welcome," Tom told Kevin.

Bless you. Rachel wanted to hug him.

"Excuse me while I stash my gear." With practiced movements, Tom pulled his large Sig Sauer pistol from its holster, pointed it at the floor while he popped out the cartridge, then stowed weapon and ammunition on the top shelf of the hall closet. Kevin, Rachel noticed, zoned in on the gun, his eyes following it until it was out of sight. He seemed equally fascinated by the duty belt, with its attached handcuffs, radio, and extra ammunition, when Tom unbuckled it and put it away on the same shelf.

"That stuff must weigh a ton," Kevin said.

Tom laughed. "You ought to see what I keep in the car. I'm always glad to ditch everything at the end of the day." Tom's gaze shifted beyond Rachel and Kevin to the kitchen doorway at the end of the hall. "You must be Michelle."

"Tom, this is my sister," Rachel said as Michelle walked up the hall to join them. "Michelle, this is Tom."

"So I finally get to meet you," Michelle said, offering a hand. "Needless to say, I've heard a lot about you." She smiled up at Tom with an expression that was almost flirtatious but could be defended as simple friendliness. That perfectly calibrated look always made Rachel want to roll her eyes, but she'd rather see her sister behaving this way than scared and withdrawn.

To Rachel's relief, Tom didn't tell Michelle he'd also heard a lot about her. "It's nice to meet you," he said, with a smile that couldn't be construed as anything other than polite and welcoming. He told Rachel, "I'm going to change out of my uniform. I'll be down in a couple of minutes. Dinner smells great."

When he headed up the stairs, Michelle leaned close to Rachel and whispered, "Wow."

"Glad you approve." Rachel smiled, relieved that Tom's arrival had coaxed the real Michelle out from behind that lifeless mask. "I need to go upstairs for a second. I'll be right back."

Following Tom to the second floor, she felt a moment of longing for a quiet, private evening, just the two of them. She was sure Tom felt the same way. Working seven days a week was exhausting enough without having to cope with the company of strangers when he came home.

She closed the bedroom door behind her and leaned against it, watching Tom strip off his uniform shirt.

"Hey," he said, giving her that penetrating look that made her feel exposed, every thought and emotion laid bare. "How's it going?"

"I'm not sure." *Michelle and I weren't alone three minutes before we went at each other.* Thank god Kevin had changed his mind about taking a long walk around the farm and returned to interrupt them when he did. "I really want your professional opinion of what's happening with her."

"We can talk about it after we eat." He pulled a clean shirt and jeans from the closet. "Dinner first. I'm starving. Are jeans okay, or do you want me to put on something else?"

"Wear whatever's comfortable." Rachel smiled, touched by his sweetness. She wished she could calm the fluttery feeling in her chest, make her heart stop taking off at a gallop every few minutes. "Did the great Detective Fagan arrive on schedule?"

"Yeah, he got in this morning. I spent most of the day with him." Tom's eyes met hers. "He asked about you right before I started home. I got the feeling he was angling for an invitation to a home-cooked dinner."

Rachel gave a humorless laugh. "As if."

Grinning, Tom sat on the bed to tug off his boots. "I gave him directions to the Mountaineer. Have a little pity on the man."

"Oh, the poor thing, forced to eat restaurant food. Is that enough pity? Where's he staying? So I can avoid going anywhere near the place."

Tom hesitated about answering. He stood and unzipped his uniform pants.

"What?" Rachel asked. "Please don't tell me your aunt and uncle are putting him up, or he's on the farm next door."

"No, I asked Joanna to let him stay at her place." He stepped out of the pants and laid them across the bed. "In your old house."

Rachel groaned. For more than a year after moving to Mason County, she had lived in a tiny four-room house on Joanna McKendrick's horse farm. "Since when do you have something against Joanna?"

"It'll be fine." Tom pulled on his jeans. "If I know her, she'll be feeding him breakfast and dinner every day."

"And pumping him for details about what happened to me back in McLean. I love Joanna, you know I do, but she enjoys finding out everything she can about people."

"Does that matter?" Tom tucked his shirttail into the jeans, zipped up and buckled his belt. He sat down to pull his boots back on. "You've already told her about being shot, and Fagan doesn't know about any of the other stuff, does he?"

The other stuff. My life. Even Tom didn't know all of it. Rachel said, "No, not that I'm aware of." Unless he'd been digging around in her past for some reason. But Fagan had no reason. Besides, she doubted he was a sharp enough detective to put all the pieces together even if they were laid out in front of him. She had to stop being so paranoid. "You're right. There's nothing to worry about. As long as I can avoid him while he's here, everything will be fine."

"Come on." Tom put an arm around her shoulders, opened the door, and sniffed the aromas rising from the kitchen below. "I'm ready to do serious bodily harm to that chicken."

Downstairs, they found that Michelle and Kevin had set the food on the table and filled the water glasses. Rachel was relieved to see that the change in Michelle's mood was holding, and she was her normal vivacious, chatty self. She would probably knock herself out to charm Tom, and that was fine with Rachel as long as Michelle didn't overdo it in front of her husband.

After they'd all taken servings of chicken and vegetables and reached the point where they had to find something to talk about, Michelle turned to Tom with a smile. "I hear you're running for sheriff. Are you busy making speeches and debating with your opponent?"

"He doesn't have an opponent," Rachel said.

Tom gave her wry look.

"Not a serious one, anyway," Rachel amended. "Just some idiot with no law enforcement experience and a lot of ridiculous opinions. Tom's already running the department with the sheriff on sick leave. He deserves to have the title and the pay."

"Get Rachel to make speeches for you and you'll be a shoo-in," Michelle said. "She can be very persuasive."

Tom laughed. "Oh, don't I know it."

So far, so good, Rachel thought.

Then, to her dismay, Michelle said in a suddenly sober voice, "That George Mason law student who disappeared last month was found here, wasn't she? It was on the TV news in Washington last night."

Her question struck everybody dumb for a moment. Tom glanced at Rachel as if hoping for a signal to guide his response. She frowned and shook her head slightly. The last thing Michelle needed now was a lot of talk about a girl who might have been murdered by a stalker.

"Yeah," Tom said. "That's taking up all my time right now, but I can't really discuss the investigation. Kevin, what kind of law practice do you have? Corporate law, I think Rachel said. Is that right?"

Rachel trusted Kevin to catch the ball Tom tossed his way and run with it, but before Kevin could answer, Michelle spoke again. "It's awful. That beautiful young woman—There are so many crazy people in the world, and you never know when one of them will—"

"Honey," Kevin said, reaching for Michelle's hand. "Let's not talk about that now."

She let him take her hand, but it lay limp in his. When she lifted her eyes toward Rachel, they shimmered with tears. "I shouldn't have come here. I'm such a mess. I'm sorry."

Was she going to burst into tears? *Oh, god, don't cry.* "I'm glad you came," Rachel said. "We'll talk about…all that after dinner. Please eat something. You haven't touched your meal."

Michelle nodded and picked up her fork, but she looked as if the last thing she wanted was the food that went into her mouth.

Kevin seemed determined to keep the conversation afloat at a friendly, superficial level. "So, Tom," he said, in a jovial tone that sounded painfully forced to Rachel, "is this a working sheep farm you have here?"

"No, not really." Tom sounded relaxed, but Rachel caught his quick assessing glance at Michelle. "I don't have the time for it. I keep the sheep because they were like pets to my mother. She worked as a nurse, but she liked to dye and spin the wool, and she always had knitters wanting to buy it. There's a retired deputy down the road who looks after them for me, and his wife uses the wool."

Rachel watched Michelle push food around on her plate. After a couple of bites, she ate no more.

Kevin kept up a stream of questions about Mason County, about winters in the mountains, about Rachel's veterinary practice. Michelle didn't utter another word for the rest of the meal.

◇◇◇

After dinner, Kevin and Tom carried the dishes into the kitchen, then went to sit in the living room while the two women loaded the dishwasher. Tom wished he could hear what, if anything, Rachel and Michelle were saying to each other.

"Listen, Tom," Kevin said, leaning forward from the sofa and speaking quietly. "I'd really like to get a professional's honest opinion. You must have handled stalking cases, harassment, that kind of thing."

"Yeah, a few times. But it's not the easiest kind of case to deal with." Tom hoped Kevin and Michelle hadn't come out here thinking he could magically fix this problem for them just because he was a cop. Even if he had the time to devote to it, he wasn't sure how much help he could be.

Kevin glanced toward the door and lowered his voice to little more than a whisper. "But can you tell whether it's actually happening, or if it's, you know, imaginary?"

So Rachel hadn't misjudged Kevin's attitude. He believed his wife might be making it all up. But why would Kevin suspect Michelle of inventing the story? This was murky territory, and Tom didn't want to venture into it. He chose his words carefully. "You have to take a lot of things into consideration. And if there's no physical evidence, like fingerprints, and you don't know the stalker's identity, there's not much the police can do."

"Right. I see that, I understand." Kevin scrubbed his palms on his knees and grimaced as if in pain.

It was a very real sort of pain, Tom knew, when the woman you loved was hurting and you couldn't do anything to help. He liked Kevin, despite the guy's less than overwhelming support of his wife. Tom wasn't sure what to make of Michelle yet. But for everybody's sake, especially Rachel's, Tom hoped they could resolve this situation quickly.

When Rachel and Michelle joined them in the living room, Rachel took the chair next to Tom's. Frank jumped onto her lap and settled down. Sitting beside Kevin on the sofa while he held her hand, Michelle looked like a small bird, frozen by terror under the eyes of a predator. What scared her most, Tom wondered—reliving her experience by putting it into words or the possibility that no one in the room would believe her?

A moment passed in uneasy silence. Tom cleared his throat. "Why don't you start at the beginning? I know you've told Rachel some of it, but I want to hear everything directly from you. When did you first notice something was wrong?"

Michelle pulled in an audible breath as if steeling herself for an ordeal. Instead of meeting Tom's gaze, she seemed to focus inward on scenes replaying in her memory. "It started about a month ago. The first thing that happened was so subtle I didn't give it much thought. I noticed one morning—it was a Monday, I remember—that some of the things hanging on my office walls had been moved around. Prints, and framed copies of my degrees and certifications. I thought the cleaning woman had done it on the weekend. Maybe she'd taken things down to dust them and got confused about where everything went."

"Okay," Tom said. "What else?"

"The next day, I received an anonymous letter at my office. It said, *You're not as special as you think you are, you little bitch.*"

Rachel gasped, and Tom realized she hadn't heard this before. "What was the postmark on the envelope?" he asked Michelle.

"Maryland. It was mailed in Montgomery County."

"What happened next?"

"Nothing until the next Monday." Michelle squeezed her free hand into a fist in her lap. "I went in that morning and all the magazines in the waiting room had been removed from the rack and dumped on the floor. And everything on the walls in my office had been taken down and thrown on the floor. The glass in all the frames was shattered."

"Was there any sign of a break-in?"

Michelle shook her head, her hair brushing her neck and cheeks. "It was as if somebody got in with a key. But nobody except the cleaning service and building management has a key."

"Did you question them about it?" Tom asked.

"Yes, I did. The same woman always cleans my office, and she swore she wasn't responsible. She cleans for the last time each week on Friday night and doesn't come again until Monday night. She insisted that when she left Friday, everything was in its proper place. The very idea was so bizarre anyway. Why would the cleaning woman do something like that? But if it wasn't her, who else could have gotten in?"

"Locks can be picked without leaving any sign of it. Most office door locks aren't much of a challenge. I would recommend you have something stronger installed even if you weren't having any problems."

The mantel clock began ringing the hour and Tom saw Michelle flinch at the sharp sound. Again she drew a deep, shuddering breath, and she gripped Kevin's hand so tightly her knuckles went white. Whether she was imagining the threat or not, she was terrified and barely holding herself together. "You reported all this to the police, didn't you?" he asked.

"An officer came out, but he acted as if I were making it all up. He wouldn't even check for fingerprints because there was no evidence of breaking and entering. He said to call again if anything was stolen, but he was very condescending."

Tom felt an irrational impulse to apologize for the unknown cop's behavior. But he knew he wouldn't have been able to do anything under those circumstances either. "You've been getting phone calls too?"

"She had one today," Rachel said, "after they got here."

"Really? Can I see the list of incoming calls on your phone?" Tom asked Michelle.

"The number's always blocked, so the list probably won't tell you anything, but you can look at it if you want to." Michelle pulled an iPhone out of her slacks pocket, pressed a couple of buttons, and passed it to him over the coffee table.

The silver metal casing felt warm from her body heat. Tom scrolled the past incoming calls on the device and saw several Caller Unknown listings.

"I've tried to find out from my service provider where the calls are coming from, but all they could tell me is that they're coming from different places."

"You're sure it's the same person calling you every time?"

"Yes. I'm positive."

"The phones might be throwaways that couldn't be traced to the owners." But why, Tom wondered, would a stalker go to the trouble and expense of buying a batch of untraceable phones just to harass Michelle? He laid the phone on the coffee table. "When did the calls start?"

Michelle hesitated, moistening her lips with the tip of her tongue.

"Tell us everything," Rachel urged in the gentle tone she might use with a fearful child.

"They started three weeks ago." Michelle's voice quavered with building emotion. "At first it was just breathing on the other end, then it was whispering. Then—" She broke off, gulping a breath.

Kevin put an arm around Michelle and pulled her against him.

To Tom, Kevin looked tired and baffled, showing none of the anger he would expect a husband to feel when his wife had been reduced to a nervous wreck by harassment. If Kevin thought Michelle was imagining things, why wasn't he trying to get help for her at home? Why bring her out here?

Rachel shifted the cat off her lap and moved to the couch. She placed a soothing hand on Michelle's arm.

Tom had hoped this whole situation would turn out to be nothing, but his gut told him Michelle was telling the truth. And if her story was true, she had good reason to be scared. Stalking could escalate to assault—and worse. He waited until she seemed a little calmer, then asked, "Can you think of anybody who'd want to upset you? Somebody you've had an argument with, a disagreement—"

"No!" Michelle cried. She squeezed her eyes shut for a second, visibly willing herself to calm down. "I haven't done anything to cause this. Don't you think I've lain awake at night going over every conversation, every encounter, every person I've come into contact with?" She looked at Rachel. "Do you think I brought this on myself?"

"Of course not," Rachel said. "Tom wasn't implying that."

"I'm just looking at the possibilities," Tom said. "Could it be related to your work somehow? If it started in your office—"

Michelle shook her head. "I work with very young autistic children. I do initial evaluation and diagnosis. I don't see adults or even teenagers. My patients aren't capable of doing something like this."

"Any problems with a patient's parent or guardian?"

"No. Never."

"Has the caller left any threatening messages? Do you have a recording of his voice?"

"No. I've always answered, so they've never gone to voice mail."

"Don't answer next time. Let's see if we get a recording of his voice. I'll have to think about this, but for now, you're safe here with us. I know it's not easy, but try to relax."

"I don't feel safe anywhere." Michelle rose. "Excuse me. I'm sorry, but I—Excuse me." She hurried from the room, with Kevin following.

Rachel stood as if to go after Michelle, then sat down on the sofa again and bent forward with her head in her hands.

◇◇◇

"What do you think?" Rachel asked Tom after Michelle and Kevin were out of earshot. Tom had seemed dispassionate, professional, when questioning Michelle. Part of Rachel wanted him to *care*, to be as concerned about her sister as she was, but she knew that was asking too much. It was enough that he believed Michelle. "Your unbiased opinion."

Tom left his chair and came to sit beside her on the couch. "Something's going on, but I'm not sure how bad it really is or what can be done about it."

Rachel sighed and shoved her hair back from her face with both hands. "My sister's not crazy—"

"I didn't—"

"I know, I know. I was about to say, she's not crazy, but I'm not surprised the police didn't want to get involved. She can't prove any of this really happened. Something has to be done about it, though. This scares me to death, so I can imagine how it makes her feel."

"Like I said, I'll have to think about it. Harassment isn't always easy to prove, and I'm afraid it's not easy to stop either."

Rachel wrapped her arms around him and laid her head on his chest. He hugged her closer. She wanted to stay there in his warm, strong embrace, listening to the reassuring beat of his heart. "Thank you for taking her seriously. I'm sorry to dump this on you now, when you're so busy."

"Don't worry about that. I want to help."

"I love her so much," Rachel said. "She drives me crazy sometimes, but I love her and I hate seeing her like this. She's all I have, Tom."

"No." He pulled back and lifted her chin with a finger. "You've got me. You're always going to have me."

"I—" Before Rachel could pull any more words out of the jumble in her head, he cut her off with a kiss.

The buzzing ring of a cell phone startled them. Not her phone, not Tom's. She looked around and spotted Michelle's phone on the coffee table where Tom had placed it.

"Let's see who it is." Tom picked up the phone and checked the display. "Caller unknown. This could be him. We'll let it go to voice mail. I want to hear this creep."

Rachel held her breath as voice mail cut in. *Don't hang up, don't hang up. Say something.*

"I think he left a message," Tom said when the call ended. "Let's hope it's more than heavy breathing."

He punched the buttons to retrieve the message and put it on speaker.

The sinuous voice was quiet and low. "I know where you are, Michelle. You can't get away from me by running off to your sister. I'm watching you."

Chapter Eleven

Kevin looked skeptical. He swung his overnight bag into the trunk of his car, slammed the lid, and turned to Tom with a frown. "You actually heard it yourself?"

"Rachel and I both did." Rachel had insisted on not telling Michelle about the call the night before, and Tom hadn't found an opportunity to fill her husband in until morning, when he was preparing to drive back home. Kevin's reaction baffled Tom. What was going on with this guy? "What did you think, that Michelle made it up?"

"No. I just—" Kevin's boyish face colored with—what? embarrassment? confusion? "I don't know what to believe. Look, I feel guilty about dropping this in your lap. I hate to leave her here and go back home."

"But you have some kind of commitment at work?" Tom said. He was trying not to judge Kevin, but that didn't seem like much of an excuse for abandoning his wife when she was going through a frightening ordeal.

"Yeah, I do," Kevin said, "but it's not just that. If Michelle wanted me to, I'd find a way to get out of it and stay. But she doesn't want me to stay. She's made that clear. And she really doesn't seem to feel safe at home. But if she's being stalked and the guy knows where she is, then how safe is she here?"

Kevin looked so miserable that Tom relented and took pity on him. Something, he suspected, was going on in Michelle and Kevin's marriage that had nothing to do with the stalker, although the threat was probably exposing the underlying problem. "I'll do everything I can to keep her safe," Tom said. "And I'll see what I can do about identifying this guy who's bugging her."

Kevin headed back home, and Michelle tagged along with Rachel because neither Tom nor Rachel thought she should stay at the farm by herself all day.

Tom didn't normally escort Rachel to work, but today he wanted to make sure she and Michelle arrived at the animal hospital safely. Chances were the man on the phone was hundreds of miles away, but Tom wouldn't bet on it when Rachel's safety—and her sister's—might be at stake.

Driving behind Rachel's SUV on the road into Mountain-view, he caught occasional glimpses of Rachel gesturing, pointing out the farmhouse where Tom's aunt and uncle lived, a hillside where dogwoods bloomed, a black vulture perched on a fence with its massive wings spread along the rail to catch the sun. Light flooded the landscape, softening the stark branches of trees that hadn't leafed out yet. Rachel loved the mountains, and Tom guessed she was trying to make her sister see this place the way she did. The high-backed seat blocked his view of Michelle, and he couldn't tell whether she was responding to Rachel or ignoring her. He doubted that she'd been favorably impressed by the vulture.

Michelle was an odd one, about as different from Rachel as an orchid from a sunflower. She didn't seem like a good match with her husband either, although Tom couldn't put his finger on the reason he felt that way. Kevin seemed to love her. But he was having trouble believing her story about being harassed. Why would he doubt his own wife? Why wasn't he doing anything to help her?

They all expected him to fix Michelle's problem. For Rachel's sake, he wanted to try, but how the hell would he find the time when an active murder investigation demanded all his attention and he also had an out-of-jurisdiction detective to keep tabs on?

That was the least of his worries, though. A lot of Rachel's past remained a mystery to him, but he was afraid that having her sister around would stir up memories and feelings Rachel couldn't handle. She loved Michelle, but in Tom's opinion she was better off when she kept her distance.

They left farmland behind, drove past houses set closer together, and turned onto Mountainview's two-lane Main Street. Rachel pulled into the parking lot outside the animal hospital and waved to Tom. He drove on toward the Sheriff's Department headquarters, where Dr. Gretchen Lauter would go over the Shelley Beecher autopsy results with him and Detective Fagan.

◇◇◇

"I feel like a child who can't be left alone," Michelle said as she and Rachel walked into the vet clinic. She carried her laptop computer in a blue nylon bag. "But I won't be underfoot, I promise. I have plenty of work to do on a paper I'm writing. I'll sit in your office and stay out of the way."

"It's not a problem." Rachel wanted Michelle where she could see her and be sure she was safe. After the call the night before, they had proof this madness wasn't a product of Michelle's imagination. If the stalker knew where she was, he might follow her. Maybe he had a job that tied him down during the week so he couldn't take off anytime he liked, but if not, they had to be prepared to deal with him in Mason County.

The two young women at the front desk broke off their conversation and turned openly inquisitive gazes on Michelle when she came through the door with Rachel. Rachel introduced her sister to Shannon, the plump, rosy-cheeked receptionist, and Holly Turner, a beautiful olive-skinned girl with long black hair who worked as an assistant.

"Oh, my goodness," Holly exclaimed, giving Michelle her megawatt smile. "It's so great to meet you."

"I'm happy to meet you too, Holly." Michelle's smile seemed genuine despite the tension that haunted her eyes. "Rachel's told me so much about you."

Holly beamed. She wasn't one of those people who would respond with a self-deprecating remark about hoping it wasn't all bad. She would be flattered that Rachel liked her enough to tell Michelle about her.

"Michelle's going to do some work on her computer in my office while I'm seeing patients," Rachel said.

"Can we do anything for you?" Shannon asked Michelle. "Would you like a cup of coffee?"

"I'll get it," Holly offered. "How do you like it?"

"Oh, I don't want to be any trouble—"

"Sure, if you wouldn't mind," Rachel told Holly. "A little cream, no sugar. Bring it to her in my office."

"Okay!" Holly said, and spun away to hurry down the hall to the staff lounge.

Now to get Michelle settled so Rachel's own work day could begin.

In her office, Rachel pulled on her white lab coat while Michelle set her laptop on the desk and turned it on. Holly brought the coffee, asked Michelle to taste it and make sure it had just the right amount of cream in it. She obviously wanted to hang around and talk to Michelle, but she left when Rachel reminded her to get out the acupuncture tools for an arthritic German shepherd that had the day's first appointment.

"I don't suppose you have a wireless Internet connection in the building, do you?" Michelle's hands trembled as they hovered over the keyboard, waiting for the machine to boot up. "One of the other partners in the practice is taking my patients while I'm gone, and I'd like to stay in touch. I hate doing e-mail on my telephone's little screen."

"Believe it or not, we do have wi-fi. Your browser ought to pick it up." Rachel pulled her stethoscope from her lab coat pocket and hung it around her neck.

"Oh, there it is. I've got it." Michelle glanced up from the computer, amused. "You named your office's wireless network after Tom's bulldog?"

Rachel shrugged. "Why not? Well, I'd better get to work. Let me know if you need—" She broke off when she saw the stricken look on her sister's face. "Mish? What is it?"

Michelle shrank away from the computer, her gaze locked on the screen, color draining from her face. "He never sent me e-mail before," she whispered.

"What? Let me see." Rachel stepped behind Michelle and read over her shoulder.

You don't belong in the country with a bunch of fucking sheep! You belong with me, my beautiful Michelle. I'll show you what it's like to make love to a real man. I'll hold you in my arms soon, and I'll never let you go. Never never never never let you go.

"My god," Rachel said. This was a outright threat, worse than anything Michelle had reported before.

"I don't want this garbage on my computer." Michelle reached for the keyboard.

"No!" Rachel caught Michelle's hand. "Don't delete it. Tom has to see it."

"He won't be able to find out who sent it. Look." Michelle pointed a shaking finger at the *From* line. The sender's address was given as *ImWatchingYou@yahoo.com*. "It's one of those free accounts, and every bit of information on it is probably fake."

"Yeah, you're right." Rachel drew a deep breath and laid her hands on Michelle's shoulders. "Tom will want to see it anyway. Leave it. I know it's hard, but try to forget it's there and focus on writing your paper."

Twisting in the chair, Michelle looked up at Rachel. "Is Tom right? Did I bring this on myself? Did I make somebody angry, did I—"

"Tom never said you brought this on yourself. Don't you dare blame yourself. For god's sake, Michelle, you're a psychologist. This guy is a textbook nut case, and he seems to have a split personality. One day he's calling you a bitch and the next he sounds like he's in love with you. You know better than anybody does that he's living out his own crazy fantasies."

"But I don't work with people like this," Michelle said. "I don't treat psychotic patients, and I've never known anybody who would do such a thing."

"But you know, in your head, that it has no real connection to you. It's his problem. You just happened to attract his attention for some reason and he's attached all his fantasies to you. Your rational mind knows that, and you have to make yourself believe it in your heart." *Why do I have to explain this to a trained therapist?* Fear seemed to have stripped Michelle of her professional expertise and made her incapable of applying her knowledge to her own life.

Michelle's cell phone buzzed. They stared at her purse, lying on the desk next to the laptop.

"It might be somebody from my office," Michelle said, but she made no move to retrieve the phone.

Rachel grabbed the purse and dug out the phone. The display told her the caller's number was blocked. Michelle didn't try to stop her when she pressed the button to answer.

"Did you get my message, sweetheart?" the whispery voice asked. "Did you—"

"Shut up and listen to me, you pervert," Rachel said. "If you don't leave my sister alone, you're going to end up in prison. You're not a real man, you're a freak and a coward who gets his kicks by sneaking around and trying to scare women. No woman would want slime like you anywhere near her. You're disgusting, you're a sick little boy playing nasty games."

She paused, gulped a breath, waited.

Silence.

"What's the matter?" Rachel's heart pounded against her ribs. "Have you run out of things to say?"

His voice was quiet, cold, flat. "Be careful, Rachel. Don't get in my way."

The connection went dead.

"Rachel?" Michelle gripped her arm. "What did he say?"

"Nothing worth repeating." Rachel dropped the phone back into the purse. How could they stop the stalker if they had no idea who he was or why he was doing this? If Michelle had angered someone without realizing it, how could they track down her tormentor before he harmed her? "I have to get to work. Will you be all right in here?"

"Sure, I'll be okay," Michelle said, brushing her hair off her cheeks and forcing a smile. "Go see your patients. You don't have to babysit me."

"I'll only be a few feet away if you need me." Rachel turned to leave, but something caught her eye and made her freeze with a hand on the doorknob.

Three framed documents hung on the wall next to the door. Copies of her college degree, her doctorate from Cornell, her certification in veterinary internal medicine. They hung side by side as always, but all three frames were upside down.

"Is something wrong?" Michelle asked, a note of alarm in her voice.

"No, no." Rachel stepped in front of the framed certificates, and before her sister could get a good look she set them right again. She fought to keep her voice casual. "These things are always shifting a little bit. I think it's the motion of the air when the door's opened and closed that causes it."

"I've seen that happen too. It's annoying."

Michelle bought the simple explanation, but Rachel knew she have would panicked if she'd seen the frames wildly askew.

The creep had followed Michelle to Mason County, and he'd done it quickly. He had been in Rachel's office during the night. And she'd just royally pissed him off. He was going to turn their lives upside down, like the frames on the wall.

Chapter Twelve

Tom yanked the cord to close the conference room blinds, blocking the reporters' view from the parking lot outside. Twice as many were out there today. A news crew from a Washington, DC, television station had parked their truck so close to the building that they could aim a camera directly into the room if they had the nerve. And Tom was sure they did.

He motioned Detective Fagan into the chair next to his and tried to ignore Dennis Murray's scowl across the conference room table. Brandon Connolly, beside Dennis, eyed the out-of-town detective with open fascination, as if he were an exotic creature in their midst.

With more formality than he would employ if no guest were present, Tom said, "Dr. Lauter has the preliminary autopsy report from Roanoke for us. Dr. Lauter?"

Gretchen, at the head of the table, handed off a folder of photos to Tom. "There's nothing new in the pictures, but I thought Detective Fagan would want to see them."

Tom flipped the folder open and, with Fagan leaning close to share the view, looked through them as Gretchen spoke.

"The pathologist confirms that Shelley Beecher has been dead for several weeks," Gretchen said, "possibly since the day she disappeared. He believes the body was tightly wrapped from the beginning, and stored somewhere cool. In fact, he sees indications that the body was frozen for at least part of that time."

"Oh, man," Dennis muttered.

"The jargon's all in the report," Gretchen went on, "but that's what it amounts to. The apparent cause of death was strangulation. Her neck bears the mark of a thick, semi-flexible ligature one inch wide, a leather belt or something similar."

"Anything under her fingernails?" Fagan asked.

"Sorry, no," Gretchen said. "No skin scrapings, no evidence of any kind. Her hands were completely clean, and so was her clothing. So clean, in fact—This is speculation on my part, but I'm inclined to believe her hands were washed and her clothes were brushed or even vacuumed to remove trace evidence such as fibers or hairs."

"Shit," Fagan said. "People watch too damned much television. They know exactly how to clean up after themselves, if they've got the time and the presence of mind."

"This killer obviously had both," Tom said. "He wasn't in a hurry and he stayed calm. And he had a place picked out to hide her body. That's not typical for a crime of passion—an angry boyfriend, say. This was planned."

"I've thought from the start," Fagan said, "that the killer is someone who knew her schedule. He picked the perfect time and place to snatch her without being seen. We haven't found a single witness who saw or heard a thing. I don't have any doubt she was abducted in Fairfax County, and she was probably killed there."

"But we're still left with the question of why she was dumped here," Tom said. "The more I think about it, the more I believe the killer, or killers, put her in a place where she would be found right away."

Fagan frowned. "Why would anybody expect her to be found right away? That spot's pretty rugged. How many people go down into that ravine in an average week?"

"None," Tom said, "but we're not talking about an average week. Civic groups and high school kids do the road cleanup every year. This year's schedule's been posted in stores, on utility poles, all over the place, so anybody who wanted to help out could contact a group leader to volunteer. It wasn't hard to find out a cleanup crew would be in that ravine on Saturday."

"A crew led by the county's chief deputy and acting sheriff," Dennis pointed out.

"Hey, that's right," Brandon said. "You think the killer wanted you to find her, Captain?"

Fagan shook his head, a dismissive little smile on his face.

"You think that's far-fetched?" Tom asked him. "You'd rather believe in pure coincidence?"

"Why would the killer want to put the victim in your path? Seriously. Why you?"

"If I knew that, I'd probably know who killed her. But there's some reason he brought the body here. Why *they* brought it here. I think it's possible more than one person was involved. If she was murdered in Fairfax County, they took a big risk in transporting her out here. They could have been stopped for a traffic violation, the vehicle could have broken down on the interstate, they could have had an accident. A dozen different things might have happened, and her body could have been discovered in the vehicle. For some reason he—they—were willing to risk it to bring her body here. And it's possible they dumped her where they did because they wanted her found this weekend."

"By you," Fagan said. "I repeat, why? What's your connection to this girl?"

"None in particular. I know the family, that's all."

"So this notion you've got about the killer wanting you to find the body doesn't really hold water."

"Not in terms of my having a special connection to her." Tom tried to stifle his irritation with Fagan, but he heard it loud and clear in his voice. "They could have wanted a cop, any cop, to find her, for whatever reason, and it was easy to find out where I'd be that day."

"Yeah, right." Fagan shook his head again. "For whatever reason."

"If you've got a theory, I'd like to hear it."

"Remorse," Fagan said.

"Remorse?" Dennis asked. "Whose remorse?"

"The killer's. He brought her close to home so her family would know what happened to her. So they'd have closure, a body to bury."

Everyone sat silent for a moment. Then Dennis huffed a laugh. "We don't come across a lot of murderers with tender hearts."

Tom sensed Fagan stiffening, heard him draw breath to fire an answering shot. He cut Fagan off as the detective started to speak. "We're just guessing at this point. We don't have evidence to back up any theory." He asked Fagan, "If her boyfriend and roommates all have solid alibis for the night she disappeared, who else are you looking at?"

"We need to widen our scope. Like I said, it was probably somebody who knew her schedule, knew where and when he could snatch her without being seen. That doesn't mean he knew her well. He could be somebody who met her casually and got fixated on her, started fantasizing about her."

"A stalker." Tom's thoughts jumped to Michelle, but he pulled his attention back to the case in front of him.

"Yeah," Fagan said. "Maybe he never even met her, just saw her somewhere and started following her. But she didn't get around much. She didn't party, she went to school and she worked, and seeing a movie with her boyfriend was about the biggest social event on her calendar. We've looked at everybody who works in that business strip where the innocence project's office is, and they've all accounted for their whereabouts at the time she disappeared."

"I've got plenty of angles to work here," Tom said, "but I want to go to Fairfax County and talk to a few people myself."

"I've done that," Fagan said. "I've filled you in. What else do you want to know?"

"I'd rather talk to people directly."

Fagan shrugged. "Whatever suits you."

Why was Fagan in Mason County? If he was sure his case was in his own county, why wasn't he there working it? "We've got some departmental matters to discuss," Tom told him, "if you don't mind."

Fagan's eyebrows went up in surprise. "You want me to leave?"

"If you don't mind."

Shaking his head, Fagan rose and walked out. As he pulled the door shut with one hand, Tom heard him jingling his keys in his pocket with the other.

"All right," Tom said when he was gone. "Brandon, did you find out whether Skeet was working the day Shelley went missing?"

"He wasn't. He called in sick to the lumber mill four days that week—before and after she disappeared. There was some bug going around at the mill, a lot of workers were out with it. Whether Skeet was really sick or not, I don't know."

"Can't say I'm surprised." Tom raked a hand through his hair. Instead of the excitement he'd normally feel when a suspect lacked an alibi, he felt sad. What would it do to the Hadley and Beecher families if it turned out Skeet was Shelley's killer? Then there was the question of who helped him hide the body and place it in the ravine. "Was his dad at work that week?"

"Yeah, every day, regular hours. And Blake and Skeet both worked every day last week too."

"The body was probably moved at night," Dennis pointed out.

"I don't think it was in the ravine longer than a few hours," Dr. Lauter said, "so I would guess it was moved sometime Friday night, early Saturday morning."

They all fell silent for a moment, and Tom knew everybody was dreading what lay ahead. Gathering criminal evidence against people they'd known all their lives was hard on all of them and would stir up a lot of anger in the community. Tom blew out a sigh. "See what you can find out about Skeet's movements at night for the last week. I'll drive to Fairfax County early tomorrow, but I don't expect to come back with much that'll help us."

As they all rose to leave the room, Tom asked Dennis to stay for a minute.

Pulling off his glasses, Dennis held them up to the light for examination, rubbed one lens on his shirt sleeve, and slid them back on. "What's up?"

"I want you to try to find out where somebody was when he made a phone call."

"This something to do with the Beecher murder? I've already put in our request for her phone records, and I'm going to get a warrant for Skeet Hadley's too."

"No, this is…Some creep is stalking Rachel's sister. He got into her office in Bethesda, and he's been calling her too."

"Oh, man," Dennis said. "I'm sorry to hear that. Can't the police where she lives—"

"She went to them, they didn't offer her any help. Thought she was imagining things, I guess. Besides, she's here now, staying with us. And she's getting calls. I want to know where this guy called from, whether he's nearby. Whether he followed her here. I've got Michelle's number and the service provider information." Tom drew a slip of paper out of his shirt pocket and handed it to Dennis. "If you need her signature on anything, I'll get it."

Dennis nodded. "This sounds like a bad time for you to be leaving the county, even for a day."

"Yeah, it is. Can't be helped, though."

Tom's cell phone rang. When he pulled it from his shirt pocket and answered, Rachel said without preamble, "I think somebody broke into the clinic last night."

"What?" Tom said, jolted. "Was something stolen?"

Dennis frowned. "What's happened?"

Tom raised a hand to silence him.

"You're going to think I'm crazy." Rachel spoke quietly, and Tom heard a blue jay's harsh call in the background. She was outdoors, not in her office.

"Just tell me," he said.

"My degrees, the ones on the wall in my office—" She broke off.

Her degrees? Where was this headed? "What about them?"

"They were all turned upside down and hanging at an angle."

Tom took a minute, trying to process this. It didn't make sense.

"*Tom.*" Rachel's voice with urgency. "Say something. This is the same sort of thing that happened to Michelle in Bethesda. It started this way. Now it's happening here."

This quickly? How was that possible? "Did you see signs of a break-in? Did any of the locks look like they'd been tampered with? Any scratches or—"

"No. It's as if somebody got in with a key. The only thing I've seen so far that's not normal is the way the frames are turned on the wall."

"Could the cleaning woman—"

"Oh, please, Tom, why would she do something like that? At the very same time my sister's being harassed in the same way?"

"Yeah, you're right," Tom agreed reluctantly. "That would be a pretty wild coincidence. If Michelle's stalker did it, he's really on the ball. He knew she was coming to see you, and he was right on her heels. Okay, I'll come over and—"

"Don't come right now. Michelle's here. I don't want to upset her. She doesn't know about this."

"It's a little late to start keeping things from her."

Rachel sighed. "I know, but I have a lot of patients to see today. I don't have time to hold my sister's hand."

"It'll probably be pointless to look for fingerprints on the doors anyway," Tom said. "So many people go in and out."

"I'm the only one who's touched the frames on my office wall, though. And I only touched the corners."

"Good. Go on about your business, and let me know when you and Michelle leave for the day. I'll come over after you're gone and see if I can lift prints from the frames. In the meantime, get your locks looked at. This worries me, Rachel."

"I've already called the locksmith. He's on his way."

Chapter Thirteen

The young locksmith crouched outside the animal hospital's front door, turning a key to lock and unlock the dead bolt repeatedly. After a couple of minutes, he rose, brushed his wavy brown hair off his forehead and shifted his puzzled gaze to Rachel. "Ma'am, it's working the way it's supposed to. This is a rock-solid deadbolt. Just like the ones on the doors in the back. I can't find a thing wrong with any of them."

Rachel hated the way he looked at her, as if he thought she might be a little crazy. She wished his father had come instead, but Jordan Gale Senior and his wife had just left for a two-week vacation in Florida. Jordan Jr., as he was identified by the embroidered script on the pocket of his gray shirt, seemed intelligent and knowledgeable enough, though. He'd taken a professional attitude toward checking the integrity of the locks. He was around Rachel's age, early thirties, and good-looking in a wholesome country boy way, with large brown eyes that made her think of a cocker spaniel.

His frown deepening, Jordan asked, "What made you worry about the locks? Have you had some trouble? These locks can't be picked. Nobody can get past one without a key, so if somebody broke in—"

"No, nothing in particular. Just being cautious." The last thing Rachel wanted was a rumor going around about a break-in at the animal hospital. Small town gossip was enough to drive her batty.

"Well, you've got top-of-the-line hardware here," he said. "And my dad installed it, so I know it was done right."

"It's not that I don't trust the locks." The truth was that Rachel had hoped he would find a glaring defect, something to explain how the stalker got into the building without leaving a trace of evidence. She'd wanted him to find something that could be fixed.

"Rachel?" Michelle had appeared on the other side of the glass door. She pushed it open a few inches and asked, "Is something wrong? Why are you having the locks worked on?"

"Nothing's wrong." Another two minutes and the guy would have been gone without Michelle seeing him. She could tell Michelle didn't buy her explanation. "Jordan, this is my sister, Dr. Goddard."

He grinned. "Another Dr. Goddard, huh? You a vet too?"

"Good heavens, no." Michelle's little laugh sounded both forced and condescending.

Rachel stifled her irritation. She knew her sister very well. She had no right to be surprised by Michelle's haughtiness toward a mere locksmith or by the implied disdain of Rachel's own profession. "She's a psychologist."

"Oh. Hey, that's interesting. So you—"

"Thank you for coming over," Rachel broke in. "Should I pay you now or wait for your parents to come back and bill me?"

"Aw, forget about it. I didn't do anything but look around. But you know, if you want more security, I can install an alarm system for you." Jordan's face was alert with the hope of more business.

"Thank you, but I don't think we need that." Who would be around to hear it anyway? Downtown Mountainview went dead after nine o'clock at night. Rachel would not surrender to paranoia, and she didn't want to communicate her anxiety to Michelle. Maybe there really was a simple explanation for what had happened to the frames on her office wall. Maybe it was just a coincidence.

As Jordan Gale Jr. walked off toward his truck, Michelle said, "You're afraid the stalker's going to come after me, aren't you? Just by being here, I'm putting you at risk, and your business—"

"Don't talk that way. Don't think that way. I'm just being cautious." Was she wrong to try to lull her sister into feeling safe here? Was Michelle as vulnerable here as she'd been at home? Whatever the situation might be, Rachel couldn't deal with it now. "I have a patient waiting. Please try to stop worrying, okay?"

◇◇◇

Rachel was in an exam room finishing up an appointment with a tiny Maltese-and-who-knew-what-else named Max, but she was aware of Ben's arrival as soon as he showed up at the clinic. Through the window in the door, she saw white-coated staff and clients with dogs and cat carriers hustling along the hallway to the front lobby.

Holly popped her head in and exclaimed, "Ben Hern's here!" as if announcing the sudden appearance of Prince William and Kate. Then she was off with the others.

"The artist who draws the comic strip?" asked Mrs. Rose, Max's owner. She scooped up the little dog. "I'm dying to meet him. I still can't believe he actually lives here. Would you introduce me to him?"

"Sure. We're finished anyway." Ben had come to Mason County to live a quiet, anonymous life, but as the only celebrity in a rural mountain community, he attracted attention everywhere he went. "Come with me."

Ben held court by the front desk, having effectively brought the whole place to a standstill. Shannon, the receptionist, regarded him with dreamy eyes. Holly flushed with pleasure at having Ben's arm around her shoulders, marking her as a friend. The other vets, along with their clients, peppered Ben with questions about Hamilton and Sebastian, his Maine coon cat and dachshund, whose fantasy lives he chronicled in the wildly popular syndicated comic strip *Furballs*. Michelle looked on with a smile. Ben's arrival, Rachel was happy to see, had done wonders for Michelle's mood.

Rachel introduced Mrs. Rose as promised, but Ben focused on the dog rather than the owner. Although he was friendly and polite with people, almost any animal interested him more than humans did. In that way he was a lot like Rachel.

"This is Maximilian," Mrs. Rose said.

"Hey, little guy, that name's longer than you are," Ben told the dog, scratching its head. "You're more like a maximillionth."

Everybody laughed. Rachel rolled her eyes.

"Sorry to break this up, folks," she said, "but my sister and I have a lunch date with this gentleman, so we're going to take him away from you now."

With parting words and smiles, the crowd around Ben started drifting away. Only Holly remained, standing awkwardly at the edge of their little group.

"Holly," Michelle said, lightly touching her arm, "would you join us? You and I should get to know each other better."

Holly beamed. "Oh, I'd love to! Thanks for asking me."

That's my sister, Rachel thought. You never knew whether you were going to get a prima donna or sweetness itself. Then she realized Michelle probably had another motive for inviting Holly. With her along, they could get through the meal without talking about the stalker.

Rachel took a minute to give Mrs. Rose's bill to Shannon, then stashed her white coat in her office and grabbed her shoulderbag. As she rejoined the others at the front desk, the main door opened and Detective Nate Fagan walked in.

He spotted Rachel a few feet away and headed toward her. She took a step back. What the hell was he doing here? How could he dare to come to her place of business, to sail right in as if he had a right?

A smile that looked more like a grimace appeared on Fagan's face. He held out a hand to Rachel. "Dr. Goddard. It's good to see you. I was hoping you'd have some time to talk to me."

"I don't have any information to give you about the Shelley Beecher case, if that's why you're here." She ignored his outstretched hand, and after it hung in the air between them for an awkward moment he withdrew it.

"No, it's not that. It's, uh, something else."

What would that *something else* be? Did he want to discuss all the ways he had failed her after Perry Nelson tried to kill her? "I'm sorry, but I'm on my way out to lunch," Rachel said.

By now Fagan had recognized Michelle. He didn't bother offering his hand to her, probably because she was glaring at him as if he'd sprouted horns and cloven hooves. "I didn't realize you were in Mason County," he said. "I'm glad to see you. How are you?"

Michelle stepped closer to Rachel and laid a hand on her back, a gesture of solidarity Rachel found a little surprising but comforting. "We'd like to go now, if you don't mind." Michelle's tone said what she would never say aloud, *Get the hell out of our faces, jerk.*

Holly threw a questioning glance at Rachel, but Rachel wasn't about to explain anything or introduce her to Fagan.

He stuck the rejected hand in a pocket and started jingling his keys. He still had that damned annoying habit. "One minute?" he said to Rachel. He darted a glance at Michelle. "Actually, I'd like to talk to both of you."

Both of them? What the heck was he up to? For a second Rachel wondered if he wanted to discuss the stalker, but Fagan worked in Fairfax County, Virginia, not in Mason County and not in Bethesda, Maryland, where Michelle lived. He probably didn't know Michelle was being stalked, and if he did it wouldn't concern him professionally.

"Why do you want to talk to me?" Michelle asked.

"Because I have some—"

"I'll give you one minute," Rachel told Fagan. She might as well surrender. If she didn't, he would keep coming back. "There's no reason to involve my sister. Step into my office, please."

She strode toward her office with Fagan close behind. Once there, with the door closed, she faced him and said, "Well?"

"How have you been? You have a nice business here." Fagan scanned the office as if he could assess the entire veterinary practice from this small space.

Was she imagining his nervousness? No. Fagan had a tight, jittery look about him, from his slightly flushed face to his stiff posture. "I'm doing very well, thank you," Rachel said. "Could we get to the point, so I won't keep my sister and our friends waiting?"

He drew a breath, let it out, met her eyes for the first time. "Look, Dr. Goddard—Rachel. I know you blame me for Perry Nelson getting off, and maybe it was partly my fault—"

"You did a great job of defending him. His lawyer hardly had to say a word."

"Maybe my testimony wasn't what—"

"The damage is done, it can't be changed. What's the point of discussing it now?"

Fagan sighed. "I'm glad things worked out for you."

"Is that what you came to say? If it is, I'd like to join my sister and our friends now."

He held up a hand. "No, Rachel, listen to me. Please. I need time to talk to you properly, we need to sit down together, someplace where we won't be interrupted."

A prick of apprehension kept Rachel silent, frowning at him.

"If you don't have time now, could we arrange to talk later? You and your sister both. She really needs to hear this too."

"No," Rachel said. "I don't know what you're getting at, but I'm sure there's no reason to drag my sister into it. Whatever you have to say, you'd better say it right now, because you won't get another chance."

"It's important," Fagan said, pleading. "It's probably the most important information anybody will ever give you. And it's just as important to your sister. It's about..." His voice fell and softened. "...your mother."

Rachel shivered as if she'd plunged into freezing water. She wanted to turn and run, but she felt rooted to the spot, unable to move. When she spoke, some detached part of her mind noted with surprise that her voice sounded firm and calm. "You don't know anything about our mother. You have nothing to tell us."

"Rachel, just listen to me, please." Fagan stepped closer, but she moved back, refusing to let him within three feet. He gave up, stood still. "I do have something to tell you. Something you deserve to know. I've thought about you off and on, I knew Nelson was harassing you even after he went to the hospital, and I felt bad about that. Anyway, I learned a little about your family when I was working that case, and I'll admit I was curious enough to want to know more. Being curious is what I do for a living, I guess you could say. I'm a born snoop."

Fagan tried a self-deprecating little smile, but Rachel's face felt as if it were carved from stone. She gripped the shoulderbag's strap with both hands, her fingernails biting into her palms.

Fagan's short pause passed in silence. Rubbing a hand over his stubbly dark hair, he said, "God, this is hard. I knew it wouldn't be easy, but—I have to get it out, though. I've kept it to myself too long already. What happened was, I remembered how your mother—how Judith Goddard died, and I wondered what might have led her to do that. I started looking into her life, her marriage, the family's background—"

"Stop." Rachel's mouth had gone dry. She backed up against her desk, sought the edge with her hands, grasped it to steady herself. "I don't want to hear any more."

Fagan stared at her. "Good god. You already know, don't you?"

"You started digging around in our family history because you were *curious?*" Rachel heard her voice rising and fought to stay calm.

Holding up both hands defensively, Fagan said, "I put the pieces together. They're all there for anybody who wants to look."

The same way I did it, Rachel thought. *Piece by piece*. But she'd had a reason. It was her life, hers and Michelle's. "What right did you have? It's none of your business."

"Are you serious? Rachel, a crime was committed. A crime against you and your sister and your family."

"And the person who did it is dead. You can't arrest her. What do you want from me? Why are you here?"

"I assumed you didn't know. I mean, your sister was just three, but you were six when Judith Goddard abducted you, so I thought you might have some memories of your real family, but I didn't see any indication that either of you knew the truth."

"And you wanted to be the one to tell us." The cold shock she'd felt at first was melting into fury. "You thought you'd walk in here and drop this bomb on us, and then—what? We'd fall on our knees in gratitude?"

"I guess I expected—" Fagan broke off, frowning, looking baffled. "Well, I sure didn't expect *this* reaction."

"Who else have you told?" Rachel demanded. "Have you informed the police in Minnesota that you've solved their cold case? Have you told—" She couldn't make herself say *our mother.* "Have you told the family?"

"No, I haven't told anybody. I thought you and your sister deserved to hear it first."

Thank god, thank god for that, at least. But what would Fagan do now? "I want you to keep this to yourself," Rachel said. "You won't be doing anybody any favors if you bring it out in the open."

He shook his head. "Why, Rachel? You were raised by a woman who stole you from your real family. I know she treated you well, and you probably loved her—Is that it? You want to protect Judith Goddard's memory? You don't want her exposed? But don't you want to know your real family?"

"My sister is my family, and I'm hers," Rachel said. "Can't you leave us alone and forget about us? You seem to think you're helping us, but you're not. Believe me, you're doing a lot more damage than good right now."

"I don't understand."

"No, you don't." Rachel felt herself veering out of control, and she paused, squeezed her eyes shut for a moment. She tried to breathe deeply, but she couldn't force enough air past the tightness in her chest.

"Then explain it to me," Fagan said.

He sounded like Tom. How many times had Tom said those words? *If I don't understand, then explain it to me.* With Tom she knew she would find understanding if she could get the words out. But how could she make Fagan see that he couldn't trample all over other people's lives and expect gratitude in return?

When she didn't speak immediately, Fagan started filling the silence. "Regardless of how well she treated you, what Judith Goddard did to you was…monstrous, that's the only word I can come up with. I've got kids of my own, and I can't even imagine what it would be like to—How did you figure it out? Did you remember your real family and start looking for answers? How long ago did you—"

"I'm not going to confide in you." Rachel stood straighter, squared her shoulders. "I'm not going to spill out my whole story for you, no matter how many questions you ask. But I will tell you that I know who my birth mother is and where she lives. I know my birth father is dead, that he killed himself after we disappeared because the police hounded him, trying to prove he was responsible. I know all that. I've chosen, and my sister has chosen, to continue living the only lives we know. As Rachel and Michelle Goddard. That's who we are. We won't take on new identities at this stage."

"But they're your real identities. You have a family—"

"No." Rachel held up a hand to stop him. "Those people are strangers to us. We don't have any emotional ties to them, and we don't want to be forced into pretending we do while the whole world looks on. We don't want to open up the past. We don't want to be on television and in magazines and newspapers as the long-lost children who came back home."

Fagan stuck a hand in his pants pocket and began jingling his keys. "Man, I really called this one wrong."

"What are you going to do with the information? Are you going to use it, or will you forget it and leave us in peace?"

Fagan took an agonizingly long moment to answer. While he stared at the floor and ran a thumbnail back and forth over his lower lip, Rachel had to stifle an urge to grab him and shake him until he said what she wanted to hear.

His eyes met hers. "I don't know how you can be so cold."

Cold? She almost laughed. "You have no idea what my life has been like, and you have no right to judge me. You haven't answered my question. Are you going to—"

"Tell me something, Rachel. Does Bridger know any of this?"

What Tom knew was none of his concern, but maybe Fagan would back off if he realized she had Tom's support. "Yes," she said. "Tom knows."

Fagan looked expectant, as if he wanted her to expand on that, but Rachel said nothing more. Let him wonder what she and Tom had said to one another. He didn't have to know.

Fagan shrugged and turned to leave. At the door, his hand on the knob, he paused to look back at her. "Like I said, all the pieces are there, for anybody who wants to look and put them together. Someday somebody else might have a reason to look, and when you least expect it, everything could come out. Including the fact that you knew and you made the choice to keep it hidden. I think that's going to cause a world of pain. Well, you have a good day, Rachel."

Have a good day? If they'd been anywhere else, Rachel would have thrown something at him.

Chapter Fourteen

Raymond Morton, Commonwealth's Attorney for Mason County, swallowed a mouthful of roast beef sandwich and dabbed his lips with a napkin while Tom waited for an answer. Tom had found him eating at his desk during the lunch break in an assault and battery trial. A thin, balding man approaching old age, he sat in front of a hanging photo of himself being sworn in when he first took office decades before. Morton had been the county's prosecutor longer than Tom had been alive.

"Yes," Morton said, "Shelley Beecher came to see me about the Lankford case. I thought she was wasting her time, but I figured the experience of making a stupid mistake would be good for her in the long run, if she was going to be a defense attorney. You want a bite to eat? The Connollys have started making takeout sandwiches at the bakery, and I'll tell you, they're something special."

Morton pushed a wrapped sandwich across the desk. Giving into hunger, Tom took it and peeled away the paper. The stack of beef, lettuce, and tomato between fat slices of bread made his mouth water. "Thanks. Looks good."

"I never knew whole wheat bread could taste like this." The prosecutor took another bite as Tom started on his sandwich. He chewed, swallowed, and added, "My wife makes bread sometimes. It's heavy as a brick and it's got about as much flavor."

"So," Tom said, "you didn't discourage Shelley? Did she tell you why she was so sure Vance Lankford didn't kill Brian Hadley?"

"She was sure because she wanted to be sure. She was a kid, Tom. Idealistic. Thought she was going to right a terrible wrong. She liked Lankford and thought he was telling the truth. Frankly, I believe that was all it amounted to."

"You never asked her for details about what she was looking into?"

"No. But I did warn her not to go around talking about other people who might have had some quarrel with Brian. I told her she could get herself into a lot of trouble that way, if people thought she was accusing them of murder." Morton paused, frowned at Tom. "To tell you the truth, the Hadleys are the ones that worry me. Especially that hothead Skeet. He seemed pretty determined to stop Shelley."

"Right. Don't worry, they're on my radar."

Tom and Morton both bit into their sandwiches and ate in silence for a moment.

"Where's your colleague from Fairfax today?" Morton asked.

Tom chewed and swallowed. "I don't know where he disappeared to. I'm just glad to be rid of him for a while."

"Is he still convinced the killer's in Northern Virginia?"

"Yeah. Who knows, he could be right. I'm going to Fairfax County tomorrow to talk to a few people myself. To get back to the Hadley case, nobody saw Lankford attack Brian Hadley, right?"

"Now don't tell me you're starting to think we got the wrong man."

"No, I just want to clarify some things."

"That's right, there weren't any witnesses to the murder. It happened at the fairground, out behind the tent where the band gave a concert. The concert was over, the rest of the band had packed up their instruments and taken off, and Brian was about to leave too. The night guard at the fairgrounds found him lying dead next to his car a couple hours after he should have left."

"And Vance Lankford was the prime suspect from the start?" Tom asked.

"Oh, yeah. Lankford and Hadley had been fighting over Rita Jankowski for weeks, and they'd also started fighting over the record contract the band was offered. They were arguing that night in front of a lot of people, before the concert started. But we had a strong case on the physical evidence too." Morton sipped from his coffee cup and took another bite of his sandwich.

"You mean the tire iron?" Tom said.

"Yep. Your dad searched Lankford's car and found it under the carpet in the trunk. It had been washed, but there was enough blood left on the business end to give us Hadley's DNA. More than enough. Lankford claimed the tool wasn't his, he didn't know how it got in his car. I guess I don't have to tell you that wasn't a compelling argument. He beat that boy's head to a pulp, practically pulverized his skull—they had to have a closed casket at the funeral—and now he's paying the price."

Tom's mind filled with the image of two young men on a darkened fairground, one of them swinging the heavy tool again and again as his victim dropped to his knees and then collapsed on the blood-splattered ground. His appetite suddenly gone, Tom folded the wrapping paper around the rest of his sandwich and set it on the desk. "It's strange he'd be so careless about cleaning the weapon. And why did he keep it around? Why didn't he throw it in the river?"

"People do stupid things when they're scared and under pressure. I don't have to tell you that. You see even more of it than I do." Morton sat forward and met Tom's eyes. "You read the transcript if you think it might help you in some way, but in my opinion your time's better spent doing two things: pinning down Skeet Hadley's whereabouts on the dates in question, and finding out who the Beecher girl was accusing of murder."

◇◇◇

After Fagan left her office, Rachel took a couple of minutes to calm down before she rejoined Michelle, Ben, and Holly.

Holly looked madly curious, but she didn't ask any questions. Michelle leaned close and whispered to Rachel, "Are you okay? What did he want?"

"Nothing. It's not important. Let's go eat."

The four of them walked in silence down Main Street to the restaurant.

Rachel didn't see Fagan anywhere along the way, but she couldn't relax. When she forcibly expelled him from her thoughts, another brand of anxiety seized her and she found herself studying the faces of the few strangers they passed. Was Michelle's stalker right in front of them? Following them? She glanced back but saw only a middle-aged woman she knew as the owner of one of her patients. Rachel made herself smile, and she got a wiggly-fingered little wave and a "Hi, Doctor Rachel" in return.

When they walked into the Mountaineer, the first person she saw was Detective Fagan in a booth near the front.

"Oh, no," Michelle groaned.

"Do you want to leave?" Ben asked.

"No," Rachel said. "We're not letting him drive us away." Besides, this was the only decent place to eat in Mountainview. Rachel led the group past Fagan to the back of the room, walking under the big wagon wheels that hung from the ceiling and served as lighting fixtures. She sat in a booth facing forward so she could keep an eye on Fagan. Not beneficial to her blood pressure, she supposed, but turning her back on him and wondering if he was watching would be worse.

Sliding in next to Rachel, Holly whispered, "I sure would like to know what's goin' on, but I guess it's none of my business, huh? Do y'all want to talk without me bein' here?"

"Of course not," Rachel said. "I don't blame you for being curious."

Michelle leaned forward and spoke quietly to Holly. "That man is a police detective in Fairfax County, and he arrested the maniac who shot Rachel when she still lived in McLean."

Ben didn't bother to lower his voice when he continued the story. "Instead of doing his job and standing up for her, he got on the witness stand at Nelson's trial and made excuses for him. He made it sound as if Nelson wasn't responsible for his actions.

So the jury acquitted a guilty man and he was sent to a mental hospital instead of prison, where he belongs."

"Oh, that's awful." Holly laid a consoling hand on Rachel's arm. "That must have been so hard on you."

Rachel glanced toward Fagan, wondering if he'd heard Ben. The waitress, a heavyset woman with wiry gray curls, blocked Rachel's view, standing by his booth and taking his order.

"What was the story about Fagan's brother?" Ben asked Rachel. "He was an addict, died of an overdose? Or did he kill himself?"

"That's no excuse," Michelle said. "He was an experienced law enforcement officer. He shouldn't have let his misguided pity for addicts color his testimony. Nelson tried to *kill* Rachel, and he knew exactly what he was doing. In my professional opinion, that's not insanity or diminished capacity. It's a crime. He should be in prison."

"Could we please not talk about it?" Rachel said. Fagan's role in Nelson's trial wasn't what had her tied in knots now. Fagan *knew*. He was one more person, one person too many, who knew that Rachel and Michelle's so-called mother had abducted them when they were small children and raised them as her own.

The waitress arrived with glasses of water and menus.

After she took their orders and left, Ben asked, "Did Fagan have anything to say about Shelley's case? That's why he's here, isn't it?"

"No, I'm sorry, he didn't." Rachel could see grief reclaiming Ben, his face settling into a mask of sorrow, his eyes growing distant. She suspected that by now his sense of guilt had solidified: he had steered Shelley toward the innocence project, somebody had killed her because of her work for Vance Lankford, therefore Ben felt responsible for her murder. Rachel knew the police had no proof whatever that Shelley was killed because she was trying to free Lankford, but she also knew that trying to reason Ben out of his guilt would be pointless.

The four of them sipped their water. Rachel glanced at Fagan, who seemed engrossed by the Roanoke newspaper. The silence around the table lasted a couple of minutes, until Holly spoke up. "That man is still in the hospital, isn't he?" she asked Rachel. "He can't hurt you now, can he?"

Rachel suppressed a groan. "Yes, he is, and no, he can't. Now can we please change the subject?"

"He's still in the hospital," Michelle said, "because Rachel has fought very hard to keep him there. But he's never stopped harassing her."

That dragged Ben out of his thoughts and back to the here-and-now. "You never told me that," he said to Rachel. "What's he doing? How is he harassing you if he's still in the hospital?"

When Rachel hesitated to answer, Michelle jumped in again. "He's sent her letters, and—"

"*Please* stop." Rachel wanted to stuff her napkin in Michelle's mouth to gag her. What had taken possession of Michelle to make her chatter like this? Maybe her sister's volubility on the sensitive subject of Rachel's stalker was a way of blowing off the tension her own tormentor generated. Rachel was in no mood to allow it. "Can we drop the subject?"

Holly made a quick apology. "I'm sorry. It's my fault. I ask too many questions."

Ben reached across the table to squeeze Rachel's hand. "Hey, kid, you want me to kill Fagan for you?"

Rachel burst out laughing. "He's not worth the trouble, but thanks."

Her laughter attracted Detective Fagan's attention, and when he glanced their way he met Rachel's gaze for a second before he turned back to his reading.

"Rachel can deal with it," Michelle said. "She's one of the strongest people I know. She's always been my rock."

Rachel shot her a surprised glance, only because she rarely heard direct praise from her sister. She knew Michelle depended on her and had faith in her inner strength. She also knew she was nowhere near as strong as her sister thought she was.

Chapter Fifteen

Rita Jankowski, the only cashier on duty, was flinging groceries into a plastic bag when Tom entered the supermarket. Neither her sour expression nor her shapeless supermarket smock succeeded in making her blend into her drab surroundings. With wavy red-gold hair, creamy skin, and doll-like features, she was a knockout who turned heads everywhere she went.

Her customer, an elderly woman with white hair, fluttered her hands and begged, "Please be more careful!"

Rita tossed two big cans of baked beans on top of eggs, bananas and lettuce. She dropped in glass jars instead of carefully placing them, and piled so much into each bag that Tom wondered whether the customer would make it into her house without one of them splitting and spilling everything.

The customer looked ready to weep by the time Rita read out the total of the bill in a bored monotone. The woman wrote a check with a shaking hand and Rita took it without once looking her in the face. Pushing her groceries out past Tom, the customer yelped in distress as one overstuffed bag tipped sideways and cans and bottles rolled out into the cart. Tom stopped to help her re-bag everything before he moved on.

"Hey, Rita," he said as he approached the checkout, "who taught you that bagging technique? I don't think I've ever seen anything like it."

She turned icy blue eyes on him. "What do you want?"

"Just need to talk to you for a few minutes. Can you take a break?"

She folded her arms and leaned a hip against the counter. "I don't get many breaks and I don't want to waste one of them. Do your talking right here and now before another customer comes through."

"You've heard about Shelley Beecher's death?"

"Who the hell hasn't? I'm sick of hearing about the poor sweet angel. A whole month of that was enough."

"Did you have something against Shelley?"

"Hey, now wait a minute." Rita drew herself up straight. "I know how you cops think. If you're desperate for suspects, go look somewhere else. I didn't have a thing to do with it."

"But you didn't like her."

"I didn't hardly know the girl, but she was making a damned nuisance of herself. I was tired of her pestering me. I know it sounds awful to say it, but I was kind of relieved when she went missing, because she wasn't bothering me anymore."

"What did she want from you?"

Rita ran a hand under her hair and lifted it off her neck with a self-conscious movement she'd probably perfected in front of a mirror before she hit puberty. "What do you think? She wanted me to help her prove Vance was innocent. Her big cause."

"Why did she believe you could help?"

Rita expelled a long sigh. "She had this idea that if I kept going over and over what happened, I'd remember something she could use. But I don't know anything I haven't already told the police." She leaned a little in Tom's direction, and her voice dropped to a confidential tone. "Don't you think she could've been killed by some man she hooked up with? Maybe they were together, you know, and things got a little rough—I heard she had marks like she was strangled, and you know some people go in for that kind of thing when they're—"

"No," Tom said, stifling the desire to strangle Rita. "We're sure that's not how it happened. She was abducted. She was murdered. I'm trying to find out why."

"Well, we're right back where we started, I guess. I don't know a thing that's gonna help you." Settling her hip against the counter again, Rita folded her arms, looking both casual and defensive at the same time.

"Did Shelley say she had evidence against somebody else for Brian's murder? Did she name anybody?"

"Oh, she was sure she was gonna prove somebody besides Vance did it, but she was real cagey about it, you know? I kept trying to find out who she had in mind, you can't blame me for being curious, but she'd just smile or she'd say, *You'll find out soon enough. Wait and see.*"

"Did you believe her?"

"What, that she was gonna clear Vance and get him out?" Rita shrugged. "I didn't know what to believe."

"Do you believe Vance killed Brian?"

For a moment Rita said nothing, avoiding Tom's eyes as she brushed specks of lint from her smock. "I hate that he's locked up, that's all."

"I hear he's doing okay," Tom said. "He stays out of trouble and nobody bothers him."

"Yeah, because he's a teacher. He helps guys write letters and study for their GEDs, stuff like that. I heard he even taught a couple of guys to read. He's doing something for them, so they let him be."

"Sounds like you keep in touch. Do you visit him?"

"I've been to see him now and then since they moved him closer to home. The place gives me the creeps. And the guards look at me like they're taking my clothes off in their minds. I get these awful nightmares afterward, every single time." She shook her head. "I'd go crazy if I was locked up."

"Were you involved with anybody else back then, besides Vance and Brian? Was there anybody else who might have had it in for Brian?"

Rita gave a harsh laugh. "Believe it or not, two at a time's my limit."

"It must have been…uncomfortable, all of you being in the band together."

"To tell you the truth, I thought it made us better. Lots of sparks flying around on stage when we played."

"That's one way to look at it, I guess."

"You don't understand. You have to give the music everything you've got. It has to come out raw, you know? That's what made us special. We didn't get up and sing pretty little mountain folk songs. We mostly sang what Brian and Vance wrote, and we really tore into it. We got the audience buzzing like we'd thrown a live wire at them." She broke off with a sigh. "We were special. Everybody said so."

"Why did you stop singing after Brian's murder? You could have gone to Nashville or wherever and gotten started on your own. You could go on one of those TV talent shows and become a star overnight."

Eyes downcast, Rita pulled a cloth from under the counter and wiped away a wet spot left by the last customer's sweating ice cream carton. "I don't know. I was good with the band. I was part of something special with them. By myself I'm just one more wannabe girl singer. I'd get lost in the crowd."

"I've heard you sing, Rita. You don't need Brian Hadley's band to make you sound good. And your looks will always make you stand out."

A faint smile tugged at one corner of her mouth, but she said, "I couldn't make it on my own. Like Jordy says, if you don't know when to cut your losses, you'll never be happy."

"Jordy Gale? Are you back with him again?"

Her cheeks flushed and the look she gave Tom mixed defiance and shame. "I don't need to hear your opinion about it. I hear enough of that crap from my mother."

"I wasn't going to—"

"He's the only man in this county who doesn't treat me like trash. I can't even walk down the street without some creep sidling over and brushing up against me. Even men coming through the grocery line whisper dirty stuff at me while I'm ringing up their beer and junk food."

"I'm sorry to hear that," Tom said.

"Jordy treats me with respect. He knows what it's like when people won't give you a chance. Last time he was in rehab, back in the winter, he got fired from his job in Manassas, can you believe that? They said they couldn't have a junkie working for them and going into people's houses and maybe stealing from them."

"That's a legitimate concern with an addict," Tom said. "I like Jordy, but if I thought he was using again, I wouldn't let him in—"

"You're as bad as everybody else!" Rita cried. She glanced around as if afraid customers had overheard, but nobody was nearby. She went on in a quiet, urgent tone. "Can't you give him credit for trying to change and do better? He stayed in that damned hospital two whole months the last time. He's back home now, so I can help him stay clean. God knows his mom and dad won't. They're just fine with him working and making money for them, but he has to live over the shop, they don't want him living at home."

"I hope things work out for both of you." Tom had his doubts about that, but at the moment he wasn't interested in either Jordan Gale's drug problem or Rita's social status. "To get back to the subject, did anybody besides Vance have problems with Brian? Not over you or the record contract, but over anything at all?"

"I don't *know*," Rita snapped. "So you might as well stop asking. Go ask Saint Grace what was going on with Brian. She was always snooping on him, keeping tabs on everything he did and who he did it with."

"Saint Grace? Brian's wife?"

"Yeah. That was his nickname for her, not mine." Rita glanced past Tom, and her face brightened with relief. "Here comes a customer. I can't talk to you anymore."

She turned her back on Tom and gestured to a woman who hesitated at the entrance to Rita's aisle.

Tom left with more questions than he'd brought. Taking Rita's advice, he set off toward Grace Hadley's house.

◇◇◇

Good timing. Grace Hadley was turning into her driveway when Tom approached her house from the opposite direction. He pulled up behind her car and parked. Grace got out and held the rear door open for her young son and daughter, but she was watching Tom with that baleful *What do you want?* expression he'd seen a lot of lately.

The kids scrambled from the car, dragging book bags behind them, and Grace shooed them toward the house as if she wanted to get them away from Tom. She wore white nylon pants, white athletic shoes, and a gaudy flowered tunic, her uniform as a dental hygienist. With her brown hair scraped back and caught in a clasp at the nape of her neck and her pale face lacking makeup except for lipstick, she appeared tired and older than her late twenties.

"Hey, Grace," Tom said as he rounded the front of his cruiser. "Got a few minutes to talk to me?"

"I'm just bringing Mark and Lucy home from school. They'll need a snack now." The children had reached the front porch.

"I don't mind waiting," Tom said.

Grace's lips formed a hard red line, and for a second he thought she was going to argue with him, but instead she wheeled around and marched toward the house. Tom took that as an invitation, however grudgingly extended, and followed her up the steps and inside.

The living room of the small house looked like a toy store in the aftermath of a tornado. Stuffed toy pandas and penguins crowded the couch and chairs, and a miniature truck, a six-car train, a helicopter, and three green plush dinosaurs scattered on the rug rendered foot traffic nearly impossible. Grace kicked the train aside and said, "I'll be back in a minute. Find a spot and sit down."

That sounded like an order, but Tom ignored it and trailed her to the kitchen, which opened off the living room.

When she noticed him leaning in the doorway, Grace paused with a gallon jug of milk in one hand. "Can't you give me a minute to get the kids settled?"

"Go right ahead. Pretend I'm not here."

"As if," Grace muttered. She plopped the milk jug onto the wooden kitchen table between the boy and girl, grabbed two glasses from a cabinet, slammed the door shut, retrieved a box of oatmeal cookies from another cabinet. The house didn't seem to have a dining room, so this must be where the family ate every meal.

The children's placid faces showed no surprise or concern at their mother's agitated behavior. They must be used to it, Tom realized.

When the children had full glasses of milk and the cookie box lay open between them, Grace pushed past Tom into the living room. She scooped a family of five pandas, large and small, off a chair. "Sit down."

Tom waited for her to sit first, but she stayed on her feet. With her arms full of black and white bears, she moved to a plastic bin in a corner and tried to lift the lid with the toe of her shoe. Tom stepped in to raise it and got a glare for his trouble. Grace dumped the pandas into the bin, on top of a jumble of other toys.

"Will you *please* sit down?" she said.

"If you will. Come on, aren't you tired? Haven't you been on your feet all day at work?"

Grace rubbed at her forehead with her fingertips as if she had a headache. Tom pushed toys aside on the couch and Grace sat in the cleared space without acknowledging his gesture.

He took the chair she'd cleared for him, across the coffee table from her. Trying a wry grin, he gestured at all the toys. "I'm guessing overindulgent grandparents?"

Her little laugh came out sour and hollow. "You have no idea. I don't know how to stop them. And there's more of this junk over at their house. Well, you saw for yourself. What do you want? I've got a million things to do before I start dinner."

"I need to know what contact you've had with Shelley Beecher and what the two of you talked about."

Grace grabbed a plush dinosaur from the couch and began plucking at the raised plates along its spine. As if speaking to the toy, she said, "I never had a real conversation with her because I didn't have anything to tell her. I couldn't make her leave me alone, but it was all one-sided. I hated her raking up that stuff and trying to drag the rest of us into her stupid little—"

An angry squeal from the kitchen cut her off. With the toy still in her hand, Grace jumped up and rushed to investigate.

Sighing, Tom sat back and waited. Maybe he should have gone to see her at the dental office, pulled her away from work for a private talk. But then she would have been hurried and annoyed that he was throwing off her schedule.

After a couple of minutes of hushed instructions to her children, the words inaudible but the no-nonsense tone unmistakable, Grace closed the door between the two rooms and returned to the sofa. She stroked the plush dinosaur absentmindedly and spoke before Tom had a chance to say anything. "You know what I think about Shelley? I think she was one of those girls who get a kick out of being involved with a man who's in prison. She might have started working on Vance's case to get some legal experience, but it was pretty clear she got real involved with him on a personal level."

Tom raised an eyebrow. Nobody else had said anything remotely like that. "What made you think so?"

"It was the way she talked about him, her whole attitude. She said she'd gotten to know him and she believed he had the soul of an innocent man." Grace snorted. "The *soul.*"

"Did she give you any idea who she thought was guilty, if Vance didn't do it?"

Tom expected a no, but he felt disappointed anyway when Grace shook her head.

"She thought Vance was innocent, that's all I know. One thing she said was it didn't make sense for him to keep the murder weapon and leave it in his car. Well, if he was high on drugs and couldn't think straight enough to cover his tracks, that's all the explanation I need."

"Drugs?" Tom said. "Do you have some reason to think Vance was using drugs the night Brian was killed? Did you see him? Did he act like he was high?"

"They *all* smoked weed before their concerts." Grace glanced toward the kitchen, where the kids still seemed to be arguing about something, their exchange muted by the closed door. She lowered her voice to a near-whisper. "I think they were getting into stronger stuff too."

Tom also spoke quietly. "The whole band, including Brian?"

Grace nodded, sorrow and anger and resignation warring in her expression. She leaned forward, closer to Tom, and he mirrored the movement. "His mom and dad'll deny it to their dying day, but he was smoking dope all the time and I think he was starting to snort coke. Wasting money on drugs when we needed things for the kids. He was all wrapped up in that show business stuff. I knew it was going to destroy him one way or another."

The children had gone silent, and Tom wondered how much they were overhearing. Grace had probably communicated her opinion of their father to the kids over the years, but Tom had to wonder why she was speaking so openly to a cop. He wasn't going to ask her and risk shutting her up. "So you didn't want Brian to pursue a career in music?"

"Do you have any idea what a dirty business it is? The music business? Drinking, drugs, women throwing themselves at the men in the band. I mean, all Brian's band had were CDs they put together themselves and sold on the Internet and at concerts, but they were already acting like stars. That was what my husband wanted. To be a star. His big dream was being up there on the stage with a whole big crowd of women screaming his name."

"Wasn't that dream about to come true? Weren't they about to sign a deal with a music label?"

She turned her eyes toward a side window, and when Tom followed her gaze he saw Blake and Maureen Hadley's house a hundred feet away. Close quarters. Her in-laws—former in-laws—could keep track of everything she did, every visitor she had.

Grace didn't acknowledge Tom's question about the record deal. She went on, "Whenever we had an argument, he'd throw it in my face, he'd tell me he could have a dozen women every night of the week if he wanted to. What was I supposed to say to that? How could I compete with it?"

Maybe a blunt question would get her attention. "Did you feel like you were losing your husband because of his career?"

Grace stayed silent for a moment, eyes still fixed on the window, her fingers kneading the soft little dinosaur. When she spoke, she sounded weary and deeply saddened. "If he'd lived, he would've left me by now. He'd be living somewhere else in a fancy house. But I never would've let him walk away from his kids. He was their father, and he had responsibilities. I would've made sure he lived up to them."

"Did you know at the time that he was involved with Rita? Was he going to leave you for her?"

She shifted her gaze to Tom. "That won't work, deputy. It didn't work when Vance's lawyer tried it, and it won't work now."

"What won't work?"

"Trying to make it look like I could've killed my husband out of jealousy."

"I wasn't implying that. Vance was tried and convicted, and I haven't seen any reason to doubt that he's guilty. We've gone way off track here. All I'm interested in is whether Shelley was doing something that might have ticked somebody off. Are you positive she never pointed a finger at anybody else for Brian's murder?"

"Sorry, no, she didn't. And you want to know something? I don't give a shit who killed Brian. If it turned out to be somebody besides Vance Lankford, it wouldn't change a thing for me. " She tossed the toy aside and it tumbled off the sofa onto the floor. "All I ever wanted was to get married and stay home and raise my kids. Now I've got two kids to raise by myself, and I'm just barely scraping by with a job I hate. Sticking my hands in other people's mouths, cleaning their dirty teeth."

"You could try something else, get some training, maybe move someplace where the pay's better."

"Are you kidding? The Hadleys would fight me tooth and nail if I tried to take the kids somewhere else. They're always saying Mark and Lucy are all they've got left of Brian." In a sudden burst of energy, she jumped up and started plucking toys off the floor and tossing them into the bin. "God forbid I'd ever want to get married again. They wouldn't let some other man be a father to Brian's children. Not that I'd want to marry anybody around here."

"Grace, I need to know whether anybody in Brian's family had anything to do with Shelley's death. I can't turn a blind eye to the way they all felt about what she was doing. Skeet acts like he would have done just about anything to stop her. Help me out here, so I can move on and leave you alone."

She stooped, lifted the string of connected train cars with both hands, straightened and met Tom's eyes. "Even if I knew for sure that one of them was responsible, I wouldn't tell you. I depend on them, do you understand? I don't own this house. Brian built it, but he didn't own it, it belongs to his parents. As long as I've got their precious grandkids, we can live here for free. My family can't take us in, and I don't see how I'll ever be able to afford a place on what I make. So I need things to stay just like they are."

"You've said a lot of things to me today that the Hadleys wouldn't like."

"Nothing I haven't said to them, more than once. But I didn't accuse them of murder, and I'm not going to. I'm stuck with Blake and Maureen." She let out a long sigh and her shoulders slumped. "And Skeet too."

Chapter Sixteen

Rachel's last client of the day rescheduled, so she was free to go home early, taking Michelle with her. She called and left a message for Tom, telling him the coast was clear if he wanted to come over and take fingerprints from the frames on her office wall. When they left the clinic Michelle seemed upbeat, almost cheerful. Just as well, Rachel thought, that she hadn't told her sister that she believed the stalker was here in Mason County and had already proved that locks couldn't stop him.

As they neared the farm, though, Michelle began the slide into anxiety again. She fidgeted with her hair, her seat belt, the computer on her lap. "It's so isolated out here. What if something happened? How would we get help?"

"The same way we would anywhere else. Pick up a telephone and call the cops."

"But it's so far out in the country. And the Sheriff's Department is so small, they can't have many officers on duty at a time. How long would it take—"

"Nothing's going to happen, Mish. Besides, Tom lives in the same house, remember?"

"He can't always be there."

"He's there at night, when we are." Rachel could only hope his work wouldn't keep him out late tonight, running around and unreachable. Tomorrow night he might have to stay in Northern Virginia, but she didn't want to tell Michelle about that yet.

When they walked into the house, Michelle seized on something new to fret about. Watching Rachel pet Frank, who had greeted them at the door, she asked, "Where's the dog? He was here this morning. What's happened to him?"

"He's with Tom's Uncle Paul. He picks Billy Bob up and keeps him most of the day."

"Oh." Michelle clutched her laptop to her body like a shield, standing immobile in the hallway as if reluctant to venture farther into the quiet house. "Maybe you should check and make sure Tom's uncle has him?"

"He'll be driving up any minute with the dog." Rachel wasn't worried about Billy Bob, but Michelle's general apprehension had infected her. She stepped into the living room and flicked the wall switch, and when light flooded the room she glanced around to see if anything was out of place. *If he got into my office, he could get in here.*

Everything looked normal. Again she told herself not to give in to paranoia.

But sometimes paranoia is just good common sense, the cautious part of her countered. *Sometimes somebody really is out to get you.*

She had to stop this.

While Michelle went to her room, Rachel fed Frank and Cicero, then started upstairs to change clothes. Normally she would go for a run if she had spare time between work and dinner, but she couldn't leave Michelle in the house alone.

She rapped on the door of Michelle's room and opened it when her sister responded. Michelle stood in front of the bookcase as if she were choosing something to read.

"Want to go for a run?" Rachel asked.

"A run? Me?"

"Okay, I guess not. I'll skip it."

"Oh. Is that what you'd do if I weren't here? It's all right. Go ahead, don't let me stop you." But Michelle seemed to be folding into herself, crossing her arms, hunching her shoulders. A fearful note crept into her voice when she asked, "How long will you be gone? It'll be dark soon. You don't run around outside in the dark, do you?"

"I'm not really in the mood for it." Abandoning all hope of exercise, Rachel crossed the room to her sister. She gestured at the bookcase. "If you want something to read, I can drive you to the county library, but they have a pretty small collection. I have a stack of new books, but I'm not sure any of them would appeal to you. History and biography, mostly."

Michelle shook her head. "No, I brought my e-book reader with me, and it's loaded with books. I was just thinking about Tom's parents, sitting up in bed side by side at night, reading before they went to sleep. Mysteries for her, I'm guessing, and the books on history and the military were his. It's strange, I hardly know anything about them, but I can almost feel them in this room." She looked at Rachel. "Were they happy? Did they have a good marriage?"

"I never knew them, but Tom and his brother Chris had a happy childhood, so it must have been a happy home. I'm sure they had their problems now and then, like any couple." Problems like the other woman Tom's father had been close to, the arguments Tom had overheard late at night. Sharing those memories with Rachel had been painful for him, and she wouldn't casually pass any of it on to her sister. What concerned her at the moment was Michelle's rapid descent into melancholy after an uneventful afternoon.

Michelle moved around the room, examining the framed renderings in embroidery of an autumn mountainside, a pair of hummingbirds, a monarch butterfly. She stopped at the dresser and picked up a photo of Tom and his brother Chris as boys. "Perfect family," she murmured.

"No family is perfect," Rachel said. "Perfection is an unrealistic goal."

Michelle set the picture back on the dresser and folded her arms as if she felt chilled. "That's certainly the truth."

Rachel touched her shoulder. "Mish, what's wrong? I mean, well, is something *else* bothering you, in addition to the obvious? Is it Kevin?" An easy enough guess.

Tears pooled in Michelle's eyes, but she blinked rapidly until they were gone. "I wish he were with me. I wish he *wanted* to be with me. But when he doubts everything I say, being around him is unbearable."

"I'll admit I'm disappointed he's not being more supportive," Rachel said. "But he loves you. You'll get past this."

"I'm not so sure." A shudder ran through Michelle. "My stalker would probably be very happy if he knew what he's doing to me. All this anxiety, the stress I've been under, it's made me see just how insubstantial my life is. I feel as if everything is falling apart and crashing down around me. Believe me, I know how melodramatic that sounds, but I don't know how else to say it."

Michelle turned away, walked to the window, and spoke with her back to Rachel. "Kevin wants a family. He's been talking about it nonstop for a year. He wants to start having children before we get any older."

"Ah." Rachel joined Michelle at the window. Outside, the growing dusk had robbed the hillsides of color and detail and reduced them to a series of gentle scallops that surrounded the farm like the crust of a pie. "And you don't want children?"

"He can't understand why. I work with children, I love kids. He can't understand why I don't want a houseful of my own." Michelle paused. "But you understand, don't you?"

Their eyes met, and again Rachel felt the ghost of Judith Goddard hovering between them. Respected psychologist, secret child snatcher. Tall and auburn-haired, looking so much like Rachel that no one had ever doubted they were parent and child. But this moment of shared memory felt shockingly different, because Michelle seemed to be offering something she had always before stubbornly withheld: an admission that Judith had done irreparable damage to her life as well as Rachel's.

"I'd be such an overprotective mother that my kids would hate me," Rachel said. "I'd be constantly terrified that I couldn't keep a child safe. I might get distracted or turn my back for one minute…"

"And the child would be gone," Michelle finished in a whisper. "Gone forever."

Like us. And children weren't safe even after they reached young adulthood. A girl of twenty-two could still disappear, could end up murdered, discarded like trash along the road.

They stood in silence, looking not at each other but out the window, into the darkening afternoon. The momentary closeness between them tasted bittersweet, purchased with painful memories. Rachel knew she was risking this delicate connection, but she had to ask, "Does Kevin know? Have you told him yet?"

Michelle flinched and she seemed to pull into herself, hunching her shoulders and wrapping her arms tightly around her waist, like a small animal under attack. She shook her head.

"Oh, Mish," Rachel said. "You have to. You're married to him. Don't you think he has a right to know? It might help him understand why you're reluctant to have children."

"He thinks he knows who I am. How can I tell him—"

"It's not as if you'll change into a different person," Rachel said. "You are who you are, regardless of who your parents were."

"Then what's the point of telling him some sordid story about being kidnapped? What if I told him and he insisted that I have to go to the police, I have to hand them the solution to this old crime that everybody's forgotten about? Rachel, I know Kevin. That's how he would react, I can promise you. I can't face it, you know that. You aren't going to tell him, are you?"

"No, of course not. It's between you and Kevin. I would never interfere." If Michelle was right about the way he would react, Rachel could only be relieved that her sister planned to keep her husband in ignorance.

"Does Tom know?" Michelle asked, throwing the question at Rachel like a challenge.

"Yes, he does. Not every single little detail, but the basic facts. I told him before I moved in with him."

"He's a policeman," Michelle said, her voice tinged with alarm. "Doesn't he want you to bring it out in the open?"

"He wants me to do what feels right to me." Rachel's mind jumped to their real family, the ordeal they had suffered, the uncertainty she and Michelle had deliberately chosen not to end. "I told him about going to see Barbara. Our…mother. I told him I didn't like her, I didn't feel any connection to her. And I think—I *know*, I remember—that she was a lousy mother to us. If she hadn't neglected us, Judith couldn't have taken us. I don't want her in my life, and Tom understands that. I don't have a mother. That's just the way it has to be."

Michelle startled her by sliding a hand into hers. "Does Tom want to have children?"

Oh god, yes. Desperately. Rachel saw it in his face every time they were with his little nephew Simon. But instead of answering, Rachel deflected the question with a forced laugh. "Tom and I aren't even married. It's a little premature for us to talk about having children."

"Are you going to marry him?"

"I don't know." Why were they talking about her and Tom getting married and having babies? Michelle was the one with the problem. *Yeah, right. And everything in my life is perfect.* Rachel added, "People around here are pretty conservative, and I guess it would be easier for Tom if we got married. With him running for sheriff, I mean."

"Oh, Rachel, you can't marry him just to help him get elected sheriff."

"No, but—"

"Don't let him push you into anything."

"He isn't pushing me." Not quite the truth. But Michelle made Rachel want to defend Tom, defend her relationship with him. She pulled her hand from Michelle's grasp.

"You have to do what's right for you," Michelle said. "And so do I. Even if it means…"

Michelle didn't finish her thought, but her fear of losing her husband was clear enough. As if signaling an end to the discussion, she grabbed the cord on the blinds, snapped them shut, and yanked the curtains closed. She brushed past Rachel and stepped around the bed to the window on the other side.

"Hey," Rachel said, "you haven't had any more of those phone calls or e-mails since this morning, have you? That's something to be glad of."

"No, not a one." Michelle moved to the double window that looked out onto the front yard and closed the blinds and curtains there. She tried to grin but didn't quite manage it. "You were so ferocious on the phone this morning. Maybe you scared him off. You put the fear of Rachel in him."

"Ha. I wish it were that easy to stop him." How could they stop somebody who never showed himself, who seemed able to come and go at will, a shadow that could walk through locked doors, leaving no trace of himself behind?

Chapter Seventeen

"So he did follow me. He's here." Michelle dropped her fork onto her plate with a clank and turned accusing eyes on Rachel. "Why didn't you tell me he got into your office? Why didn't you tell me this morning, when you saw what he'd done? Why do I have to hear about it from Tom?"

Rachel reached to lay a hand on her sister's arm, but Michelle shook it off. "I wanted to be sure first," Rachel said. "I didn't want to upset you unnecessarily."

Michelle's hands curled into fists on each side of her plate. "Will you stop protecting me? Stop treating me like a child, Rachel. This concerns me more than anyone else. *Me.* I have a right to know."

Rachel huffed a sigh and muttered, "When will I ever learn?" She wadded her napkin and threw the rumpled cloth on the table. "All right, you've got it. I won't spare you a thing from now on."

"Look," Tom said, "there's no point in arguing over this. Let's look at the facts and go on from there." Before either of them could speak, he told Michelle, "I don't know how he caught up with you so fast. Maybe he was watching your house when you left and tailed you out here. That level of stalking indicates we're dealing with somebody dangerous. Anyway, the call you got this morning came from inside Mason County. We've only got one cell phone tower, the one outside Mountainview, and the signal originated nearby."

"Was he watching me through the window when he called?" As Michelle grew more agitated, blotches of red bloomed on her pale cheeks. "Can you tell how close to me he was?"

"No, we can't pinpoint a location. All we have is the information Sergeant Murray got from the service provider, and it's not that detailed."

He could be anywhere at any time, Rachel thought. *He might be a man on the street, the driver of a passing car.* She caught herself before she plunged headlong into panic. She might be annoyed as hell with her sister right now, but the lifelong instinct to protect Michelle was too strong to stifle. She had to stay calm and reassuring. "You're never alone, Mish. He's not going to get to you."

"Sergeant Murray wants to talk to you tomorrow," Tom told Michelle. "And he wants to take a look at that e-mail message. We'll do everything we can to stop this. Meanwhile, as long as you're careful and stay around other people, you'll be safe."

Unless this lunatic has a gun, Rachel thought. Tom had to be thinking the same thing, and she was grateful he didn't say it aloud.

With trembling fingers, Michelle lifted her napkin from her lap and folded it in half, then in quarters, then eighths. When she tried to force it into a tinier fold, Rachel touched her hand and murmured, "Mish."

Michelle jerked away as if Rachel's fingertips had burned her skin. Breathing audibly, she tucked the wad of cloth under the edge of her plate and pushed back her chair. "Thank you, Tom," she said, her voice tight. "I know how busy you are, and I appreciate your taking the time to look into this. Excuse me, please." She left the room with her head high and her back rigid.

When Michelle was gone, Tom said, "She's right, you know. You need to stop trying to protect her. She can't deal with this if she doesn't have all the facts."

"I know, I know." Rachel leaned her forehead into her palm. "It's a reflex I can't seem to control."

"She might be stronger than you think, but you'll never find out if you don't take off the kid gloves. Well, she knows now that the guy is close by. It's better for her to be aware of the danger than to think she's outrun it."

"This is awful," Rachel said. "And I probably made it worse this morning."

"What are you talking about?" Tom's voice took on an all too familiar edge of apprehension. He frowned. "Rachel, what did you do?"

She couldn't look at him while she told him about grabbing the phone when the stalker called and launching into a rant.

"Oh, good god," Tom groaned. "That's the worst thing you could have done. Promise me you won't do it again. Don't engage him in any way."

"I realized at the time that I was making a mistake, but I was so angry I couldn't stop myself."

"This is a bad time for me to go to Fairfax County." Tom pushed his plate away and dropped his napkin onto the table.

"You don't have to change your plans," Rachel said. "You wouldn't be watching over us every second even if you were here. We'll be at the clinic all day, and Ben's coming for dinner tomorrow night. Then Brandon will be here until you get back. What could possibly happen?"

Tom looked doubtful, but he said, "I can't ignore the fact that Shelley disappeared in Fairfax County. And my gut is telling me Fagan missed something when he talked to the people who knew her."

"I wouldn't be at all surprised. He does have that tendency. Go and do your job. We'll be fine." Rachel tried to tamp down her own uneasiness and keep Tom from seeing it. Everything she'd said was true, after all: Michelle would be as safe with Tom gone as she would be if he were here.

"I'll be back sometime during the evening, probably pretty late," Tom said. "By the way, I postponed that civic club dinner we were supposed to go to. They'll schedule it for later on."

Rachel grimaced. "I wish we could cancel the damned thing. I hate being on display. I hate having to smile at people who think my soul needs to be saved because I live with a man I'm not married to."

"There's an easy fix for that, you know," Tom said with a grin. "All you have to do is say yes."

Why was he making a joke of it? Did he think he could jolly her out of her bad mood? Rachel pushed her chair back and stood. "Do you think it's funny when people tell us how to live our lives? Oh, wait. They don't hold it against you, do they? I get all the criticism. They think you're a good man and I'm the scarlet woman leading you astray."

"Rachel, for god's sake." Tom rose to face her. "Don't you think you're making it sound worse than it is?"

"I am not exaggerating." Or was she? Maybe Tom was right and she was being overly sensitive. But no. Since she'd moved in with Tom, she'd had to put up with personal questions and disapproving attitudes from people who had no right to meddle in her life. She started clanking dinner plates and bread plates together on the table in a haphazard pile. "I'm tired of people I barely know asking me if we've set a date yet. What business is it of theirs?"

"None," Tom said. "But people in a small community are nosy. It comes with the territory. And with me running for sheriff, well, it's going to be worse for a while. I'm sorry about that. There's not much we can do except put up with it."

Irritation flared into anger, and she turned it on him. "Why should I put up with people prying into my life? Don't you know how I feel about that? And just so we're clear about it, I won't let you pressure me into getting married just so a bunch of small-minded people will elect you sheriff."

As soon as the words left her mouth, Rachel felt stupid, selfish, cruel. How could she say such a thing to him? "Oh, god, Tom, I'm sorry."

He looked as if she'd hit him. Shocked. Hurt. "Is that what you think? That I expect you to marry me because it'll help me get elected to an office I don't even want?"

"No, no, of course not." She stepped closer, laid a hand on his chest, pulled it back when his frown deepened.

"Where did that come from, Rachel? It didn't even sound like you, but you wouldn't have said it without a reason."

It came from my sister. I'm letting her infect my mind, my life. "I'm sorry," she said again. "I'm totally stressed out because of this thing with Michelle. But that's no excuse."

"Are you sure it's just Michelle? Are you having second thoughts about me? About being with me?"

"No. Please don't think—" Rachel broke off, sank back into her chair. She couldn't find words to describe the darkness that lived inside her, the fear that wounds inflicted in the past would bleed into the new life she had created. Most of the time that fear floated along the outer edge of her consciousness, but Fagan's visit coupled with her sister's presence had energized it, and now it beat frantically inside her, bat wings flapping against cold black air.

"Rachel?" Tom sat down again across the table. "What's really got you so upset?"

He wanted a coherent explanation, something concrete he could point to as the trigger for her agitation. He would think she was crazy if she let him glimpse the depth of the turmoil inside her.

She gave him what he wanted, simple cause and effect. "Detective Fagan paid me a visit today. He came to the clinic at lunchtime."

"Aw, for god's sake. I wish the bastard would go back where he belongs. What did he want? What did he say to you?"

"He wanted to be sure I knew he's been digging around in my past. My family's background." Rachel pushed the stacked plates aside, clasped her hands on the tabletop. The words shuddered out of her. "He knows everything, Tom. He said he'd keep it to himself, but I don't have any reason to trust him. Right now, I don't know who scares me more, Fagan or the guy who's stalking my sister."

Chapter Eighteen

It was too damned early in the morning to have to deal with this crap. Tom grabbed a couple of notebooks and fresh pens from his desk drawer and slammed the drawer shut. "You stay the hell away from Rachel," he told Fagan. "You crossed the line, and I won't let you do it again."

"Look," Fagan said, verging on exasperation, "I thought I was doing the right—"

"She doesn't want you deciding what's right for her. She feels like you were threatening her."

"Threatening her?" Fagan laughed. "Look, I'm sorry, but that's paranoid. I never implied—"

"Don't call her paranoid." Tom pointed a finger at Fagan. "Stay away from her. Don't go to the animal hospital, don't even speak to her if you pass her on the street, and you'd sure as hell better stay away from our house."

"Okay, okay, I hear you.." A red flush of anger crept up Fagan's face. His hands dove into his pants pockets, and he started jingling his keys.

"Do you have to—" Tom broke off, told himself to cool down. "I'm going to Fairfax County today. I plan to talk to everybody I can who knew Shelley Beecher. I've notified your chief's office that out-of-county law enforcement will be working in his jurisdiction."

"We'll go together," Fagan said. "I'll take you around—"

"I'd rather work on my own. Whether you go back home or not is up to you. Just stay away from Rachel."

"I'm going to collect my stuff, then I'll be right behind you. I'll see you in Fairfax County, Captain."

◇◇◇

On the long drive northeast, Tom tried to collect his thoughts, organize the questions he wanted to ask Shelley's friends and her coworkers at the Virginia Innocence Project, but his mind slid back to Rachel and the situation he was leaving behind in Mason County. He'd found no fingerprints on the frames in Rachel's office except those of Rachel herself, but that proved nothing. Anybody who was savvy enough to get into a locked building without leaving evidence of a break-in wouldn't handle objects with his bare hands.

He passed the turnoff to Roanoke and drove through rolling farmland toward Lexington, feeling more uneasy with every mile he put between himself and home.

Tom understood why the Montgomery County Police hadn't pursued Michelle's complaint after they found no hard evidence. But he knew Rachel wouldn't concoct a story like this. If she believed someone entered the animal hospital while it was closed for the weekend, that was good enough for him. Last night she'd demonstrated, using pictures in their bedroom, the way the frames in her office had been repositioned. It couldn't have happened accidentally, and the cleaning woman wouldn't have done it.

The report from Michelle's phone provider clinched it: the stalker had followed her to Mason County. He'd been in Rachel's office once and might do it again. He could show up at the house in search of Michelle. *So why the hell am I on my way to Northern Virginia?*

When he approached Interstate 81, Tom almost swung off the road to turn around. But he crossed into the merge lane. He had to do his job. Rachel understood that. The longer Shelley's murder went unsolved, the more damage would be done to all the families affected by her attempt to free Vance Lankford.

If Tom could prove her death had no connection to her work for the innocence project, that would be the best outcome for everybody concerned.

The drive to the suburbs of Washington, D.C. took four hours, and Tom was ready for lunch when he exited the interstate and entered Fairfax City. Navigating the narrow, traffic-clogged streets, he passed several restaurants in converted Federal-style townhouses but didn't see anywhere to park. The small city, at the heart of a huge, sprawling urbanized county along the Potomac River, dated back to the early 1800s, and a lot of the buildings looked as if they'd been around that long.

Deciding to ignore his hunger pangs for a while, Tom consulted a map while he was stopped at a red light, then headed over to the innocence project office, just outside the western edge of the city limits. It occupied a storefront in a strip mall, and he grabbed a parking space reserved for patrons. He pushed the swinging door. Locked. He peered inside and saw no one. A long counter divided the outer room in half, a row of empty plastic chairs lined one wall.

No bell, no knocker. Tom rapped his knuckles on the glass door. After a moment, an inner door behind the counter opened a few inches and a young woman stuck her head out, angling her neck so her blond hair fell in a smooth sheet.

Tom raised a hand in greeting and waited for her to look him over, take in his uniform. He'd talked to her on the phone and told her to expect him.

She walked around the counter to let him in. From the sound of it, the door had a slide bolt and a chain lock as well as the deadbolt.

"Come in, Captain Bridger. I'm Morgan St. James." She glanced around outside before shutting the door and relocking it. A perfect example of a modern professional woman, she wore a sexless black suit that hid a slender figure but enough makeup to bring out the striking contours of her face, its high cheekbones and wide mouth.

He took the hand she offered. She had a firm handshake.

"Come on back." She led him around the counter and through the doorway into a large back room dominated by a conference table with a dozen chairs parked around it. File boxes and stacks of bulging file folders sat on the table. "Detective Fagan called about an hour ago and asked if I'd heard from you."

"Oh?" Tom moved around the room. Cork bulletin board covered the top half of the rear wall, and along its length the stunned eyes of a dozen prisoners stared back from mug shots. Grouped under each prisoner's photo were blown-up snapshots of men, women, and children Tom assumed to be victims. He spotted Vance Lankford's mug shot, and Brian Hadley smiling from a photo underneath. "Did Fagan tell you not to answer my questions?"

He glanced at the woman in time to see one corner of her mouth lift in a humorless smile. "Not in so many words, but I got the message. He doesn't control who I speak to. I want justice for Shelley. I only wish I could help more." She shook her head, her eyes drifting away from Tom. "It's dreadful what happened. Horrible. I kept hoping she would turn up alive somewhere."

Tom stepped over to study Vance Lankford's picture, which had been taken when he was arrested and booked in Mason County. With his lean, angular face and thick brown hair, he was just as good-looking in his own way as the boyish Brian Hadley, but in his mug shot he looked like he'd been slammed up against a reality he couldn't quite grasp. Tom saw only bewilderment and fear in his deep-set eyes.

He told himself he was reading too much into a photo that captured one second of the man's life. Vance had probably been stunned by his own behavior, disgusted that he'd been stupid enough to kill Brian in a rage, careless enough to get caught.

Tom turned away from the pictures to find Morgan St. James watching him with catlike intensity.

"I'm sure that when you look at him you see a guilty man," she said. "But Shelley believed very strongly that he was innocent. She put in a phenomenal amount of work on his case interviewing everyone involved and going over the evidence presented at the trial."

"Did she go see Lankford in prison?"

"Of course, several times. That was the first thing she did, when we were evaluating whether to take on the case. That initial meeting with him was what sold her on his innocence."

"You mean she liked the guy and thought he sounded credible," Tom said.

Morgan's patient little smile told him she was used to this kind of skepticism. "Don't you ever rely on gut instincts in your work, Captain?"

"Sure, but I'm a professional with more than ten years on the job. Shelley was a first-year law student."

"A lot of our volunteers are young and idealistic. If they believe in something strongly enough, we allow them to pursue it. Passion and a fresh perspective can lead to breakthroughs. Shelley was serious about the work, and she seemed to be making some progress. I was willing to let her work on it as long as she needed to."

"She was making progress in what way?" Tom asked. "Did she tell you she suspected somebody specific of killing Hadley?"

"No, she didn't. But she did say that she had talked to a woman who might have information that would help Vance Lankford. She wasn't even sure what the information might consist of. She was planning to continue talking to the woman until she could persuade her to tell what she knew. Before you ask, no, she didn't tell me the woman's name."

"Is that normal," Tom asked, "for your volunteers to keep you in the dark the way Shelley did?"

"No, it isn't." Morgan sighed. "And you have no idea how I've beaten myself up for not insisting that she tell me absolutely everything."

"Well, if it makes you feel any better, you're not the only one having an attack of hindsight where Shelley's concerned." Tom gestured toward the door. "Would you show me where her car was parked the night she disappeared?"

Morgan led him outside and paused to lock the office door before they moved away from it. As they passed a hair salon, a pawnbroker, and a computer repair shop, Tom checked the positions of security cameras. He spotted one at each end of the strip. "Are those the only cameras?"

"Yes, I'm afraid so," Morgan said. "The businesses are concerned about robberies. They don't care what happens in the lot. This is where Shelley was parked."

They stopped at a parking spot along one edge of the lot. At the moment a blue Honda occupied it. Traffic streamed past on the street.

"Is it busy like this at night, around the time Shelley went missing?"

"No, unfortunately. It's fairly quiet here at night. When she arrived, the lot was busy, which is probably why she parked over here. By the time she left, all the shops were closed and rush hour was over." A light breeze blew Morgan's hair across her face and she pushed it back behind her ear. "We've offered a reward to anybody who might have seen something, but the only people we've heard from are the usual head cases."

"Are you going to keep working on the case without Shelley?"

Morgan lifted her chin. "Absolutely, unless we hit a wall and can't find any reason to pursue it further."

"Do you believe she was murdered because she was trying to help Lankford?"

"It's hard not to believe there's a connection." Her green eyes glinted with sudden anger. "We're used to people trying to put roadblocks in our path, but no one's ever resorted to murder before."

"Aren't you afraid the person who killed Shelley might come after you if you continue the investigation?"

"That's why I keep the door bolted, Captain."

"Do you have anything of Shelley's, any of her notes on the case, anything that points toward somebody she was investigating?"

Morgan sighed. "All we have are the public documents, the trial transcript and so on. Shelley held on to her documentation. Every bit of evidence she gathered, every piece of paper, every computer file, vanished when she did."

Chapter Nineteen

Something else had happened. Michelle waited, wide-eyed and rigid, by the front desk when Rachel walked her client and the woman's dog out. Rachel smiled through her goodbyes to owner and pet, then grabbed Michelle by the elbow and steered her toward the office. "What's wrong?"

"Another e-mail." In Rachel's office, Michelle stood away from the desk, her arms folded, gaze fixed on the laptop screen. "It's an instant message. It just popped up."

All Rachel saw was a screensaver, a constant swirl of bright colored lines. Dreading what might appear, she tapped the navigation pad. The screensaver faded, two lines of type came up.

The cops can't help you. You can't get away from me.

Rachel sighed. "Call Dennis Murray and let him know about this."

"What good will that do? He won't be able to tell where it came from."

True enough. Somebody using a free e-mail account from a gigantic international server could remain unidentifiable and untraceable.

"He might be out there watching me right now." Michelle's gaze flicked to the window and the street beyond. She shifted a couple of feet sideways, putting the wall between herself and anyone looking in. "I wish we didn't have to be alone in the house tonight."

"We won't be," Rachel said, trying to sound reassuring although she knew she would feel vulnerable as long as Tom was absent. "Brandon Connolly will stay all night if necessary. Nothing's going to happen."

Michelle nodded too many times. "I'm trying to hold it together. It's not easy."

"I know it isn't." Rachel frowned, distracted by a whiff of a foul odor. She'd first noticed it when they arrived, but she'd quickly forgotten about it as she got caught up in work. This was the first time she'd been back in the office. "Do you smell something?"

"Yes, I've been smelling it all morning." Michelle seemed to struggle to pull her mind away from the nastiness on her computer screen to the unpleasantness in the office. "I don't know what it is. It's getting stronger."

Now that Rachel gave it her full attention, she recognized the odor. Where was it coming from? Sniffing like a tracker dog, she moved around the office, trying to pinpoint the source. She couldn't. "Hold on a minute," she told Michelle.

She walked out to the waiting room, where a small dog with a thick, fluffy black coat scrambled to his feet, nails clicking on the vinyl tile, as she approached.

"Hey, Loki." Rachel scratched the dog's head. He was a Schipperke, a breed she didn't see often, and he looked like a black fox with his pointed ears and snout. She smiled at the owner, an older woman with dark hair. "Hi, Mrs. Stevens. I'll be ready to give him his shots in just a minute, but first, would you mind if I borrowed him? There's an odor in my office that I can't track down, and I need a dog to show me where it's coming from."

Mrs. Stevens laughed. "I'm sure he'll be happy to help out. Can I come too?"

"Of course."

They trooped back to the office, Loki's owner tugging him away from intriguing scents in his path. Inside the room, Rachel and Michelle stood back while Mrs. Stevens unclipped the leash and allowed Loki to snuffle around the space. In less than thirty seconds, he zeroed in on the cabinet underneath the window. Sniffing loudly, whimpering, he scratched at the cabinet door.

"No, no." Mrs. Stevens grabbed his collar and tugged him away, but he strained forward, trying to get at the source of the tantalizing odor. "Don't destroy the furniture."

Rachel leaned down to take a whiff. "I think this is what we're looking for. Good boy, Loki. I'll reward you with a rabies shot in a minute."

Loki whined in protest as Mrs. Stevens dragged him out of the office.

Rachel opened the cabinet and released a sickening stench.

"Oh, my god." Michelle clamped a hand over her nose and mouth. "What is it?"

Rachel shifted a box of stationery to one side in the cabinet. "It's something…" She broke off, staring at what she'd uncovered. "Something dead."

The biggest rat she'd ever seen lay on the cabinet shelf, its throat and belly slit open, its entrails spilling out.

Michelle took a look, gasped and stumbled backward.

Rachel slammed the cabinet door shut. "Mish, listen to me. Don't panic."

"It's him. *He* put that thing in there."

Rachel grasped Michelle by the shoulders, felt her body trembling. "It's just a dead rat. Don't start imagining all sorts of—"

"Are you trying to tell me it died a natural death? Look at it!" Michelle twisted out of Rachel's grip. "You heard Tom yourself. That man followed me. He's here."

Rachel scrubbed her fingertips across her forehead. She was getting a heck of a headache. "I'll ask Dennis to come over and look for fingerprints on the cabinet, but I doubt he'll find any."

"What are you going to do with that thing?"

"Dennis can take it. Meanwhile, I'll get something to put it in. Dennis will probably give me a lecture about disturbing a crime scene, but I can't leave it here, decompos—" Rachel caught herself. Why didn't she just saying *rotting* and maximize

Michelle's reaction? "You can take your computer into the staff lounge while the office airs out."

In the supply cabinet Rachel found a plastic, airtight container. She deposited the dead animal in it, folding the rat's body to make it fit. She tried not to think about what the mutilated rodent meant, but she couldn't silence the buzz in her head, the echo of Michelle's words. *He's here. He's here. He's here.*

◇◇◇

On the telephone Shelley's boyfriend, Justin Reidel, sounded eager to talk to Tom and told him to come straight over. When Tom knocked twenty minutes later, the apartment door swung open immediately.

"Hey, I'm Justin. Thanks for coming to see me." The skinny, dark-haired young man stuck out a hand. His palm felt sweaty against Tom's. "Have you arrested anybody? You've got suspects, right? You've got some idea who did it, don't you?"

Tom stepped inside and waited for him to shut the door. "We're following up on some leads."

Justin crammed his fists into the pockets of his khaki cargo pants and bounced on his toes. He wore a blue tee shirt with the Hard Rock Cafe's circular gold logo printed on it. "Oh, man, I still can't get my head around this."

His boyish face and slight build made him appear younger than twenty-four, the age Tom knew him to be. And he was rattled. About to jump out of his skin. Tom checked the pupils of his brown eyes for a sign he was high on something, but they appeared normal.

"Can we sit down and talk?" Tom asked.

"Oh. Oh, yeah, man, sorry."

Justin led Tom to the seating area in the living room. The sparse, shabby furnishings made the images that crowded the walls all the more dramatic. Most were photos of wild birds, eagles and hawks, colorful songbirds and several species of woodpeckers. No photos of Shelley, Tom noted. If Justin had been a possessive boyfriend, he wasn't displaying any evidence of it.

Instead of sitting on the small couch, Justin took one of the wooden captain's chairs that flanked the coffee table. Tom sat in the other.

Leaning forward with his head in his hands, Justin muttered, "I can't believe this is happening."

"When was the last time you saw Shelley?" Did the guy have tears in his eyes? Tom hoped he wouldn't have to cope with a weepy boyfriend.

"It was that day. The day she—she—"

"Disappeared," Tom supplied.

Justin nodded. "We grabbed some burgers for dinner, then she went over to the innocence project office, and that was it. Next thing I heard, she was gone." He paused only a second before adding, "I was working that night, in case you're wondering. Lots of people saw me. I was taking pictures outside a restaurant in Georgetown, there were some Hollywood people there that night, in town to talk to Congress about something. The environment or refugees, I can't remember which, it's usually one or the other with them."

"So you're the Washington version of the paparazzi?" Tom asked.

Justin laughed. "It's not just me, man. But yeah, I pick up some freelance money that way. And I do wedding shoots, kids' birthday parties, whatever people will pay me for. That stuff pays the rent so I can do the kind of photography I really want to do." He waved a hand at the extraordinary nature photos on the walls. "Anyway, I already told the Fairfax cop where I was that night, he checked it out."

"Yeah, I know. Have you remembered anything you didn't tell the police about at the time? Anybody Shelley was having trouble with, anybody she'd talked about."

He slumped back in his chair, his legs sprawled, resting his chin in his hand. "The only person who bothered her that I know of was that guy from Mason County, the one whose brother got murdered. He was up here about once a month, putting pressure on her."

Skeet Hadley again. "Was he here close to the time Shelley disappeared?"

"Oh, yeah. Couple days before."

"Did she ever say that he threatened her? Was she afraid of him?"

"No, man, he didn't scare her. It was kinda like, you know, a routine with them. He'd come see her, yell at her for a while, then he'd go back home. She said she felt sorry for the guy, him losing his brother and all, and he'd thank her when she got his brother's real killer put away. Hey, wait a minute, I'll show you something."

He jumped up and went to a long, low cabinet against a wall. Tom followed him. Justin pulled out a drawer containing lateral files and ran his fingers along the tabs.

"Here we go." Justin plucked the file from the drawer, laid it on the cabinet, and opened it to reveal an eight by ten shot of Skeet Hadley with his mouth wide open, his cheeks florid with anger, a pointing finger two inches from Shelley's face. "That's him. Crazy fucking dude. But look at Shel. Cool as ice. Never let him get to her."

Tom picked up the photo and studied it for a moment. Justin was right. Shelley looked unperturbed, patient, even sympathetic. "Why did you take this? Did she ask you to?"

"No, man, she didn't even know I was doing it. That was on the street, outside the building she lived in. I parked around the corner and came walking along and saw them before they saw me. I wanted Shelley to get a restraining order on his ass. I gave her that picture to use, but she wasn't interested. Said he was harmless."

"Can I keep this?" Tom asked.

"Sure. Let me put it in an envelope for you. Do you think he could be the one who did it? Killed her?"

"I don't know." While Justin grabbed a manila envelope from a box on the cabinet, Tom asked, "Did she say who she thought the real killer was? Who committed the crime Vance Lankford was convicted for?"

"No." Justin took the photo and slid it into the envelope, handed it to Tom. "She wouldn't have told me sensitive information like that. I'm not sure she even had somebody in mind. To tell you the truth, I thought she might be doing all that work for nothing."

"Did you know that all her notes relating to the case have disappeared?"

Justin straightened his slumped shoulders. "What? Are you kidding me?"

"No. They're all gone. Do you know anything about who had access to them?"

"Nobody, man, and I mean *nobody*. I don't think she even told her boss at the innocence project about everything she was working on. She didn't make copies of stuff, she didn't leave papers all over the place, some at home, some at the office, like that. She kept it with her. Carried it around."

"All of it?" Tom asked.

"All of it. I told her it was risky. I mean, what if somebody stole her car? What if she had an accident and stuff got lost?" He paused, a shadow passing over his eyes. "I never thought about something happening to *her*." He looked at Tom. "You think whoever killed her took the files?"

"We're not sure, but it makes sense. What did you think had happened to her notes? Before I told you they're missing?"

"Well…I guess I never thought about it. I mean, I've been worried about Shelley, not some pieces of paper. But I guess if I'd thought about it, I would've guessed the police or her boss had them. Got them out of her car. Wait a minute, though." Justin frowned at an enormous photo of a white pelican, hanging over the file cabinet, as if the bird had provoked a sudden insight. "She left the building that night and never made it to her car. So if she was taking the files back home after the meeting, she couldn't have put them in the car. She was still carrying the files when—" He broke off.

"When she was abducted." Tom watched Justin's expressive face twitch and scrunch as thoughts passed through his mind. "How close were you and Shelley?"

"Huh?" Justin refocused on Tom, but confusion clouded his face at the abrupt change of topic. "Close? Oh. Pretty close, I guess. I mean, we weren't about to get married or anything. We had fun together, we didn't let it get heavy, you know?"

"Did she see other guys too?"

Justin shrugged. "If she did, I didn't hear about it. She wasn't real social, you know? I mean, she wasn't shy or anything, but she had too much to do, she didn't have time to party. She was real busy all the time, with law school and the innocence project."

"But she spent time with you."

"When she could, yeah, but I didn't expect to hang out with her every day or anything. I just about had to get her in a choke hold and drag her with me to a movie now and then." He broke off, his face crumpling. "I can't believe I said that. That's probably what happened. Some guy grabbed her and dragged her—"

Tom waited while Justin pulled in a shaky breath and got himself under control. His emotions seemed real to Tom, the seesawing between normal and grief-stricken, the calm recounting of memories punctuated by the stab of realization that Shelley was dead. Murdered.

"Aside from this guy," Tom said, holding up the envelope with the photo, "are you sure you can't remember her being bothered by anything, or anybody, before she went missing? Did you ever see her upset, apprehensive?"

Justin didn't answer the question quickly this time. Tom saw in the fluid movements of his features that he was trying to decide whether to reveal something.

Tom prodded, "Anything you can tell me might help. I don't care how insignificant it seems. Let me decide whether it's important or not."

"She never actually *said...*"

"But?"

"I got the feeling something was going on, you know? It was just a vibe, though." He gave Tom a beseeching look, as if afraid he sounded silly.

"It sounds like you knew Shelley pretty well, so if you were getting a negative vibe, there was probably something to it. Did you tell the Fairfax cops about this?"

Justin shook his head. "Everything was so crazy, people searching and the cops wanting to know what Shelley did *that day*, who she saw *that day*, what kind of mood she was in, I didn't even think about what was going on before then. I didn't have much of anything to say anyway, and it never occurred to me they'd want to hear it."

"I want to hear it," Tom said. "Tell me."

"Well, sometimes when I saw her, she seemed nervous, you know? Looking around like she expected to see somebody. I asked her one time, just joking, if she thought she was being followed. She kind of shivered and said, *God, I hope not.* Then she just laughed and changed the subject."

"Could she have been worried about Skeet Hadley?"

"No, I told you, she wasn't scared of him. This was something else."

"Did that kind of thing happen more than once?"

"Yeah. Yeah, it did." Justin nodded. "Maybe her roommate can tell you what was going on. It's kinda hard for me to describe, you know? I mean, you're a cop, would you take it seriously if I told you she wasn't acting like herself but I can't say exactly what was wrong?"

"Yeah," Tom said. "I'm taking it seriously."

Chapter Twenty

The apartment Shelley Beecher had shared was on the top floor of a narrow federal rowhouse that had been cut up into three residences. Tom climbed the stairs, hearing every decade of the building's age in the creaks and groans of the wood underfoot.

He knocked on a door painted bright red. A beautiful young woman with glossy black hair and olive skin as dark as his own opened the door.

Tom introduced himself.

"Oh, hello." The girl almost smiled, then caught herself and turned solemn. She spoke in the lilting accent Tom recognized as Indian. "I am Supriya. I was so terribly shocked to hear about Shelley's death."

"You lived here with her?" Nobody fitting this girl's description had turned up in the interview notes Fagan had shared with him.

"Oh, no. Not at all. I've only lived in this apartment for one week. I didn't know Shelley well, although I believe she was a lovely person."

"Does somebody named Maria Lima still live here?"

"Oh, yes, she does. She and Shelley lived here together."

Maria, as it turned out, was working at her day job behind the counter at the nearest Starbucks. Before Tom headed over there, he asked Supriya, "Have you heard about anybody harassing Shelley? Has there been any gossip about who might have abducted her? You don't have to be able to prove it, and I'll keep it confidential."

"There have been many rumors. Gossip and innuendo." The girl fussed with her long hair, sweeping a strand off her cheek and tucking it behind her ear. "But I can't tell you whether any of it is true."

"What have you heard?"

"Oh, I shouldn't say. I didn't hear anything firsthand from Shelley herself. I don't want to gossip."

Yes, you do. The eagerness in her eyes begged him to talk her into spilling it all. "Anything you can tell me might lead to the arrest of her killer."

He'd spoken the magic words. With a little smile, she said, "Then of course I'm very happy to help. I've heard that a man came here to the apartment several times and made quite a fuss. I've also heard that Shelley received frequent telephone calls that upset her, and she was afraid to go out at night alone."

"She was out alone the night she disappeared, wasn't she?" Tom said.

Supriya sighed, her shoulders slumping. "Yes. Indeed she was."

◇◇◇

The roommate, Maria Lima, had a line of customers to serve at the Starbucks counter, and she wasn't getting much help from the lanky, spiky-haired young man working with her. A miniature dynamo with a long black ponytail, she whisked back and forth, producing lattes of every description, scooping cookies and slices of lemon pound cake into bags, plucking proffered bills from outstretched hands and depositing change in palms, filling three orders for every one her fellow server completed.

Most of the customers wore jeans and t-shirts, some had book bags slung over their shoulders. Students just out of afternoon classes at George Mason University, Tom assumed. He waited a few minutes until the crush dwindled. When he approached the counter, Maria glanced at him and asked, "What can I get for you today, sir?"

Tom ordered coffee and paid before he introduced himself. "I'd like to talk to you about Shelley Beecher."

She turned her large dark eyes on him, truly seeing him for the first time, and he watched all the energy drain out of her pretty face. "Oh, god," she said. "I've been trying so hard not to think about Shelley."

From her name and appearance, Tom guessed she was no more than one or two generations removed from Cuba or Latin America, but she had a pure Middle Atlantic accent, with no trace of Spanish influence.

"Can you take a break for a few minutes?" he asked. "Looks as if you deserve one."

"You're right about that." Casting a scathing look at the young man working with her, she told him she'd be back shortly. She ignored his mumbled protest as she came around the end of the counter and led Tom to one of the small round tables by the window.

Before he was in his chair, she said, "You'd better catch the bastard who did this to Shelley. And I want to see him get the death penalty. Life in prison is too good for pond scum like him."

Her angry words sounded especially harsh coming from such an attractive, petite young woman.

Taking a seat, Tom said, "I know you've talked to the local police—"

"Just once, and that was a month ago, when she disappeared."

"Have you remembered anything else about the last days of Shelley's life that might point us toward her killer?"

She sat back, folded her arms and pursed her lips as she gazed out the window. Around them, a couple dozen people sat drinking their coffee and eating their afternoon snacks, and the place bubbled with conversation and laughter. Refocusing on Tom, Maria said, "I wish to god I'd taken it more seriously. I'll never forgive myself. I should have made her report what was going on."

"And what exactly was that?" Tom pulled his notebook from his jacket pocket and plucked a pen from his shirt pocket.

"Well, for one thing, there was that guy whose brother was murdered. He came to see her at the apartment a couple of times when I was home. He was a mess. Both times I saw him, he came in all mad and threatening, and Shelley just talked him down. Before you knew it, he was crying over his brother and she was feeding him cookies and milk."

Skeet Hadley was starting to sound downright sympathetic. "So you don't think Shelley was afraid of him?"

"Not a bit. She said if it helped him to yell at her, then he could yell at her all he wanted to. She was way too soft." Maria made a scoffing sound and shook her head. "I would've thrown him out on his ass. Hell, I wouldn't have let him get a foot through the door in the first place."

"You said that was one thing. What else was going on?"

Maria leaned over the small table and lowered her voice. "Somebody was stalking her. She was freaked but she didn't want to admit it. I got in her face about it, but she said the cops probably wouldn't do anything, and if her boss at the innocence project found out and thought she was in some kind of danger, she'd lose her case. It'd be taken away from her and given to somebody else. She couldn't stand the thought of that."

"Stalked by somebody else? You're not talking about the same guy who came to talk to her?"

"No, no. That guy, the victim's brother, he was upfront about it. This was something way different."

"Like what?"

"Like weird notes in the mailbox. Like phone calls with nothing but heavy breathing on the other end."

"Did you ever see the notes or answer one of those calls yourself?"

"Yeah, I saw one note. It said something like *I'm always watching you.* Creepy. There must have been five or six more, but she wouldn't let me read them."

"What about the calls? Did you answer any of them?"

Maria shook her head. "They went to her cell phone. We don't have a land line in the apartment."

"Do you know how often she got them?"

"It was kind of cyclical, I guess you'd call it. She'd get a couple a day for a few days in a row, then nothing for a while, then they'd start again. At first, she thought it was somebody who kept getting the wrong number, maybe they'd written down somebody's number with one digit off or something. But it kept happening. I could always tell when it was one of those calls, just from the look on her face. But she said it was nothing, she wasn't going to let it get to her."

"You say it happened several days in a row, then it stopped, and it started up again later. Do you remember what days of the week she got the calls?" Any kind of pattern might tell him something.

"Days of the week? I don't—Hmmm." She frowned and chewed on her full lower lip as she considered the question. After a moment her face cleared, her expression brightened a little. "Maybe on the weekends? I couldn't swear to it, though. My schedule's so crazy half the time I don't know what day it is."

"Today's Tuesday," Tom offered.

She laughed, a little burble of amusement. "Thank you, sir. Look, I'm sorry. I'm not being much help."

"Yes, you are." Tom scribbled a note: *Weekend calls?* Somebody whose work during the week didn't allow time for harassing girls?

Just then he heard a familiar sound from behind him. Jingling keys. Tom twisted around in his chair.

Detective Fagan, hands in his pockets, grinned back at him. "I figured I'd run into you somewhere."

"Are you back here for good?" Tom asked.

"Maybe, maybe not." Fagan pulled out a chair and sat at the table with them. "I might have to go back to Mason County, but right now I think I'll make more progress here." He looked at Maria. "Hello again, Miss Lima. How have you been?"

"Mad as hell," she said. "What kind of a world is it where a girl can't walk from a building to her car without being grabbed and murdered? Are you gonna find the person who did this?"

"We're doing our best," Fagan said.

"Well, excuse me for being a cynic," Maria said, rising from her chair, "but your best really sucks, detective."

She strode back to the counter, her head high and her shoulders squared, making her look a little taller than she was.

"It's always good to have support from the community," Fagan said with a bitter twist to his lips.

"Don't blame me," Tom said. "I haven't been on this case long enough to take responsibility for the foul-ups."

Fagan grunted. "You learn anything from her that I didn't already tell you?"

"Not much." But it was something. After hearing what Maria had to say, Tom believed more strongly than ever that Shelley's abduction and everything that happened to her afterward had been well-planned in advance.

Another stalker. Tom couldn't help thinking about Rachel's sister. No connection, but the similarities made him cringe. He didn't want Michelle to end up like Shelley. But most of all, he didn't want Rachel hurt because she happened to be at her sister's side.

Chapter Twenty-one

"Let's go. I'm done for the day and there's somebody I want you to meet." Rachel stripped off her lab coat and hung it on the coat rack in the corner of her office. When Michelle looked up from her computer with a doubtful frown, Rachel said, "Turn that thing off and let's get out of here."

"Where are we going? I'm not sure it's safe for us to be driving around."

"It's broad daylight and we'll be on the busiest road in the county. You can't let that freak rule your life. I want to see you smile before the day is over."

Michelle turned off her laptop and rose, her face pinched with anxiety. Rachel shoved down and locked the window that had stood open to air out the room. She still detected a faint hint of the dead rat's odor, but it would dissipate by tomorrow morning. A few smears of black fingerprint powder remained on the cabinet despite Dennis Murray's effort to remove all of it. He'd found no fingerprints except the ones Rachel left when she opened the cabinet.

◇◇◇

The smile Rachel wanted to see appeared on Michelle's face as soon as they turned into the driveway of Grady and Darla Duncan's big Victorian house. Simon, Tom's eight-year-old nephew, barreled toward them across the lawn.

"Oh, he's adorable," Michelle said. "And he looks so much like Tom."

Rachel jumped out and braced herself for Simon's high-impact hug. She managed to stay on her feet with a minimum of wobbling. "Hey, you," she said, "I brought my sister to meet you. This is Michelle."

"Hey, Michelle, I'm Simon." He grinned up at her and stuck out a hand.

"I'm so happy to meet you, Simon." Michelle offered her own hand and Simon gave it a vigorous shake. "Rachel has told me a lot about you."

Michelle's response to children never failed to amaze Rachel. All the defenses came tumbling down, some childlike part of her shone through and made an instant connection. It was easy to believe Michelle could reach autistic children when no one else could. Anybody would expect her to be a natural, confident mother. They might think that of Rachel too, but they would be wrong in both cases.

"You want to meet Mr. Piggles?" Simon asked, eyes wide and hopeful.

Momentary alarm bloomed in Michelle's face. "A pig?"

Now that was something Rachel would like to see: Michelle meeting a pig.

Simon giggled. "He's a guinea pig."

Michelle visibly relaxed. "Oh, well, in that case, I would love to meet him."

"Do you mind meeting me first?" Darla Duncan, in jeans, sweatshirt, and athletic shoes, walked toward them with a smile and an outstretched hand. "I'm Darla, this little whirligig's grandmother. Glad to meet you at last, Michelle."

Rachel, knowing her sister so well, could see the small signs of emotional withdrawal as Michelle greeted this middle-aged woman with a makeup-free face and brown hair secured in a ponytail with a rubber band. Michelle's smile froze in place, the warmth Simon had ignited in her blue eyes cooled and faded. She placed a perfectly manicured hand in Darla's, which was rough from working in the yard without gloves. Rachel was sure Michelle noticed the bit of gardening dirt Darla had failed to remove from under a couple of fingernails.

"How do you do?" Michelle murmured.

"You girls come in and I'll make us some tea," Darla said.

"But I'm gonna show her Mr. Piggles," Simon said. "You have to come too, Rachel." He grabbed Rachel's and Michelle's hands and tugged them forward.

Rachel laughed. "Okay, first things first."

Simon charged into the house and up the stairs, pulling them along, chattering as if he wanted to tell Michelle everything about himself as quickly as possible. Rachel noticed the warmth returning to her sister's eyes and smile as she heard about Simon's school, his teacher, his best friend, and what he liked most for school lunch.

In Simon's bedroom, Rachel leaned close to speak to the brown and white guinea pig, while Michelle stood back a couple of feet. "Hey, there, Mr. P," Rachel said. "How's Simon treating you?"

The fat little animal responded by lifting a tiny dish in his teeth and bobbing it up and down. Rachel reached into a bag on a shelf under the cage and pulled out a peanut. She slid it through the mesh and dropped it into the dish. Mr. Piggles scurried to his hutch in one corner with it.

"Oh, that's funny," Michelle exclaimed. "Simon, he's very handsome and very smart."

"I didn't even have to teach him," Simon said. "He learned to do that all on his own."

"Then he's even smarter than I thought."

"He wants more." Rachel pointed to the cage, where the guinea pig had reappeared with the now empty dish in his teeth. "Mish, why don't you do the honors?"

She hesitated, half-smiling. "He doesn't bite, does he?"

"No," Simon said, in a fresh fit of giggles. "He's not *danger-ous* or anything."

"I guess I'm being silly, huh?" Michelle said.

"That's okay." Simon shrugged. "Girls are scared of a lot of stuff."

"Hey, watch it," Rachel teased. "I'm a girl. I'm not scared of much."

"You're not a girl. You're a *grownup*."

Michelle raised an eyebrow at Rachel in amusement.

"Anyway," Simon said, losing a fight to hold back a grin, "you're not all that brave. You're scared of spiders."

"Busted." Rachel hung her head in shame.

Michelle laughed, a genuine, out-loud laugh, something Rachel hadn't heard from her in...How long? Years. Since before Mother died and their whole world fell apart.

The chime of Michelle's cell phone sounded from her purse. She froze, staring down at the bag hanging over her left shoulder.

"Let it go," Rachel said.

"That's a telephone ringing, isn't it?" Simon asked.

Michelle unzipped the top of her shoulderbag.

"Don't," Rachel said. "Mish, don't answer it."

"Why don't you want her to answer her phone?" Simon caught Rachel's arm to get her attention.

Rachel met her sister's gaze and shook her head. But Michelle extracted the phone. When she glanced at the caller ID, her pale face went bloodless and she drew a shaky breath.

"Let me." Rachel grabbed the phone from Michelle's hand. The readout said "Caller unknown." She pressed the button to answer but said nothing, just listened to the low, raspy voice.

"Our time is coming, Michelle. We'll be together very, very soon. Be ready for something special."

Chapter Twenty-two

Late that night, Rachel lay in bed in the dark, listening to the wind fling twigs at the windows and set the old house to moaning and creaking as air pushed in through the attic vents.

Downstairs, Brandon Connolly stood guard, armed and ready to handle any threat. Billy Bob, always a sharp watchdog, snored in his bed by the bedroom door, but at the slightest abnormal sound he would waken in an instant. Tom would be home within the hour.

Rachel knew Michelle was safe here, that nothing would happen to her sister tonight, yet she felt as agitated as the wind, unable to be still. She kicked off the sheet and blanket, felt chilled after a couple of minutes, pulled the covers back up. Was Michelle lying awake too? Probably. The house's isolation frightened her so deeply that Rachel doubted she'd slept much since arriving on Sunday.

Only three days since Michelle arrived. Four days since Rachel, Tom, and a group of teenagers had discovered Shelley's body. Rachel felt as if a lifetime had passed, and her raw nerves begged for an end to it.

True to her word, Rachel had repeated to Michelle exactly what the caller said on the phone when they were at the Duncan house. Michelle had gone rigid and hadn't spoken a word on the drive back to the farm. Throughout dinner with Ben as their guest, she'd remained mostly silent, giving brief, distracted answers when Rachel or Ben asked her a direct question. She disappeared into her room before Ben left.

Lying in the dark without Tom beside her, Rachel couldn't keep the stalker's words from cycling through her head. *Our time is coming... We'll be together...Be ready.* Soon, he'd said. But most men who tormented women with anonymous phone calls, messages, and gruesome "gifts" were cowards, weren't they? They didn't always graduate to physical violence. When one of them did, though, a woman ended up hurt or dead.

She wouldn't be able to go to sleep until Tom came home. Sighing, she threw off the covers again, swung her legs off the bed, found her slippers with her toes. When she tugged her robe out from under Frank at the foot of the bed, he bleated in protest.

At the window, Rachel pulled back an edge of the curtain and stared out like the lonely wife of a sea captain, searching for her husband's ship on the horizon. The outside security lights cast a cold, bright glow around the perimeter of the house, and clouds passing over the full moon played shadows across the front yard. The trees thrashed in the wind as if trying to tear free of the earth.

No sign of Tom's car coming down the road. No sign of life anywhere. Rachel was turning away when she caught a movement from the corner of her eye. Leaning closer to the window, she peered into the yard.

A figure darted through the shadows, racing from the house and across the yard and driveway to the road. Rachel's breath caught in her throat. Man? Woman? She couldn't tell. Torn between yelling for Brandon and watching the fleeing figure, she let too much time pass. In seconds, it was gone, swallowed up by the woods across the road.

Rachel ran from the room, pounded down the hall and the stairs. "Brandon!" she screamed. "Somebody was here. He was at the house."

Brandon stood at the bottom of the stairs, one hand on his pistol. "What? Where?"

"He ran into the trees across the road. I saw him from the bedroom window."

"Stay here. Stay inside." Brandon tore out of the house through the front door.

A second later Rachel heard a thud and a shout of surprise. She ran to the door, yanked it open. Under the porch light, Brandon sprawled on his back. Her heart racing, Rachel pushed the screen door open. "What happened? Are you all right?"

"Don't come out!" Brandon shoved himself to his feet. "Don't step in it."

"Step in what?" Rachel looked down. At the same moment when she saw the pool of dark liquid on the porch floor, she registered the rank, meaty odor. "Oh, my god. Is that blood?"

"Yeah. Not too fresh either." Brandon rubbed his left elbow and frowned at the woods. "No chance of catching him now. I'll call for backup."

Bile rose in her throat and Rachel swallowed it down. She was around animal blood all the time and had long ago stopped reacting to it, but the mess on the porch made her want to vomit.

She stepped back and closed the screen door while Brandon called dispatch on his cell phone. Michelle's voice behind her startled Rachel. "What's going on?"

Rachel spun around. Billy Bob had come downstairs with Michelle and now skirted Rachel's legs to get to the screen door. He snuffled and snorted, taking in the odor, and lifted a paw to push at the screen. Grabbing the dog's collar, Rachel said to Michelle, "Stay back. You can't go out there."

"What is that smell?" Michelle's face knotted with revulsion and horror as she peered around Rachel and Billy Bob. Her voice rose in alarm. "It's blood, isn't it?"

"I'm pretty sure it is," Rachel said. "But nobody got to you, that's the important thing."

"But somebody came right up to the house and poured blood on the porch." Michelle's voice rose and thinned. "Even with a police car parked out front and the security lights on."

"Whoever did it, he's gone now." Still gripping Billy Bob's collar, Rachel shut the main door. She tugged the dog into the living room and Michelle followed. "Brandon's calling for more deputies."

"I hope you aren't going to tell me I'm perfectly safe and I shouldn't worry."

Rachel sank onto the couch, exhausted. "Okay, it worries me too, I'd be crazy if it didn't, but let's not panic, okay?"

Michelle sat next to her. "Speaking as a psychologist, I'd say panic is a perfectly reasonable response to this event."

Rachel burst out laughing, and after a second Michelle joined in. They leaned against each other, surrendering to the absurdity of the situation.

"Are you two okay?"

Brandon's voice from the doorway stopped their laughter abruptly. Wiping tears from her eyes, Rachel said, "I guess this is making us a little loopy."

"Yeah, I guess so." His grim expression aged his young face by years. He held his boots in his hands with the blood-smeared soles turned up. Billy Bob trotted over and started sniffing the back of Brandon's uniform pants, where the fabric had soaked up blood after his fall. "I've got a couple of cars out looking for a man on foot. They're going around the other side of the woods in case he parked over there."

Anxiety flooded back, replacing gruesome hilarity. Rachel stood and pulled the dog away from Brandon. "I'll clean your boots for you. Would you like to change into a pair of Tom's jeans?"

"Oh, no, I couldn't do that. I'll just stay on my feet. I won't get this stuff on your furniture."

Rachel stepped over and tried to take the boots from him, but he held on. "You don't have to clean them. Just tell me which sink to use."

"It's the least I can do," Rachel said. "You should stay here anyway, so you can keep an eye on the yard."

"Yeah, right." Brandon let go of the boots.

Handling them carefully, avoiding the blood, Rachel carried them to the basement and dropped them in the laundry sink. Her hands shook so badly she had trouble pulling on rubber gloves. *Calm down,* she told herself. *Breathe. Tom will be home soon.*

She tried to wash off the soles without wetting the uppers, but she couldn't control her hands and kept splashing water on the leather. Muttering in self-disgust, she turned off the water and began swabbing the boots with damp paper towels, wiping away streaks of blood that had already begun to dry.

"I should leave," Michelle said from the doorway. "You shouldn't have to go through this because I'm here."

Without looking around, Rachel said, "Nobody's asking you to leave."

"I know, and I appreciate it. But if I go, this person, whoever he is, will follow me and you won't be subjected to this kind of thing anymore."

Rachel tossed the soiled paper towels into the trash can, stripped off the gloves and threw them in too. She faced Michelle. "And where will you go? Back to your husband, who doesn't believe you're being harassed? Back to a place where the police won't do anything to help you?"

Michelle slumped against the door frame as if she needed its support.

Rachel hated the mean-spirited sound of her own words, hated the look on Michelle's face, the mute plea for mercy that made her think of a beaten dog. "I'm sorry, Mish. I shouldn't have said that. The situation's stressful enough without me adding to it."

"I don't know what to do," Michelle said. "I can't hide here forever. I have a career, I have patients. And you have your own life."

"Give Tom and Dennis a chance to help."

"They have more important matters to deal with." Michelle pushed back a strand of hair that had fallen across one eye. "It isn't fair to ask you and Tom to put up with things that are aimed at me."

"Listen." Rachel gripped her sister's shoulders. "This mess tonight could be totally unrelated to you. Tom's investigating a murder, he's getting under people's skins. Somebody could have decided to get back at him."

Did she really believe that? Rachel was no longer certain what she believed. All she knew was that she would go crazy worrying if her sister were out of sight, hundreds of miles away.

Michelle looked doubtful. "I'll sleep on it."

"Good. Don't rush to do anything. Don't make a decision because of what happened tonight."

Chapter Twenty-three

Flashing lights up ahead. A light bar on a Sheriff's Department cruiser parked on the road in front of the house.

"Aw, god, no," Tom muttered. Tightening his fingers on the steering wheel, he sped up. When he drew closer he saw a second cruiser parked on the roadside, its lights off. Probably Brandon's vehicle. But two cruisers meant trouble. Tom barely slowed as he passed the cars and swung into the driveway.

He slammed the door behind him and jogged to the house, where Brandon waited at the bottom of the steps. Before Tom could speak, Brandon held up both hands to stop him. "You don't want to go in this way, Captain."

"What's going on here?" Tom could smell it. Blood, rank and faintly metallic. What had happened since he'd phoned Rachel from the road ninety minutes ago? "Where's Rachel? Is she hurt?"

"I'm right here," Rachel called from the doorway, standing behind the screened door. "We're all okay. Nobody got hurt."

The clutch of dread around Tom's chest eased a little, and he was able to take a deep breath again. He peered at the porch. Light from the fixture above the door glinted off a dark crimson pool three feet wide. "Who did this?" he asked Brandon.

"I don't know." Brandon shook his head. "I didn't see anything or hear anything."

"Are you telling me somebody came right up to the house while all these lights were on, and threw, what, a gallon of blood on the porch, and you didn't see a thing?"

"I was inside, where you said you wanted me to be." Brandon sounded a little defensive. He'd argued in favor of staying outside the house all evening. "I made the rounds over and over, looking out all the windows. This happened while I was checking the back yard from the kitchen."

Tom dialed back his anger. He wasn't being fair to Brandon, who had followed orders. "Nobody got in the house, that's the important thing." And blood on the porch was minor compared to what could have happened. He glanced toward the door again, reassuring himself that she was really there, unhurt. Michelle stood beside her, an arm linked with Rachel's, looking like she'd been zapped by a stun gun.

"I saw somebody running away." Rachel pointed across the road. "He disappeared into the woods."

"Keith Blackwood's over there now, looking around," Brandon said. "We had a couple of cars on the other side of the woods pretty soon after it happened, but they didn't see anything. I guess he got to his car fast and he was long gone by the time our guys showed up. Rachel was the only one who saw him—"

"And I didn't get a good look," Rachel said. "I can't even say for sure it was a man."

"All right, I'm here now. Brandon, why don't you go and see if Keith's found anything? But I doubt the guy dropped any evidence for us to trip over. Look around for a while, then give me a call and go on home."

"Will do, boss."

As Brandon started off toward the woods, Tom surveyed the porch again, infuriated by his own helplessness as much as the thought of someone defiling the home he shared with Rachel. Was this the work of Michelle's stalker, or was somebody trying to warn him away from the Beecher case? "I'll come in through the back door," he said.

Rachel waited for him there, and she stepped into his embrace. "I'm so glad you're home," she whispered.

Tom pulled her close and pressed his face against her silky hair.

Rachel's voice was muffled against his shoulder. "If you hold me any tighter you're going to break a rib."

"Sorry." Tom pulled back to look into her face. Smoothing her auburn hair off her brow, he said, "You'd better tell me what you saw while it's still fresh in your mind."

"I think this night will be fresh in my mind for a long time."

When they moved to sit at the kitchen table Tom noticed Michelle in the doorway from the hall. She looked haggard, her hair hanging in disheveled strands, her blue eyes haunted. "Hey," he said. "You all right?"

"I was telling Rachel right before you got here that I think I should go home. I'm so sorry I brought all this on the two of you."

"We don't know that this was meant for you. It could be connected to the murder case I'm investigating." Tom paused. "Would you feel safer in Bethesda?"

He thought Michelle's departure was the best idea he'd heard in a long time, and he hoped she would say yes. But she dropped her gaze and shook her head.

"Then stop talking about leaving," Rachel told her. "I'm sure nothing else will happen tonight. Go back to bed and try to get some sleep."

Silently Michelle turned away and disappeared down the hall toward the stairs.

Tom closed the door, sat down again. Speaking quietly, he said, "She ought to be with her husband."

"He won't help her," Rachel said, her voice low and furious.

"You can't fix this for her," Tom said. "She's got money. She can hire security."

Rachel's mouth dropped open. "That's your solution? Hire a bodyguard? For how long? The rest of her life?"

"She has to go back to the Montgomery County police with this. I'll give them a report on what's been happening here. I'll get them to take it seriously."

"Can you get her husband to take it seriously?"

"He knows this is real. He knows you heard the stalker on the phone."

"But he still went home and left her here."

"And we know why. She didn't want him to stay."

Rachel leaned closer over the table to whisper. "They're having problems. Aside from this stalker stuff. He's not going to make her feel safe. He makes her feel even more vulnerable."

Tom scrubbed a hand over the stubble on his chin. He was worn out. He wanted to take a hot shower and fall into bed. "Okay, let's put that aside for now. Tell me what you saw tonight."

Rachel described the figure she'd glimpsed sprinting toward the woods. "Like I said, I don't know if it was a man or a woman. From the height and the way he was running, long strides, I'd say it was probably a man. But a lot of women are tall and powerful runners, so I can't swear to it. Slender build, I'm sure about that. Average, really. Not skinny, not overweight."

"You couldn't see the face or hair?"

"No." Rachel paused a moment, examining the brief memory. "I don't believe I saw any skin, now that I think about it. The hair was covered. I'm sure of that. Dark clothing, head to toe, and a hood over the hair."

Tom sighed. "Great."

"I watched until he, she, ran into the woods, but altogether it wasn't more than a few seconds." Rachel spread her hands. "Sorry. That's all I can tell you."

"That's a lot better than nothing. If this is the same person who's been harassing Michelle, it's a man."

"He called again this afternoon." Rachel repeated what the caller had said: *Our time is coming, Michelle. We'll be together very, very soon. Be ready for something special.* "There's one more thing you need to know about. I was going to wait until morning to tell you, so you could get some rest first, but that seems pointless now that we've got blood all over the front porch."

A chill ran through Tom. "What is it?"

He listened with growing apprehension as Rachel told him about finding a dead rat, its throat and belly slashed open, inside a cabinet in her office. "Jesus Christ. He's escalating, Rachel. This is a dangerous situation. I'm starting to think Michelle ought to get away someplace where he can't follow her."

"Go into hiding?" Conflicting emotions flitted across Rachel's face. "How would that help you catch him?"

She was right about that. He needed to lure the stalker into revealing himself, and that wouldn't happen if the guy lost sight of his quarry. "Dennis will keep trying to track down the calls and the e-mails. We're getting the word out that we want to know about any strangers who've shown up in the county lately, even if it's just somebody who stopped at a gas station to tank up. That might help us with the Beecher case too. Let me think about this a little more when I'm not so beat."

"You do look a little tired." Rachel smiled at him, one of those soft smiles so filled with love that Tom had no doubt about how lucky he was to have her in his life. "Did you make any progress today?"

"Some, I think. I didn't want to believe it at first, but everything I've heard makes me think Shelley was murdered because she was looking into Brian Hadley's murder."

Rachel frowned. "Do you think it's possible the wrong man was arrested and convicted? That would mean your father made a colossal mistake."

"I don't care," Tom said. "I can't put on blinders because my dad was the cop on the case. If Vance Lankford didn't kill Brian Hadley, the real killer is still free, and he had a strong motive for killing Shelley. I don't think I can solve Shelley's murder unless I take another look at the Hadley case."

Chapter Twenty-four

Tom halted in the doorway of the conference room, taking in the six bulging cardboard file boxes on the table. "Oh, man," he said to Dennis. "I didn't think it was going to be this much of a slog."

From the far side of the table Dennis surveyed the material with a bemused expression. "It was an open and shut case, but Vance Lankford kept saying he didn't kill Brian, so your dad talked to just about everybody in the county to make sure he didn't miss anything. The clerk's office is printing out the trial transcript for us. Are you real sure we need to look at all this stuff again?"

"Yeah, I'm sure." Tom stripped off his uniform jacket and draped it over the back of a chair. "By the way, I'm sending a bottle of blood to Roanoke for analysis. As soon as the report comes in, I want to know about it, even if you have to track me down."

Dennis was staring at him. "Back up a little, will you? A bottle of blood?"

"It's evidence, but I don't know whether it has to do with the Beecher case or Michelle Goddard's stalker." Tom pulled out a chair and sat down. Dennis sat across from him and listened without questions as Tom described what he'd returned home to the night before. "I'm telling the lab that it's evidence in the Beecher case, so they'll get to it faster. I want to know what kind of animal it came from. If it turns out to be cow blood or pig blood, that could narrow down the source."

"But if it's deer blood," Dennis pointed out, "almost anybody with a hunting rifle could have collected it."

"Right. That's what I'm afraid of."

"Rachel told you about the rat, I guess." Dennis pulled off his glasses and rubbed one lens on the sleeve of his uniform shirt. "I put it in the fridge in the break room in case you want to take a look. You think the same person's responsible for the blood on your porch? Could be somebody trying to scare you off the Beecher case."

"He'd have to be an idiot to think it would work. But I don't know who's doing what." Tom shook his head. "I don't like this kind of thing getting so close to home. Close to Rachel. The stalker's after her sister, not her, but when Rachel's with Michelle she's going to get sideswiped by anything he does. God, I wish Michelle would go back to Bethesda, but Rachel wants her to stay here."

"How's the guy getting into the animal hospital without leaving any sign of a break-in?" Dennis slid his glasses back on.

"Good question. The tumbler locks could be picked, but not the deadbolts."

"Maybe one of the employees is forgetting to turn the dead-bolt," Dennis suggested. "Don't some of them go in after hours, to walk any dogs that are being boarded or check on animals recovering from surgery? Somebody leaves a deadbolt unsecured, the stalker comes along, testing the locks, finds a door that's easy to get open."

Tom nodded. "That occurred to me too. I want to question the employees myself, but Rachel says no, she has to do it."

"Nobody's going to admit to it." Dennis pulled one of the file boxes closer and removed the lid. "They don't want to get fired."

"But if that really is the problem, just talking to them ought to take care of it, and the guy won't get into the building again." Tom half-rose to reach for another of the boxes and dragged it over. "He'll keep up the phone calls and e-mails, though, and he might try something at the house again. Following Michelle here was pretty extreme behavior. I think he's got more in mind than just scaring her."

"You got any idea what's behind it? What set him off?"

"No," Tom said. "He's not dropping many clues to his motivation. He sent an e-mail that sounded like a love letter, then he put a dead rat in Rachel's office, where Michelle's spending her days. He could be the one who threw blood on our porch. Not the most romantic gestures I've ever seen."

Dennis tapped his fingers on the table. "So what are we going to do?"

"Make sure nobody gets hurt, hope the guy trips up and lets us know who he is." Tom pried the lid off the overstuffed box in front of him. "Right now, we need to go through my dad's records on the Hadley murder."

◇◇◇

Rachel had cleared an hour of her schedule so she could speak to all the staff members one by one, in the privacy of her office. With Michelle temporarily shunted to the staff lounge, Rachel steeled herself and opened the door to the first person she'd summoned.

She told Dr. Diane Davis, a wisp of a young woman who had joined the staff recently, that an intruder had been getting into the building at night, apparently through an unlocked door.

Dr. Davis drew herself up straight in the visitor's chair, making herself appear a little older. With her slight figure and makeup-free face, her brown hair pulled into a ponytail, she usually looked around fourteen. "I hope you don't think I've been leaving doors unlocked. I'm always very careful about—"

Rachel held up a hand to cut her off. "Whoever did it, I know it wasn't deliberate. I'm sure none of you would knowingly leave a door unlocked. But the fact remains that somebody has gotten in at least twice without having to break in."

"What did they take? Meds? None of the equipment's missing, is it?"

Rachel sighed. How much should she tell the staff? She didn't want to drag Michelle's problems out in the open for everyone's scrutiny. She was amazed that she'd been able to keep the staff from finding out about the dead rat. "Nothing has been stolen that I know of. Not yet, anyway. But there's been some minor vandalism in my office." She went on, talking over another question from Dr. Davis. "I hate to do this, and I hope you won't take it personally, but I'm going to limit the number of people who have keys to the building. Of course, if you know you'll need to get in after hours on a particular night, you can take a key. I'd like you to sign for it, though, so I'll always know who has one."

The young vet's cheeks flushed pink as she reached into the pocket of her white coat and pulled out a key ring. She detached a key and slapped it onto Rachel's desk.

"Thank you," Rachel said, feeling miserable about offending the other doctor. "I'm glad you understand."

"What good will it do, if the cleaning woman's got keys? She comes in here at night when nobody else is around. Are you sure it's not her or somebody in her family?"

"I plan to talk to her about it," Rachel said.

So it went with the other three vets—denials, protests, indignation, and suggestions that the cleaning woman was to blame. Rachel moved on to the rest of the staff.

Shannon, the front desk manager, would be allowed to keep her key to the front door because she was always the first to arrive in the morning, she never came to the clinic after hours, and Rachel considered her totally trustworthy about safeguarding her key. The clinic's farm vet, who went to his clients instead of the other way around, and came in only when he needed supplies, would keep his key too.

Holly handed over hers promptly and without argument, as did another aide and a second young woman who worked behind the front desk with Shannon. However, the clinic's technician, a taciturn middle-aged woman named Marjorie, greeted Rachel's request with silence and an incredulous expression.

"This is just temporary," Rachel told her.

Marjorie pulled her key ring from her pants pocket, yanked off two keys, and dropped them into Rachel's palm, her lips set in a hard red line. Catching Rachel's eye, she conveyed in one blazing glance the depth of her outrage at being treated as untrustworthy.

Marjorie spun and walked out, back straight and head high. She slammed the office door behind her. Rachel squeezed her eyes shut for a moment and drew a deep, calming breath before following Marjorie. She would have to salve the woman's bruised feelings. She couldn't afford to lose the clinic's only licensed tech.

Before she could catch up with Marjorie, though, Rachel encountered Jordan Gale, who had just walked through the front door with his locksmith's tool kit in hand. Rachel had asked him to come over and install additional locks on both front and rear doors.

Shannon, behind the desk, gave the locksmith a flirtatious smile. "Hey, Jordy. You just can't stay away from us, can you?"

He grinned back. "Hey there, Shannon. How're you doing?"

"Oh, just fine, thanks."

Rachel hadn't paid much attention to the locksmith's appearance before, but now she noticed how attractive he was, with his boyish face and wavy dark hair. Older than Shannon by a few years, but apparently available. Married men around here always wore wedding rings, and Jordan's ring finger was bare.

He turned his attention to Rachel. "You know we're always glad to get more business," he said, "but are you sure you need new locks? Like I told you before, what you've got is the best on the market."

"I'll feel better if we add to what we already have."

"The customer's always right," he said cheerfully.

Rachel was relieved that he didn't press her to tell him what had inspired her sudden concern about security. Rachel didn't want the stalker story to get around, and she knew if she told a single person, half the county would be gossiping about it by this time tomorrow.

An hour later, all three doors to the outside—front, rear, and the door leading to the dog run—had been equipped with additional heavyweight deadbolts. Rachel sent Holly to the hardware store to have copies of the new keys cut.

After Jordan Gale left, Rachel fingered the new mechanism on the front door and wondered if she'd wasted her money. Reclaiming keys from the staff and urging them to be careful might have been all that was necessary. But how could she be sure?

The only thing she knew for certain was that somebody who scared her half to death had gotten into the building. The frames being askew—that might have an innocent explanation. A mutilated rat in her office cabinet was a different matter.

"Dr. Goddard?" Shannon said. "You've got a call. The Sheriff's Department dispatcher."

The dispatcher? Rachel's first thought was that something had happened to Tom. Instead of taking time to return to her office to take the call, she crossed the lobby to the desk in five quick strides and grabbed the receiver from Shannon. "This is Dr. Goddard. What's wrong? What's happened?"

"My goodness," the dispatcher said with a laugh, "I didn't mean to scare you. I got a report about an injured hawk—a Cooper's hawk, I think the man said. He sounded real upset about it. He said he saw somebody shoot it and break its wing, but he wouldn't give me any names because he doesn't want to get anybody in trouble."

Rachel blew out a breath. Her heartbeat was dropping back to a normal pace, but anger replaced alarm. Some people thought shooting at wild birds was great sport, and they couldn't care less if they were maiming and killing protected species.

The dispatcher went on, "He wants somebody to save the hawk and he asked me if we've got any wildlife rehabbers around here. I thought you'd want to go out and get it."

"Did you call the animal warden?" Tom would not be thrilled if she went out by herself in search of a bird.

"Yes, I did call the animal warden first, but he said you're the only one he knows of who could handle a bird like that when it's hurt. He doesn't think he could."

Of course not. She glanced at her watch. She could manage an hour away from the clinic to pick up the bird. And the stalker was focused on Michelle, not Rachel. Without her sister around, she had no cause to be afraid. And she had to do her job, after all. "Okay, tell me where it is."

She took notes on the location. A familiar road, one she'd been on last Saturday with Tom and the teenagers doing litter cleanup. She paused, her fingers tightening on the pen, when the dispatcher told her which milepost to look for. It was no more than a quarter mile from the ravine where Shelley's lifeless body had been found.

Chapter Twenty-five

Hawk, hawk, where'd you go?

Rachel stood on the shoulder of the road, pulling on her elbow-length leather gloves and scanning the woods. A net on a long pole lay at her feet. She'd spotted the bird flopping around in the ditch, one wing wrecked and useless. By the time she'd pulled ahead thirty feet and parked, the hawk had disappeared. Finding it might not be easy in a patch of woods made up mostly of pines and other evergreens.

There. A movement through the underbrush.

She scooped up the net and held it aloft as she pushed into the woods, to keep it from snagging on the cat briers that caught at her jeans. She grimaced with every snap of a twig under her thick-soled athletic shoes. But the racket she made hardly mattered. The bird knew she was after it.

The woods enveloped her, shutting out the midday sun and chilling the air.

The high school kids had cleaned the roadside along here on Saturday morning, before they moved north to the ravine where they'd discovered Shelley's body. The image of the beautiful young woman shrouded in plastic burst full-blown into her mind, and her throat closed up with anger and sorrow. *Don't think about it. Shut it out.*

A flutter directly ahead caught Rachel's eye. The hawk scrabbled from beneath a rhododendron, beating its good wing furiously, trying to get airborne. A blue jay screamed alarm from the treetops. The hawk collapsed onto its chest, pushed itself up again and took off, dragging the damaged wing through the leaf litter. It was definitely a Cooper's hawk, larger than a crow with steely blue-gray feathers across its back, a cap of gray, thick dark bands on its tail, and fine reddish streaks across a pale throat and chest. It could tear an unprotected hand to shreds with its beak and talons. Rachel followed, using the net's pole to slap aside low evergreen branches. The bird disappeared into a thicket of vines that hadn't yet leafed out.

"Oh hell," Rachel muttered. "You just had to go in there, didn't you?"

A rustle alerted her that the bird had thought better of the hiding place and was emerging from the other side. She crept forward. Up ahead, beyond the thicket, she glimpsed a shallow pool, no more than a collection of rainwater in a depression. The hawk dragged itself toward the water.

The bird stopped beside the puddle, although it still seemed to be straining to move ahead. When Rachel drew closer, she saw a vine tangled around one of its feet. At her approach the hawk fanned its good wing frantically and yanked its trapped foot with no success.

Rachel crouched close by, the net raised. If the hawk broke free and tried to take off, she could easily get it, but she would rather wait until it quieted to avoid further injury when the net went down.

The bird stared up at her, panting through its open beak, a predator become prey and expecting death at any second.

"Just hang on," Rachel whispered. "I'm not going to hurt you."

She avoided eye contact that might seem like a threat, and gave her attention instead to the massive pine trees around her. Here and there, spindly wild dogwoods reached for the dappled sun in the shade of the evergreens. New leaves had begun emerging on deciduous trees two weeks ago in Virginia's hill country, but a chill lingered in the air, and night temperatures dipped into the forties. She still missed the glorious warm weather of spring and fall in the Washington area where she and Michelle had grown up.

Gradually, while Rachel sat motionless, the birds that had fallen silent at her intrusion took up their songs and chatter again. A squirrel paused in its descent from a nearby tree to study her before leaping to the ground and scurrying off. She heard the engine of a vehicle on the road, but she couldn't see it through the dense trees.

At last the hawk lay still, its eyes bright with fear and the knowledge that capture was inevitable. Slowly Rachel lowered the net over it. The hawk jerked just once and emitted a high-pitched cry before hunkering down, resigned.

Rachel snaked a gloved hand under the net and grasped the foot that was caught in the vine. She worked it loose slowly, gently. She peered at the injured wing through the netting. What a godawful mess. Dirt and bits of dry leaves clung to blood-soaked feathers. The humerus was shattered, its jagged ends piercing the skin, and the unnatural fold of the wing told her the radius and ulna were fractured too. She had seen bad injuries from collisions with utility lines and windows but only one thing could wreck a wing this way: a shotgun.

Rachel shook her head and swore in disgust. "Human beings," she said to the bird, "are capable of anything. But I guess you've already come to that conclusion on your own."

She caught both of the hawk's legs in one hand and, holding the net down over him, got to her feet. He went limp and flopped over backward. "Oh, come on now. Don't give up that easily."

She righted him and he settled in her grip, glaring at her through the netting. If his talons and beak could get to her bare skin he'd show her what he thought of her intrusion into his life.

"Hang on to that fighting spirit, pal. You're going to need it." Rachel could take the hawk to the vet clinic, repair its wing to the best of her surgical ability, but thanks to some idiot with a gun this bird would never fly again.

As she turned back toward the road, a shot rang out.

The hawk panicked and flapped wildly inside the net, straining to break free. Rachel held onto his feet and keep the net over him at the same time she looked around for the shooter. She didn't spot anybody among the trees. Her heart pounding, her mouth suddenly dry, she stood still and waited. Every bird and squirrel had frozen in silence.

No more shots came. She heard no movement through the brush.

The gunfire had sounded like a shotgun blast. Maybe the hunter who had wounded the hawk was still around. She couldn't linger. She had to get out of his way before she ended up full of buckshot too.

Holding the bird against her chest to prevent another attempt at escape, Rachel headed for the road. She swept the woods with her gaze as she went. If a hunter glimpsed her movement through the trees, he might mistake her for a deer and shoot. This wasn't deer hunting season, but around here such fine distinctions hardly mattered to hunters.

Emerging from the woods, she raced toward her parked vehicle. She swung the rear door up and spent a few agonizingly long minutes maneuvering the hawk out from under the net and into a cage. The bird appeared weak and dehydrated, and the stress of being captured was bad enough without the added exposure to her palpable fear. She blew out a breath in relief when she snapped the cage door in place.

She trotted around to the driver's side, yanked open the door, climbed in, and stared at the windshield.

What on earth?

Words. Written on the glass. Rachel gripped the steering wheel. While she'd been in the woods a hundred yards away, someone stood here painting this message on her windshield.

Viewing the words backwards, she needed a moment to make sense of them.

With red paint—she hoped to god it was paint—someone had written: YOU'RE NEXT

Chapter Twenty-six

Furious and frightened at the same time, Rachel stared through the message on her windshield all the way back to Mountainview, forcing herself to focus outward, on the road, instead of the letters in front of her. She flicked her eyes to the rearview mirror over and over, making sure no one was following her. Each time she passed another vehicle, she saw the driver's head snap to the side as he or she caught sight of the Range Rover's windshield.

Was Michelle's stalker after her now? Had she brought this on by telling him off on the telephone? *Be careful, Rachel,* he had said. *Don't get in my way.* A clear threat, but she hadn't taken it seriously because she was so focused on protecting her sister. She was crazy for driving out to the middle of nowhere by herself.

Where had he been when she'd returned to her vehicle? She hadn't seen another car, but she'd heard one while she was in the woods. Had he driven away, or did he hide nearby to watch her reaction? The thought nauseated her. He must have followed her out there. Or maybe he'd known exactly where she was going because he'd shot the hawk himself and called it in. How could he be sure, though, that the Sheriff's Department dispatcher would summon Rachel when he asked for a rehabber? That wasn't hard to answer. He was obsessed with Michelle, and he'd probably collected as much information as he could about her life and the people in it, including Rachel.

She wished she could find Tom right away, but she had to think first of the wounded bird in the back of her vehicle. She drove into Mountainview and parked in the vet clinic's lot. Before hauling the cage out she draped a large towel over it to help keep the hawk calm. The bird remained still and quiet until Rachel encountered a client who was leaving the building with his little beagle-terrier mix. While the man held the front door open, the dog sniffed the cage, smelled the bird, and went crazy, barking and dancing on his hind legs, trying to get at it. The hawk let out a high-pitched screech and scrabbled around in the cage. Rachel held it aloft and hurried into the clinic as the dog's owner dragged him away by his leash.

Inside, Rachel raced down the rear hall to the hospital room, with Holly on her heels.

When Rachel placed the cage on a steel operating table and pulled off the towel, Holly exclaimed, "Oh, my goodness, the poor thing."

"Somebody shot it," Rachel said. "I have to get that wing fixed right now. Go tell Shannon to rearrange my schedule."

For the next hour, she gave all her attention to the bird. She repaired the wing as best she could, but the buckshot had done ruinous damage to the bones. After he recovered she would find somebody in the Raptor Society to take him permanently.

She didn't think about the message on her windshield until she was latching the cage where the sedated hawk would rest and recover. When the memory hit her, it brought back all the sick fear she'd felt out in that remote area, with no help nearby, knowing the person who had threatened her had been so close.

This time she couldn't hide anything from Michelle. She couldn't protect her sister from bad news anymore, not if she wanted to keep both of them safe. She flung her latex gloves into the hazmat can and dropped her surgical gown in the laundry hamper, then walked back to her office to tell Michelle what had happened.

Michelle was gone. Her laptop wasn't on Rachel's desk.

Rachel walked out to the front desk and asked Shannon, "Where's my sister? Did she say where she was going?"

"Mr. Hern came and got her and took her to lunch."

"Oh, right." Rachel glanced at her watch. "I completely lost track of time."

"No, wait a minute." Shannon tapped her chin with a fingertip. "I remember seeing them come back from lunch, but I got busy on the phone and I didn't notice…" Shannon frowned, thinking. Her face cleared and she smiled. "Oh, she's probably just in the restroom."

With her laptop? "I'll check," Rachel said.

When Rachel rapped on the restroom door, she got no response. She swung the door open. The tiny room with its single commode and sink was empty, the light off. The staff lounge made more sense. Michelle might be getting a cup of coffee or hot tea.

She wasn't there either.

This is ridiculous, Rachel told herself. Michelle had to be here—unless she'd gone somewhere with Ben. In that case, she would have left a note or a message for Rachel. She and Ben both knew what a worrier Rachel was. No note, no message— Michelle must be in the building.

But she wasn't. No one Rachel asked had seen her.

Rachel paused in the hallway, wondering where to look next. *Oh, come on, I don't need this aggravation. Where the hell are you?* Then she had a *duh* moment: call Michelle's cell phone. What was wrong with her? Why hadn't she thought of that earlier? She pulled her own phone from her shirt pocket and selected Michelle's number.

The call went to voice mail.

The dread Rachel had tried to fight off with impatience seized her in a grip that took away her breath. *Michelle. Mish. What's happened to you?*

She called Ben's phone and got voice mail.

She rushed to the front desk and told Shannon, "I'm going over to the Sheriff's Department. If my sister comes back, tell her to call me on my cell phone right away, and I mean *immediately*."

Out in the parking lot, she found an elderly woman holding a cat carrier and frowning at the Range Rover's windshield. "What is the meaning of this?" the woman asked Rachel.

"Hi, Mrs. Webster." Rachel pressed her electronic key and the door lock popped. "Just vandalism. No real harm done."

"But it's terrible. Teenage boys, most likely. I wouldn't put up with it for one minute."

"I'm trying to find out who did it." Rachel opened the door. "Dr. Davis will see Cleo, if you want to take her on in. I have to make a quick stop somewhere."

"Well, you be careful, dear. These teenagers…" The woman shook her head as she walked to the door with her cat.

"How I wish," Rachel muttered. At the moment, adolescent vandals sounded like an easy problem to deal with.

She drove down the narrow street, her windshield attracting curious glances from pedestrians and other drivers. Was *he* one of them, watching her every move?

She turned into the lot beside the ornate old courthouse and drove around back to the low cinderblock building that housed the Sheriff's Department. As soon as she pushed open the door, the middle-aged woman at the front desk said, "Captain Bridger's not here."

"Then I'll talk to somebody else. Is Sergeant Murray—" Rachel broke off when Michelle appeared, walking up the hallway from the squad room, flanked by Dennis Murray and Ben Hern. The tight panic in Rachel's chest dissolved. As Michelle reached her, she said, "Mish. Where have you been—Well, obviously you've been here, but why? Are you okay? Why didn't you leave me a message?"

"I'm fine." Michelle held her laptop computer under one arm.

"I should have left a message for you," Ben said. "I'm sorry. Michelle was upset and I didn't think of it."

"Upset about what?" Rachel looked from Ben to Michelle. "Did something happen?"

"More e-mail," Michelle said. "A really nasty one. I called Sergeant Murray and he asked me to bring my laptop over so he could see it."

"I haven't been able to trace the sender," Dennis said, "but I'm doing my best."

Rachel wished she could sit down. Emotional extremes exhausted her. "I'm afraid I'm bringing you a new problem," she told Dennis. "Come out in the parking lot and I'll show you."

The three of them trailed Rachel outside. When Michelle saw the writing on the Range Rover's windshield she gasped and clamped a hand over her mouth. Dennis and Ben both scowled as if a piece of filth had been flung in their faces. Rachel was explaining what happened when Tom drove into the lot. He pulled up next to them and got out.

"What's going on?" Tom slammed his car door. "Why are you all here? What's happened?"

Dennis gestured at the windshield.

Tom stepped closer to look at it. "Good god, Rachel. Who did this? When?"

She launched into her story again from the beginning. As she talked, she watched Tom's expression harden into fury.

"I'm going to find this creep, and when I do—" Tom broke off and seemed to be trying to rein in his temper. "All right, that's it, you're not going anywhere alone again, and I don't want to hear an argument about it."

For once, his bossiness didn't rankle. "You're not getting one," Rachel said. "Believe me, I'm not interested in being alone right now."

"I'll go with you, both of you," Ben said, "anywhere you need to go."

Michelle shook her head. "No, I was right, I should leave. I brought this problem out here with me, and I'll take it away if I leave."

"Don't talk that way." Ben wrapped an arm around Michelle's shoulders. "This isn't your fault."

"But now he's harassing Rachel too. I can't let this go on."

"Why do we have to keep discussing this?" Rachel said. "We all want you to be safe, and you know you wouldn't be any safer in Bethesda than you are here."

Tom was looking around the parking lot, the hills beyond, as if he might find the culprit in plain sight. "Who the hell is this guy, and what does he want? How long is he going to keep playing these juvenile pranks?"

Tom met Rachel's eyes, and in her mind she heard the rest of his question, the part he didn't speak aloud. *When will he move on to something a lot worse?*

Chapter Twenty-seven

After Tom took a statement from Rachel about the shot she heard in the woods and the writing on her windshield, he read a print-out of the latest e-mail to Michelle from the stalker—*I'm coming for you, blondie. I'm going to fuck you blind.* It had been sent during the time Rachel was out looking for the hawk, he noticed. That didn't necessarily mean anything. An outsider sending e-mail from within Mason County probably had a 4G connection that could be accessed anywhere and wasn't dependent on local cell service. Maybe the stalker sent the e-mail while waiting for Rachel to emerge from the woods. But Tom believed it was also possible that two different people were behind the e-mail and the warning to Rachel. The incidents could be unrelated.

He escorted Rachel and Michelle down the street to the vet clinic, then returned to headquarters and called Dennis and Brandon into his office.

Pacing back and forth in front of his desk, he told the deputies what he hadn't said to the two women. "The threat to Rachel might be connected to the Shelley Beecher case. Somebody warning me that Rachel will get hurt if I look into Shelley's work for the innocence project. I get the same feeling about the blood on our porch."

"This is the way a coward operates," Dennis said. "He won't tackle you directly. He threatens somebody you care about."

"I wouldn't be surprised if Skeet Hadley did something like this," Brandon said.

"Neither would I," Tom said. "Find out where he was the past few hours. If nobody outside his family can vouch for him, let's get him in here for questioning."

Dennis and Brandon were leaving his office when Tom's desk phone rang. Ben Hern was on the line, sounding angry. "Somebody broke into my house while I was out," he told Tom.

Tom sat in his desk chair and picked up a pen to take notes. "A robbery? What's missing?"

"No, it wasn't a robbery. I think they were looking for something Shelley might have left here when she used my computer. There wasn't anything to find, but I think that's what they were looking for."

"I'll be right over," Tom said. "You can fill me in when I get there."

◇◇◇

Tom drove up the curving, tree-lined driveway and into the parking circle outside Ben's front door. A coal company executive had built the stately brick Georgian-style house at a time when coal was still a booming industry in the area. The man's widow lived out her life there. When Ben wanted a quiet refuge from fame and people with outstretched hands, he followed Rachel, a childhood friend, to the mountains and bought the house and ten surrounding acres—paying for it in full up front, Tom had heard.

Ben stood on the stone steps, his face grim. When Tom climbed out of the cruiser, Ben said, "I thought I had a state-of-the-art security system. Whoever got inside knew what he was doing. Even the damned cameras were turned off."

Following Ben's gesture, Tom glanced up at a tiny lens over the door lintel that he wouldn't have spotted without direction. Hern opened the front door and led them in. "I'm relieved he didn't hurt my dog and cat."

The pets in question sat side by side in the foyer. Hamilton, the gray Maine Coon cat, was as big as the dachshund, Sebastian. Tom patted Sebastian and rubbed his knuckles against Hamilton's head. The dog had always been friendly, but Tom had visited several times with Rachel before the cat allowed him to get close.

"This is starting to sound like the same guy who got into the vet clinic," Tom said. "But why would anybody think Shelley left something in your house?"

"Like I said, she used my computer when she needed to do research. Her family doesn't have an Internet connection at home. And in case you're wondering, Angie was always here when Shelley came over. I was usually upstairs in my studio and didn't even see Shelley except when she stuck her head in to say hello and goodbye."

Tom scanned the living room off the foyer on the right. "Everything looks okay. They didn't exactly trash the place."

"No, that's the creepy part." Ben gestured for Tom and Brandon to follow him down the hall. "A straightforward break-in and robbery, that's one thing. But this was something else. I was surprised the alarm was off when I got home—I always set it when I leave the house—but nothing seemed to be missing or out of place, so I thought maybe I'd forgotten to do it for once. I didn't know for sure somebody had been here until I saw my office."

Tom followed him to the office, across from the kitchen at the rear of the house. Ben stood back while Tom studied the room from the threshold. The desk drawers were closed, the few papers on the desktop next to the computer lay in a neat stack. Small sofa, coffee table, book-filled shelves—all of it looked to be in order. "What made you think somebody was in here?"

"My computer was on, for one thing." Ben edged past Tom into the room, walked to the desk and rolled the trackball with one fingertip. The black screen sprang to life in brilliant color. "I never leave it on. I haven't even used it since yesterday, and I turned it off then."

"Okay, come on out and don't touch anything else." Tom wasn't persuaded that Ben had turned off his computer and an intruder had been there using it, any more than he was convinced that Ben always set the alarm. People often made firm statements about their habits that proved to be exaggerations. "Why do you think this has something to do with Shelley?"

"That drawer on the bottom was standing open a few inches." From the doorway. Ben pointed at the lower right desk drawer. "I closed it without thinking after I found it open. I'm sorry, it was just a reflex. Anyway, that's the drawer I let Shelley use."

And why the hell haven't I heard about this before? Tom pulled latex gloves from his back pants pocket and drew them on. "What did she leave here? Is it all missing?"

"I gave everything she left behind to her parents."

"When?"

"A couple of weeks ago. I tried to believe she'd turn up okay, but after two or three weeks, I was giving up hope. I thought her parents would want her stuff."

It wasn't likely, Tom thought, that the super-secretive and careful Shelley Beecher had stored anything of value in a drawer at Hern's house. But he would go see the Beechers after he left here and find out what Ben had turned over to them.

"You know," Ben said, "the computer being on, the drawer being open—I wonder if he, whoever it was, if he was still in here when I got home. He probably would have turned the alarm back on if he'd had the chance. Maybe I interrupted him, and he got out through the back."

"That's a pretty good assumption," Tom said. "By the way, where's Angie? Wouldn't she normally be here this time of day?" Angie Hogancamp served as Ben's secretary and general assistant.

"She hasn't been in today. Her mother and father both have the flu."

Tom slid the bottom drawer open. Empty. "I'll get somebody over here to take prints." Maybe this guy was sloppier than Michelle's stalker and had left something of himself behind.

◇◇◇

Tom drove directly from Ben's place to the Beecher family's house. When he pulled into the driveway, Megan stood on the lawn, tossing a ball for Scout. The dog did all the playing, charging after the ball, pouncing on it, racing back to drop it at Megan's feet and look up at her with a panting, wide-eyed appeal for another round. After tossing the ball again, Megan turned toward Tom, her pretty young face solemn.

Tom didn't want her to think he had come with news, so he said quickly, "I just need to ask your mother something."

"About what?" Sarah spoke from behind the screen door. When Tom mounted the steps, she pushed the door open to let him enter. "What do you need to know now?"

Inside the house, Tom said, "Ben Hern told me Shelley left some research material at his house, and he gave it to you and Dan. I'd like to see it. I don't know that it can help us, but I want to make sure I don't miss anything."

Sarah's weary sigh made Tom wonder how close she was to breaking. The slightest request, the simplest effort, could be the final weight that would crush her fragile heart and mind. Without speaking, she began climbing the stairs. Tom followed, keeping pace with her laborious steps, pausing when she needed to stop for a few seconds.

She opened the door to the room Shelley and Megan had shared. Blue walls, fluffy throw rugs over sisal carpet. Four black and white stuffed panda toys sat on shelves among books. An ancient computer with a bulky CRT monitor occupied a wooden desk. The machine looked barely adequate for typing school papers. After Shelley disappeared, Tom had thought Shelley's Internet and e-mail activity might yield clues to a stalker or to men in her life, but the Beechers had never had Internet service.

Sarah opened the closet, reached to the shelf and pulled down a small cardboard box. Clear tape sealed its flaps. "Here it is. This is all Ben gave us. We haven't even looked at it. I forgot we even had it until you mentioned it just now."

Tom felt a stab of impatient anger. Why hadn't they turned this stuff over to the police? He quickly suppressed the reaction. Sarah and Dan could barely function these days. He shouldn't be surprised that they had put this box away and forgotten it.

"I'd like to take this to my office and go through it."

Sarah gave a half-hearted shrug. "Sure, go ahead."

Didn't she wonder what was in it? Now that she knew her daughter was dead, maybe nothing else mattered.

They didn't speak again until they were at the bottom of the stairs and Sarah held the door open for him.

"The funeral home is going to get her tomorrow," Sarah said, her voice soft. "So we can say a proper goodbye. We're having her cremated. She always said she didn't want to be buried in the ground."

Tom waited, but she said nothing more.

He touched her arm. "I'm sorry, Sarah."

She nodded, and Tom left with the box.

Chapter Twenty-eight

Megan Beecher sat in the waiting area at the animal hospital, her head bowed, her pale hair falling forward over her cheeks and hiding her face. She didn't seem to notice Rachel's approach, and she started at a touch on her shoulder.

"Hi, Megan." Rachel took the chair beside her. Two white-haired women waited with their dogs to see other vets, and Rachel kept her voice down so they wouldn't overhear. "What can I do for you?"

Megan's blue eyes, enormous in a delicate face ravaged by weight loss and grief, glistened with unshed tears. "I know you're busy. I won't take much of your time. I can't stay long anyway. I have to do the grocery shopping for Mom."

Waiting for her to work her way around to the point of her visit, Rachel watched Megan fidget with several keys attached to a keyless remote for a car. She was always a little surprised when reminded that this petite girl, whose appearance and quiet manner made her seem younger, was seventeen and could do things like driving the family car to the grocery store.

"I have a little time." Rachel glanced at the nearby women, a pair of elderly sisters who openly regarded Megan with pity while they restrained their sweet-faced little mongrel hounds from venturing over to give her a sniff. "My next patient isn't even here yet. Come back to the pharmacy with me while I get some vaccines ready."

In the small pharmacy room, a narrow space with a sink, a counter, and three walls of cabinets containing drugs and supplies, Rachel gave Megan her full attention instead of preparing the vaccines. "What is it, sweetie?"

"Shelley used to talk to me about things," Megan began, then broke off and bit her lower lip so hard Rachel was afraid she would draw blood. After a moment, she cleared her throat and continued in a tremulous voice. "She never treated me like a kid, you know? She always said I was her best friend, and she could trust me to keep secrets."

Rachel's skin prickled. When Megan paused, Rachel asked, "Did she tell you something that you think other people ought to know about now?"

Megan nodded. "She made me promise never to tell anybody, because Mom and Dad would've been worried, and they would have made her quit what she was doing."

"Do you mean her work for the innocence project?"

"Yeah. She was home the weekend before she disappeared, and she told me she was sure she knew who really killed Brian Hadley. But she couldn't prove anything yet, and she needed real solid proof or nobody would believe her." Megan drew a deep breath and released it, her body shivering. "She said she was afraid the killer knew she'd figured it out. But she thought she was real close to getting a witness to talk, and it would all be over soon."

So there it was. Tom was on the right track. "Did she tell you who the real killer was? Or the witness?"

"No. I'm pretty sure she didn't tell anybody. I tried to get her to. I mean, I was freaked out of my mind that he was going to hurt her. But she said she could take care of herself. I almost told Mom and Dad so many times. But every time I was about to, I didn't, because I knew they'd stop her, and it meant so much to her. You can't imagine how important it was to her to save an innocent man and put the real killer in jail. She just needed a little more time. Then, the next thing I knew, she was gone." Tears spilled down Megan's cheeks. "If I'd just told Mom and

Dad, they would've made sure she was safe. She'd be mad at me, but she'd still be alive."

◇◇◇

Brandon shoved aside the mountain of files on the Hadley murder to make room for Tom to set the cardboard box on the conference room table.

"Don't expect much." Tom slit the tape over the flaps with his pocket knife. He could feel the buzz of Brandon's excitement and hated to see it crushed, but he knew it probably would be in the next few minutes. "Everybody says Shelley kept the important material with her, and it all disappeared when she did. This is incidental stuff."

"Hey, you never know," Brandon said. "I say it's about time we caught a break."

Tom lifted out the contents of the box piece by piece and spread them on the table. Mostly photos, with a few newspaper and magazine clippings. "Looks like it's all about Brian Hadley's band. No notes about the case."

The two of them leaned over the table to study the pictures and clippings. Candid as well as posed photos showed the entire band, with Rita always beside Brian, a tambourine in her hand. Brian played guitar and fiddle, Skeet played both guitar and banjo, and Vance Lankford was on bass. Rita played piano when one was available at a concert site. Brian and Rita were the lead singers, together and solo, and Skeet and Vance sang backup.

"Man, they were good," Brandon said. "They had this kind of polish, you know? Like they'd been doing it forever. You could tell they were going places. You heard them play, didn't you?"

Tom nodded. "I wonder where they'd be now if Brian was still alive, if none of that mess had happened."

"Top of the charts, that's where they'd be."

They were silent a moment. Tom thought of Rita slamming groceries into customers' bags, her expression as sour as her life had become, her dreams nothing but memories. "It's crazy how much people will throw away in a fit of jealousy."

"Crazy love, it'll get you every time. Hey, I've never seen this before." Brandon picked up pages that had been clipped from a newspaper and stapled together. "It's from the Leesburg paper. A long story and some pictures."

"Published while Vance Lankford was on trial." Tom took the pages from Brandon and pointed out the date in the lower corner of the top sheet. Flipping through, he saw photos of the band members talking backstage and performing. One large picture showed a cheering concert crowd. Attached to the page was a Post-it note on which Shelley had written *Last performance, night of the murder.*

Brandon leaned closer. "Something's written on the picture too. What is that, names?"

In tiny block letters, Shelley had jotted names across the chests of many people in the audience. The overflow crowd filled the space at the rear, but shadows obscured their faces and Shelley had named only one person, a man who stood out because he was the only one not clapping or cheering. A dark baseball cap cast its own shadow over the man's face, and Shelley apparently hadn't been positive about his identity. Above his head, she'd written *Jordan Gale?*

"You see anything that rings your bells?" Brandon asked.

Shaking his head, Tom dropped the clippings onto the table. He swept his gaze over the photos, considering the fates of these people who had seemed on the brink of stardom. Brian was the one who lost his life, but the other band members had been profoundly affected by his death. Vance was in prison, Skeet was consumed by bitterness and anger, Rita had nothing left but memories and, Tom suspected, the self-contempt that came from knowing she helped set the catastrophe in motion. Two other guys had moved to Nashville in search of success, but from what Tom had heard, they'd struck out.

"We ought to talk to Jordan Gale, though," Tom said. "A lot of people from the audience were interviewed, but I don't remember seeing a statement from him in the files. You never know when something useful will turn up. He might have seen or heard something that night that could help us."

Tom's cell phone rang, and he dug it out of his shirt pocket. Rachel was calling. "Can you come over here right away?" she asked. "Megan Beecher's here, and she has something to tell you about Shelley."

◇◇◇

Tom knew he was inviting trouble. Standing just inside the front door of the animal hospital, he told Rachel in a near-whisper, "I shouldn't be talking to her without one of her parents present. Dan's going to have a fit."

"He wants to know who killed Shelley, doesn't he?" Rachel said. "If this can help, why on earth would her father object? Look, she's here, she wants to talk. Don't put obstacles in the way."

Tom blew out a sigh. "Where is she?"

"I put her in the staff lounge. Michelle's using my office." Rachel led Tom down the rear hall to the so-called lounge. It looked more like a closet to Tom, with four wooden chairs, a table, and a small fridge crammed into it.

Megan sat on one of the chairs with her knees drawn up and her arms wrapped around her legs. When Tom walked in she uncoiled, brushed her hair back behind her ears, and assumed a stiff posture with her hands clasped in her lap.

"Hey, Megan." Tom and Rachel sat down. "Dr. Goddard said you wanted to talk to me."

The girl's words poured out in a rush. She told him about Shelley's concern that Brian Hadley's real killer knew she had identified him.

"But she didn't tell you who it was?"

"She said it wasn't safe for me to know," Megan said. "She said it would all be over soon, though, because she was real close to making a breakthrough. She said there was one person who could set Vance Lankford free if she would just come forward and tell what she knew."

"But she didn't tell you who that was either?"

Megan shook her head.

Tom had heard only one detail that might open a small crack in the case for him. "You're positive she was talking about a woman? This person who could help clear Vance?"

"Yes, I'm positive."

"Megan," Tom said, trying to keep his voice level and non-judgmental, "why haven't you said anything about this before now? Why didn't you tell somebody when Shelley went missing?"

Tears welled in her blue eyes and she screwed up her face in anguish. "Mom and Dad kept saying she was okay, she was going to show up. And I prayed every day that she'd come back. I couldn't stand thinking she might have been hurt by the same person who killed Brian Hadley, and I could have prevented it. But that's true, isn't it? If I'd told somebody, she would've been mad because I broke my promise, but she'd be safe now."

Megan bent double, her arms over her head as if protecting herself from an expected blow. Tom felt like a louse for making this grief-stricken girl feel worse than she already did.

Rachel left her chair and stooped next to the girl, an arm around her shoulders.

"I didn't want Mom and Dad to know it was my fault," Megan gasped between sobs. "But I can't keep it to myself anymore. They're going to hate me, and I deserve it."

"No, no," Rachel said. "Your mom and dad aren't going to hate you."

"But I could've saved Shelley and I didn't."

"You mustn't blame yourself. It's not your fault."

Tom wasn't so sure that Daniel and Sarah Beecher would forgive Megan for withholding the information. Right now they were consumed with grief for their older daughter, and they might lash out at their younger child if they thought she could have intervened and prevented Shelley's death. He could imagine Megan carrying her guilt around the rest of her life, letting it destroy her self-respect and undermine every relationship she formed.

Megan's future wasn't his concern right now, though. He had to scrape her memory bare in search of something he could use to catch her sister's killer. "Did Shelley say anything at all that could help us identify the person she suspected?" he pressed. "Think about it. Did she give you even a hint of who it was? Did you get any impression of what kind of man she was talking about? Think hard, Megan. It's important."

She clamped a hand over her mouth and struggled to calm herself. After she dropped her hand, she stared into space for a long moment, grimacing as if combing through her memories was physically painful. At last she looked at Tom, her eyes widening. "I do remember something else. I didn't even think about it until now."

"What is it?"

"You remember I told you she said it would be dangerous for me to know who really killed Brian Hadley?"

"Yeah. What about it?" Tom's heart took off at a gallop, although his rational mind was telling him that a bombshell revelation was the last thing he could expect from Megan.

"She said if she told me, I might give myself away when I saw him. Because he's somebody I know."

Chapter Twenty-nine

"It's better all around if I leave." Michelle laid a folded blouse in her suitcase and smoothed out the slightest wrinkles with both hands. "If I were the only one being harassed, that would be different, but I can't let this spill over onto you."

"Don't worry about me. I'll be fine. It's your safety I care about." Rachel, standing by the dresser, wanted to scoop everything out of the suitcase on the bed, grab the clothes that lay ready to be packed and stuff them back into the closet and dresser drawers. Instead, she crossed her arms and kept her distance.

Michelle added a pair of slacks to the suitcase, giving them the same meticulous attention she'd shown the blouse. Why did she bother? Everything would get wrinkled, Rachel thought, regardless of how carefully she packed.

"I'm sure Tom will be happy to see me go." Michelle reached for another blouse.

"What? Has he said or done a single thing to make you feel that way?"

That provoked a humorless little smile. "He doesn't have to express his feelings overtly. You know what I mean."

"No, I don't," Rachel protested, hoping she sounded convincing. "Tom's trying to help you. He wouldn't have Dennis Murray looking into it if he didn't care about you."

"He's doing it for you. And he probably thinks that solving my problem is the only way he'll get me out of your home."

Privately, Rachel couldn't deny the truth of Michelle's perception—hadn't Tom suggested that Michelle go back home and hire protection if her husband and the police refused to help her? But she wouldn't, couldn't, tell her sister about that. And she wouldn't turn Michelle away. The stalking episode, and Michelle's confidences about her marriage, had made Rachel realize how alone her sister was, what a barren and friendless life she led. She need someone she could depend on. She needed Rachel.

Without bothering to contradict Michelle's statements about Tom, Rachel said, "You have to stay until you're safe again. Do you want me to go out of my mind worrying about you?"

Michelle began tucking underwear into the little pockets around the inside of the suitcase. "I'm leaving, Rachel. I'm sure Ben will let me stay at his house tonight, and I think he'll drive me home tomorrow if I ask him to."

Rachel crossed the room and laid a hand on Michelle's arm to make her stop her systematic packing. "You haven't heard what happened at Ben's house this afternoon. While he was with you."

Now Michelle looked at Rachel, eyes wide. Her voice came out faint and fearful. "What are you talking about? What happened?"

"Somebody broke in while he was gone. That's the safe place where you want to spend the night. He has an alarm system, but somebody got into the house."

Michelle sank onto the bed, shoulders slumped. The folded nightgown she held fell open and draped her knees and legs with pink nylon and lace. "Oh no. Do you think it was because he was with me, because we're friends?"

Pushing the suitcase aside, tempted to shove it all the way into the closet, Rachel sat next to her sister. "Will you stop seeing yourself as Typhoid Mary? It has nothing to do with you. Tom thinks it's connected to the murder investigation. Ben knew Shelley, he was helping her, letting her use his computer equipment. The person who broke in might have thought Shelley left something there. My point is that Ben's house isn't secure. I'd worry about you a lot more if you were over there instead of here."

Michelle clasped her hands in her lap so tightly that it seemed to Rachel she would crush the delicate bones. Frustration and desperation flooded her pale face. "I keep going over and over every person I've ever met, trying to figure out who would do this to me. How could I matter that much to somebody and not even know who he is or what he wants?"

"We'll find out eventually." Rachel patted Michelle's shoulder. "I wish I could help you more. I hate seeing you so anxious."

Michelle bowed her head and spoke in a near-whisper. "All the anxiety and stress…It's doing something to my mind."

"You're letting Kevin's doubts get to you. Don't start doubting yourself, Mish."

Michelle straightened and pushed her hair away from her face with both hands. "It's not that. I'm not talking about Kevin. I feel as if…" She turned to Rachel, her eyes begging for understanding. "I feel like a door has cracked opened in the back of my mind. And memories are slipping out. I think I'm remembering things from—from back then."

Rachel went cold inside. *If a secret door swung open in your memory, what would you see?* She had silently asked Michelle that question many times, when she wondered what, if anything, of their life before Judith remained in the recesses of her mind. But now she felt a surprising resistance, an urge to flee before she heard the answer. "You can't remember," she said. "You were too young."

"I was three—"

"Just barely."

"Old enough to remember a little, at least. And it is just a little, flashes now and then."

The same way it happened to me, Rachel thought, dread squeezing her heart. She had already experienced the cataclysm of losing her identity, discovering that her life was a lie, and she had spent the last several years rebuilding her sense of self. She didn't want to go through that again vicariously, through Michelle.

She forced herself to ask, "What do you remember?"

Tears spilled over, but Michelle swiped them away before they could run down her cheeks. "A sad house. A terribly unhappy house. Shouting. Anger." Michelle looked at Rachel. "Is that what it was like?"

Rachel nodded.

"They were fighting about me, weren't they?" Michelle said. "Because she had an affair and got pregnant with me."

Rachel had promised not to protect Michelle from the truth anymore, but this was one reality she couldn't bring herself to confirm. She didn't need to. She saw in her sister's eyes that her silence was confirmation enough.

"But we were happy with Mother, weren't we? She took us out of an unhappy home and gave us a wonderful life."

Rachel stiffened and drew away from her sister. When Michelle reached for her hand, Rachel snatched it away. "*You* were happy. You were the one she loved. You looked like the daughter she'd lost, she gave you her name, she made you her replacement. She doted on you. Of course you were happy."

Michelle pressed her hands to her chest as if trying to stanch bleeding from a wound. "She cared about you too. I know she did."

"I was nothing but collateral damage. I just happened to be on the playground with you, so she had to take me too. You were her dead husband's child, after the car crash you were all that was left of him. But I was a different man's daughter, and I didn't fit into her fantasy. The very sight of me must have reminded her every single day that her husband had betrayed her and you weren't hers either. A child knows when she isn't loved, Mish."

Tears flowed freely down Michelle's face now, but she cried silently, her body rigid. When she spoke, her voice had a bitter edge, a hardness Rachel had never heard before. "Were you any happier when you uncovered the truth? Was it worth it, what you put us all through? Was it worth Mother's life?"

The question, the accusation in it, cut like a knife to the heart. Rachel had heard it before from her sister, but not for a long time, and she hadn't expected to ever hear it again. "She killed herself. I didn't kill her."

"She killed herself because you made life unbearable for her, you dug it all up and threw it in her face."

Rachel sat still for a moment, then she rose, fighting to stay calm. "If you still feel that way, if you're always going to feel that way, I don't see how we can go on. I don't see how we can ever trust each other."

Panic bloomed in Michelle's upturned face. She grabbed Rachel's hand and squeezed it tightly. "No, don't say that, please, Rachel. I'm sorry. I do trust you, you're the only person I trust, and I love you so much. Please don't shut me out of your life."

Rachel didn't try to stop her own tears. "I love you too," she said. "You're my sister, and I'll always love you."

"Tell me how you did it," Michelle begged. "You put your life back together and went on. Tell me how you got that door closed again."

"I didn't," Rachel said. "Once it's open, you'll never be able to shut it again."

Chapter Thirty

The locksmith shop, a two-story, flat-topped box of a building covered with brown siding and sitting alone by the road, appeared deserted when Tom and Brandon walked in. A voice said from somewhere behind the counter, "With you in a sec."

Tom peered over the counter and found Jordan Gale crouched next to a steel cabinet, rummaging on a lower shelf.

Jordan raised his head, seemed momentarily startled when he saw who had come in, then smiled and said, "Hey, guys. Be right with you." He plucked something off the shelf and stood. "Here's what I need. Okay, sorry, what can I do for you?"

"We need to ask you about the night Brian Hadley died," Tom said.

Jordan's mouth fell open. Then he laughed. "Whoa. Where'd that come from?"

"You know Shelley Beecher was looking into the case? Trying to get Vance Lankford out of prison?"

"Yeah, sure, everybody knows about that." His expression sobering, Jordan set a small box on the counter and wrote *Atkins* on it with a felt-tip pen. "What's it got to do with me?"

"For some reason I thought you weren't living here at the time," Tom said.

"I wasn't. I was living in Manassas."

"But you were at the concert that night."

Jordan frowned and shook his head. "No, I wasn't. Where'd you get that idea?"

"Did my dad ever talk to you about what happened that night?"

"No. Why would he? Like I said, I wasn't there. I wasn't even in Mason County."

"You sure you weren't here visiting your parents?"

Jordan leaned on the counter with both hands and shook his head. "Yeah, I'm sure. Why are you asking about it?"

Tom pulled a photocopy of the newspaper picture from his jacket's inside pocket and spread it on the counter. He'd used correction fluid to cover the name Shelley had written on it. He pointed. "Is that you?"

Bending close to the paper, Jordan squinted and studied the photo. After a moment he shook his head. "Naw, that's not me."

"Have you ever seen this picture before?"

"I don't think so. I mean, it's just a picture of a crowd. I don't think I'd remember it anyway. What's this about?"

Ignoring the question, Tom asked another of his own. "When you came home to visit your folks, while you were living in Manassas, did you ever see Rita, or Brian, or Vance?"

Jordan's large, sincere eyes held Tom's gaze as he answered. "Yeah, I always got together with Rita, even if it was just to say hello. But Brian and the rest of them, that wasn't my crowd. I didn't know any of them real well."

The guy appeared and sounded as guileless as a puppy, but Tom could swear Jordan was holding back something. He couldn't guess what. He doubted that pressing him about the newspaper photo would be useful. The picture was so grainy that Tom couldn't claim with any certainty that it showed Jordan at the concert. Shelley's question mark indicated she'd had her doubts too. When Tom had called the editor to ask for the original so he could have it enhanced, he'd learned that all the photos were taken by a stringer who had long since moved out of the area.

He changed direction. "So you and Rita stayed friendly after you broke up? Even after you moved to Northern Virginia? That's kind of unusual for couples that have been married."

"Yeah, Rita and me, we've always been good friends. We never should've tried to take it any further than that. We didn't have any business getting married right out of high school. Big mistake, but it wasn't any reason for us to stop being friends."

"She must have talked to you about what was going on with Brian and Vance."

"Uh…" Jordan seemed suddenly uneasy, his gaze jumping around, avoiding Tom's eyes. "What do you mean exactly?"

"Did she talk about their disagreements? Their rivalry over her?"

Jordan considered the question for a moment, then cleared his throat. "You know, there's one thing I never told anybody about. It didn't happen the night Brian died, so I never thought the cops would be interested. I mean, they had plenty of evidence against Vance as it was, so…" His voice trailed off.

"What is it?" Tom asked.

"Well…" Jordan picked up the box on the counter, seemed to be reading the label absentmindedly, set it down again. "There was this time a few months before Brian—uh, before he died, the band played in Manassas at some kind of fundraising thing. Up where I was living with my sister, you know? Rita told me to come on over when they were rehearsing, and we could hang out. So I went, and when I got there everybody was standing around listening to Brian and Vance yelling at each other. Rita told me Brian just had his first meeting with somebody from a record company about making an album, and Vance went apeshit about not being included."

"He thought he ought to have some say in it?"

"Well, yeah. You see, Brian and Vance started the band together, they were supposed to be partners, now here Brian was acting like he made all the decisions, and Vance thought he was getting screwed out of his share,. Brian said him and Rita singing together, that was what brought in the audience, that was what the record company was interested in. Who played backup didn't matter much."

"And Vance didn't like hearing that," Tom said.

"Oh, no, not one bit. I heard him say…" Jordan paused. "Hell, none of this matters now. I don't know what the point is, repeating it."

"Tell me," Tom said. "Let me decide whether it matters."

Still looking doubtful, Jordan scraped a hand over his chin and frowned, thinking, before he went on. "I heard Vance say Brian was lucky that he—Vance, I mean—didn't have a gun on him, 'cause if he did Brian would be a dead man."

"Was that the only time you ever heard Vance threaten Brian?"

"Yeah. I mean, like I said, I wasn't around them much. Rita told me it didn't mean anything, Vance was just blowing off steam. But…"

Tom waited, and when Jordan didn't go on, he said, "But what? What were you about to say?"

"Well, it seemed to me like Brian was bound and determined to show Vance who was boss, who was the big man, you know? Rita told me that was when Brian started coming on to her, and they had a triangle kind of thing going right up to the day Brian died. To tell you the truth, I'm kinda surprised it took Vance so long to kill him." Jordan shrugged. "And that's all I can tell you about those two."

"All right." Tom folded the photocopied picture and tucked it back into his inner pocket. "Let me know if you think of anything else."

"Sure will." As Tom and Brandon turned to go, Jordan added, "Oh, hey, how're the new locks working out at Dr. Goddard's place?"

"Fine. No problems. I think it's secure now."

"Glad to hear it."

When they were back in the cruiser, Tom asked Brandon, "So? What do you think?"

"He's lying about not being at the concert. And he's lying about something else too, but I'm not real sure what."

"Yeah, same here." Tom had to smile at how much alike he and Brandon were in their assessments of people. He always liked to have Brandon along to reinforce or contradict his perceptions, but he seldom heard a contradictory opinion.

"You think he's the one Shelley suspected?" Brandon asked. "Maybe she showed him that picture and spooked him?"

"Could be." Tom started the engine and pulled onto the road. "The fact that he was there doesn't mean he killed Brian, though. Did you notice he never answered my question about what Rita told him?"

"Yeah, I noticed. And that story he gave us about Brian and Vance arguing is old news. He was trying to distract us."

"You know," Tom said, "I think it's time I went to the state pen to see Vance Lankford. I'll drive over there in the morning."

◇◇◇

That night, Tom fell asleep quickly, and his rhythmic breathing made Rachel feel lonely as she lay beside him staring at the ceiling, replaying their argument in her head. They had fought about Michelle, speaking in whispers to prevent her from overhearing.

"It's you I'm worried about," Tom had said. "You were out there alone in the woods today, and some maniac with a shotgun was right there with you. Anything could have happened."

"I realize that. But you said it wasn't necessarily the stalker. It could just as easily have been somebody who wants to derail the Beecher investigation."

"We don't know anything for sure," Tom said. "But we could eliminate one possibility if Michelle went home."

"My sister needs help. I can't ask her to go home and take her problems with her."

Tom sighed. "We'll tackle this tomorrow, okay? Right now, all of us need some rest."

Sometime after two in the morning, Rachel finally drifted off, only to be awakened by the ringing telephone. The dispatcher was summoning Tom to an emergency at the home of Vance Lankford's parents.

Chapter Thirty-one

Deputy Keith Blackwood stood at the open gate when Tom pulled up in front of the Lankford house.

He climbed out of his cruiser, Maglite in hand, and stared at the chaos laid out before him.

The moon and a dim porch light illuminated a scene that looked more like a landfill than a front yard. Tom switched on his flashlight and swept it over the mounds and layers of trash, picking out beer cans, banana skins, pizza boxes, used tea bags, and garbage he couldn't identify. He caught the stench of rotting meat from somewhere in the mess. Styrofoam packing peanuts lifted a couple of inches on a breeze and blew across the front walk like scuttling white beetles.

On the porch Jesse and Sonya Lankford, both in robes and slippers, stood two feet apart. The front steps dripped a red liquid that immediately made Tom think of the blood thrown on the porch of his and Rachel's house.

"Christ, what happened here?" Tom asked Keith Blackwood.

The deputy shrugged. "Nothing new, just worse than ever before. Whoever did this spent a lot of time getting their act together. Looks like they raided the county dump."

Gritting his teeth against an explosion of fury, Tom strode up the walk, kicking aside the peanuts—god, whoever invented those damned things deserved a special place in hell. He leaned over the steps and sniffed at the red liquid. Paint, not blood.

"You don't want to step in that while it's wet," Sonya said. "Go around to the back door if you want to come in."

She met him at the back door and double-bolted it again once he was inside. Then, without warning, she burst into tears. "I can't do this anymore," she sobbed. "I've had enough. It's just too much."

Her husband entered the kitchen from the hallway. "We're not giving in to them now. They're not going to win. You shouldn't have called the police."

"I don't care about winning!" she screamed. "I just want one day, one night, of peace and quiet. I can't stand this anymore. We're not safe in our own home."

"Did you see who did this?" Tom asked. "It must have taken a while."

The husband and wife glared at each other across their kitchen. "I wanted to call you while they were still here. You could've caught them in the act. But *he* wouldn't let me."

"Filing a complaint will just make matters worse," Jesse said. "We still have to live in this county."

"You call this *living?*"

"I don't want to hear that kind of talk anymore," Tom said. "The Sheriff's Department was called, we're here, and I expect cooperation—from both of you."

"It was the Hadley boy." Sonya spoke to Tom, but her angry eyes never left her husband's face. "I'll sign any papers you need me to sign. I've had enough of this torment."

"Well, if you think it's been bad," Jesse said, "just wait, because it's about to get hell of a lot worse." He turned and stalked out of the room.

Sonya began to cry again, a hand pressed to her mouth, her shoulders shaking. "This is *hell*," she said, her voice muffled.

"Come on and sit down." Tom took her by the arm and urged her toward a chair at the kitchen table. "Tell me what happened."

She sat in the chair, clutching the collar of her robe tightly around her neck, and rocked back and forth. Her gray hair was messy from sleep and a strand fell down her forehead and over one lens of her glasses, but she seemed not to notice. "The sounds woke us up. They weren't yelling like they usually do—"

"They? Who?"

Sonya sniffled, pulled a tissue from the pocket of her robe, and blotted her nose. "Skeet and his friends. Marty Bohannon and Billy Hodges. Usually they're drunk and yelling. But this time they didn't say anything. I woke up and thought I heard somebody moving around outside. I woke up Jesse. We both looked out, and there they were in our front yard."

"All three of them were trespassing?" Tom asked.

"Well, Skeet was in the yard. He must have climbed over the fence. The other two were throwing trash bags over, and he was cutting them open and dumping out the trash. They'd been at it for a while before I woke up, I guess, because the yard was already full of garbage. They came in a pickup, and they must have had the whole truck bed full of trash bags. Skeet emptied it all, then he picked up a can and came up to the house and poured the paint on the steps. He climbed back over the fence and they all got in the truck."

"How long after they left did you call it in?"

Sonya shook her head. "They didn't leave right away. They got back in the truck and we thought they were leaving, but—" She broke off, choking up.

"What happened? Did they do something else?"

Her voice fell to a whisper, as if she feared anyone overhearing. "They shot at us, Tom. *He* did, Skeet. He was in the passenger seat of the truck, and he rolled down the window and stuck a rifle out and started shooting at our house. Shooting at the window where we were standing. He almost hit us. Another few inches and we'd both be dead."

◇◇◇

Bathed in the light of the full moon, the Hadley house looked peaceful, closed up and darkened for the night. Tom sent Keith Blackwood around to the back door with his gun drawn. Standing to the side with his own pistol in one hand, Tom banged a fist on the front door.

It took a few minutes for Blake Hadley to appear, wearing a tee shirt and boxer shorts, his hair rumpled from sleep. "What the hell? What do you want? Do you know what time it is?"

"I'm here for Skeet. Where is he?"

Blake's eyes narrowed and his face hardened. "What do you want with him?"

"Just get him—"

"Captain!" Keith yelled from the backyard. "He's running!"

Tom leapt off the porch and darted around the house. In the moonlight he saw Keith sprinting toward the woods on Skeet's heels. Skeet stumbled, righted himself, stumbled again and went down. As he scrambled to his feet again, Keith tackled him and knocked him onto his back. Skeet writhed under Keith's weight, flailing with his fists.

Tom dropped to his knees, yanked plastic cuffs from his equipment belt, and helped Keith flip Skeet face-down so they could cuff him.

"You get off my son!" Blake yelled, marching toward them.

Maureen was right behind him, screaming, "Don't you hurt my boy!"

Tom and Keith dragged Skeet to his feet.

Blake and Maureen came to a stop in front of them and stood there, both with their fists on their hips, as if defiance would be enough to stop the arrest.

"Stay out of the way," Tom told the parents. To Skeet, he said, "You're under arrest for assault with a deadly weapon. And we'll be adding a few more charges to that."

"Go fuck yourself!"

"Let's get him in the car," Tom said to Keith. "Maybe he'll be ready to cooperate after he's spent some time in a cell."

"You're not taking him anywhere," Blake said.

"Get out of the way," Tom warned, "or you'll go to jail with him."

Tom and Keith kept moving, shoving past the Hadleys, pulling Skeet with them as he resisted every step. A strong odor of whiskey and beer came off him, and Tom knew he was unsteady, too out of control to summon his full strength. Sober, he would have been a lot harder to handle.

Maureen hustled alongside them. "He didn't do anything. You've been persecuting him from the start. He didn't kill that girl."

"I haven't charged him with killing anybody," Tom said. "He's under arrest for shooting at Jesse and Sonya Lankford tonight."

"What on earth are you talking about? Are they claiming that? It's a damned lie. "

Tom didn't bother answering her. He and Keith wrestled Skeet into the back of Tom's cruiser and slammed the door on him. Tom told Keith to stay behind and stand guard over Skeet's truck until Dennis Murray could wake up a judge and get a warrant to impound the vehicle and confiscate the rifle that hung on a gun rack behind the seats.

With Blake and Maureen yelling at him, Tom got in his car. The Hadleys tried standing in front of the cruiser to block it, but when Tom started the engine and crept forward, they jumped out of the way.

He listened to his passenger's drunken rant all the way to town, hoping he would hear something useful, but Skeet seemed most interested in running through his entire vocabulary of four-letter words and other curses. Tom winced when he heard Skeet pause to retch. The odor of vomit from the back of the car forced Tom to lower his window and let in the cool night air.

◇◇◇

Tom let Skeet stew in a cell for a while after he was booked before having him cuffed again and hauled over to the Sheriff's Department. By the time Tom entered the conference room to question him, Skeet's truck and gun were securely in police hands, along with the brass casings from the ammunition he'd used.

When he saw Tom, Skeet jumped up, knocking his chair over backward.

Tom righted the chair and pushed Skeet back into it with a heavy hand on his shoulder. Switching on a small tape recorder,

Tom walked around to sit opposite. He placed the recorder in the middle of the table.

Before Tom could speak, Skeet blurted, "My folks'll have a lawyer over here to get me out."

"I wouldn't count on seeing a lawyer until morning. This isn't exactly an emergency."

"I don't have to talk to you without a lawyer."

"No, you don't." Tom shrugged. "Want to go back to your cell? It doesn't make any difference to me."

Skeet glared, tried to hold Tom's gaze, but couldn't. He shifted his gaze.

"Come on," Tom said, "stop wasting my time. What's it going to be? If you're not in the mood to answer questions, I'll be just as glad to go back home to bed. I'd rather be getting a good night's sleep than sitting here looking at you."

"You gonna take their word over mine? People that raised a killer?"

"Since you can't seem to make up your mind, let's make this official in case you decide to say anything." Tom recited the Miranda warning and asked, "Do you understand your rights?"

"Yeah, Sherlock, I'm not stupid."

Tom let that pass without comment. "Why don't you just tell me your version of what happened?"

Skeet leaned forward and spat out his words. "Nothing, that's what happened. I never went near their house tonight."

"Then I guess the bullet casings we picked up there won't match your rifle. Which we've got here under lock and key, by the way. The weapon and the brass will all go to the ballistics lab in Roanoke for testing first thing in the morning."

Skeet looked startled by that, his face going slack for a moment, and Tom could see he was beginning to sober up. "You didn't have any right to take—" He broke off, frowning as if doubting his own statement.

"Why can't you leave those poor people alone?" Tom asked. "Their son's in prison. What more do you want from them?"

"I want them to quit trying to get his guilty ass out. He killed my brother."

"It's the innocence project that's working on Vance's appeal for a new trial. I don't think his parents have been involved in it."

"They could stop it if they tried hard enough."

"It's not up to them. They don't have any say in it. The innocence project is working for Vance, not for his parents."

Skeet shook his head. "I thought with Shelley gone, the whole thing would fall apart. But I called up there today, I talked to the woman who runs that outfit, and she said nothing's changed, they're going right on ahead with it."

Stifling an urge to grab Skeet and shake some sense into him, Tom settled for raking a hand through his own hair. "Did you really believe if you got rid of Shelley, that was all it would take?"

"Hey, now, don't go twisting my words. I didn't say—" Skeet raised his cuffed hands and in an awkward movement swiped the sweat off his upper lip. "Aw, hell, your mind's made up. You're gonna think what you want to, no matter what I say."

"I know you don't have an alibi for the evening Shelley disappeared."

"I was sick! I was sick all that week. Ask my mom. But oh, wait a minute, cops don't believe mothers, do they?"

"I know you'd been harassing Shelley for months," Tom continued. "Calling her, going to see her in Fairfax. Plenty of people saw you together, heard the two of you arguing." Tom paused. "Heard you threatening her."

"That doesn't mean I killed her."

This was progress, Tom thought. No one had told Tom about overhearing a specific threat, but Skeet's response confirmed that he had threatened Shelley in some way.

"I wasn't really going to hurt her," Skeet added. "I just wanted her to stop what she was doing."

"But she refused to stop."

"Damned stubborn girl," Skeet muttered.

"I can imagine how frustrated you got, begging her to—"

"I never begged anybody for anything in my life."

"Okay, then. You threatened her, you warned her about what might happen if she didn't stop."

"I didn't threaten her." Skeet had turned sullen, his voice flat.

"Exactly how would you describe your conversations with her? Calm and reasonable discussions? That's not what witnesses have been telling me." Tom leaned forward. "In fact, you know what I heard? Sometimes you broke down and cried and Shelley patted you on the back like you were a little kid."

Chewing on his lower lip, Skeet stared at the wall behind Tom and didn't answer.

Tom stood. "I'll get somebody to take you back to your cell. If you decide you've got something to say to me about Shelley or what you've been doing to the Lankfords, it'll have to wait for daylight. I'm going home to bed."

When Tom glanced back at him before leaving the room, Skeet's face was stripped bare of bravado and pretense, exposing an expression of naked fear.

Chapter Thirty-two

"I don't know if I buy it." Tom leaned back on the desk next to Dennis Murray's in the squad room. He'd come in at eight o'clock, after just enough sleep to leave him groggy. "It feels too obvious."

"Sometimes," Dennis said, "the obvious answer really is the answer. Skeet lost it and killed the girl. I don't know where he kept her body for a month, but I wouldn't be surprised if his father helped him get her to the bottom of that ravine."

"Well, for now we've got Skeet for what he did to the Lankfords, and I've got a feeling the judge is going to set his bail pretty high because of the gun charge, so we might have him here for a while." Tom stood. "Meanwhile, I've got some other questions that need answering, like why it's so important for Jordan Gale to make us believe he wasn't in Mason County the night Brian was killed. And who Shelley was talking about when she told her sister she was trying to get a woman to come forward and tell what she knew."

"Do you think it's Rita?"

"Possibly," Tom said. "Being straight with cops goes against Rita's moral principles, but I'll swing by and see if I can get her to talk to me before I head over to the prison. I'll be out of touch for a few hours. I ought to be back in time for Skeet's arraignment."

◇◇◇

Rita Jankowski shared a house with her widowed mother in a sparsely populated area a few miles outside Mountainview. The narrow road they lived on had been graded and paved at some point but hadn't been touched in years. Tom bumped over ruts and broken slabs of asphalt for a quarter mile before he arrived at the house. The one-story wooden structure, painted white and faded to gray, occupied most of its small lot. Although the driveway Tom pulled into had a fresh layer of chunky gravel, the weeds-and-dirt front yard looked as if it had never been tended.

Mrs. Jankowski opened the door and eyed Tom with a frown. She had a face like a dachshund's, with a long nose and a receding chin. Her frizz of orange hair looked like a wig added for comic effect and made Tom think of a circus clown. Hard to believe this mother had produced a beauty like Rita.

Before she could speak, Tom said, "Good morning. I need to talk to Rita. I see her car's here."

Mrs. Jankowski hesitated, then jerked a thumb to the right. "In back. Hanging out the wash."

She shut the door in Tom's face.

By the time he walked up the gravel driveway and around to the backyard, Mrs. Jankowski was over by the clothesline, talking to Rita.

When her mother gestured at Tom, Rita glanced his way, a twist of wet blue towel dangling from one hand. Although the night's chill lingered in the air, she wore a tee shirt and cutoff jeans, both a little too snug on her voluptuous figure. As he approached, she turned her back on him and flapped the towel before hanging it.

"Hey, Rita," Tom said.

"What is it now?" She stabbed a plastic clothespin onto the line to hold a corner of the towel. "Don't you think it's a little early in the day to be pestering people?"

Mrs. Jankowski narrowed her eyes at Tom and pressed her lips into a grim line, as if backing up her daughter's demand that he explain this intrusion.

"I need to ask you a few more questions," he said to Rita. "Can you give me your attention for five minutes?"

"Oh, for god's sake." Rita had grabbed another towel to hang on the line, but now she flung it back into the yellow plastic basket. "What *is* it? Why are you bothering me?"

Tom looked pointedly at Mrs. Jankowski. Her return gaze said clearly that she wasn't going away. Tom hoped she would at least keep quiet. Looking around the small yard, he saw a set of aluminum chairs and a table on a square of concrete outside the back door. "Can we sit down over there and talk?"

"I'm busy." Rita plucked the towel from the basket again. "I need to get this done before I go in to work."

"All right then," Tom said. "We'll talk here. Did you see Jordan Gale the night Brian was murdered?"

The wet towel slipped from her fingers and landed on the ground. "Shit," she muttered, stooping to pick it up. She shook it, obviously her idea of getting it clean again. "No, I didn't. And why do you keep raking up ancient history?"

"Jordy Gale," Mrs. Jankowski put in, "is nothing but a waste of space on this earth."

The remark jerked Tom's attention back to Mrs. Jankowski. Jordan's quiet and mild-mannered personality couldn't have provoked that harsh judgment from the woman who had once been his mother-in-law for a few months. She was probably condemning his drug use.

He started to ask, but Rita cut him off with a groan. "For god's sake, Mama, will you shut up?"

"Don't you be disrespectful to me!" Mrs. Jankowski sounded more like a peeved child than a parent.

Tom could imagine how his mother and father would have reacted if he'd ever told one of them to shut up. Regardless of his age, a lecture would have followed, leaving Tom thoroughly ashamed. Rita appeared unrepentant for saying something she probably said every day, and her mother didn't push for an apology.

"I keep raking all this up again," Tom said, "because some-body's not telling me the truth. You say Jordan wasn't at the concert that night. He says he wasn't. But I've got a newspaper picture that shows him in the audience."

"That picture Shelley was waving in my face?" Rita sneered. "I told her, it's not him. I don't know how anybody can look at that and say for sure who's standing way in the back in the dark."

"We can get the original and enhance it." That wasn't going to happen, but Tom might as well try to get some mileage out of the threat. "If it's him, we'll be able to tell."

"But why? Why do you care so much about whether Jordy was there or not?"

"I'm more interested in why he's lying about it. When people lie to me about things that don't seem to matter, I start thinking maybe they do matter after all."

Rita didn't answer, but hauled a wet bed sheet out of the basket and draped it over the line. Tom grabbed a corner that threatened to graze the ground. Together he and Rita tugged the sheet straight on the line while her mother stood idle, looking on.

"If Jordy's been withholding evidence all this time," Tom said as they arranged the sheet, "the sooner I find out about it, the less trouble he'll be in. The same goes for you. Think of yourself, Rita."

Mrs. Jankowski gave a short, harsh laugh, but Tom wasn't sure what had provoked it.

"Be quiet," Rita snapped at her mother. Her fingers curled into a tight ball around one edge of the hanging sheet, squeezing free a drop of water that fell and disappeared into the grass. She looked at Tom, her face screwed up as if she wanted to cry. "I'm not going to let you drag me back into that mess. You know how people have been treating me ever since it happened."

"You reap what you sow," Mrs. Jankowski said, nodding as if she'd uttered a nugget of profound wisdom.

Fury sparked in Rita's eyes, and her expression hardened into defiance. "No, I didn't see Jordy at the concert that night," she told Tom, "and I don't know why it would matter if he was there. Everybody heard Brian and Vance arguing. Everybody knows Vance killed him. Seems to me your dad already solved that murder. Why don't you stick with solving the one that happened on your watch?"

"That's what I'm trying to do. I'm on my way to see Vance. Want me to give him a message from you?"

For a second Rita's lively face went slack, her reaction unreadable. She turned back to her chore. "No, I don't have any message. Now I'm done talking. Leave me alone."

Tom had no choice but to give up for the moment. Returning to his car, he had the strong feeling he'd heard nothing but lies, and the uneasy sensation that the ground he was treading on might break open any second and reveal a chasm he hadn't suspected was there.

Chapter Thirty-three

The tabby kitten cringed in terror as Rachel peered into his ears through an otoscope, but he didn't try to escape. A family named Williamson had found the starved, flea-ridden little creature stuffed into their roadside mailbox. They'd dubbed him Lucky, which Rachel thought was fitting. He couldn't have landed with more caring people.

She tried to ignore the noise of a commotion elsewhere in the clinic—somebody's dog causing trouble, a cat eluding capture after escaping from its owner? Then she heard a scream. She dropped the otoscope on the steel table, flung open the door, and sprinted toward the sound.

Holly, Shannon, and two vets had gathered around Michelle in the hallway outside Rachel's office. Michelle covered her mouth with one shaking hand and groped at her trouser-clad right leg with the other. But Holly was the one who had screamed. Pointing into the office, she cried, "A diamondback! I saw it too. That's what scared her."

"A what? A snake? Close the door." Nobody moved. "Will somebody close the damned door before it gets out?"

One of the vets, Diane Davis, leaned into the office, grabbed the doorknob, swung the door shut.

Rachel gripped Michelle's shoulders, momentarily disoriented by the sensation that they had become children again and Rachel was trying to reassure her silly sister that the creature she feared most couldn't hurt her. "It's okay. It's trapped in there. We'll get rid of it."

Michelle's eyes appeared unfocused, and she seemed not to hear. Rachel almost shook her, but that seemed superfluous when her sister's body was already trembling from head to toe. "Michelle? Look at me. Michelle!"

At last Michelle's blue eyes fixed on Rachel's face. She reached toward her leg again. "I moved my feet—I felt something, my foot hit something—I heard a strange noise and I looked down and it—I think it bit me."

Horrified realization flooded in. "Oh my god. Where did it bite you? Show me."

Hoping fervently that her sister, in her phobia-fueled panic, had imagined the bite, Rachel stooped to look where Michelle pointed. She pulled up the leg of Michelle's linen slacks, rolled down the thin trouser sock. Blood seeped from two puncture wounds just above her ankle. The skin around them had already begun to redden and swell.

"Oh, no," Rachel said. "Shannon, call an ambulance. Tell them it's a diamondback rattlesnake bite and she'll need anti-venom serum the second she gets to the hospital." As Shannon rushed toward the front desk to make the call, Rachel added, "Then call the hospital and make sure they're ready with it. We have some here, but it's for dogs and I don't know what the dose would be for a person."

Michelle had begun to sag, and Rachel had to put both arms around her to hold her up. "Somebody get her a chair and bring me a pan of warm water and some soap and a fresh pair of gloves. Hold on, Mish. Don't you dare go into shock."

In two minutes Michelle was sitting in a wooden chair fetched from an exam room. Her face had gone dead white and perspiration stood on her forehead and upper lip. "It hurts," she whispered, looking up at Rachel with frightened eyes. "This could kill me, couldn't it?"

"You're going to be fine. Just stay calm." When Holly brought what she had requested, Rachel pulled on latex gloves and stooped in front of Michelle. "I'm going to clean the wound. We have to keep your leg below your heart and you need to keep absolutely still. The more you move around, the quicker the toxin will spread."

"Okay. Okay." Michelle breathed in quick gasps, and her whole body went rigid.

"Relax, breathe normally. You'll be okay. The snake had to bite through your pants leg and your sock, so it might not have injected a full load of venom." The angry wound, though, made Rachel think Michelle had taken in enough poison to do serious damage.

With as little jostling as possible, Rachel rolled up Michelle's trouser leg, slipped off her shoe, and removed her sock. By the time she had washed the wound, the ambulance medics were in the building. They elevated the head of the gurney and shifted Michelle onto it while Rachel held her foot to minimize movement of her leg.

"You're coming with me, aren't you?" Michelle reached for Rachel's hand.

Rachel squeezed Michelle's hand and brushed strands of hair off her perspiring brow. "I'll be along in a few minutes. I need to catch the snake first, okay? You're going to be all right, Mish." *You have to be all right. I love you so much.* On impulse, she leaned down and kissed her sister's forehead.

Tears welled in Michelle's eyes. "He did this. He wants to kill me."

"Don't think about that. Don't upset yourself. I'll be with you soon."

After the ambulance left with Michelle, Rachel heard a buzz of voices from all directions. Everybody in the place, employees and clients, chattered with excitement, and several small dogs added their high, sharp barks. She asked Dr. Davis to finish examining the cat named Lucky and give her the necessary vaccines. "I have to get something to catch the snake with," she told Holly, "and something to put it in. Stay right here, and don't let anybody open that door."

"Oh, I'm real sure nobody's gonna try to," Holly said. She gave an exaggerated shudder. "I can't abide snakes. It scares me just knowin' it's in there."

Hurrying down the hall to the basement door, Rachel seethed with anger and frustration and worry about Michelle. How the hell did somebody get into the building to leave a snake in her office? She ought to call the locksmith over here and dump the rattler at his feet and tell him to deal with it. Had she wasted the money she'd paid for those supposedly tamper-proof locks?

She flipped on the basement light and headed down the stairs to the equipment storage area. Somewhere down here she had a snake hook and a pincer tool, but she couldn't recall the last time she'd used them or where they were stored. She moved to the outer wall where loops of various sizes, attached to poles, hung on a row of hooks. There they were, the two snake-catching tools, hanging together.

As she reached for them, the basement window caught her eye. Something didn't seem right about the window, high on the wall at ground level at the rear of the building. Rachel walked over to examine it. She could have sworn it had a screen on it. Where was the screen now? She looked around, didn't see it. Who had pulled a metal cabinet from its normal place against the adjacent wall and pushed it underneath the window?

Frowning, Rachel examined the window more closely. The simple twist lock was in the open position. It had a keyed lock too, and that should be providing the real security, but when Rachel tugged on a section of the window, it slid open sideways.

"Damn it!" She felt like slamming a fist into the concrete block wall. She felt like kicking herself. How could she be so stupid? All the time she'd been worrying about the locks on the front and back doors, this little window in the basement was available to anybody who wanted to get into the building at night. She turned the twist lock into the closed position. The small key to the other lock was probably on the key ring she kept in her desk drawer, the one that also held an assortment of cabinet and drawer keys.

She would worry about the lock later. Right now she had to remove the snake from her office and get over to the ER to be with Michelle. She grabbed the tools she needed and looked around for a secure container to put the snake in. Rummaging through the supplies on the shelves, she found a plastic box with a snap-on lid that should be large enough. She dumped the container's contents, dozens of bags of syringes purchased in bulk, onto the shelf. Next she located elbow-length gloves of thick leather and pulled them on.

Upstairs at her office door, she realized she had an audience of staff and clients crowded together at a safe distance to watch. "I want all of you to move back," she told them. "If I can still see you, you'll be too close."

They seemed reluctant, but they dispersed.

Clutching both the snake hook and pincer tool in one hand, Rachel pushed the door ajar, moving cautiously in case the snake waited just inside. Although she wouldn't say she was afraid of poisonous snakes, she had a healthy respect for their cunning and the damage they could do. Knowledge and common sense should protect her, yet she felt her heartbeat speed up and her breath quicken.

She poked her head into the office, her gaze sweeping the floor. She saw nothing. If she couldn't locate it, she would be vulnerable to attack from any angle. She grabbed the plastic container, stepped into the office, and kicked the door shut behind her.

"Come out, come out," she whispered, "wherever you are."

A faint sound of movement, something sliding on the floor. Under the desk?

Drawing a deep breath, she told herself to stay calm. She pushed the plastic container ahead of her and removed the lid.

"Okay now," she murmured. "Come on out and let's get this done." Leaning down, she peered under the desk. What she saw made her jerk back. A rattler at least four feet long lay coiled on the floor in the open center space under her desk. The snake raised its head in her direction, and its muscular body, covered with gray and black blotches and ending in a black tail, began to contract, pulling itself taut as if preparing to strike. As Rachel stared into its cold, unblinking eyes, the snake's tail lifted and began to vibrate, producing a soft rattle. This was a male, she noted, with a long, thick tail that tapered gradually to the black tip.

Rachel ran her tongue over her dry lips. The instant she went for him, he would go on the offensive. He was big enough to get at her beyond the protective gloves.

She didn't want to get down on hands and knees because she couldn't move out of that posture quickly. Bending from the waist, she stuck the snake loop tool under the desk, slow and easy. The rattling grew louder. She felt the end of the pole make contact with the snake's body.

The snake's head shot out, mouth agape, fangs going for Rachel's hand. She gasped and jumped back out of the way, and the snake hit the pole hard enough to knock it out of her grip. Then the snake took off, slithering out from under the desk, its body writhing rhythmically, propelling it across the tiled floor. It aimed for the space between the wall and the back of a filing cabinet.

Standing, trying to catch her breath and slow her heartbeat, Rachel watched the snake wedge its head into the space. "Good luck with that, pal." She swiped perspiration off her upper lip with the back of her hand. "You don't seem to know how big you are."

The snake worked the first foot of its body between the cabinet and the wall before it got stuck.

Rachel watched for a couple more minutes to make sure it wouldn't decide to back out. But it curled its lower body into a loose spiral and lay still, apparently feeling safe as long as its head was hidden. Rachel approached cautiously. Starting at the tail, she worked the loop up over the snake's body as far as she could and tightened it. She held the pincer ready in her other hand as she slowly pulled the rattler out of the narrow space.

When its head came free, the snake twisted to strike, but Rachel clamped the pincer on and immobilized its head. Holding the snake's thrashing body with the hook and pincer, she lowered it into the plastic container. By the time she got the front half into the container, the rear half was out again. She worked with the hook until all of the snake was inside. Hanging on with the pincer until the last second, she pulled off the loop and lowered the lid onto the container. Holding the lid down with one foot, she shuffled it closer to the desk. Her copy of Merck's veterinary diagnostic manual looked hefty enough to match the snake's strength. She grabbed it off the desk and dropped it onto the lid.

Leaning against her desk with her face in her hands, she felt every drop of adrenaline abruptly drain from her body.

The snake changed everything.

She knew who had put it here, she knew it wasn't an anonymous stalker, and she knew Michelle wasn't the target.

Chapter Thirty-four

Total silence in the cruiser for ninety minutes felt like a blessing to Tom, and the spring landscape of mountainsides dotted with blooming dogwoods and rhododendrons was a bonus. Out of radio and cell tower range, he didn't have to answer questions, respond to demands, issue any orders. He let himself relax for the first time since he'd seen Shelley Beecher's plastic-wrapped body lying in a ravine on Saturday.

The respite didn't last. Without distractions, he had to face his own bedeviling questions about the case. If he blamed Shelley's murder on her attempt to prove Vance Lankford innocent, he had to ask who would be willing to kill her in order to stop her. If Vance didn't kill Brian, Hadley's murderer was still walking around free, and desperate to avoid suspicion. That was as strong a motive for killing Shelley as Tom could ask for—but to believe it, he also had to believe his father had arrested the wrong man in the Hadley case six years before and helped to put him behind bars for life. John Bridger hadn't been perfect, he'd made mistakes, but he was a fair-minded investigator, and Tom couldn't accept a mistake of these proportions without rock-solid proof.

Swinging around a curve on the narrow road, Tom encountered a coal truck coming from the opposite direction and realized with a jolt that he'd strayed over the center line. He pulled the cruiser back on course and sped past the truck.

His thoughts shifted back to the case. If Vance had killed Brian Hadley, what could he hope to gain from the innocence project's investigation? If it was a charade, they wouldn't find evidence to clear him because that evidence didn't exist. And it could backfire on him—they might turn up additional evidence to reaffirm Vance's guilt.

Where did all this leave Tom? Because the killer had brought Shelley's body back to Mason County, he had trouble believing she'd been the victim of a random abduction and murder. But if she was killed by somebody who knew her, who had a strong enough motive to do it? The Hadleys were infuriated by Shelley's work for Vance, but would they kill the girl to stop her? Did anyone besides the Hadleys care that much about what she was doing? Who was the woman Shelley was trying to persuade to come forward, and what kind of evidence could she offer? If it wasn't Rita, what other woman was close enough to the events to know anything of value? Grace? Was she protecting the Hadleys, out of self-interest?

Tom chewed over these questions for more than an hour as he drove, until the prison came into view.

Vance had begun his life sentence in a maximum security institution on the other side of Virginia, but three years of model behavior won him a transfer to Harper Ridge, a medium security prison closer to home. Miles before he reached it, Tom could see the place from the road, a collection of buildings inside an octagonal wall, sitting on a leveled mountaintop surrounded by deep ravines. More than a thousand men lived inside that wall.

Tom braked at the turnoff and locked his service pistol in the glove compartment before he started up the steep, curving road to the prison. At the gate into the parking lot, he spent a few minutes proving his identity and waiting for the guard to get the warden's okay for him to enter. He parked where he was told to and approached the gate into the prison compound on foot. From there, he moved through the layers of security and into the main building without incident.

The warden, a tall, chunky man with white hair and a rumpled brown suit, appeared at the final checkpoint to shake Tom's hand, exchange a few words with him, and turn him over to a young guard.

The guard had big hands and a muscular body that probably earned him the respect of the inmates. He didn't bother with chitchat as he led Tom down a hall. From behind them, Tom heard the automated steel mesh door slide shut with a grinding noise and lock with a clang. He didn't see anyone else, but a hum of indistinct voices seemed to seep through the walls and ceiling and gave him the sensation that the building itself was alive around him. Prisons always made him think of the Borg, those cybernetically-enhanced beings in *Star Trek* who functioned as mindless drones in a vast collective that forcibly sucked in new victims. *You will be assimilated. Resistance is futile.* Tom had known more than a few people who were destroyed or changed for the worse by prison. For that reason alone, he hoped to god Vance Lankford was guilty and deserved to be there.

The guard showed Tom into a small room that contained only a metal table, bolted to the floor, and two chairs. When the guard gestured at a chair, Tom sat down. He'd had enough of sitting in the car, though, and as soon as the guard left him alone, he rose, stretched, and walked to the window.

Thirty feet from the building, a couple dozen men wearing orange prison clothes were locked in a small yard surrounded by a six-foot chain link fence. They had divided predictably along racial lines, with whites, blacks, and Hispanics forming separate groups. One young white man, though, marched alone around the perimeter of the yard, his face set in a determined expression, as if he had to meet an exercise goal before his time outdoors ended.

Vance Lankford wasn't among the men in the yard.

Tom had been waiting almost twenty minutes, long enough to watch the men shuffle back inside and another group take their place outdoors, when he heard the distant rumble of motorized doors. Footsteps sounded on the tiled hallway floor, drawing closer. A different guard, this one a balding middle-aged man, opened the door to the room where Tom waited, poked his head in and glanced around. Apparently satisfied that everything was as it should be, he ushered Vance Lankford inside.

"Go on and sit down," the guard told Vance, "and don't get up unless the deputy says you can." To Tom he said, "I'll be right outside, deputy. Yell if you need me."

Vance, without cuffs or shackles, kept his eyes downcast as he approached the table. His gaunt frame acted as little more than a clothes hanger for his prison uniform, and he hitched up the loose waist of his pants before he took a seat. Tom didn't know him well, but he'd seen him around often enough in the past to be shocked by the change in his appearance. His cheekbones and jaw looked like carved stone beneath taut, colorless skin. A buzz cut that had left his dark hair less than an inch long accentuated the stark angles of his face. Vance was barely thirty. He looked fifty.

Tom almost asked him how he was doing, but thought better of it. He could see the answer in Vance's dull eyes and the way he slumped in his chair. This was a man who had given up on himself. Maybe he realized Shelley's death meant the end of his hope for freedom.

"I'm Tom Bridger. We've met a few times. I don't know if you remember me."

Vance's gaze flicked over Tom and the right edge of his mouth lifted a fraction of an inch. "I'm not likely to forget anybody connected to John Bridger. And you look just like him."

"You know Shelley Beecher's dead, don't you?"

Vance turned his head to look out the window at the men in the yard. "Yeah," he said, his voice as flat and empty as his expression. "The woman from the innocence project got in touch. But I heard it from the guards first. They got a real kick out of telling me."

"She was murdered," Tom said.

"Well, I've got a good alibi, so you can't pin that one on me."

Tom watched Vance for a moment, trying to detect some emotion on his face. Distress, anger, disappointment, fear—all of that would be understandable. Did he feel any grief for Shelley herself, any sympathy for her family? Did he recognize the indirect role he might have played in her death? Whatever Vance felt, he hid it behind an impassive mask.

"You didn't kill Shelley," Tom said, "but her work for you might have been responsible for her murder."

Vance leaned forward, meeting Tom's eyes and showing a spark of life for the first time. "What the hell is that supposed to mean? She was the only person who ever took the time to listen to my side of the story. Why would I want her to get hurt?"

"Were you pushing her to investigate some other person in particular? Dig around for dirt that might make somebody else look guilty? Was she threatening somebody who still lives in Mason County?"

Vance slumped back in his chair, and his face went blank again. "Look, whatever you're here for, I can't help you. I don't know who she was investigating."

"Are you saying she didn't she tell you anything? That's hard to believe. She was doing it for you, after all. You were her client."

"Believe what you want to. But she didn't want to talk about it until she could prove it."

"And you didn't give her any ideas about who else could have killed Brian? How did you persuade her to get involved in the first place?"

Vance folded his arms tightly over his waist and raised his chin. "All I know is that I didn't kill him. And after Shelley heard me out, she believed me. She thought I was telling the truth, and she was willing to look into it."

"The people at the innocence project don't have any of the information she collected. It all disappeared when Shelley did. They don't have anything to start over with."

"I know that," Vance mumbled. For a second his mask slipped and Tom glimpsed the despair behind it.

Tom had heard protestations of innocence from a lot of guilty people, many so earnest that they might have been persuasive if hard evidence against them hadn't existed. Some seemed to have convinced themselves that they'd done nothing wrong, and Tom was beginning to wonder if Vance was one of those. But he wasn't here to debate Vance's guilt or innocence. "There's something else I wanted to ask you about."

Vance regarded him with suspicion. "What?"

Tom reached into his uniform jacket to pull the photocopied newspaper picture from an inner pocket. He spread it open on the table. "Did Shelley ever show you this?"

Vance shot a cursory glance at the photo. "Yeah, a couple of times. What about it?"

"Why did she show it to you? What did she want to know about it?"

"She wanted me to identify some of the people. I don't recognize most of them. The light's bad, the picture's not all that clear, and some of them were probably from outside the county anyway. But that's Jordy Gale." Vance shifted in his seat and tapped the picture.

"So Jordy was there that night?" If Vance had seen him, so had a lot of other people, Tom thought. "You told Shelley that?"

"Sure I did."

"He claims he wasn't at the concert," Tom said. "Why would he lie about it?"

"Hell, I don't know. Maybe he just didn't want to get dragged into a police investigation."

"Rita says he wasn't there."

Vance laughed and shook his head. "She knows he was there. I saw her talking to him."

"Why would she lie about something like that?"

"Don't ask me to explain Rita. I'd have to be a psychiatrist to even try. But I've been over every second of that night a million times in my head. I can tell you what happened minute by minute. I saw Jordy before the concert, I talked to him, I told him to get the hell out of my face. And I think he was gone by the time we wound it up. I didn't see him afterward, anyway. But why does this matter to—"

"Are you saying you had an argument with Jordy that night too?" Tom broke in. "Was that before or after your fight with Brian?"

"I wasn't *fighting* with either one of them. An argument's not a—Aw, hell, I don't have to put up with this crap." Vance pushed himself to his feet.

Tom rose too. "Sit down, Vance. We're not finished."

"Oh, yeah, we are. Just leave me alone and let me serve out my time in peace. That's what you want, isn't it? Me stuck in here for the rest of my life. You sure as hell don't want anybody proving your daddy got the wrong man." He turned away.

"I said *sit down.*"

The door swung open and the balding guard appeared. "What's going on in here? Didn't I tell you to stay put, Lankford? Do I have to cuff you to the table?"

"Take me back to my cell."

The guard looked past Vance to Tom. "Deputy? You done with him?"

Before Tom could answer, Vance said, "Yeah, he's done with me, whether he thinks so or not."

Tom sighed and waved a hand. "All right. Take him."

On his way out, Vance paused at the door and looked back at Tom. "I'll tell you what I told Shelley. If you really care about finding the truth, go ask Rita your questions. Keep after her, break her down. I think she knows stuff about that night that she's never told anybody."

◇◇◇

Tom followed another correctional officer, retracing his steps through the prison to the outside. Ninety minutes to get here, ninety minutes to get back home. What a goddamn waste of time. He'd confirmed that Jordy Gale was on the scene the night Brian was murdered, but so what? Maybe Vance was right and Jordy had lied for the simple and obvious reason that he didn't want to get caught up in a police investigation. Maybe Rita had backed him up out of friendship. It could meant nothing.

In his cruiser in the parking lot, Tom grabbed his cell phone from the glove compartment and held it out the window to see if he could get a signal. Might as well check in and find out whether he'd missed anything important while he was on his wild goose chase.

He picked up a weak signal and found a couple of voice mail messages waiting. One was from Rachel, who sounded like she was clinging to self-control by her fingernails. What the hell? A rattlesnake at the animal hospital? Michelle in the ER?

Tom yanked on his seat belt, swung it around his body and fastened it with a click. He revved the engine, but before he shifted into drive he clicked on the other voice mail message. He had to play it twice before he was sure he'd heard right.

Dennis Murray wanted him to know right away about the crime lab report on the blood that was thrown onto Tom and Rachel's porch. "It's deer blood," Dennis said. His voice faded in a burst of static, and when it became audible again it sounded faint and distant. "...heard Blake and Skeet Hadley shot a buck last weekend...out of season, so they're not going to admit it... stalker probably didn't do it...I'm betting on Skeet...boy's out of control."

Chapter Thirty-five

Rachel found Michelle, propped up and looking groggy, near the end of the row of beds in the emergency room. The only other patients were a teenage boy with a broken leg and worried parents, and an infant who screamed in his frazzled mother's arms while a doctor struggled to examine his throat. Curtains drawn on both sides of Michelle's bed gave her privacy.

"Hey," Rachel said, laying a palm against her sister's ashen cheek. Michelle's skin felt cool to the touch even though it was moist with perspiration. An IV dripped fluid into her, delivering the antivenom to a vein on the back of her left hand as rapidly as possible. Not much more left in the bag. "How are you feeling?"

"Kind of loopy from the pain meds. I can't stay awake." Michelle sighed and her head lolled to the right. She wore a light green hospital gown, and a sheet covered her to the waist.

"Are you in much pain?"

Michelle ran her tongue over dry lips and murmured her reply, so that Rachel had to lean within inches to catch her words over the racket the baby made. "…gave me Percocet. You could flatten me with a bus right now and I wouldn't feel it."

Rachel forced a smile and tried to answer, but a lump of guilt sat in her throat like something hard and sharp-edged that refused to go down. She brushed a strand of damp hair off Michelle's cheek. *It should have been me. This was meant for me.*

Whispery words drifted from Michelle's mouth. "Doctor wants me to stay overnight…That necessary?"

"Yes, it is. You have to be watched for a while." The baby's cries ceased abruptly. In the startling silence, Rachel lowered her voice. "Do you mind if I look at your leg?"

Michelle gave a little gust of a laugh and waved a hand. "Oh, go ahead. Everybody else has. I drew a crowd when they brought me in. Doctors, nurses, residents…I was a teaching moment, I guess."

Michelle must have had a heck of a dose of the painkiller if she could laugh about being displayed as a teaching aid for strangers.

Rachel pulled down the sheet. Several inches of skin around the two fang punctures were as tautly swollen and shiny as a red balloon. The antivenom would prevent further damage, but it couldn't reverse the destruction of tissue that had already taken place. Necrosis would follow the inflammation, and Michelle would always have an ugly scar on her leg. Rachel drew the sheet up again, folding it at Michelle's waist.

A dark-haired nurse dressed in blue scrubs bustled into the curtained-off space, asking, "How are we doing here?" She brushed past Rachel to reach the IV bag. Her boyish figure and ponytail made her look about twelve, but she was all business. In seconds, she assessed the level of fluid, checked Michelle's pulse, stripped away the sheet to check the wound, yanked it back up. "We'll be moving you to a room soon, Michelle. Let us know if you need anything in the meantime." With a nod at Rachel, she marched out.

Rachel rearranged the sheet, making it as neat as it had been before the nurse breezed in.

"I hate it when they call me by my first name," Michelle whispered. "There ought to be a rule against it."

Ah, the real Michelle surfaces. "Kevin will be here in a few hours. I called him before I came over here."

"Oh, no." Michelle pushed away from the slanted bed, tried to sit up straight. "Why did you—I don't want—"

"Stay still, please, Mish." Rachel caught her by the shoulders and used gentle force to press her back against the pillows. "He's very worried about you. He'd never forgive me if I hadn't called him, and there's no way he's going to stay in Bethesda while you're in the hospital. He wants to be here with you."

"No, he doesn't."

A piercing scream from the baby a few feet away cut through the quiet.

Michelle winced at the noise, then all her defenses crumbled, her face puckered, and she seemed to become a child too, alone and frightened.

But she wasn't alone. *You have me. You'll always have your sister.* Trying to ignore the screeching infant, Rachel took Michelle's hand and said, "Just rest now. That's all you need to do."

Michelle seemed not to hear her. "Mother thought Kevin was all wrong for me. You knew that, didn't you?"

Rachel winced. "You're stressing yourself when you should be trying to relax."

"She was right." Michelle's fingers tightened on Rachel's hand. "But she was blaming him, when it was *me*. I'm the one who's all wrong. I shouldn't have married him. He deserves a real wife, not somebody like me. I'm broken, Rachel. She ruined me."

Would the woman they'd called Mother never let go of them? Would she always be reaching out from the grave to twist their minds and make them doubt their own worth? "You've had a shock and you've got a narcotic in your system. This isn't the time to try self-analysis. You don't know what you're saying."

Michelle seemed trapped in memories and regret and wasn't listening to Rachel. "If she hadn't died, I never would have married him. I couldn't bear disappointing her. I was the one who always pleased her. I was the little princess, prim and proper, and you were the tomboy getting dirty in the woods and coming home with leaves stuck to your clothes and your hair a mess. You never could please her, no matter how hard you tried. And I liked being her favorite. I'm so sorry, Rachel. I wasn't a good sister."

"None of it was your fault, or mine. When you're stronger, we'll talk it all out." Rachel knew how it felt to be drowning in a flood of memory and regret and guilt, and she wanted desperately to save her sister from that ordeal, but the past couldn't be held at bay forever. At last it was bleeding through into the present, and its stain would never be erased.

The buzz of her cell phone made her jump. By the time she'd pulled it from her shirt pocket the brisk young nurse had appeared, scowling. "Not in the hospital," she snapped. "Take it outside."

Rachel was about to silence the ringtone and let the call go to voice mail when she saw the caller ID display. *Private caller.* The name and number had been blocked. She didn't have to wonder who it was. She knew.

"I'll be right back," she told Michelle.

She rushed for the door to the outside, hoping voice mail wouldn't take the call before she could. Shoving open the glass door, she punched the button to answer just in time.

"Hello, Perry," she said.

No response. Unable to stand still, Rachel paced back and forth outside the ER door. "Nothing to say? You seemed to have a lot to say to my sister. But it's really me you're after, isn't it? When are you going to stop hiding like a coward and come out in the open?"

The sound from the other end began as a soft chuckle and built to a laugh, louder and louder until Rachel had to hold the phone away from her ear. Then the connection went dead.

◇◇◇

Tom peeled strips of fingerprint tape off the basement window and the area around it and pressed each one onto a white card. Rachel stood watching with folded arms and a grim expression.

"Don't get your hopes up," he said. "This guy hasn't left a fingerprint behind yet. Or a footprint or a hair or anything else that might identify him."

"Oh, yes, he has," Rachel said. "That rattlesnake told me exactly who he is."

Tom frowned at her. "What do you mean? What does the snake tell you except that he's not afraid to handle deadly reptiles?"

"Finish your work here, then come up to my office."

If she had some kind of theory about Michelle's stalker, Tom was willing to listen. He and Dennis had gotten nowhere by checking e-mails and phone calls and putting the rest of the deputies on alert for strangers in the area. The stalker had turned dangerous. Michelle could have died from the snakebite. If Rachel had sat down at her desk before Michelle did, she could be the one in the hospital.

Tom finished collecting the prints, put his kit back together, and joined Rachel upstairs.

"Okay, what's your theory?" he asked, closing the door to her office behind him. Rachel stood at the window, her auburn hair gleaming in the slant of sunshine.

"It's not a theory. I'm positive. Just hear me out, okay?" She sat behind her desk and gestured for Tom to take the visitor's chair. "You know about some of the threatening letters Perry Nelson sent me—"

"What does he have to do with this?"

"Just listen, please. I showed you some of the letters he's sent me. But not all of them."

"What? Why not?"

"I told myself I shouldn't obsess about him, I shouldn't let him interfere with our lives."

"I thought the letters stopped after the last time you made a complaint. Or did you just stop telling me about them?" Rachel was good at keeping secrets, and she could withdraw into an impenetrable shell when she wanted to.

"Actually, they did stop. Late last year."

"So…?"

"The last one he sent came here, to the clinic. I still have it." Rachel pulled open a bottom drawer in the desk and riffled through the files. She pulled out a folder and handed it across to him. "He hasn't sent me anything since."

Inside the folder Tom found a single envelope, addressed to Rachel at the animal hospital. It had no return address but bore a generic Northern Virginia postmark. The envelope had probably been through so many hands that any fingerprints on the paper would be meaningless, but still Tom handled it with care, touching only the edges. He did the same when he pulled out the sheet of paper and spread it on Rachel's desk. The paper bore a realistic drawing of a rattlesnake, with tail raised, mouth open, fangs dripping venom.

Underneath the drawing, a message had been printed in thick block letters: *YOU'LL NEVER KNOW WHEN THE SNAKE IS GOING TO STRIKE.*

The ugliness, the raw menace of the drawing and the words hit Tom with a visceral punch. "Why did you keep this to yourself?"

"I just told you why. Can we argue about that later, please?" Rachel waved both hands, palms-out, as if erasing the subject from the conversation. "I know a lot of time has passed since he sent me that drawing, but the snake under my desk this morning—I can't prove it, I can't even prove he sent the drawing, for that matter, but I know he's responsible."

Tom chose his words carefully. "I believe Nelson sent you this drawing, but—"

Rachel released a tremulous breath. "I knew there would be a *but.* Tom, he called me today while I was with Michelle at the ER. He called *me* this time, not her."

"You mean the stalker called you?"

"Perry Nelson *is* the stalker. I'm convinced of it."

Tom could see that she was, and he hated questioning her reasoning, but he had no choice. "I don't see how he could be the stalker, if he's in a hospital."

"We don't know for sure that he's hospitalized right now," Rachel said. "Nobody keeps me informed about him anymore. The prosecutor who handled my case always looked out for me, she told me what was happening, but she's moved on. After I got that drawing, I called the prosecutor's office and found out they're not even keeping track of him now. All they could tell me was that he'd been moved from a state hospital in central Virginia to the Northern Virginia State Hospital in Fairfax County, so he could be closer to his family."

"I'll check on him myself, I'll make sure he's still in the hospital."

"You're going to find out he's not. They've either let him go or he's walked away, and nobody went to the trouble of telling me."

"One thing at a time. I'll let you know what I find out."

Tom rose and went to her, pulled her against him. Her body was rigid with tension and although they wrapped their arms around each other he didn't feel he was holding her. What if he learned that Nelson was safely inside the walls of the hospital, had been nowhere near Mason County? Would she accept that? Hoping he could make it true, he said, "We'll get to the bottom of this, I promise. Whoever the stalker is, I'm not going to stand by and let him hurt you."

◇◇◇

As Tom feared, his promise to Rachel was easier made than kept. When he returned to his office and called the hospital director, the man refused to cooperative.

"I can't share information about a patient with you," the doctor protested. "I would need a compelling reason to violate a patient's privacy, and I certainly can't answer questions over the telephone from someone I've never met, whose official position I haven't verified."

"Then verify it," Tom said. "Do whatever will satisfy you. Look up the number of the Mason County Sheriff's Department and call and ask for Captain Tom Bridger."

"It would be better for you to come to my office with a warrant in hand, and—"

"I don't have time for that," Tom snapped. "Nelson could still be harassing Dr. Goddard. That trumps any concern you have for his privacy. I know what the law is. You have to provide information to law enforcement if a patient is a potential danger to anybody's safety."

"It's up to our staff to determine whether that is the case, and I don't consider Mr. Nelson to be—"

"All I'm asking you to tell me is whether Nelson is in the hospital right now, today, yes or no."

A long pause followed. Tom rapped a pencil against the edge of his desk, seething as he listened to the man's breath, in and out, on the other end of the line. *Come on, come on, I don't have all day.*

At last the doctor huffed a noisy sigh. "Mr. Nelson was granted a leave to visit his parents, who live in McLean, just a few miles from the hospital."

"How long has he been out?"

Another hesitation, another sigh. "Since Friday morning of last week. He's due to return to the hospital on Friday evening of this week."

"Is he checking in with you? Do you know where he is all the time?"

"Well, no, of course not. There's hardly any point in granting a patient leave if we're going to place onerous conditions on him. Captain Bridger, I feel sure that your concern is misplaced. Mr. Nelson has made considerable progress, and he's not a danger to anyone anymore."

Tom tried to keep his temper in check and his voice level. "Is this the first time he's been out?"

Again the doctor hesitated before answering. "No, it isn't. We wouldn't suddenly send a patient home for a week without first assessing his ability to cope."

Now maybe they were getting somewhere. Tom grabbed a notepad, ready to write down dates. "When did you start letting Nelson out on furloughs? I need the exact dates of every overnight furlough he's had in the last six weeks."

"I didn't say he'd been out overnight. I'm not sure that he has been. He's probably been given passes for lunches and dinners with his parents. I don't have the details of his case in front of me."

Tom flung down his pen. It landed on the desktop with a thwack and rolled a couple of inches before stopping. "Could you locate those details for me? I need to know if he's been out of the hospital overnight before this week. Can you check the records and tell me so I'll have accurate information?"

The doctor said, in a long-suffering tone, "If you insist."

Tom gave him a clipped, "Thank you."

The doctor put him on hold. No music, no recorded message, just dead air that made Tom wonder if he'd been cut off.

Then the doctor was back on the line, telling him, "I'm afraid I was in error when I spoke from memory. Mr. Nelson has, in fact, been out on overnight leave before."

His heart suddenly racing, Tom grabbed his pen and poised it over a notepad. "Tell me the dates."

His excitement deflated when he heard the dates.

"Is that all, Captain Bridger?" the doctor asked.

"Yes, it is, for now. Thank you."

"Goodbye then, Captain Bridger."

Tom ended the call, feeling as if he'd walked into a wall. Nelson could be in Mason County now, he could have followed Michelle there last Saturday. He could have put the snake in Rachel's office. But he'd been in the hospital every time something happened at Michelle's office in Bethesda. Common sense said Nelson wasn't the stalker, but Tom knew Rachel wouldn't be satisfied with that conclusion.

First things first. He had to find out whether Nelson was where he was supposed to be right now, with his parents in Fairfax County. He didn't want to make a cold call. He couldn't trust anything Nelson's parents might tell him, in any case. Perry was their son. From what Rachel had told Tom, he guessed they would protect their boy and insist on his innocence even if they found him standing over Rachel's dead body with a smoking gun in his hand.

Tom knew somebody he could turn to for help. He snatched up the receiver again while he pulled a telephone/address book from his desk drawer and flipped through it. He dialed Detective Bernard Fagan's cell phone number. It rang five times and went to voice mail.

"Damn it," he muttered. When Fagan's voice told him to leave a message, he said, "This is Tom Bridger. If you still want to do something to help Rachel, give me a call as soon as you get this."

Chapter Thirty-six

Mrs. Jankowski greeted Tom with the same degree of enthusiasm he would have expected from her daughter.

"Rita's not here." Mrs. Jankowski squinted at him through the screen door. Her bright red hair was pinned up, the curls sitting atop her head like strawberries heaped on a plate.

"They told me at the store that she's not working today. Do you know where I can find her?" The cell phone signal in this part of the county was unreliable, and Tom was afraid he would miss Fagan's return call if he stayed out here too long. At the same time, he couldn't sit in his office and wait while he had so many things to follow up on.

"Find Jordy Gale and you'll probably find her." She snorted in disgust. "He's been going through a *hard time* and Rita says she's the only one who *understands* him. Why she'd want to understand a sick puppy like him is more than I can figure out."

Tom regarded her with interest. He might learn more from Rita's mother than from Rita herself. "Can I come in and talk to you for a few minutes?"

She jutted her sharp little chin as if brandishing a knife. When she took a step backward Tom was afraid she would shut the door in his face, but instead she said, "You got no business with me."

"I just want to ask you a few questions."

"What are you up to?" She folded her arms. "Tryin' to trick me into sayin' something against my daughter? You think my girl had something to do with Shelley Beecher dying?"

"No, I don't."

"Just what are you gettin' at, then? Why are you doggin' her like this?"

"I'll explain if you let me come in."

"No. You can't set one foot in my house without my say-so. I know my rights. No reason you can't talk to me right where you're standin'."

"Okay, fine. You don't seem to be a big fan of Jordy Gale. What do you have against him?"

Mrs. Jankowski raised her eyebrows in surprise. "You know he's mental, don't you?"

"Mental?"

"Crazy. Not right in the head. He's been locked up. Lord, are you as dense as you seem to be?"

"I know Jordy's been in drug rehab two or three times," Tom said. "Like a lot of people. But he seems to be straightening out his life."

"Ha! Shows how much you know. He's always been a junkie. That's the reason Rita got herself unhitched from him just about as fast as they got hitched. But it wasn't just drugs. He went off the rails, had a nervous breakdown. His sister that he was stayin' with up in Manassas, she caught him with a shotgun in his mouth, ready to blow his head off. She put him in the nuthouse, the state hospital up there."

"When did that happen?"

She pursed her lips and seemed to be debating whether to share the information. When she spoke, she sounded cagey, as if she didn't want to say too much. "Oh, about six years ago, I reckon." She paused and averted her eyes, gazing off beyond Tom. "While Vance Lankford was on trial for murder."

That explained why Tom hadn't heard about Gale attempting suicide. Tom was working for the Richmond Police Department at the time, Jordy Gale had been living in Northern Virginia, and they'd barely known each other. His ongoing drug problem was what the gossips focused on. Suicidal moods weren't unusual among addicts, and Tom wasn't surprised Jordy had crashed on meth and crack. But Mrs. Jankowski seemed to be hinting that there was more to the story.

"State mental hospitals have units where they treat drug addicts," he said. "If Jordy didn't actually hurt himself, that's where he would have gone, to a substance abuse facility."

"Facility," she scoffed. "Everything's a *facility* these days. Well, to me it was the nuthouse. Yeah, they got him off drugs, and they blamed the dope for him wanting to kill himself. But I think he's got a screw loose. Anyway, that was just the first time he landed in that place. I tell you, he's bad for Rita. I thought so when they run off and got married straight out of school, and I think so now."

Mrs. Jankowski was hardly the first mother to take against a daughter's boyfriend. "If they're back together now, maybe that means they belong with each other. They shouldn't have split up the first time."

"No, sir, she don't belong with the likes of him." Mrs. Jankowski shook her head so vigorously that a red curl pulled loose from the pile atop her head and dangled over her right ear. She swiped it back into place and folded her arms. "I've been beggin' and beggin' Rita to cut him off, steer clear, but she won't listen to me."

"Don't you believe he's kicked his habit?"

She looked at Tom as if she couldn't believe somebody so dumb was walking around loose. "There ain't no such thing as kickin' a drug habit. You oughta know that, bein' a cop. Once they're hooked, they stay hooked. You might as well cut your losses and let 'em go."

"You're a hard woman, Mrs. Jankowski."

She sniffed and rubbed at her nose with the back of a hand as if scratching an itch. "Anyway, like I said, it's not just the drugs. It's the way he makes Rita feel about herself. He just sucks the life out of her, you know what I mean? Makes her think she's not worth a thing, and he's the only man who appreciates her."

Rita had said as much to Tom in slightly different words— *Jordy treats me with respect. He's the only man in this county who doesn't treat me like trash.*

Mrs. Jankowski was wound up now, the words spooling out of her. Through the screen door Tom watched a kaleidoscope of emotions play across her face. Anger. Bewilderment. Frustration. And fear, deep and genuine.

"It wasn't so bad long as he stayed up there with his sister, but every time he landed in the nuthouse, Rita had to go see him, didn't let a week go by. Spendin' money she couldn't afford on motels so she could stay over. Missin' work. Nearly lost her job over it that last time, back in the winter. Now he's right here underfoot, and he's just shot her plans all to hell."

"What plans?"

Tom watched in surprise as Mrs. Jankowski's eyes filled with tears. "She could be on her way to something good if it wasn't for him. You know them TV shows where people sing and everybody that's watchin' calls in to pick the winner?"

Tom nodded, recalling his own question to Rita about auditioning.

"Well, she was all set to go and try out, and you know what her voice is like, she coulda got on the show like that." Mrs. Jankowski snapped her fingers, then sniffled and swiped at her nose with the back of her hand. "She was keepin' it a secret, so she wouldn't be embarrassed in case it didn't work out. But she told Jordy, and by the time Jordy got through, she was sayin' she wasn't ever gonna sing again. He's a loser, and he's makin' sure she'll be one too, so she won't get above him. He's tryin' to get her to run off with him, start over somewhere. If she does that, she'll never come back, I just know it. I'll never see her again."

"Are you afraid he's going to hurt her?" Tom asked. "If she won't do what he wants?"

"Now, I didn't say that. I—" She broke off, frowning. Then she produced a little smile and her tone changed abruptly to a wheedling plea. "You know, you could do Rita a lot of good if you'd talk to Jordy, tell him to leave her alone."

"Sorry, but keeping Rita and Jordy apart isn't in my job description."

She huffed in frustration. "Well, I'm gonna find a way."

Mrs. Jankowski's feelings about her daughter were all over the place, shifting from resentful to protective without signaling a turn. The prospect of her daughter being tied to a man with a history of drug abuse was enough to worry any mother. But Mrs. Jankowski was in the grip of much darker fears for Rita, and Tom was beginning to think she might have good reason.

He pulled the photocopied picture from his inside jacket pocket and unfolded it. "Is that Jordy there, at the last concert?"

She stared at the picture for a long moment, chewing on her bottom lip so vigorously that Tom was afraid she would draw blood. She flipped the latch, pushed the screen door open a few inches, and grabbed the paper from Tom. He waited out the silence while she studied it. At last she shifted her eyes to Tom. "Ain't this proof enough he was around that night? The Beecher girl wanted Rita to say he was there, put it in writin'. But you don't have to drag her into it, do you? This picture ought to be enough."

"It's nowhere near enough," Tom said. "It's not even a clear picture of him. Are you sure it's him?"

She opened the screened door again and thrust the paper at Tom. "Maybe I said too much already. I'm not gonna get my girl in trouble. Jordy Gale's gonna do a real good job of that."

"I don't know what kind of trouble you're talking about," Tom said. He didn't let himself stop to wonder about the meaning of her statements. At the moment he wanted to keep her talking and get as much information out of her as he could. "If Rita didn't tell the police Jordy was at the concert that night, so what? Nobody was investigating Jordy. There was no reason for her to say anything about him being there. Or was there?"

Mrs. Jankowski sniffled and her mouth puckered as if she might start bawling in earnest. Tom stayed silent while she dragged a wad of tissues from her pants pocket and blew her nose. He thought she was working her way around to telling him something, but instead she stepped back, shaking her head, and closed the door.

Chapter Thirty-seven

Ben Hern, Rachel's appointed escort and guardian, stayed downstairs to play with Frank and Cicero while she collected a few things to take to Michelle at the hospital.

She opened the closet in Michelle's room to find it empty except for a single pink blouse. Michelle had brought plenty of clothes with her. Where were they?

Rachel's gaze dropped to the suitcase on the floor. She hauled it out, dropped it on the bed, and snapped it open. Inside, still neatly folded, lay the clothes her sister had packed when she'd been determined to leave. Despite their argument, Rachel thought she'd talked her out of going home, but clearly Michelle wanted to be ready to leave at any minute.

I should have let her go. She's not safe around me.

Was that true? Sinking onto the bed beside the open suitcase, Rachel gave in to the accumulated tension of the past few days, allowing her shoulders to sag as her emotional defenses fell away.

Because of a drawing sent to her months ago, she'd become convinced Perry Nelson was the one tormenting Michelle, that the snake picture had turned out to be a literal warning. Tom didn't seem sure, though, and his doubts made Rachel question her own conclusion. It must sound crazy to Tom. And if Rachel were the target, why would Nelson involve Michelle? Why didn't he come after Rachel directly? Because it was more fun this way? Stretching it out, savoring the thought of stupid Rachel worrying about her sister instead of herself? Yes, she could imagine Perry Nelson thinking that way.

Even if Rachel were the ultimate target, she had been right to worry about Michelle. The calls and threatening e-mails terrified Michelle, destroyed her emotional equilibrium. The snakebite could have killed her.

If all this happened because of me—

She banished the thought—this was all Perry Nelson's doing, not hers. She rose to gather necessities for her sister. Toothbrush and toothpaste, comb, fresh underwear, a change of clothes, a bar of the triple-milled coconut oil soap Michelle couldn't live without. She placed it all in a little pile on the bed. One of her canvas shopping bags could hold everything. Leaving most of Michelle's belongings packed in the suitcase, Rachel returned it to the closet floor. Michelle and her husband would decide when she should go home to Bethesda, but Rachel knew it would be soon. Although Kevin was a sensible and even-tempered man, Rachel had a feeling he would be outraged if it turned out she was the indirect cause for Michelle's fear and anguish over the past month.

Where was Nelson right now? Was he following her around, always just beyond sight? He had the kind of unremarkable good looks, a smooth boyish face and dark hair, an average build with no striking features, that would allow him to be a chameleon, blending in anywhere. Rachel hadn't seen him in a while, and she might not recognize him instantly if he had changed his hair color or grown a beard. Maybe she'd seen him on the street in Mountainview, looked straight at him without knowing him.

She walked to the window and gazed out across the acres of rolling land that made up Tom's small farm. For a moment she almost forgot her fear as she took in the beauty of the scene. The spring grass had a vibrancy that would fade when the heat of summer set in. Half a dozen mature dogwood trees near the house were losing their white flower petals to the breeze. On a hillside in the distance, Tom's flock of sheep grazed, slowly making their way down toward their paddock as the day drew to a close.

Nowhere out there for Nelson or anyone else to hide. Rachel felt safe at home during the day. Night was a different matter. Even with the security lights creating an illuminated perimeter, someone—Nelson?—had dared to walk right up to the house and throw a gallon of blood on the front porch.

What had Tom found out from the mental hospital? Why hadn't he called her? Rachel was supposed to wait for him to get back to her with news, but she couldn't keep her hand away from the cell phone in her shirt pocket. She was fingering it when its ringtone startled her.

Certain Tom was calling, Rachel didn't check the display before answering. "Hello? Tom?"

The caller chuckled, a low, derisive sound. "So sorry to disappoint you, Rachel, but it's not your darling Tom."

She balled her free hand into a fist, wanting to hit him, frustrated that she couldn't get at him. "You won't get away with this," she said.

"Oh, but I will. I'll see you soon, Rachel."

He was chuckling again when he broke the connection.

◇◇◇

Skeet Hadley lay on his bunk, hands clasped behind his head, glaring at the ceiling as if he had something personal against it. Stubble covered his jaw, and he still wore the clothes he'd been arrested in, although his mother had brought over a fresh shirt and pair of pants. Skeet didn't look over when Tom spoke to him through the wall of bars enclosing the small cell.

"Your lawyer will be by to see you in a while, but I thought I'd let you know that your bail hearing's tomorrow morning."

That got Skeet's attention. He jerked upright and jumped to his feet. "*Tomorrow?* I've been sitting here waiting all day. I'm not staying in this shithole another night."

Tom shrugged. "Sorry. The judge has a busy docket. That's the best he can do."

Skeet brought up a fist and swung, but not at Tom, who was out of reach in the corridor. The punch smacked into an iron bar. Skeet yelped in pain and cradled the hand against his chest with the other.

"You ready to cooperate yet?" Tom asked. "We can wait and talk when your lawyer shows up if you want to."

"Go to hell."

"You're up against some serious charges here." Tom took a step closer and immediately regretted it. Skeet gave off a sour odor of perspiration and stale beer. "I'd advise you to start thinking about how you can make things go a little easier. I expect your lawyer will tell you the same thing."

"You think you can find a jury in this county that'll put me in prison for going after the Lankfords? It's not gonna happen. Everybody despises them and their murdering son."

Tom wasn't in the mood to argue that point again. "I'm wondering where you got the idea to throw red paint on their porch and steps. Did you use up your whole supply of deer blood at my house?"

Skeet's expression had turned wary. "I don't know what you're talking about."

"We both know you did it, so let's stop playing games. Throwing blood and paint on people's porches, spreading stinking garbage everywhere. That's crazy behavior, Skeet. You know that, don't you? Sane people don't act that way. And shooting at the Lankfords, my god. Does that sound like a reasonable thing for anybody to do? You could be sitting here on double murder charges right now, and for what?"

"I wasn't trying to—Ah, hell." Skeet turned away, scrubbing a hand across his mouth. He took six steps to the far end of his cell, turned and paced back to the bars. He jammed his fists into his jeans pockets. "I was drunk, okay? We were all drunk. And I was mad and wanted to do something about it."

"Is that your excuse for all the other times too?"

Skeet rocked back and forth on his heels, stared at the floor, and didn't answer.

After every other crazy thing Skeet had done, Tom was more than willing to believe he was capable of murder. But if Skeet had killed Shelley, hidden her body for a month, then dumped it in a ravine, he hadn't acted alone.

"I'm not talking anymore without my lawyer," Skeet said, regaining a little of his belligerence.

"Fine." Tom had plenty of other things to do. "See you later."

When he returned to his office he found a call-back message from Detective Fagan waiting. They had talked briefly an hour before and Tom had asked him to go to the home of Perry Nelson's parents and find out whether their son was there. "Got some news" was all Fagan's message said. Tom phoned him back.

"The father's at work, and I had to go round and round with the mother." Fagan's voice sounded tight with anger. "But I finally got an answer out of her. Nelson's not there. He got out of the hospital Friday morning, then he borrowed his mother's car and said he was going to see a friend and took off. They haven't seen him since."

"God damn it. They didn't report it to the hospital?"

"Oh, no, no, they don't want to get their darling boy in trouble. The mother says he's off somewhere with a close friend, having fun, and he's entitled to a little freedom without the police harassing him. She doesn't see any reason to help us track him down. I'll tell you, I've never come so close to throttling a woman."

"What friend?" Tom asked. "Did she mention somebody by name?"

"It's some guy he met in the hospital, but she claims she doesn't remember his name. I'm outside the house right now, but I'm going back in to see if I can get more information out of her. If she'll let me back in. Look, I made some calls and put out a BOLO, but from what you told me, I don't believe Nelson's still in this area. Our department's faxing you a picture of him, and I'll e-mail you a description and the license number of the car he's driving. Just to be on the safe side, you'd better start looking for him in your neck of the woods."

◇◇◇

She'd forgotten Michelle's Darjeeling tea bags. At the front door, Rachel thrust the canvas tote bag filled with supplies for Michelle into Ben's hands. "Here, take this to the car for me, and I'll be right out."

Her cell phone rang as she walked down the hallway to the kitchen. Tom. Finally. *Please, please, tell me Perry Nelson is safely locked up.*

"I'm afraid it's not good news," Tom said when she answered. "Nelson's on the loose. He's been out since Friday morning, and his parents haven't seen him since then."

A blast of cold fear blew through Rachel. Stopping in the kitchen doorway, she grasped the door frame for support. "So I was right. He's been doing all these things."

"I'm afraid it's not that simple," Tom said. "The hospital director told me Nelson was definitely in the hospital on all of the dates when the stalker got into Michelle's office. He couldn't have done it, Rachel."

"But he's here!" Rachel beat her palm against the door frame. "And he's done things here. He called me less than an hour ago." While she repeated her brief telephone exchange with Nelson, Rachel walked to the kitchen window and peered out into the gathering darkness. How close was Nelson right now?

"I've put out a bulletin with his picture and description," Tom said, "so the State Police and our guys will all be looking for him. Fagan's still talking to the mother. I want you to stay at the hospital with Michelle until I tell you it's okay to leave. I'll get Uncle Paul to come to the house and look after things there."

"Okay." Rachel restrained herself from peppering him with questions. She didn't need to know everything he was planning, didn't want to slow him down. "I'm leaving now with Ben. I won't be able to use my cell phone in the hospital, but please get a message to me if you have any news."

She fetched half a dozen tea bags for Michelle, then retraced her steps to the front door. Frank had already curled up and fallen asleep on a living room chair. Cicero had retreated to his big cage in the den and pulled the door shut behind him, ready to settle down for the night. Tom's uncle, who had Billy Bob with him, would be there soon. Everything would be all right at the house. But that knowledge didn't lift the crushing sense of dread that sat on Rachel's chest, heavy as a boulder.

She switched on the front porch light, locked the door behind her and started toward Ben's low-slung black Jaguar, crouched on the driveway as if it were about to pounce on her Land Rover's back. She didn't see Ben. Pausing on the walk from house to driveway, she scanned the yard and the fields beyond. Ben enjoyed the hour when the day ebbed away and night crept in, and she expected to see him standing somewhere, watching the sky fade from blue to black.

She didn't spot him anywhere, and she wasn't in the mood to go searching for him in near-darkness. "Ben?" she called. "Where are you? I'm ready to go."

A faint sound made her spin around, back toward the car. "Ben?"

The sound came again, a low moan.

Rachel ran to the car, rounded its front end. She found Ben sprawled on the driveway, face down, arms splayed above his head as if he'd tried to break his fall. The canvas bag lay next to him, Michelle's hairbrush and shampoo spilling out.

Rachel gasped and dropped to her knees. "Ben, can you hear me?"

With one hand she fumbled in her jacket pocket for her cell phone, with the other she touched the dark blotch on his neck. Her fingers came away wet. Blood.

A strong arm closed around her waist and yanked her upright. She opened her mouth to scream, but no sound escaped before a hand clamped a reeking cloth over her face.

Chapter Thirty-eight

This time the state mental hospital director dug in his heels. "I can understand why you wanted information about Mr. Nelson's whereabouts, but I have to draw the line at this. I can't give you a list of patients who were released months ago. I see no justification for your request."

"This information could help us locate Nelson," Tom said. "He's with a friend, somebody he met in the hospital."

"Then I don't think you have anything to worry about. I don't know the details of all our patients' interactions, who's friendly with whom, but I do know that Mr. Nelson's treatment team regarded the formation of a friendship as an excellent sign. He had finally reached out to someone, and that milestone was a long time in coming."

"If you'll just look at his records, or ask somebody on his treatment, and get me a name—"

"I'm sorry, but no, I can't do that. I've told you too much already. You're on the wrong track. Mr. Nelson is no longer a danger to anyone. Now it's time I left for the day, so I really have to cut this short. Goodbye, Captain Bridger."

When Tom dropped the receiver into its cradle on his desk, Dennis Murray turned from the window. "No luck?"

"No." Tom leaned back in his desk chair and raked both hands through his hair. "Are the State Police cooperating?"

"Yeah." Dennis took a chair in front of the desk. "I got a quick okay on road blocks, and they're on it now. I faxed over Nelson's picture. Anything else we ought to be doing?"

"We have to find out who that friend of his is. I'm starting to think he's important in all this. But we're not going to get a name from Nelson's mother or the hospital. Nelson has used outside people before to send threatening letters to Rachel. Of course, his lawyer claimed he couldn't have sent the letters because the mail he sends from the hospital is monitored by the staff. But the original prosecutor on the case proved that Nelson was giving letters to patients who were being discharged or going on leave, and paying them to drop the envelopes in the mail."

"Breaking into Michelle's office for Nelson is a lot different from mailing a letter for him," Dennis said.

Tom nodded. "He's been in a mental hospital for years. Sooner or later he had to come across somebody as twisted as he is. Or willing to do anything for money. If he's got an accomplice, that could explain—" Tom broke off when Daniel Beecher appeared in the doorway.

In a barn jacket flecked with bits of straw and hay, Dan looked as if he'd come directly from work at the horse farm. Tom could smell the manure clinging to his boots.

Dennis stood and acknowledged Dan with a nod.

Before Tom could speak, Dan blurted, "When are you going to get around to charging Skeet Hadley for killing my daughter? What's taking so damn long?"

Tom got to his feet before he answered. "I know you won't like hearing this, but we don't have any evidence that Skeet killed Shelley."

Dan charged toward the desk so suddenly that Tom braced for an assault. Dennis raised a warning hand and said, "Whoa there."

Dan stopped short, glaring at Tom. "How much evidence do you need, for god's sake? He's been threatening her since she started working on Vance Lankford's case. Now I hear he tried to kill Jesse and Sonya Lankford. Why haven't you—"

"I understand why you're upset," Tom said. "But we can't talk about it unless you calm down a little."

Dan stabbed a finger at Tom, and his voice rose to a shout. "Don't you take that tone with me, Captain High-and-mighty. God damn it, does he have to murder somebody right in front of you before you'll do something?"

"He's in jail right now," Tom said. "He's being charged with the crimes against the Lankfords."

"But you're gonna turn him loose."

"That's not up to me. It's up to the judge, and it depends on whether his family can raise the money for the bond."

Dan snorted in disgust. "If Sheriff Willingham was still on the job, he wouldn't be letting other people decide whether a killer goes loose. He wouldn't let the Hadleys buy their boy's way out of jail."

"Sheriff Willingham would handle this situation exactly the same way I am. I'm recommending against release, and so is the prosecutor, but the final decision—"

"Well, you do that," Dan said, "you *recommend against* it. Just remember, everybody's watching you. You screw this up and you can forget about being elected sheriff."

Although the office door hadn't been closed before, Dan slammed it on his way out.

"Gotta feel for the guy," Dennis said.

"I do. Believe me, I do." Tom dropped heavily into his chair and swiveled around to glance out the window to the parking lot. He'd expected the news crews to drift away as the days passed, but instead their numbers had swelled, and now he counted two dozen reporters and camera operators out there, clustered around their vehicles. The TV trucks had satellite dishes on their roofs to provide live reports.

Swinging back around to his desk, Tom confronted a stack of callback memos impaled on a spike. Some from reporters, some from county supervisors. All boiled down to the same complaint: after almost a week, Tom hadn't caught Shelley's killer yet.

He yanked the message slips off the spike and dropped them into the plastic recycling bin next to his desk.

"Can't say I blame you." Grinning, Dennis took his seat again.

"They ought to try their luck catching this guy if they think it's so damned easy," Tom said.

"To get back to Rachel and Michelle's stalker," Dennis said, "I think we…"

Dennis continued speaking, but Tom wasn't listening. He stared at the expanse of his desktop, now bare except for a head and shoulders photo of the deceptively boyish and innocent-looking Perry Nelson. A scenario was taking shape in Tom's head as bits and pieces of information came together.

"Tom?" Dennis said. "What is it?"

It was crazy. Tom couldn't see any obvious connections.

But maybe that was the point. No obvious connections meant no suspicions.

Yet it made sense. In the warped brains of psychopaths and killers, it would make perfect sense.

He was about to try his theory on Dennis when the phone rang. He was startled to learn that Rita Jankowski's mother was on the line. "What can I do for you?"

She broke into sobs. Tom had to wait for her to calm down a little and draw a gulping breath. "I can't find my daughter. She won't answer her phone. She promised to be home by this time. Nobody answers the phone at the locksmith shop. But I know she's with him. He's got her."

"Look," Tom said, "Rita and Jordy are two adults. They have a right to—"

"You don't understand!" she yelled. "He's gonna hurt her, I know he is."

Tom's own suspicions about Jordy made him hesitate. This woman knew something Tom needed to hear. She'd been on the verge of telling him earlier. "I'll make a bargain with you," he said. "Tell me what you're hiding, what you wanted to tell me when I was at your house, and I'll go find Rita and bring her home."

She keened as if she faced a choice between the devil and an abyss. "You'll put Rita in jail," she cried.

By this time, Tom wasn't surprised at what he was hearing. "If you really believe Jordy might hurt her, I don't think this is the time to worry about jail. Do you want me to find her or not?"

She stalled a little more, sobbed and snuffled. Then she blurted, "He came over here that night after the concert, came lookin' for Rita. Woke us up in the middle of the night, beggin' her to help him. And she did, like she always does. I saw them down in the basement. They didn't know I was on the steps. watchin' and listenin'. Rita was washin' blood off that tire iron and tellin' Jordy what he had to do with it so he wouldn't get caught."

◇◇◇

The inside of Rachel's nose burned, as if she'd breathed in pepper. She swallowed and tasted something musty, but familiar, at the back of her throat. When she opened her eyes, she saw only darkness. She felt a blanket, soft and light, covering her entire body, including her face.

Where am I? Her foggy brain took a moment to register the hum of a car engine and the bumps in the road beneath the vehicle's tires.

He's got me. Dear god, he's got me.

She shivered violently and bile rose in her throat. She lay on her right side, and her arms seemed to be caught behind her, unmovable. She tried to shift her legs, push herself upright, but her ankles were bound together and something hard pressed against her stomach. The metal buckle of a seat belt, she guessed. Although she was lying down, she felt the belt running over and under her body, holding her in place. She wasn't gagged. Thank god for that, at least, but the blanket was smothering her.

Focus, focus. Don't panic.

Thrashing her head from side to side, Rachel worked the blanket off her face. As she'd suspected, she lay on the back seat of a car. Her movements hadn't made much noise, but surely the unseen driver had heard, was aware she'd awakened. Yet he said nothing, didn't look around.

Rachel gulped in air, swallowed, and tasted the familiar mustiness again. Isoflurane? An anesthesia gas she used on animals all the time. Now someone had used it on her.

Not *someone*. Him. Perry Nelson. It had to be him.

The faint glow from the dashboard, glimpsed between the front seats, provided the only light in the car. The high headrest blocked her view of the driver. Why hadn't he spoken? Why hadn't he reacted to her movements?

Rachel squirmed around, trying to reposition herself for a better look without drawing his attention. When she raised her head from the seat, nausea swept through her, made her gag. Laying her head down again, she closed her eyes until the sickness subsided. It was an aftereffect of the anesthetic and would go away.

That struck Rachel as funny—god only knew what Nelson would do to her, or how much longer she had to live, but she was thinking about waiting for her nausea to pass. She almost laughed, but caught herself before any sound could escape. She had no time to waste. She swallowed again, clenched her teeth, and raised her head.

Still fighting off nausea, she craned her neck until she caught a glimpse of the driver in the dim light. What she saw made her gape. She dropped her head to the seat again. How was this possible? What on earth was going on?

The side of the driver's face was barely visible, hidden by a cascade of shoulder-length, wavy dark hair that gleamed in the dashboard light. She had expected to see Perry Nelson. But her silent kidnapper was a woman.

Chapter Thirty-nine

Dennis and Brandon, seated in front of Tom's desk, exchanged doubtful looks.

"I'm having a little trouble wrapping my head around this," Dennis told Tom. "Your instincts are usually right on target, though. We know Jordan Gale and Perry Nelson were in the same hospital at the same time, but what makes you think they cooked up a murder plot together?"

"Jordy had motive and opportunity to kill Brian Hadley six years ago," Tom said. "He thought Brian was going to break Rita's heart. And he was there, at the fairgrounds, at the concert, the night Brian was murdered. He never came under suspicion because all the evidence pointed at Vance Lankford from the word go. Nobody ever had any reason to question Jordy or check up on his movements."

"Then why did Shelley suspect him?" Brandon asked.

"Because he tried to cover up something simple, something an innocent person wouldn't lie about. We know Shelley found that picture and was trying to identify people who were present that night but were never questioned. She showed the picture to Vance and he recognized Jordy. Then she showed it to Rita and got a reaction that made her think Rita was lying when she said it wasn't Jordy. Finally, she went to Jordy himself and he denied it was him, denied he was even in the county that night. If Jordy had nothing to do with Brian's murder, why would he or Rita lie about him being around that night?"

"If all that's true," Dennis said, "and Jordy thought Shelley was onto him and wouldn't quit until she proved he was guilty, then I can see him killing her to shut her up. But the trouble is, I just checked his alibi for the day Shelley went missing, and it's solid. He was here in Mason County, and he can prove it with witnesses and work records."

"I don't think Jordy killed Shelley," Tom said. "I'll bet you anything I own that Jordy Gale is the friend Nelson made at the hospital during the winter."

"But you said the hospital director wouldn't verify it," Dennis said.

"No, and he's left for the day. Nobody's in the admin offices right now, but I'll call him again in the morning and fax Jordy's driver's license picture to him. I know I'm right."

"So let's assume Jordy killed Brian Hadley," Dennis said, "and he's been covering it up all these years. It would have been a hell of a scare when Shelley started poking around in the case."

"He was so afraid Shelley was going to expose him," Tom said, "that he started using again or started talking about killing himself, and he ended up back in the hospital, not long after Nelson was transferred there. Nelson's always blamed Rachel for ruining his life. Both men had women in their lives they wanted to hurt. Suppose they decided to team up and help each other get even?"

Brandon leaned forward in his chair. "You think what happened to Michelle was really aimed at Rachel? Just to get under her skin and torment her for a while before Nelson focused on her?"

"That's what Rachel believes," Tom said, "and it's starting to make sense to me too."

"But Nelson was in the hospital while most of that stuff was happening to Michelle," Dennis pointed out.

"He's got an alibi for the times Michelle was harassed in Bethesda," Tom said, "but he was out of the hospital on the night Shelley was snatched."

"Yeah, that's right," Dennis said, the doubt beginning to fade from his eyes.

"And Jordy," Brandon said, "was out of the hospital and living back here, so he was free to drive to Bethesda on the weekends and mess around in Michelle's office."

"Nobody would ever suspect Jordy because he had no history with Michelle, no reason to harass her. Nobody would suspect Nelson of killing Shelley because he had no history with her." Tom stood. "We need to pick up Jordy right now. Rita's probably with him. Her mother thinks he might hurt her, but I think it's more likely they'll take off together if we don't get to them first. Bran, you come with me. Dennis, put a couple of our guys on alert in case I call for backup."

By the time they hit the road, Brandon was excited about the connection Tom drew between the stalker and the Beecher murder. "Man, that is really slick. And *sick*. So you think they cooked it up together, before Jordy got out of the hospital?"

The cruiser's headlights bored into the darkness as they left the lighted streets of Mountainview. Hills loomed on both sides of the road, their ridges rimmed with moonlight. Tom hoped to god he was right, that he wasn't chasing the wildest goose that ever took flight. "I'm not sure Jordy's smart enough. But from what Rachel's told me about Perry Nelson, he's got the brains to plan something like this. I don't know where Nelson is, but Jordy's weak, he might give Nelson up if we put on the pressure. You sure he's living in the rooms above the locksmith shop?"

"Positive. I remember him telling me his folks didn't want him to move back in with them. He acted kind of put out about it, but he said at least he's got privacy and Rita can stay over if she wants to."

Rita. Tom could understand why Mrs. Jankowski had kept quiet about what she'd seen and heard in order to protect her daughter, but why would Rita let an innocent man go to prison for life? Had she protected Jordy ever since because she loved him, or was she simply looking out for herself?

The small building containing the locksmith business, and apparently Jordy's living quarters too, wasn't far from town. As Tom swung the cruiser into the narrow parking strip in front of the shop, his headlights illuminated Rita's old car, sitting next to the shop's van. The shop downstairs was dark, but lights blazed in the second floor rooms.

"Let's try to do this without anybody getting hurt," Tom said. He and Brandon climbed out of the cruiser and closed their doors slowly, silently. Tom was reaching for his pistol when his cell phone rang. "Damn," he muttered, angry at himself for not thinking to silence it. Afraid the shrill tone would cut through the quiet and alert Jordy, he yanked the phone from his shirt pocket and pressed the button to answer.

His uncle was calling, and it took Tom a minute to make sense of what he was saying. Paul had found Ben Hern bleeding and unconscious on the driveway at the farmhouse. "I called an ambulance, they're on the way—"

"Where's Rachel?" Tom demanded.

He heard his uncle let out a long, shaky breath. "I don't know, Tommy. I found her cell phone on the driveway, but Rachel's gone."

◇◇◇

They must be somewhere in Mason County, but this was countryside with no lights along the road, no landmarks to help Rachel orient herself, and the shadows of the surrounding hills blotted out most of the moonlight. When she twisted her head to look up and out the car's side window, she saw only darkness.

The driver remained silent, a mysterious, malign presence who held Rachel's fate in her hands.

The car turned, swinging sharply to the right. It slowed as it bumped along, and she guessed they'd left the pavement for a dirt road.

With a spike of panic, Rachel realized they must be nearing their destination. What would happen when they stopped? The time was coming when she would have to act, do something to keep herself alive. Her head was clearing, she'd quelled the nausea. She didn't know who her captor was, but she believed she had better odds of freeing herself from a woman than from a man.

She had to get the woman to talk to her so she could get some idea of what was happening and what her chances were. She ran her tongue over her dry lips and asked, "Where are you taking me?"

No answer.

"Are you a friend of Perry Nelson? His girlfriend? Is he waiting for you to bring me to him?"

"Shut up."

Rachel gasped. A man's voice. *Oh, my god. It's him.* Her heart banged in her chest. *Think. Focus.* She knew she had the strength to save herself. "Perry? Where are you taking me?" she asked again.

"Shut the fuck up!" He snatched the wig off his head and flung it into the passenger seat.

They emerged from the shadows, and moonlight flooded the car. Rachel heard weeds scraping the undercarriage. The car stopped.

No, no. As long they were moving, she'd been safe.

Nelson shifted the car into park, turned off the engine, and unlocked his seat belt.

The impossibility of escape threatened to overwhelm her. *One thing at a time,* Rachel told herself. He was crazy, but she wasn't, and that gave her an advantage as long as she could stay calm and focus.

Nelson slid out of the car, slammed his door.

Twisting on the back seat, Rachel searched with her bound hands for the seat belt latch. Her fingertips brushed over metal but couldn't grasp it.

Nelson opened the back door closest to her feet. He rolled her forward on the seat a couple of inches, then leaned on her legs with one hand to steady himself so he could reach behind her and unsnap her seat belt.

Kick him. Kick him in the balls. If she could pull her knees up—But his hand, and the force behind it, pinned down her legs.

Then he was hauling her out of the car feet-first, so roughly that she banged her head on the door frame. He seemed to expect her to stand on her own, but with her ankles bound she couldn't get herself upright and balanced. She toppled against Nelson, then crumpled to her knees. He swore, hoisted her to her feet, and shoved her against the car.

Her breath coming in gasps, Rachel shot a look around. They were on a dirt road in a deserted area. Under silvery moonlight she saw an old farmhouse thirty feet off the road. Small and dark, it listed to one side. Abandoned. A place no one was likely to come to anytime soon. Dead, dry weeds from years past covered the ground between the house and the road. Rachel saw nothing that resembled a driveway. From somewhere in the distance came the raspy bark of a fox.

Nelson hadn't gagged her, which probably meant no one was close enough to hear her scream. Did he have a gun? Where was it? If he didn't have a gun, she stood a chance of escaping. He wasn't much bigger than Rachel, and she was strong, in good shape. Her heart raced with excitement.

He took away that hope when he leaned into the car and removed a pistol from the glove compartment. He stuck the gun into his waistband.

She had to get Nelson to talk, keep him talking until she figured out how to free herself. "What is this place?"

A mocking smile contorted his face. He wore no makeup, and he was dressed in jeans and a sweatshirt. The wig alone had been his disguise, enough to deflect the attention of anyone passing on the road who might be looking for a boyishly handsome young man with close-cropped dark hair. Rachel caught a whiff of mint on his breath, an aroma so familiar and harmless that it made her mind reel with the insanity of the situation.

"This," he said, "is the place where you're going to die."

Chapter Forty

"You think they've got Rachel in there?" Brandon whispered.

"Anything's possible. Let's find a way in."

Guns drawn, they edged around the corner to the back of the building, staying close to the wall so they couldn't be seen from the second floor. Tom was betting Jordy and Rita didn't know they were here. Where was the entrance to the second floor stairwell? If the only way to get up there was through the shop, they would have to take a different approach and call for backup.

Tom blew out a breath of relief when he spotted two doors at the rear of the building. Slowly, quietly, he turned one knob. Locked. Probably the door into the shop. He stepped over to the other, three feet away. Again, he took care to make no noise when he tried the knob.

It turned.

Tom gave the door a gentle push. The hinges creaked, and he jerked his hand away.

They waited, listened. Tom heard no sounds from upstairs, not even the murmur of a TV set. He stepped into the dark stairwell, keeping his gun up, praying the steps weren't as noisy as the door. He felt Brandon close behind him. The door at the top of the stairs was closed, but a strip of light glowed along the bottom.

Tom and Brandon were halfway up when Rita screamed from above, "He's got a gun. He'll shoot you. Don't come—" She broke off as if a hand had clamped her mouth shut.

Tom froze. Who was with her? Jordy, Perry Nelson, both of them? Was Rachel up there too? He leaned against the wall, Brandon beside him. What the hell would they do now?

◇◇◇

Instead of wading through the thicket of weeds in front of the house, they followed what Rachel recognized as a deer trail that wound around the side of the structure to the back.

She could barely walk with rope tying her ankles, but she exaggerated the difficulty, deliberately stumbling again and again as Nelson, cursing and sweating, dragged her along the path. Only his painful grip on her arm kept her from falling. Perspiration trickled down her face and back.

He ran out of patience after her third or fourth stumble. "Damn it, Rachel, stay on your feet."

"How can you expect me to walk with my ankles tied? If you want me to go faster, untie me."

"Aw, fuck it." She heard a *snick* and a flashlight came on, a shock of clear, bright light. He pulled a folding knife from his pants pocket and pressed a button to make the blade pop out. "Don't get any ideas about running when your feet are loose," he said. "You try it and I'll shoot you in the back."

When the knife sliced through the rope, the blade caught on Rachel's sock and nicked her left ankle, but she sucked in a breath and didn't let him see a reaction.

Nelson stood and tucked the knife back into his pocket. "You don't have anybody to blame for this but yourself, Rachel, I hope you know that. You wrecked my life. I lost everything because of you. The girl I was going to marry. Law school. I'll never get any of it back. I'll always be that crazy guy who shot the animal doctor. Well, now I'm about to take your life away from you. How does it feel, Rachel? Huh?"

You're not taking anything away from me. She would find a way out of this, if she could buy enough time. "If it's me you're after," she said, "why did you have to torment Michelle? What has she ever done to you?"

"That snotty bitch had it coming. Do you think I didn't notice her sitting in the courtroom every day? Watching me, looking at me like I was a piece of shit, passing judgment on me. They *all* pass judgment." Drops of spittle flew from Nelson's mouth and hit Rachel's face. "Psychologists, psychiatrists. They sit around deciding who's crazy and who's not, who's going free and who's going to rot in the nuthouse. They don't have any idea how easy they are to fool."

"You're a little confused, Perry. You're not thinking clearly. My sister has nothing to do with the hospital or your treatment." Rachel couldn't stop herself from adding, "Anyway, you *are* a piece of shit."

He pulled back his hand and hit her hard enough to knock her to her knees.

◇◇◇

Tom crept up the stairs, slowly, expecting Jordy to throw open the door and fire on them at any second. As he and Brandon got closer, Tom heard Rita and Jordy arguing in low, urgent voices. They might have Rachel in there, bound and gagged, a prisoner. If Perry Nelson was with them, he could be armed like Jordy.

Tom and Brandon couldn't wait on the stairs forever. As long as things stayed quiet, maybe the best tactic would be to wait for backup. Tom could stay here and send Brandon outside to call for reinforcements.

Tom was turning to give Brandon the order when Rita screamed, "Jordy, don't!" Something hit the floor with a thump.

A split second later Tom heard a gunshot.

He charged up the stairs, swung a booted foot, kicked the door open. Jagged strips of wood flew into the tiny sitting room and landed inches from Jordy and Rita. He was on top of her, pinning her to the floor, trying to wrestle a pistol from her hands.

"Drop it!" Tom shouted.

Rita let go and Jordy caught the gun when it fell free. He scrambled off her, and still on his knees, hooked an arm around her neck and jammed the gun barrel against her temple. "I'll shoot her," he said. "You back off right now or I'll blow her brains out, then I'll shoot myself, and you'll never find Dr. Goddard."

Chapter Forty-one

Behind the dark bulk of the farmhouse, the back yard was a broad cleared space flooded with moonlight. Why had Nelson brought her to the back instead of taking her in the front? To avoid trampling the weeds near the front door, leaving a visible sign that someone had been here?

Rachel stared at the squat hovel enveloped in darkness. She would not die there, alone. She would not die where rats could feast on her body. She was going to live a long life. With Tom. With the family they would create together.

She had slowed their progress as much as she could, but she didn't dare make Nelson angry enough to hit her again. He might knock her out next time, and she couldn't risk that.

The shadow of an owl glided over them, broad-winged and silent, and Nelson flinched as if he thought the bird might attack him. He wasn't invincible. He could be scared too.

She had to stall him while she collected her thoughts, came up with a plan. She couldn't reason with a lunatic. Begging him would get her nowhere. Taunting him would get her killed.

Say something. Flatter him. Trying to calm the tremor in her throat, she said, "Aren't you going to tell me how you did it? You fooled all of us. Me, the police. We didn't know it was you."

Nelson chuckled. The ugly, self-satisfied sound ended abruptly. "Didn't the snake tell you anything? You were supposed to make the connection. Are you so fucking stupid you couldn't figure it out?"

"Oh, I did, I finally made the connection then." Rachel rushed on, stroking his ego to stave off his anger. "I couldn't forget that drawing you sent. I'll admit it scared me."

"That damned snake was a bitch to get hold of. Then it didn't even bite you." He jerked her arm, kept her moving. "Why the hell didn't you sit down at your desk?"

So he wasn't all-seeing, all-knowing. "You didn't do your homework, Perry. If you had, you'd know I'm not in my office much. Morning's for patients and surgery. Paperwork has to wait until after lunch. Michelle's been using my desk since Monday. Didn't you know that?"

"Shit," Nelson spat out. "One more thing that dickhead got wrong. Couldn't even get your damn schedule straight. Fucking idiot. Serves me right, though. What could I expect from a guy I met in a nuthouse? I should've known better."

In the moonlight Rachel saw a mask of frustration and fury on his boyish face. "Who? Who was giving you information about me?"

Nelson didn't seem to hear. He turned his eyes to the star-speckled sky as if imploring heaven to hear his complaint. "It could have been perfect. My plan *was* perfect, I had it all worked out, every step of the way. He'd do his part, I'd do mine, and nobody would ever connect us. But that fucking imbecile couldn't get a goddamn thing right. I got rid of that girl for him, then he didn't have the stomach to take you out."

"That girl?" Rachel felt as if a vise had squeezed all the air out of her lungs. "What girl did you get rid of?"

"You ought to know, you found her body." Nelson chuckled again. "That worked out better than I expected. Perfect timing. That's the only damned thing that's gone right."

He tightened his grip on Rachel's arm and yanked her forward. "Come on."

"Who are you talking about? Who's helping you?"

"Helping," Nelson said with a scoffing laugh. "All that idiot knows how to do is get a door open without a key. And he's got a real mean talent for throwing magazines on the floor and moving picture frames around on a wall. I had to do the real work."

Rachel couldn't take time to absorb his answers, but she had to keep throwing questions at him. She didn't want him to force her into that house, didn't want to be swallowed by the shadows around it and the darkness within. "What's the real work?"

"Getting rid of women who can't mind their own fucking business. Now it's your turn. Jordy was supposed to get rid of you after I'm back in the hospital, but he pussied out, so here I am, doing everything myself. But like my dear old grandmother used to tell me, life gives you lemons, you make lemonade. I'm going to enjoy taking care of you myself."

◇◇◇

Tom and Jordy stared into each other's eyes while Rita whimpered in Jordy's stranglehold, his arm around her neck, pressing her against his chest. A strand of her bright hair fell across one eye and stuck to her tear-dampened cheek.

Tom kept his pistol trained on Jordy's head, the only exposed part of his body.

Brandon edged into the room, gun raised, and stood shoulder to shoulder with Tom. In the small space, no more than six feet separated them from the pair on the floor. Tom caught the sour odor of the sweat that poured off Jordy's body and soaked the collar and armpits of his denim shirt. Panic exploded in Jordy's eyes as his gaze darted between the two deputies, and his gun wavered as if he couldn't decide where to aim.

"Come on now, Jordy." Tom kept his voice level, casual. "You know you don't want to hurt Rita. You mean a lot to her, she's told me so, and she means a lot to you. You don't want to let her down. She deserves better than that."

Jordy glanced down at Rita's terrified face. She whispered, "Please, Jordy. I'm on your side, I've always been on your side. You can still make this right. I'll help you."

"It's too late, don't you see that? It's gone too far."

With Jordy distracted, Brandon shifted a couple of feet away from Tom, to the left.

"What are you going to do?" Tom asked Jordy. "Let Perry Nelson get away scot-free while everybody blames you?"

Jordy jerked his head up. "How do you know about him? Did he kill Dr. Goddard already?"

Any satisfaction Tom might have felt at guessing correctly vanished in a wave of despair. Nelson had Rachel, and he intended to kill her. "Where are they? Where did he take Rachel?"

"I asked you how you knew about Perry." Jordy ground the gun barrel against Rita's temple, and she cried out and tried to push his hand away. He looked down at her as if shocked that he'd hurt her.

Brandon moved again, closing in on the two from the side.

"I'm sorry," Jordy told Rita, pulling the gun away. "I'm sorry, honey."

A raving lunatic, Tom thought. Jordy's unpredictable emotions made him every bit as dangerous as Nelson. But Nelson was the one who had Rachel, and Tom didn't know where he'd taken her.

He concentrated on distracting Jordy's attention from Brandon's movements. Calmly, Tom answered Jordy's question. "I put it together. I knew you and Nelson were in the same hospital at the same time, but that didn't mean anything until I had a few other pieces of information. You were at the concert the night Brian Hadley died—"

"That damned picture," Jordy blurted. "If Shelley'd never seen that picture and started asking questions, she'd still be alive."

"And Rachel made me realize Nelson was the one harassing her and her sister," Tom went on. "Was it all Nelson's idea? Did the two of you plan the whole thing before you got out of the hospital? He'd help you, you'd help him."

Before Jordy could answer, Rita protested, "That guy bullied Jordy into it. Jordy was already scared because Shelley wouldn't leave him alone. She kept showing up at his sister's house in Manassas and asking him questions. She pushed him right over the edge."

"Then you met Perry Nelson in the hospital?" Tom asked Jody. A real meeting of minds: two psychopaths in search of reinforcement. "Is that how all this started?"

"That's right." Rita's face lit up with hope, as if she believed she was winning Tom over. "Perry Nelson took advantage of him when he wasn't strong enough to say no. He got him to talk, then he threatened to tell the police if Jordy didn't go along with him."

Jordy nodded as if agreeing with everything Rita said. "Once Perry killed Shelley, he said I didn't have any choice, I had to get rid of Dr. Goddard for him. I went in her sister's office, but I couldn't kill Dr. Goddard. I just couldn't."

"You see?" Rita said to Tom. "Jordy's a good person at heart. He was supposed to kill Dr. Goddard this weekend, when Perry Nelson was back in the hospital and nobody could blame him. But Jordy likes her, he never would've hurt her. You have to believe that."

The whole scene felt surreal to Tom, Rita pleading for him to forgive and trust Jordy while Jordy held a gun to her head. "Nelson's got Rachel now, doesn't he?" Tom asked.

"Yeah, he took her," Jordy said, his voice turning mournful. "He knew I wouldn't kill her, so he has to do it himself before he goes back to the hospital. I'm supposed to meet him, though. He told me I have to help him after he's got her."

"Where are they?" Tom demanded. "Where did Nelson take Rachel? Just tell me and this will all be over."

"If I tell you, Perry'll kill me." Jordy's face puckered, he squeezed his eyes shut and tears spilled down his cheeks.

Brandon shifted closer. He froze when Jordy opened his eyes.

"Honey," Rita said, "if they catch Perry Nelson, you'll be okay, you can get help, and he'll be in prison, he won't be able to get to you." She looked at Tom. "I know where they are. Jordy was going to shoot himself, and he wanted me to tell you—"

"They'll put me in prison for killing Brian." Jordy wailed like a child, sobbing now, pressing his face into Rita's red-gold hair. "I don't want to go to prison. I'd rather be dead."

"Jordy, honey," Rita crooned. "don't say that. You'll get through this. I'll help you. I'll never let you be alone."

Brandon was almost there. Tom saw Rita's gaze flick toward Brandon, and for a heart-stopping second he thought she would warn Jordy. He saw her consider it. He saw her decide against it, and he breathed again.

"Why did you help him get away with killing Brian?" Tom asked Rita. "Why would you let an innocent man go to prison for it?"

Her face went slack with shock, and her mouth fell open. "What—How—"

"I know everything," Tom said. "I just don't know why you did it."

She burst into tears, her body shaking with sobs as Jordy held her against him. "It was all my fault. Jordy just wanted to keep Brian from hurting me. I told him to throw the damned thing in the river. I didn't know he was going to put it in Vance's car."

"Shut up!" Jordy cried. "Don't tell him that stuff."

Brandon took a step toward them, and this time Jordy caught the movement. He swung his gun toward Brandon.

Tom sprang forward and landed on top of Jordy and Rita, knocking them both flat.

Chapter Forty-two

Rachel twisted her hands behind her back, rubbing her wrists raw in an attempt to free herself. The sisal rope had loosened, but not enough. Not nearly enough.

What was Nelson planning? Why were they just standing here? She got the feeling he was waiting for something—for someone?—before he could carry out his plan for her. That meant she still had some time, if only a little.

She had to be ready to fight for her life when her chance came, but how would she defeat a man with a gun and a knife while her hands were tied?

Keep talking. Keep him talking. "You said Jordy. Do you mean Jordy Gale, the locksmith? He's part of this? What does he have against me?"

"Nothing, and that's the problem," Nelson said, petulant now. "I didn't have anything personal against the Beecher girl either. I didn't even know her. That was the beauty of it. Nobody would connect me to her, and nobody would ever suspect Jordy of killing you. But he's a moron with no backbone. I got rid of the girl, and he got into your sister's office a couple of times, then he started wimping out."

"Jordy's the stalker?" Rachel felt as if all her perceptions had exploded into pieces and fallen around her in an unrecognizable pattern.

Nelson grunted a laugh. "Some stalker he turned out to be. I even had to tell the idiot what to say on the phone. Had to write it down for him, for fuck's sake. He doesn't even know what women are afraid of. Sex and violence, how hard is that to understand?"

He paced around her, muttering under his breath. She thought she heard him say, "...taking him so damned long?"

She was right. He was waiting. "Is somebody else coming?" she asked.

"Oh, yeah. Jordy's going to help me with you. He's going to live up to his part of our bargain."

Rachel stared at the house. He—they—would have to drag her, kicking and screaming, to get her inside it.

Nelson moved close to her. His mocking chuckle made her shiver. "You don't seem to be falling in love with this little place. It's a real fixer-upper, isn't it? Well, don't worry, sweetheart, you're not going in the house. You're going *under* it."

"What?" Rachel heard her voice rising and fought to control it, to sound calm. "What do you mean?"

"Stay right where you are and I'll show you." Nelson pulled the pistol from his waistband and pointed it at her face. "Don't even think about trying to get away. You won't go six feet before I bring you down. Do you understand me, Rachel?"

She nodded.

"Good girl." Nelson stepped over to a slanted door, jutting out from the back of the house, that obviously led to an underground space. In the beam of his flashlight Rachel saw a shiny new padlock hanging from the hook-and-strap latch.

A coal bin? A root cellar? No, no. He can't put me in there.

Her horror grew as she watched his every move. Nelson inserted a key into the lock, removed it, and pulled up the metal strap of the latch. He hung the opened padlock back on the hook. When he swung the warped wooden door up, its hinges squealed and resisted. He let it drop open to one side, exposing a black, black hole.

He shone the flashlight into the opening. "Aw, shit. That idiot left the ladder in there. What the hell was he thinking? I told him to check it out, make sure it was secure. I didn't expect—"

Nelson broke off, shaking his head, and blew out a sigh of exasperation. "Well, he can get it out again when he shows up."

"When is he coming?" Rachel asked. *How much time do I have?*

"Any minute. He'd sure as hell better show up. He knows I'll come after him if he lets me down again."

She couldn't wait until there were two of them. She had to free herself before Jordy Gale arrived.

"Get over here," Nelson said. "Take a look."

Rachel didn't move.

He took several long strides, grabbed her arm, and propelled her forward.

Rachel squeezed her hands into fists behind her back, nails digging into palms. Holding her breath, she peered into the hole. The chamber looked about ten feet deep. The flashlight beam played over dirt at the bottom.

Nelson swung the light her way, flashed it over Rachel's face, momentarily blinding her. She heard amusement in his voice when he asked, "How long do you think you'll last down there? No food, no water. Just the rats and spiders for company."

Digging deep for her last scrap of confidence and strength, Rachel said, "I thought you wanted the snake to kill me. So why do you have this place ready for me?"

"Oh, the snake was just a taste of what I had planned for you." He moved closer and spoke in a near-whisper, his breath hot and moist on her cheek. "I knew you'd get to the hospital before it killed you. Then when you were back at home, recuperating, Jordy was supposed to go and collect you and bring you here. But the fucking weasel backed out, said he couldn't do it, I'd have to do it myself. Well, your sister got the snakebite, but I can follow through on the rest of it. Here's what I'm going to do to you, Rachel."

Rachel stood still, determined not to let him see that he terrified her.

"Before I put you down there," Nelson went on, "I'm going to blindfold you and stuff a rag in your mouth. I'm going to take off all your clothes. We might take a little break then for some recreation. You up for that, sweetheart? I could get that nice soft blanket out of the car so you'll be comfortable on the ground. Would you enjoy that? Huh?"

Rachel kept silent. She wanted to fling herself at Nelson, kick him, bite him. *Kill him.* She would kill him if she could.

"Then I'll tie you up so you can't move, and I'll drop you in that hole. It'll take you days to die, Rachel. You're going to have a lot of time to think about what you did to me. You took my whole future away from me, and now I'm taking yours."

She scanned the yard, trying to readjust her vision to the moon's glow after the glare from the flashlight. She hoped to spot a possible weapon, yet she knew she could be surrounded by guns and knives and blunt objects and they would all be useless to her. When she spoke, she willed herself to keep the terror and rage out of her voice. "Somebody will find me. Everybody will be looking for me."

Nelson's face contorted with an ugly smile and he moved close enough for her to smell his breath again, that disconcerting sweet scent of peppermint. "Oh, yeah, every able-bodied person in this little hick county will be out searching for the wonderful Dr. Goddard. Hell, the sick and the crippled will rise from their beds to join in. But they'll never find you. That hole you can see—that's not all of it. There's another hole under it, with a hatch. And when it's got a couple of feet of dirt on top of the hatch, nobody would ever know it was there. You'll be tied up and gagged, and an army of people can be standing right here looking in, and you won't be able to let them know you're there."

Rachel couldn't control the shudder that shook her body.

Nelson pivoted away from her and vanished into the deep shadow against the house. All Rachel could see was the beam of his flashlight, bobbing as he walked.

Where was he going? She could try to get away right now, run into the woods. She might make it to the main road, stop a motorist, find help. But no. *Be realistic.* Nelson had a gun, and she would be slow and clumsy with her hands bound behind her back. She had to do something, though, however reckless, before she ran out of time.

She followed his flashlight beam with her eyes and saw it land for a second on an old metal lawn chair. He hauled it out of the blackness and into the moonlight where Rachel waited.

"Sit," he said. "I'm going to tie you down so you can't give me any trouble while I take care of Jordy."

"Take care of him?" Rachel said. "What do you mean? You said he was your partner."

"Well, I'll tell you a little secret. Jordy thinks he's coming out here just to help me, but he's going in the hole to keep you company. Except he won't be in any shape for lively conversation. I hope you don't mind the smell of a decomposing corpse right next to you while you're dying. I told you to *sit down*, Rachel."

Nelson shoved her and she lost her balance and dropped into the metal lawn chair. No more than five feet in front of her, the dark hole gaped. A plan of escape was forming in her mind, but she had to act quickly. She twisted her wrists, silently praying that the rope would suddenly drop away, knowing she couldn't count on a miracle like that.

◇◇◇

Locked in the back seat of the cruiser with Rita, hands cuffed behind his back, Jordy poured out a torrent of words that swept past so rapidly Tom could barely keep up. In the front passenger seat, Brandon had turned so he could keep an eye on the prisoners as Tom drove.

"My fault," Jordy said, "it was my fault, I said yes to everything, I just wanted Shelley to stop, you know? She had to stop before she started telling people I killed Brian. Perry said he'd stop her, he'd stop her for good."

If this was a confession to conspiring in Shelley's murder, Tom wasn't sure how well it would hold up in legal proceedings. Jordy had swung from depression and despair to wild-eyed incoherence in a matter of minutes. Was he manic-depressive?

Maybe bipolar was the proper term these days, but mania was the best description of Jordy's current mental state.

When Tom glanced in the rearview mirror, he saw Rita leaning her face against the window glass, an endless stream of tears flowing down her cheeks. She was cuffed too, and Tom intended to throw every charge he could justify at her. But that would be later. Right now he had to find Rachel, and Jordy and Rita were the only ones who could help him.

"Tell me something, Jordy," Tom said. "Why did you bring Shelley's body down here? Why not leave her where she died?"

"He had a plan, but I ruined it." Jordy sounded mournful, almost angry at himself. "Perry said he wanted to get double use out of Shelley's murder. He brought her here so you'd be busy investigating, you wouldn't be spending much time at home. Dr. Goddard would be alone at night and she'd be easier to get at. Easier for me to get at. But I couldn't do it." Choking up, he paused to catch his breath.

Tom wanted to stop the car, drag Jordy out and take him apart. But he needed the bastard to find Rachel. His whole body rigid with the effort of controlling his fury, Tom drove on into a part of the county that had been all but abandoned by its residents, who had moved on and left their small farms and houses behind to go to seed and ruin. Unless Jordy had invented the whole thing, Rachel was out here somewhere, trapped in a dilapidated house with a madman.

Jordy started up again. "He called me a cunt. I killed a man, I bashed in his head, I ought to be able to do anything after that. But it wasn't *me* that killed Brian. It was the meth, it made me lose control. I didn't mean to hurt him. Well, I wanted to hurt him, but not *kill* him, you know? Not like that. Then there he was, dead. I couldn't believe I did it."

"So you framed Vance Lankford?" Tom asked. "You put the murder weapon in his car?"

To Tom's consternation, Jordy burst into tears, shaking with sobs and howling in misery. "I should've listened to Rita. I should've thrown it in the river."

"Honey, don't." Rita leaned closer to Jordy, unable to embrace him because of her cuffs. "Shhh. It's going to be all right. We'll get through this together."

"Oh, for god's sake," Tom said. What was wrong with the woman?

"No," Jordy moaned. "It'll never be over. It's gonna stay in my mind the rest of my life…."

Tom raised his voice. "Jordy, pull yourself together. If you feel like talking, tell me where Shelley's body was for the last month. Did Nelson have her in a freezer somewhere?"

Tom watched Jordy in the rearview mirror, bobbing his head rapidly. "You guessed it. A big freezer at his family's place on the river." Jordy let loose a wild cackle of a laugh that seemed to echo in the car. "Boy, that'd be a surprise for his folks. Go out for a nice weekend and find a dead girl in the freezer."

Tom remembered something Rachel had said more than once about Perry Nelson. *He's a good actor. He can make anybody believe he's okay, he's perfectly normal.* The same had been true of Jordy at times. But his vulnerable mind couldn't handle the pressure of Shelley Beecher's suspicions. She'd been right, but she'd had no idea what a mess Jordy was, and she hadn't counted on him bringing a twisted creature like Perry Nelson into her life.

Chapter Forty-three

"Well, Rachel, I don't think my brilliant assistant is going to show up." Nelson stuck the pistol into his waistband. "What a surprise. I guess we'll have to do this without his help. Just the two of us."

While Rachel sat in the old rusted lawn chair, Nelson struggled to maneuver the ladder out of the narrow cellar opening. The moon rode high overhead, casting a cold glow that rendered the landscape and everything in it black and gray. The breeze felt chilly on her perspiring face.

Maybe he would exhaust himself with the ladder. Maybe this would be easy.

Yeah, right. He had a gun and a knife, and she didn't even have the use of her hands.

Did Tom know she was gone? His uncle would have found Ben, alerted Tom. Ben would be at the hospital getting medical treatment by now and Tom would have the whole Sheriff's Department looking for her. But how would they ever find her in this desolate spot?

He gave up on the ladder and let it clank back into place in the opening. Turning to Rachel, he said in a singsong voice, "I know what you're thinking." He leaned down and picked up something from the shadows next to the cellar door. "You're trying to figure out how to get away from me, aren't you? Well, you can forget about that." He stepped closer to Rachel and held up one arm, displaying a thick coil of rope. "Put your feet together for me like a good girl."

No, Rachel told herself. *This is not over.*

Standing in front of her, Nelson grasped one end of the rope and let the rest drop, uncoiling as it fell. He stuck his flashlight into the crook of one arm while he pulled his knife from his pants pocket. He began sawing at the rope, trying to cut a piece about three feet long. "Too bad you can't hold one end for me," he said with a nasty laugh.

With awkward movements he tried to hold the rope taut enough to cut it. The flashlight slipped out of place. Cursing, he grabbed it before it fell. His breathing came quick and shallow as he grew more frustrated. She braced herself against the back of the chair and pulled her feet together, getting ready.

"Damn it," he muttered. Then he solved his problem by stepping on the end of the rope, holding it straight and taut.

Rachel was out of time.

She jerked both feet up and kicked him in the gut.

He stumbled backward, his arms windmilling. The knife dropped from his hand. "Goddammit! What's the fuck's the matter with you?"

He came at her and she kicked him again. He lost his balance and went down.

Before he could get up, Rachel was on him, slamming her feet into his ribs. When he wrapped his arms around his upper body, she aimed her kicks at his groin. Bellowing in pain and rage, he rolled on the ground as he tried to avoid her blows. She heard the rattle and clink of small objects dropping out of his pockets, keys and coins and a cell phone, but what she wanted most, the gun, stayed secure in his waistband.

"You're going to pay for this," he screamed. "You're going to be sorry you fucked with me."

He struggled to rise to his hands and knees in front of the cellar opening. He reached for the pistol. Rachel swung her right leg back, propelled it forward and hit him in the face. The force of the blow knocked him backward, into the opening. But the ladder broke his fall. He hung there, one leg hooked over the top of the ladder, the rest of him invisible below. Then a hand appeared, clawing at the opening, grasping for purchase.

Rachel stomped on his hand and he jerked it back. She kicked his leg until it came free and Nelson slid down the ladder and into the cellar. She heard him land with a thud.

"Quick, quick," she told herself. "Close it, lock it."

She hoisted the wooden door up with one foot, let it slam shut over the opening. She couldn't see Nelson, but she heard him groaning. Any second he could be up and moving around, and he still had a ladder to climb out and a gun to kill her with.

She wouldn't have a prayer of escaping if she ran now, leaving him free to follow. Like an overturned turtle, she dropped backward onto the cellar door, grasping for the latch and the padlock. She found them, but it took an agonizingly long time to remove the lock from the hook, work the latch strap over the hook and get the padlock in place.

She heard Nelson grunt. Then a wordless roar rose from the dark hole.

Rachel clicked the lock shut. When she felt the snap, she went limp with relief.

Above her, the treetops swayed in a breeze. She gulped in air. She was alive.

But he still had the gun. She had to get out of here.

The knife. Where was it? She dropped to her knees and scoured the ground in front of the chair. She spotted the faint glint of moonlight off a steel blade. Still on her knees, she shifted around, leaned sideways as far as she could without tipping over, and combed the ground with her fingers until she found the knife.

A thump on the cellar door made her gasp. "You're not getting away with this," Nelson screamed. "Do you hear me? You are dead, you fucking bitch!"

Rachel gripped the knife and started sawing on the rope, ignoring the pain when she twisted her wrist, ignoring the bite of the blade when it sliced her skin.

Nelson fired a shot through the cellar door.

The rope came loose. Rachel tossed it aside and ran her hands over the ground. His keys. She was sure his keys had fallen out of his pocket.

Behind her, she heard several rapid shots. He was shooting off the lock.

She was about to push herself to her feet and run when her fingers touched metal, closed around it. His cell phone, not his keys. Where the hell were the keys? They must be close to the phone. Frantically, she shifted in a circle, searching with her fingers. When she moved, one knee came down on something hard and sharp-edged. *Oh, thank god.*

She grabbed the keys, jumped up and sprinted around the side of the house, down the narrow path toward the car. She heard the cellar door bang open. Nelson yelled, "You bitch! I'll get you for this!"

Just as she reached the car, the gun went off again and dirt flew up when the bullet slammed into the ground beside her.

Heart pounding, Rachel flung the car door open and threw herself into the seat. She was trying to get the key into the ignition when Nelson fired again and a bullet pierced a rear window.

At last the key slid into place. She started the engine and shifted into drive without turning on the lights and making herself an easy target. The car lurched forward. But she had to turn around to get out. She couldn't risk getting trapped in a dead end.

She pulled on the steering wheel and swung the car in a circle. A bullet crashed through the windshield and struck the passenger seat next to her. She floored the gas and took off.

The shooting stopped. Where was Nelson? Why wasn't he running after her? Why wasn't he trying to shoot the tires? In the rearview mirror, she saw nothing but the murk of shadows.

Rachel bounced in her seat as the car jolted into and out of deep holes in the road, and she had to slow to a crawl before she lost control of the car. She needed headlights to navigate this road. Surely it was safe now to turn them on.

She flipped the lever and the headlights blazed. A figure dashed from the trees to her left and into the light. Perry Nelson stopped in the middle of the road fifteen feet ahead, pointing his pistol at the car.

Rachel yelped and ducked. A shot cracked the windshield and bits of glass rained down on her like sand.

She lifted her head far enough to glimpse the road ahead. Nelson was walking toward the car, his gun raised. He seemed in no hurry. Did he think he had hit her with that last shot? Was he coming to make sure, to finish her off?

I am not going to sit here and let you kill me. In that moment, watching him move toward her at an almost casual pace, all the fear and rage she'd held inside for years boiled to the surface and exploded. She sat up straight, grabbed the steering wheel with both hands and found the gas pedal with her foot.

The instant the car started moving, Nelson fired again, but the shot went wide, striking the far edge of the windshield.

He didn't get out of the way. He stood there and fired another shot at the windshield, this one coming within inches of Rachel.

She stomped on the gas and plowed into him. The impact shook the whole car, and Rachel felt the shock down to her bones. She saw the gun fly out of his hand, and he seemed to take flight too, his body lifting into the air for what seemed an eternity before it crumpled to the ground.

Gripping the steering wheel, staring straight ahead, Rachel drove on and left Perry Nelson behind. She hoped to god he was dead.

Chapter Forty-four

"It looks good." Rachel, on her knees in the kitchen, finished wrapping gauze around Michelle's swollen lower leg and secured it with the strip of adhesive tape Michelle handed her. "You'll have a scar, of course."

Michelle, sitting in a chair at the table, sipped from her mug of tea as Rachel got to her feet. "You haven't answered my question."

"I was doing an internal check so I could give you an honest answer." Rachel took a seat on the other side of the table. Frank, the cat, sat upright on a third chair, his one good ear angling back and forth between them as if he didn't want to miss anything. "And I can honestly say I don't feel any guilt over Perry Nelson. Maybe it'll hit me in the middle of the night weeks from now, but I doubt it. He was trying to kill me. I defended myself."

"I'm glad you feel that way, and I hope you won't waste any time wishing it had ended differently. You're rid of him now. He can't threaten you anymore. And Jordan Gale and his girlfriend will go to prison, so you don't have to worry about them either. But if you ever want to talk about it, remember you can call me anytime."

"Sister to sister, right? Not patient to therapist."

Michelle held out a hand across the table and Rachel took it without hesitation. "To tell you the truth," Michelle said, "I wouldn't even know where to begin to analyze you."

They both laughed, and Rachel tried not to analyze the moment. She'd spent too many years doing that. She squeezed

Michelle's hand and asked, "Are things going to be okay between you and Kevin?"

"I think so. I hope so. We still have a lot to work out. We had reached a point where we were hardly communicating at all, and then when the stalking started, I was so stressed and scared, I was behaving so strangely, I can't blame him for wondering if I'd gone off the deep end."

"Now that he knows your whole story, our story, that'll make a difference, won't it?"

Michelle nodded. "It already has. I can't get over how well he took it when we told him. But that look on his face at first was priceless, wasn't it? I didn't know whether he was going to faint or get up and run away. I was scared for a minute, but I should have had more faith in him."

"My favorite moment," Rachel said, "was when he looked at both of us and said, 'This explains *so* much.'"

They laughed together again, as if it were something they did all the time.

"I was terrified of telling him," Michelle said. "I couldn't have done it without your help. And Tom's. Thank you."

"Kevin loves you. That's going to take you a long way."

Holding tightly to Rachel's hand, Michelle searched her face as if looking for some elusive answer there, to a question not yet asked. "Kevin and I had a talk last night before we went to sleep. He asked me if I thought I would ever want to know our real mother."

Our real mother. Rachel detected only a hint of the effort it cost Michelle to speak the words. "What did you say?"

"I told him I can't imagine ever wanting to know her. But are we doing the right thing? Letting her believe we're dead? Some people might think we owe it to her to let her know the truth, to give her closure. Detective Fagan seems to feel that way, from what you told me."

"She had closure a long time ago," Rachel said. "When I tracked her down and pretended I was a student doing research on missing children, I sat next to her and listened to her talk about accepting that we were dead, gone forever. We're part of the past for her. She has another family now. And we have our own lives. If you ever decide you need to see her, I'll back you up, but I'd rather leave it alone, go on the way we are." Some wounds would never heal, and slashing them open again would only bring fresh pain. They had to hope that Fagan would keep quiet about what he knew, but he would always be a vague threat hovering in the background.

"I can't even remember her," Michelle murmured. "Sometimes I think I do, but the image is all mixed up with Mother— Judith, I mean."

"I'm not surprised," Rachel said. "There's such a strong resemblance between them. I look like our biological mother, so I look like Judith too." No one had ever questioned their kinship. No one except Rachel, whose dreams and buried memories had driven her to pry the lid off the truth during a brutally hot summer several years before.

"I guess Daddy had a thing for tall redheads," Michelle said.

For a moment Rachel let the startling words float between them. Michelle had never willingly broached this subject before. Neither of them had ever met Judith's husband, who had died in an auto accident with their small daughter months before Judith kidnapped Rachel and Michelle. Throughout their lives in her house, Michael Goddard was the blond man with movie star looks who smiled from a picture frame in Mother's bedroom. They thought of him as Daddy but could never talk about him, never ask questions because Mother's grief for him ran so deep. Yet when he'd betrayed Judith by having an affair with an employee in his law office and fathering her younger daughter, he had set in motion everything that happened to them, everything that led to this day, to Rachel and Michelle being together now in this farmhouse kitchen.

Rachel waited to see whether Michelle would say more about her biological father, but she seemed finished with the subject. She took a last sip of her tea and set the cup on the table. Smiling, she reached over to scratch the cat's head. "I guess this is goodbye, Frank. Be a good boy for Rachel."

Tom appeared in the doorway. "There's somebody here who wants to talk to the two of you for a minute. Don't ask who. Just come."

They followed Tom to the living room but halted before entering when they saw Detective Bernard Fagan standing there. Kevin stood nearby, arms folded, scowling and silent.

With a glance between them, Michelle and Rachel reached silent agreement. They joined hands as they walked into the living room. Tom and Kevin took their places beside the two women, and Rachel knew they wouldn't hesitate to step in and toss Fagan out if necessary. Now that he'd been proved wrong, all Rachel wanted from the detective was an apology and a promise to stay out of their lives.

They all waited for Fagan to speak.

He cleared his throat and jammed his hands into his pockets. In a second the inevitable jingling of keys began. One day, Rachel thought, somebody who'd had enough would haul off and deck him for that habit.

"Captain Bridger and I have wrapped up all the loose ends on the Shelley Beecher case," Fagan said, "and I'm about to start home. I wanted to stop by and see you for a minute before I leave. Look, Rachel—Dr. Goddard—I realize none of this would have happened if I'd done a better job when Nelson first started threatening you back in McLean. I'm sorry he got off after he shot you. I'm sorry for my part in it. I went easy on Nelson, I sat in the witness chair and made excuses for him, and that influenced the jury's decision. I let something that happened in my own family distort my judgment. That's never going to happen again."

Rachel nodded. "It's over now. I'd like to put it behind me. Thank you for what you've said. It helps." It wasn't everything she needed to hear, though.

An awkward silence developed. Fagan jangled his keys. Rachel considered decking him herself. Nobody helped him out by speaking.

At last he said, "About the other thing, what happened when you were kids, I want you to know that nobody will ever hear about it from me. That's one cold case I have no interest in solving."

Michelle's hand tightened on Rachel's. When Rachel glanced at her sister, she saw her own relief mirrored in Michelle's face. She had to take a deep breath before she could speak. "That means a lot to us."

"Yes," Michelle whispered.

"Well, I'd better get going," Fagan said, his voice suddenly crisp and impersonal. He nodded at Michelle and Kevin. "You two have a safe trip. Captain, Dr. Goddard, you have good day."

The four of them moved aside so Fagan could leave. When she heard the door close behind him, Rachel let go of another part of her past.

She and Tom, accompanied by Billy Bob, said goodbye to Michelle and Kevin a few minutes later and stood on the porch, Tom's arm around Rachel's shoulders and her arm around his waist, watching them leave. In the car, Kevin leaned over and kissed Michelle before starting the engine. The car rolled down the driveway to the road, turned, and disappeared, taking them back to their life in Bethesda.

As her sister left, Rachel felt an old, familiar pang of loss, as if an empty space had opened inside her. She knew she would always feel that way when she and Michelle parted. Their bond was forged by experiences so extraordinary that no one else could ever fully understand their lives. Not even Judith Goddard's malign influence could break that connection. It would survive the physical distance between them.

Rachel turned her eyes to the clear blue sky, then let her gaze drift over the wooded hillside across the road and the fields that stretched away from the house. For the first time since she'd moved into the farmhouse with Tom, she could look around her and think: *I'm home.*

A squirrel dashed across the yard directly in front of them, and Billy Bob took off, woofing and bouncing down the steps on his stubby bulldog legs.

Rachel laughed and leaned against Tom. She felt the wall she'd long ago built around herself crumbling and settling as quietly and gently as dust. *A normal life*, she thought, *filled with love. That's all I want.* What a gift that would be.

"I'd like to invite them back in a couple of months," she told Tom.

"Sure." He squeezed her shoulders and kissed her forehead. "Maybe they can relax and enjoy it next time."

"A vacation wasn't exactly what I meant. I want my sister to be my matron of honor."

"What?" He pulled back to look into her eyes, and a slow smile lit his face. "Seriously?"

"If I want to help you get elected sheriff," Rachel said, grinning, "I'd better start by making an honest man of you."

To receive a free catalog of Poisoned Pen Press titles, please contact us in one of the following ways:

Phone: 1-800-421-3976
Facsimile: 1-480-949-1707
Email: info@poisonedpenpress.com
Website: www.poisonedpenpress.com

Poisoned Pen Press
6962 E. First Ave. Ste 103
Scottsdale, AZ 85251